I0593167

Grace
Arising

EMMA LOMBARD

THE WHITE SAILS SERIES
BOOK THREE

Cover Illustration © Emma Lombard, 2022
Moral Rights of the Illustrator—Vera Adxer, have been asserted
Cover Design by Jennifer Quinlan, Historical Fiction Book Covers
Interior Formatting by Nicole Scarano Formatting & Design

Come join the crew! Subscribe to my newsletter at www.EmmaLombardAuthor.com for fun giveaways and to receive advance notice about future book releases.

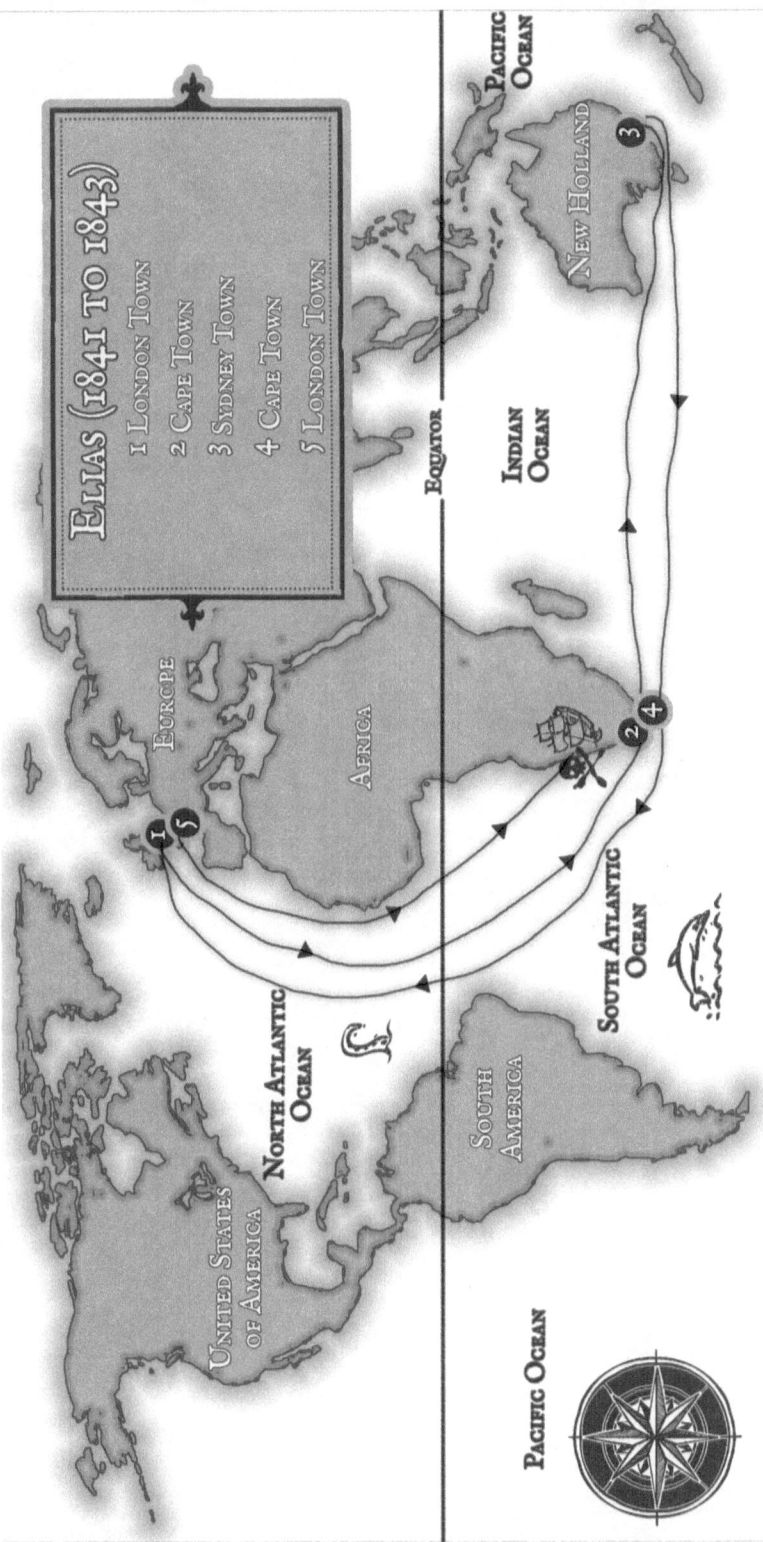

ELIAS (1841 TO 1843)

1 London Town
2 Cape Town
3 Sydney Town
4 Cape Town
5 London Town

This book is for all the fans of Lambert 'Gilly' McGilney ... may he rest in peace ... what, too soon?

Chapter One

ABERTARFF HOUSE, LONDON, 1 APRIL 1841

Grace curled into the Chesterfield lounge in Seamus's library, glad it was warm enough to not require the fire. The lantern on the mahogany Davenport desk bathed her husband in a golden glow, catching the corn-kissed strands of his hair as he dipped his chin in concentration over his letter writing. The clock on the mantel ticked loudly, and the townhouse's night-time sounds settled comfortably around Grace as she curled her legs tighter, the leather upholstery squeaking. She snapped the letter's wax seal, eager to read Adelia Barclay's latest news.

Wooloongilly Downs, New South Wales, 21 October 1840

Dearest Grace,
   It is with the gladdest of hearts that I received your letters. I wonder constantly how you and your little darlings are.

I am glad of the cooler weather, and to be relieved of the distraction of the incessant flies. Mr Barclay has begun work on Barclay Hall. He assures me it will be grand, but as long as it has a roof that does not leak with every rainstorm, and walls that keep out the winter wind and summer dust, I shall be happy. This promise of comfort has eased my restlessness. I no longer threaten my poor long-suffering husband that I shall flee back to London.

The children are well. Noah (3), Ruth (2), and Eve (1) recently welcomed their new little brother, Gideon. Mr Barclay arrived just in time to help his new son into this world after visiting the shepherds out in the pastures. I still smile at using the term 'pastures' for this brown and overgrown country, when to me, the word conjures images of sweeping green landscapes dotted with white woolly sheep. Here, our poor sheep endure just as difficult a time as we do, though they are no less stupid than their British counterparts.

Regarding shepherds, there is a significant shortage here of men with experience in sheep. Most available for employment are ex-convicts, but since the recent curtailing of convict transportation, even they are in short supply. Putting aside their criminal pasts, most are from the city and have no idea about sheep farming. Some are quick learners and hard workers, but nothing is as valuable as experience. However, these men are necessary for our survival.

Mr Buchanan is especially adept in drawing out the best of the most cynical man. I simply do not know how he maintains that level of enthusiasm! He is a treasure, for sure! The married shepherds are the hardest working, and their wives make equally good shepherds. They have even taught me how to grow Indian corn and potatoes. The shepherds and station hands suffer many injuries in the bush, though I have learned how to sew an axe wound to the leg. Alas, I am a much better seamstress of fabric than flesh.

I digress—back to the children. They are a rambunctious lot who trip me up all day. The lot of them were born bald, though all have taken on their father's russet locks, leaving me swimming in a sea of redheads. My two excellent Irish maids relieve me of sinking up to my armpits in soiled clouts.

It is your fault our children number so many! I say this fondly, though. Had it not been for your sage advice, I am sure Mr Barclay would still be offering me bows and civilities and not much more. We are truly blessed.

Mr Buchanan has embraced Nevin as a father would. Rory Buchanan would be pleased to have his son raised by such an honest and earnest man. When I shared with Mr Buchanan the wonderful news of your intended arrival, he whooped and did a jig on the spot.

Mr Barclay is quite enthused about his partnership with your husband. Having a dedicated packet to ship our wool to London shall do wonders for both enterprises. Business aside, I cannot wait to see you again. Being so hard-pressed for gentle female company makes your arrival that much sweeter.

I have fortunately kept a lovely acquaintance with Mrs Deas Thomson after our first encounter with her at the Governor's Ball all those years back. Although her father is no longer governor, she is kept frightfully busy by her commitments as wife of the Colonial Secretary of New South Wales, so our reunions are far too infrequent for my liking.

Oh Grace, if you could see how far I have come, you would be so proud of me. I have adapted to the hot weather, not just with our clothing, but preserving our bread and meat too. I gave up baking bread with natural yeasts—it does not keep in this climate. We eat the same bread as the shepherds, called damper. It is tasty enough, and the children prefer it. I look forward to receiving quality British tea. I am unsure where the merchants in Sydney Town source their supply, but Mr Barclay often jests that he could split the thick tea stalks into posts and rails! There's nary a fragrant leaf to be seen.

There are scarcely enough hours in the day to stitch clothes for all my little ones, though if the truth be known, they wear only their undershirts in the summer. I often find myself in only my shift and stays—it is too hot to bear wearing anything else. I am sure this sounds positively primitive to you, but it does not even raise an eyebrow out here.

While our children may appear to be wild ragamuffins, I do still insist on them wearing their best for our Sunday roasts. It is far preferable to eat a hearty midday meal, then have the afternoon to doze and laze on our full stomachs.

Well, my dear friend, I must be off. I hear pandemonium developing in the henhouse. Noah and Ruthie are arguing about who is to fetch the eggs. If I do not hasten, there shall be no eggs left to fetch!

Your loving friend,
Adelia Barclay

Grace laughed lightly.

"Care to share?" asked Seamus. The quill nib hovered over the inkwell as a drip of ink slid off the un-tapped point.

At his blue stare, a familiar warmth rolled through her chest —even after all this time. "Adelia. Sharing her children's antics. Oh, I can't wait to see my dear friend again." She had not yet sent word to Adelia of Elias's passing, the act of confirming it in ink still too raw.

Smiling and twirling the pen between his thumb and forefinger, he offered, "I'm finishing a letter to Barclay if you'd like to add a postscript for Mrs Barclay?"

"Yes, thank you, my love. Perhaps just a line or two." Grace rose, and excitement warmed her cheeks as she scoured over his neat loops.

Abertarff House, London, 1 April 1841

Dear Mr Barclay,

I write to you with most excellent tidings. After a successful run of advertisements in news-sheets and handbills, I have secured twenty—yes, twenty!—respectable and intelligent shepherds who all, to varying degrees, have experience in sheep farming.

They may appear a motley crew who hail from all around the world but, I assure you, I have endeavoured to learn the true nature of their shepherding skills by all means possible, including requesting letters of recommendation from previous employers or parish priests.

One thing they all have in common is a desire for a fresh start in a new country, and all have most heartily assured me of the loyalty of their service. Though, as a ship's master, I know only too well the changeable nature of some of these promises once the oath-taker is faced with the reality of an honest day's work. However, I feel assured by my investigations that the attrition rate will be minimal.

I have also procured an entire crate of sheep shears from the steelworks in Sheffield, as well as those seventy-five iron sheep-hurdles you requested. The rate at which your sheep numbers have grown is astounding—five thousand to twenty thousand in five years is no mean feat, sir.

My confidence in our new partnership is absolute. I appreciate your transparency about the offer made to you by the American, Gregory Chittenden. It is many a year since I heard that name. I saw him last aboard his reeking schooner, laden with furs and heading to Boston. He relieved me of a troublesome passenger, for which I was most grateful. I confess surprise that he is dabbling in the wool trade. The man gained quite a name in the opium game after he gave up transporting furs. Perhaps his interest in transporting wool bodes well for us all—a man with his business acumen must have a nose for predicting boons. Your loyalty to honour our original agreement is appreciated, Barclay. Especially since Chittenden undercut my price so severely. I cannot imagine how the man hopes to keep the Firelight *profitable at those prices!*

Nonetheless, with the invaluable influence of my wife's uncle, Admiral Baxter, I have secured a government supply contract to bring out the staples of soap, candles, clothing, and glassware to the colony, thereby ensuring a profitable outcome for both legs of the voyage. I feel it in my bones, sir; only good can come of our joining! As for the other supplies you requested, I have successfully acquired everything on your list, including the winnowing machine.

The Elias's *hold will fit more than five thousand bales of wool—amply adequate for your annual yield of thirteen hundred, with room for other suppliers. By the speed estimated by my shipwright, it is predicted we should make the journey from London to Sydney in blistering time. We shall have no problem transporting your clips to London in time for the February wool sales.*

I was most relieved to hear that the architectural plans for your new home arrived safely. Barclay Hall will be the envy of your neighbours. I have sourced the marble requested by your stonemason. I am sure you will have the grandest fireplaces in the district! I only hope there is a bullocky team strong enough to manage it across the rough terrain in one piece. It would be such a pity for it to have made its way all that distance only to be caught short a few miles from your new home.

I am delighted that Buchanan has adjusted so well to life on terra firma. He grew up on the Isle of Skye, you know? Son of a Scottish cotter. So, it is not surprising to hear he has knowledge of the land. And I concur with your summation of him being a hard worker. The man never shirked his duties aboard my ship.

Speaking of ships, the Elias *is undergoing the final stages of rigging. Not long now before departure.*

Yours in anticipation,

Seamus A. Fitzwilliam

Grace dipped the quill's nib in the inkpot. Perhaps it was time to let her friend know about Elias. Adelia and Elijah would likely be confused by the name of their new ship. Tapping the nib on the glass rim, she took a deep breath.

P.S. Adelia, my friend—Grace here. I have procured the coats and boots you requested for you and the children. It is also with the heaviest of hearts that I share unspeakable news. Our beloved little Elias was taken from us in a tragic accident. It is how our new ship comes to bear his name. I can speak no more of this now, the ache of it still too great. Until we next meet, adieu!

There. It was done, and easier than she anticipated. She breathed in Seamus's citrusy bergamot scent, and her heart skipped as he drew her onto his lap. Abandoning the quill on the desk's leather inlay, she stroked his stubbled cheek with inky fingers, avoiding the shaving nick beneath his right ear. He looked so untroubled.

"I can't wait to make a home with you on the *Elias*," she whispered. Speaking her son's name aloud felt more natural than it had in months.

Despite the weather-lines beneath Seamus's eyes and beside his mouth, she still found him breathtakingly striking. Nearly fifteen years since their first meeting at Mother's dinner party at Wallace House, and still he drew her in like a lodestone.

"It gladdens my heart immeasurably to hear you say so, Dulcinea." He leaned in, peppering warm kisses on her neck. "Are you ready to retire for the evening?"

"I am," Grace laughed, wriggling as the shape of him firmed beneath her. "Clearly, *you* aren't."

Her breath snagged in her chest as Seamus gripped her waist. He drew her closer and their lips met, gently at first and then with urgency. Age had not softened him, unlike her waistline. Birthing three children had put paid to that. She self-consciously gentled her kisses, extracting herself from his lap.

He held her wrist, the lantern light flicking across his flushed cheeks. "Where are you going?"

"Aren't we retiring?"

He rose slowly, his hand brushing her bare arm. "Not before I fully disrobe you and take the measure of you." He pressed her back against his desk, and she bit back a squeal as he lifted her onto it.

"You know how I feel about you seeing me in the light," she jested half-heartedly. Desire flared through her abdomen as he stepped between her knees. The sickle-shaped scar curving from rib to hip had been a necessity to save Elias at birth. That she had survived such butchery was thanks to Billy Sykes's excellent surgical skills.

"Your body is the vessel that gave our children life. That it bears evidence of this only makes me love you more deeply."

Eyeing the door, she chuckled. "Seamus. The servants."

"Have all retired." He drew her hair away from her neck with one finger, his touch light and tickly.

"But our Em and Eddy—"

"Are both asleep," he murmured, leaning down. "This"—he trailed kisses down her neck—"is the point of beginning."

He undid the first few hooks of her bodice, whispering against her collarbone, "And this is a benchmark because of its elevation."

He peeled open the edges of her gown, his lips mapping the contours of her décolletage. Another involuntary yelp escaped her, but it did not stop him. He unhooked her dress further, exposing the tops of her breasts to the warm air. She shivered.

"Seamus." She exhaled breathlessly.

He studied her intently, his eyes narrowing. Oh, Lord, she was powerless against that blue gaze. Who was she to protest? Grace rested back on her hands to grant him easier access. He continued, his caressing fingers working nimbly ahead of his exploring mouth.

"And this," he murmured, kissing her where the two curved lines of her breasts met over her breastbone. "Is the point of intersection."

She wrapped her legs around his, and he rumbled in approval.

"Oh, Dulcinea," he growled thickly. "I want you with every ounce of my being." He exhaled hard, and she breathed in traces of peach from his earlier cognac. He pulled her up for a long, deep kiss that swept her back to their first kiss beside Captain Fincham's sickbed on the *Discerning*—their passion heightened by the secrecy and spice of being caught.

"You've not kissed me like that in a while," she gasped, her lips and chin stinging from his enthusiasm. To be fair, up until now, she had not wanted to be kissed like this. How could she enjoy life when her darling Elias could not? Still, something in her shifted. Was it time to cease her self-flagellation?

He rested his forehead on hers and smiled. "Blame it on the promise of our new life."

Grace reached her arms around his neck and, threading her fingers through his hair, loosened his ribbon. "I require no excuse to love you, husband," she purred, pulling his shirt front. Her self-punishment was not fair on Seamus. He had been a constant light in the storm, and it was time for her to follow the beam back to the safety of his home shore.

Chapter Two

ABERTARFF HOUSE, LONDON, 20 *APRIL* 1841

Billy stood in the entrance of Abertarff House, hunched against the overcast day. Despite the chilliness, Grace's spirits soared. His floppy black fringe, still ink-black and unmarred by grey, fell carelessly across his brow beneath his derby. His handsome brown suit matched the paper-wrapped package beneath his elbow.

"Billy! You made it!"

"Wouldn't miss it for the world, flower." He squeezed her arm.

He was a little thicker around the waist, but Grace breathed in the familiar childhood scent of him, and a sisterly affection squeezed her ribs. Goodness, it was marvellous to see him again.

Stepping back, she beckoned. "Come in, come in. Bartel will fetch your trunk."

"Thank you." Billy lifted the black bag beside him, the glass vials and metal instruments inside chinking as he stepped into the entry.

"Apologies for the mess." She smirked, waving at the scene of domesticity.

The children's muddy shoes were lined up beside the blue ceramic umbrella stand. Her red tartan shawl hung among various-sized coats on the rack. She hoped he would not notice the line of discolouration on the wallpaper where grubby little hands leaned against it for support while outdoor shoes were swapped for indoor ones. Emily's voice floated down the stairs, in the throes of performing a puppet show. Sweet cinnamon wafts of baking apple pie filtered down the hall from the kitchen.

Billy sniffed appreciatively. "Mmm, roast pork? With crackling crisped to mouth-watering perfection!" He glanced down at her, his brown eyes softening. "'Tis good to see you again, flower."

"Seamus is in his library." She took his arm and led him down the carpeted hall. "He's leaving soon after luncheon to meet his new first mate at the dock. He wants to orient his new officer with the lay of the *Elias*. Come say a quick hello."

Grace glanced fondly at the familiar spread of charts and brass instruments of measurements littering Seamus's large desk. Books on the shelves behind him were lined up immaculately, not a single picture crooked. The spotless library offered a heartening aroma of wood polish, cold ash, and the earthy press of old books—opening a vault of memories of Uncle Farfar's visits to the nursery when she was a child.

Seamus laid down the brass divider calliper he had been using on the chart. "Dr Sykes, glad to see you again, old friend."

Billy lowered his bag and leaned the wide parcel's thin edge against the desk. "Sir. Nothing could have kept me away from another adventure with your intrepid family. Wouldn't want you having all the fun without me."

Seamus chuckled. "Adventures that bring a risk of bodily

harm. It's a relief knowing you'll be there to piece us back together."

"There'll be no bodies losing any bits, if I can help it," Grace said, quirking up one corner of her mouth. "Your company is as good a balm for ailing spirit as your liniments."

"Indeed, it is," concurred Seamus. "It's poor Dr Krantz's loss that you're abandoning the infirmary for a post upon the *Elias*."

Billy smiled congenially. "Not at all, sir. Dr Krantz retired last month. He plans to settle in his country house in the Cotswolds, content to put his days of sewing human beings behind him and indulge only in the sowing of vegetables."

"The man's had quite a career spanning the continent. I suppose a well-earned rest is in order," said Seamus. "Same goes for ship's surgeon Beynon. He too has laid down his scalpel and settled for a more sedate life in the country."

Grace tipped her head. "Is Dr Krantz terribly disappointed that you're not continuing his practice?"

"No. The last couple of years in Oxford have highlighted my preference for adventure." Billy shrugged one shoulder. "Besides, it's not the same with Krantz gone. I plan to do justice to his teachings on the *Elias*." He pointed to the parcel. "I've brought you both a gift."

"Not necessary, my good man," said Seamus. "Your agreement to accompany us is gift enough."

Armed with Seamus's miniature cutlass letter opener, Grace slit the paper packaging. It slithered to the floor with a dry rasp, and she inhaled sharply. "Oh, Billy! It's… it's…" Her voice jammed in her throat. Her husband stepped from behind the desk, and she was glad for his arm around her waist. She stared at the portrait, the pang of familiar faces tugging her heart.

"By Neptune, it's… *magnificent*," said Seamus hoarsely.

In the painting, Seamus stood smartly in a black suit. Our Em stood before him with an equally solemn look upon her face. Seamus's hand rested on her shoulder. Grace sat in a gown of soft lavender, and to her right stood Eddy, stiff-backed and staring, with his wide blue eyes peering beneath his side-swept fringe. His hand rested lightly on Grace's arm. To Grace's left stood Elias, staring back at her with a curiosity matching his twin's.

A tumbling swell of grief and joy collided in Grace's chest. She stared, unblinking, and traced a light finger over Elias's face. "My beautiful boy."

Her friend's warm voice drew her around. "I hope you don't mind that I've added Elias?"

With her throat tight with tears, she whispered, "I don't mind. It's perfect." She studied the slight elongation of her late son's head and his almond-shaped eyes that differentiated him from his twin brother. Eddy's hairline swept to the opposite side.

Billy cleared his throat. "I had enough sketches of the children from our previous voyage to be able to capture their likeness here."

Grace absorbed the face of her lost son, the memory of him like a balm across her ragged wound of grief. Too many people avoided mentioning Elias, but Billy's loving observation was as comforting as a toasty warming pan on crisp, winter sheets.

"Thank you, Billy." She sniffed. "Eddy will appreciate it too. He misses Elias terribly. He's always making allowances for his brother—an extra place at the table, insisting when he receives a new toy that the same is added to his brother's collection."

"It's the perfect final touch for the great cabin," added Seamus.

Chapter Three

NORTH ATLANTIC OCEAN, 10 MAY 1841

The *Elias*'s sleek, black hull sat low and heavy in the water, but she cut through the waves with an agility Seamus had never seen in a ship before. A familiar thrill of pleasure traced up his spine as he tilted his head back. Her three masts were full, and he squinted against the brightness of the new white canvas. The lower masts were painted black, the white mastheads stretching to dizzying heights, like the stiff fingers of a giant tickling the clouds. The wind blew the smell of her new wooden deck and fresh paint back to him, and he breathed in the familiar scents of tar and lanolin. A surge of happiness swelled in his chest. He was home.

He studied his crew—twenty-six, the tiniest contingent with which he had ever sailed. The loss or incapacitation of any of the hands would slow them down considerably, but it was a risk he was willing to take. The new packet was easy to manage with the small, skilled crew, and Seamus nodded sagely at the blend of his handpicked recruits. Familiar faces included O'Malley, Ben Blight, Toby Hicks, and of course, Billy Sykes. It had been easy enough to persuade O'Malley and Ben Blight from their respective commissions. The two red-headed sailors had been fortunate to find themselves together on Captain Preston's schooner, the *Pedantic*, which made Seamus's job of pilfering them onto the *Elias* that much easier. O'Malley and Blight jumped at the opportunity when they heard Grace would be sailing with them.

Seamus knew his wife would never have forgiven him had he not secured Hicks's services, but Seamus would have picked him even without her persuasion. Hicks had served as a shipwright alongside Old Jock Willis long enough for him to measure the man's intelligence. And his loyalty to their family, particularly Grace, was unquestionable. Seamus was confident he would make an excellent clerk, perfect for handling the many wool contracts he hoped to secure in New Holland. The new bosun, cook, carpenter, and sailmaker all came with outstanding references.

As his gaze roved critically over the billowing sails above, Seamus's mind slipped to the scene of domesticity he had left in the great cabin earlier that morning. Being only a few days into the voyage, they still had the luxury of proper bread with their bacon and eggs, even if it required toasting. Emily had pleaded with Grace to retell, for the umpteenth time, the story of how Seamus had given her the heart-shaped brooch on their first attempt at a wedding in the church ruins of Tierra del Fuego. Emily touched the Luckenbooth—always pinned to Grace's clothing—and was audacious enough to ask her mother if she could wear it.

"One day it'll be yours, Empem," said Grace, smiling serenely, her fingers tracing the polished heart-shaped brooch. "But for now, it's still mine."

Seamus looked at Miss Lissing, the striking governess. With her waist so tightly pulled in by her corset, it was a wonder she could breathe. "And what of the children's lessons this morning, Miss Lissing?" he asked.

Flowing russet locks aside, he appreciated her frank look—determined and intelligent, and not easily intimidated, not even by the fact that he was master of the ship. Her plump lips turned up. "French conjugation follo—"

Emily and Edwin groaned but grinned cheekily at the governess when she raised her eyebrows. "Careful now," she cautioned. "Or I'll add an extra two pages of handwriting to the four I've set for today."

Emily waved in surrender. "Oh no, Miss, I'm sorry, I'm sorry."

At nearly nine years old, Emily's head already reached Seamus's elbow. She had long, strong legs like him and was already taller than all girls her age. Her blue eyes glinted mischievously.

"I's sorry, Miss!" Three-and-a-half-year-old Edwin's blue eyes matched Emily's, though he had Grace's easy smile. Miss Lissing pretended to pert her lips in disapproval, but Seamus caught the smile playing in the corners of her eyes.

Grace interjected. "In addition to Miss Lissing's lessons today, I'll teach you how to read a compass. And if you're good, I might be able to persuade O'Malley to let you have a go at the helm."

Emily and Edwin quivered, pressing their lips together to tame any squeals Seamus had expressly forbidden aboard the ship.

He frowned at their untouched breakfast. "Eat up, please, children."

"I's not hungry." Edwin flicked his sister an odd look.

Seamus narrowed his eyes.

Grace tutted. "What would the hands think to see you wasting delicious bacon and eggs when they must be content with porridge?"

Emily slowly chewed another mouthful, and Edwin bit his toast, the butter and honey painting a wide golden smile up his cheeks.

Inspecting the sticky, giggling chaos, Seamus gave a silent thanks for it all. He dipped his brows. "Just remember, you two, there are always men sleeping between watches—at all times of the day. No unnecessary noise, understood?"

They replied in dutiful unison. "Yes, Cappy."

"This evening before bed, we can study the charts," added Seamus. "I'll give you the names of three islands each, and the first to find all three of their islands may stay up an extra half hour." He was habitually strict about bedtime. Emily and Edwin's instant delight wordlessly morphed into a silent challenge, their eyes narrowing at one another.

Seamus turned at a knock at the dining-room door. Hicks stood stiff and pale. "Yes, Hicks?"

Hicks fidgeted with his ear. "Um, pardon me, sir. Cook Woodhouse has a problem."

"Can't it wait? I'm in the middle of breakfast."

Hicks shifted his weight from one foot to the other. "Sir, there was a theft from the galley last night. A tray of jam tarts."

Christ above! A thief? In a crew so closely vetted? It was likely one of the blasted shepherds he was ferrying. The air thickened with the tetchiness that bristled off him. "Please, tell Cook Woodhouse to await me in the lounge," he ordered.

"Yes, sir." Hicks dipped his head.

Seamus tossed his napkin onto his empty plate and shook his head at Grace. "Not even a week into the journey, and there's already trouble afoot." He rubbed his nape. All eyes were on him. He drew his shoulders back. "I'll not tolerate thieving. The culprit has earned himself a lashing, but first, he'll run the gauntlet. Let the rest of the men teach him a lesson with fists and boots."

Grace blanched and shifted in her chair. She shook her head minutely, flicking her eyes at the children.

Seamus pressed his lips resolutely. "*Everyone* needs to fully understand the seriousness of the matter, Grace." Damn and blast that accusatory glare of hers. He knew she was thinking back to when he'd had Hicks flogged aboard the *Discerning* for stealing food. "We've barely begun the journey for anyone to feel deprived of rations."

Emily wriggled in her seat. "What if it wasn't one of the crew?"

Edwin made a slight movement, and his sister jolted as though she had touched an electric eel.

Seamus's teacup wavered before his lips. Draining the last of the cold tea, he settled the cup back on its saucer with a chink. He swung his gaze to Emily. "If it's one of the shepherds, they'll be held in irons until we arrive in New Holland." Emily's cheeks flushed as though she had a fever. He dipped his chin. "Are you unwell, Emily?"

Reddening further, she stammered, "N-no, Cappy. I'm well." She broke eye contact with him by taking a sip of her own tea. Seamus flicked his eyes towards Edwin, who bowed his head and fiddled with the napkin on his lap.

Emily shuffled upright in her chair. "How will you find out who did it?"

"First, I'll muster all on deck and ask for the guilty party to step forward. If no one does, then I'll order a full search of the ship. There are bound to be crumbs left in evidence wherever the thief ate the tarts."

Emily swallowed, glancing uncertainly at her younger brother, who gnawed on a thumbnail, his eyes fixed to his plate.

"W-what if you find no crumbs?" Her voice shrank.

Seamus cocked his head. "Then, every hand will draw straws. The man with the shortest straw will receive the punishment."

Edwin's head whipped up, his eyes as wide as his sister's.

Emily sputtered. "B-but if he's not the thief, he'll be punished for nothing."

"He'll serve as an example that I'll not tolerate dishonest behaviour." Seamus held his back rigid as both children stole guilty glances at one another. Coughing, he caught Grace's eye and waggled his eyebrows. She nodded.

Emily seemed determined to learn the full measure of his mind. "If the guilty parties come forward, will they still be punished?"

"Of course," he insisted.

"But if they're honest about stealing, you can't punish them." Her voice wobbled.

"Their honesty will save another innocent person from being punished, but by stepping forward, they'll be admitting their guilt. And *that's* what they'll be punished for."

His daughter lifted her chin, and Seamus gnawed his cheek to not smile at her bravery.

"I stole the tarts, Cappy," she said stiffly.

"You stole and ate a *dozen* jam tarts all by yourself?" said Seamus, quirking one brow up.

A crimson flush mottled her neck. "Y-yes. Well, no."

"You didn't steal the tarts? Or you didn't eat them all by yourself? Hmm?" Seamus turned on what Emily called his *captain's voice*, and she clenched her shaking hands.

Emily blurted, "*I* took them, but I shared them—with Alby."

Seamus's right eye twitched. "Alby? Your tortoise?"

Edwin's blond head flicked around in panic. His chair thrust back with a piercing wooden shriek as he shot to his feet. "And me! And we saved one for Elias." His lower lip trembled, tears brimming in his cobalt eyes.

Seamus slowly clasped his fingers together before his mouth, his elbows resting on the table as though in prayer. He let a thick silence fill the room.

"But it was *my* idea! I dared Eddy to eat them," Emily gushed. "And Alby really liked them too."

She took a deep breath, and Seamus admired the way she steadied herself.

"Punish *me*, Cappy," added Emily. "Not Eddy."

Edwin stared at his sister, his confusion apparent. Seamus wondered whether a skewed sense of sibling rivalry would have his son claim the crime. Had his daughter felt victorious sneaking back from the galley undetected by anyone on the first watch? That was no mean feat—and he was secretly impressed.

"I stole the tarts. Punish me." Edwin blinked, immediately clamping his lips.

The notion of Edwin saving a tart for his twin almost undid Seamus's resolve. The bell above sounded eight o'clock, and Seamus rose wordlessly. Dusting toast crumbs from his shirt, he leaned down and gently kissed Grace on the lips. Usually, this elicited giggles from Emily and Edwin, but not today.

Glancing at the two guilty faces, he added dryly, "I'm expected above. I'll deal with you two later." Both children sagged.

Now, on the quarterdeck, the hazy outline of Seamus's dreamy reminiscing sharpened to the present as a loud voice below caught his attention. His new first mate, Lucius Chittenden, stood over young Shelby Hicks near the water barrel. Young Hicks drew a ladle of water to his mouth, and Chittenden smacked it from his hands, sending the metal spoon clattering to the deck. Water dripped from young Hicks's square chin, darkening his blue coat front.

"I ought to slap that taste right out your mouth! Back to work, you lazy mongrel," snapped Chittenden. "No sauntering about having sips of water like you're having tea with the Queen. Where in the blazes is Carpenter Hanson anyway? You're his responsibility." Chittenden glowered around the deck, his pale green eyes cold, the edges of his sun-bleached hair tousled by the brim of his tarred straw hat.

Young Hicks was shorter than his older brother, but he carried a strength that flowed up his thighs and torso, around his broad shoulders to a thick neck. At eighteen, he was centred like a ship's mast hewn from a single tree, and he was in prime condition. His only imperfection was a skewed nose, clearly broken more than once. Knowing a little of the Hicks brothers' upbringing from Grace, Seamus deduced the disfigurement was courtesy of their father.

Toby Hicks had assured Seamus that his easy-going brother was prepared to take any position aboard the *Elias*. Seamus had witnessed the first moment that young Hicks crossed paths with Henry Hanson, the ship's carpenter. The barrel-chested man, upon loading his tools onto the *Elias,* struggled under the weight of a crate and, missing his footing, sent the utensils across the deck in a clattering wave of iron.

Young Hicks had not hesitated to bend down and help Hanson gather his tools. Seamus had seen Hanson's dark wiry eyebrows draw together angrily in embarrassment. He antici-pated a curse-filled tirade from the carpenter, but instead young Hicks, with lightning-quick humour, immediately proclaimed, "Anyone can trip over their own feet, sir. Real skill's in glaring behind you with a conviction that persuades everyone something tripped you up. Would it help if I frowned back at the deck with you, sir?"

Seamus was relieved when a loud guffaw burst from Hanson's thick, black whiskers. With the last tool in the box, Hanson shook young Hicks's hand. "You'll do, young man. If you're half as good with your tools as you are with your words, I'll make a decent carpenter of you. You interested?"

But now, Carpenter Hanson was nowhere in sight, and the young apprentice was at Chittenden's mercy. The first mate had come with an excellent letter of introduction from the Duke of

Berkshire, one of Admiral Baxter's wartime acquaintances. Upon first meeting Chittenden, Seamus had challenged him about being Gregory Chittenden's son.

Standing before Seamus's desk in the captain's lounge, Chittenden had almost glowed with impertinence. "I'm a disgrace in my father's eyes. God knows I gave it my best, but it wasn't enough for him."

"Is he aware you're seeking a position aboard my ship? We're business rivals, you know?"

Chittenden roughly scrubbed his chin. "I'd rather a position with you than with him, sir."

"I'm confused. How does the son of an American merchant come to speak the Queen's English?"

"My father blames me for my mother's death at my birth." Chittenden swallowed thickly. "He sent me to boarding school in Wales when I was five years old."

Seamus had studied the odd-looking man. He had a couple of things going for him—a fire in his belly to better his father, and that letter of recommendation. The duke had praised Chittenden's skills as a competent officer, though there was little evidence of this right now.

Down below, Chittenden's gaze fell upon young Hicks like an axe, and he lashed out his riding crop. The blow struck young Hicks's face and bowled his hat across the deck, where it stopped against a coil of rope. The young apprentice doubled over, clutching his cheek. Slowly righting himself, his nostrils flared and his jaw clenched.

Chittenden kicked the metal ladle towards him. "Pick that up."

Heavens! The gall! Seamus called out, "Mr Chittenden, a word, please."

Chittenden's eyes, pale as though they had been rinsed in briny saltwater, swung to Seamus. The first mate clicked his tongue, the stealthy expression on his lips not quite a smile.

By Neptune's forked trident, did he just *tut*? Seamus clenched his fists. He saw Chittenden hesitate. *"Now*, Mr Chittenden."

Chittenden glared balefully back at young Hicks, who scampered to pick up the ladle and his hat. The first mate trudged up to the quarterdeck, the pungent smell of onions following him across the deck. Seamus knew he ate one whole raw onion a day, declaring it would prevent him catching the bubonic plague. He had even brought his own supply. Chittenden's recent display of violence and his overpowering stench endeared Seamus to the man as much as the Devil to holy water.

Seamus clasped his hands informally behind his back and kept his voice low to reach only his subordinate's ears. "Mr Chittenden, I expect a strict hierarchy of order on my ship. Bosun Lincoln is familiar with my expectations. It's *his* duty to decide if and when the men are out of order, and *his* privilege to decide whether punishment is due or not." He glanced at Chittenden from the corner of his eye. The man's pale cheeks flared, and to Seamus's surprise, instead of contriteness, he was met with hostile incredulity. Ignoring this, he continued calmly, "I suggest you garner the men's respect through dependable leadership, and not through threats and intimidation. Drinking water isn't a punishable offence on my ship."

"Sir, I'm the forward commander on this watch. I'd appreciate being allowed to do my duty," said Chittenden.

Seamus doubled up his fists and dropped his voice dangerously low. "Chittenden, I'm commander of this *entire* ship."

"Yes, sir, and I'm first mate of her. I know my place." Chittenden smiled woodenly.

A warm slide of anger slicked across his nape. Letting his hands fall slack, he willed himself to calm. "You're an officer for only so long as *I* choose. And at the moment, you're perilously close to losing this privilege." His rage created a thirst, his thoughts flicking to the cool water in the barrel below. "Your cruelty tells me you've never held a position of authority before, despite the Duke of Berkshire's validation. I caution you against mishandling my men."

"They wouldn't require such handling if you didn't run such a lazy ship. *Sir*." Chittenden's tone was as blunt as his words.

Damn the impudent fool! Seamus drew himself up and slid his impassive mask into place. "Since you so clearly stated that your position for this watch is forward, you should head there now—before I'm forced to put you in chains."

Seamus's stomach rolled sourly as the officer made no move towards the stairs. He raised his voice a notch, loud enough that he caught Blight and Crowleigh, a new topman, peering down from the rigging in which they hung. "That was an *order*, Mr Chittenden."

"Aye, aye, sir," drawled Chittenden.

Seamus blew a long breath out of his nostrils as Chittenden strolled unhurriedly along the main deck, his gait long and deliberate. Blasted brazen bastard! He must deal with Chittenden's insubordination before the rest of the crew caught wind of it. Heavens above! He had not foreseen needing to discipline such a carefully handpicked man so early on in the journey—nor his children for thievery! His lips were drier than a year-old chunk of salt beef, and he licked them.

Just after noon, Seamus finished eating the baked fish at his desk in the captain's lounge, leaving a tidy pile of bones beside his knife and fork. He straightened the miniature cutlass letter-opener and brass magnifying glass, and he nudged the cut-glass inkwell nearer to the blotting paper. He prided himself on frugally preserving the sheet until every inch of its surface was used. Waste not, want not. Folding his hands across his lap, he waited for McGilney to load the dirty crockery onto a tray. Grace had come to depend on the maid's help with the children, and she was a welcome addition aboard his ship. "Thank you, McGilney."

The rustle of Grace's skirts announced her arrival. Her tight smile at McGilney gave Seamus an indication of the depth of her worry as she plonked into the chair opposite him.

He leaned forward. "Care for a spot of Madeira?"

"No, thank you," she replied. "Seamus, what'll you do about our Em and Eddy?"

He caught McGilney flick a sympathetic glance towards Grace. Their attachment, struck by the extraordinary circumstances of Grace being shipmates with McGilney's brother, had not wavered over the years.

"They're equally guilty," Seamus said coolly. "Therefore, they deserve equal punishment."

Grace's throat undulated as she swallowed. "How do you plan to do it?"

"I'll make an example of them." His resolve slipped slightly at the flash of pain in her green eyes.

Her chin lifted. "I'll not have them beaten in public." There was a steeliness to her voice.

Seamus regarded her carefully. She had a long-standing abhorrence of public corporal punishment—evidenced all those years back by her spectacular objection to Hicks's flogging aboard the *Discerning*. As irked as he had been as a young first lieutenant, it was also the moment this plucky lass planted a seed of admiration in him that swiftly flourished into a deep love, anchored by mutual doses of respect and passion. Releasing the knit of his brows, he came to a decision. "Very well. Emily and Edwin must publicly admit their guilt, but I'll punish them in private. A caning of six strikes each on the bare posterior." A violent wrench of guilt ravaged his bowels. He had never laid a finger on his children before, and he resented being forced into this position. If he was to demand obedience of his crew, it had to begin here—with his family.

"Thank you," she said stiffly.

Seamus ignored the peculiar disconnection blooming

between them—this was unchartered territory for them both. He nodded decisively. "Tomorrow after breakfast, I'll make the announcement."

The following morning, Seamus had Bosun Lincoln pipe all hands on deck, including the shepherds. Everyone milled in curious consternation before the quarterdeck. Most glanced warily at Chittenden from the corners of their eyes and shuffled away. His first mate fitted in like a blasted trumpet in a string quartet!

Seamus glanced down at the tiniest, most wizened woman he had ever seen. Wee Granny Mac, the only shepherdess, kept strictly to herself, declaring that the only company she preferred, besides sheep, was her own. Mindful of her being the only woman below, Seamus had ensured her a private berth—commonly a storage cupboard for sails—with a lockable latch.

At the quarterdeck rail, Seamus addressed the crowd. "There was a theft aboard the *Elias* two nights past." The men mumbled, feet shifting. Seamus continued, "The guilty parties have confessed. I call upon them now to step forward and admit their crime."

An awkwardness settled over the ship, and shifty gazes glanced around. Startled gasps accompanied Emily and Edwin as they stepped beside Seamus. By Neptune's trident, there was no going back now. Both children looked like their legs were about to buckle, and they were so ashen Seamus wondered if there was any blood left in their heads. He squeezed his scarred wrist behind his back to still the tremble in his hands. This was an unpleasant duty, but an essential one.

"Miss Emily Elizabeth Fitzwilliam, you stand accused of stealing a dozen jam tarts from Mr Woodhouse's galley and inciting your co-conspirator to consume said tarts until they were finished. How do you plead?"

Emily's chin quivered, though her voice was steady. "Guilty, sir."

Seamus turned to his son. "Master Edwin Alexander Fitzwilliam, you stand accused of consuming a dozen stolen jam tarts until they were finished. How do you plead?"

A lone tear rolled down Edwin's pale cheek, and he warbled, "Guilty, sir."

Seamus glared at the dumbstruck crowd. "For the crime of thievery, I hereby sentence you both to six strokes of the cane in the captain's lounge at midday today. Until such time, you'll remain in your berths." Some of the sailors and shepherds nodded at Seamus in admiration, and others gave his terrified children looks of sympathy. Wee Granny Mac, all four feet of her, clutched a grey, knitted cowl about her neck. Her face was weathered like a walnut, and without teeth, her lips pulled deeply into her face as she nodded up at the children. Only Chittenden remained aloof and unimpressed.

"A lesson to all," said Seamus, scanning across the sea of heads, his brows dipping. "Thievery will *not* be tolerated aboard my ship."

Beside him, Grace stood rigid and pale, tightening her red shawl across her chest. He wanted to put his arms about her. Comfort her out of her misery. Instead, he gripped Emily and Edwin by the shoulders and steered them below.

At midday, Seamus heard shuffling footsteps falter behind the captain's lounge door. Balanced on the edge of the leather-seated chair at his desk, he clasped his fingers, his thumb absently toying with the raised scar on his wrist. Bowing his head, he closed his eyes, drawing on his resolve to see this unpleasant matter through. He glanced at the panelled door, craning towards the hissed whispers behind it.

"I shan't scream," declared Emily.

"Me too," said Edwin. "Or Elias."

At their tentative knock, Seamus wrenched open the door. Two pairs of eyes darted to the wiry rattan cane in his hand.

"Who's first?" he asked, his voice low and hard. Edwin

quailed and looked at his sister, who boldly lifted her chin. Like mother, like daughter. Seamus was regularly amused by these similarities, but the weight of his current task squashed his enjoyment.

"Ladies first," Emily said, marching in. Edwin's large, terrified eyes softened with admiration—a sentiment Seamus shared. Oh, Emily—so plucky and brave. He shut the door and turned.

Emily valiantly lay over the wingchair's arm and flicked up the hem of her dress, offering him her pert, pink behind. She stiffened as Seamus settled his hand on her back. Clenching her eyes tight, she pressed her fist to her lips. For pity's sake! She really was determined not to cry out! Seamus's steadfastness dissipated like gun smoke whipped away on a high wind. He had seen his fair share of canings and floggings. He could not—would not— inflict the barbarity of it on his children. Not for a childish lark.

"Emily," said Seamus softly. His fingers on her back expanded and contracted in time with her rapid breathing. "Emily," he called again.

She peered over her shoulder, her eyes red and blurry.

He softened the muscles in his jaw. "Stand up."

Emily shook down her skirts, her fists gripping clumps of the fabric as she gazed up. Seamus knelt beside her, drawn into the blue depths of her eyes. She stepped back, but the chair's wing pinned her in place.

"Have you learned your lesson?" he asked. She nodded dumbly, her gaze fixed on him in confusion as he elaborated, "I shan't give you a thrashing today."

Emily's blonde eyebrows squeezed together. "Why not?"

He slid his hand over her shoulder, her golden ringlets feathering his skin. "It serves no purpose. I trust you're smart enough to have learned from this ordeal?" He gently squeezed her nape. "However, I can't pardon you entirely. Everyone must believe you've received your full punishment."

"S-so, I'm still getting a hiding?" Emily chewed her bottom lip and tilted her head like a confused puppy.

"No," said Seamus. "I'll strike the armchair. Every time you hear the thump, scream loudly. Understand?"

She sagged against the armchair behind her, her face creased in horror. "But I told Eddy I wouldn't scream. He'll think I'm not brave if I do."

Seamus chuckled softly, raising his eyes heavenward. Such a courageous little thing. He lowered his gaze to Emily's jutting chin.

"It'll be worse for Edwin hearing you scream while awaiting his turn. The last thing he'll remember is your vow of silence." He stood, stretching out the stiffness in his thighs, and tightened his grip on the cane. "Are you ready?" The whole scene seemed absurdly surreal.

Emily nodded.

Seamus thwacked the armchair. An explosion of fibres and dust particles erupted into the air like a fine mist.

Emily shrieked loudly.

"Louder, Emily," he whispered encouragingly.

He belted the chair again, and this time, Emily let out a bloodcurdling yell. He nodded at her, grinning and drawing her deeper into his little charade. Seamus was positive her howls and cries could be heard by all. Six strokes later, he knelt beside her, pinching her lower eyelids and cheeks gently to redden them. He also splashed her face with water to create faux tears. "Head straight to Mamam and let her know you're unharmed."

Real tears welled in Emily's eyes. She flung her arms around his neck, pressing her damp face against his skin. "I'm sorry I made Eddy eat the tarts. And that I made you pretend to hit me."

He kissed her cheek and inhaled her sweet smell tinged with salty tears. "Run along. And remember, tell no one except Mamam. Not even Edwin."

"Yes, Cappy." She sounded so young and remorseful. "I promise I shan't do anything like this. Ever again."

He hummed comfortingly, relieved to have only played the role of a pantomime villain. Pressing his lips into her fine hair, he murmured, "I believe you. Now, let's put your brother out of his misery."

Chapter Four

ATLANTIC OCEAN, 25 MAY 1841

Seamus patrolled the main deck, studying the hard-blue sky that deceptively disguised the blustering wind—perfect conditions for his ship, and even more perfect for the snowy albatrosses dipping and weaving in the turbulence above.

Emily was on all fours, racing her tortoise across the undulating quarterdeck, her movements so stilted it was clear she was letting her tart-eating accomplice win. That shelled criminal—only three inches long when Emily was gifted it by Alby Church in the Galapagos—now weighed as much as an eighteen-pound shot ball, which was nothing compared to the five-hundred-pound monster it was destined to become. Still, it was harmless enough, and in no position to throw itself overboard to a watery death like her pet chicken had. It also soiled his deck far less frequently than the hen, thereby earning itself a stay of execution.

Edwin balanced on his tiptoes atop an empty upturned crate that had once held shot balls, his stubby fingers gripped white on the rail. O'Malley stood beside the boy, near enough to grab him should he pitch himself overboard in excitement at catching his first albatross. Bobbing about in the choppy wake, a baited hook floated on a line attached to a wooden shingle. A great-winged fowl dove in curiously for a closer look, and Seamus turned sharply at Edwin's squeal of excitement at snagging it.

"Hush, Edwin. Men are sleeping," Seamus chastised in a low voice.

"Sorry, Cappy, but I got one, I got one!" Edwin whispered as O'Malley helped him reel in the trumpeting creature. The quarterdeck filled with long, flapping, black-tipped wings. Powerful feather-covered legs scrambled to escape, but O'Malley caught the bird with an expert swoop, pinning it between his knees. Gripping the snapping beak with one hand, he wiggled the hook free with his other—the bird no match against the sailor's wiry strength.

"Does a abbertross taste like chicken?" Edwin jumped off the crate, staring into the bird's round, unblinking eyes.

O'Malley's ginger-whiskered face broke into a grin. "No, Eddy, lad. We don't eat albatrosses. Ye'd bring a world of bad luck upon us if ye killed it. How about we have a wee look at this fellow, then send him back to his friends?"

"Oh." Edwin's voice shrank, and his nose rumpled. "He's stinky!"

"Not half as stinky as a fulmar," explained the Irishman patiently. "They spit their stomach oils at ye. This fine fellow's a rose compared to that mess of rotten fish and gut juice."

Edwin retched, and O'Malley laughed. Rising, he grasped the immense feathered body firmly under his arm, keeping a grip of the sharp beak. He glanced at Edwin balanced atop the box again. "Just say when."

At Edwin's nod, O'Malley released the albatross. It took

flight, the flurry of its wings sounding like the snapping of a shaken length of tarpaulin. It shook its majestic head as though in disbelief, or perhaps to rid itself of the memory of its recent unpleasant encounter.

"Look!" Edwin attempted a stage whisper, but failed. "It's flying—just like Elias can fly." Settling a distance away on the water, the white bird rose up the high, heavy swell before tipping over the top and disappearing in the waves behind.

Seamus smiled. Oh, for those carefree days as a young midshipman that delivered him such frivolities, though there was a satisfying power in now having command of a vessel. And there was also a certain comfort that Elias was never far from Edwin's mind. Far from being bowed by grief, the youngster's easy acceptance that his twin's presence was still about eased Seamus's own heartache. He shook his head clear of his daydreaming. He should be paying vigilance to how his new ship handled rather than his son's bird-catching efforts. He glanced up. The sails maximised the excellent winds currently impregnating them. Watching the billowing canvas a few minutes longer, he swung his gaze to the bank of cumulus clouds gathering in the distance and squinted at the flat, dark base. "What the devil?" he murmured. It was Chittenden's watch, and he was doing nothing to prepare for the prevailing weather.

Spotting Chittenden near the bow, he dropped below and, narrowing his eyes, strode towards him. "Mr Chittenden?"

"Sir." The man's tone dripped. His stringy hair whipped about his head in a frenzy.

"You're driving the ship too heavy. Why haven't you taken in the topsail? If there's a squall lurking in those clouds, you'll lose the lot."

Chittenden squinted up at the masts and blew out a noisy breath. "You said you wanted *maximum* speed from her. I'm only doing what *you* ordered. Sir."

A flash of anger flared up his nape. "Damn it, Chittenden!

She's smacking the waves like a drunkard servicing a dock whore. Just what in Heaven's name are you doing, man?"

"That rainbow-wielding monster two days back barely carried a stiff breeze." Chittenden licked the white film of salt from his lips and cast out a finger. "We'll blow past that little rain cloud before it even has half a chance to spit on us." He shrugged and patted the gunwale. "Besides, she'll either carry the topsail, or drag it—but I'll have the *Elias* to Sydney Town in record time."

Seamus clenched his teeth and swallowed hard. "Not by destroying *my* ship in the process, you won't!" He studied the straining canvas again, his eyes watering against the sun's glare, then scowled at the tower of clouds on the horizon. They might yet miss it, but it paid to be prepared.

Hanging onto the main topmast yardarm, new topman Crowleigh grinned dementedly at Toby Hicks as they stood swaying on the footrope, their midriffs pressed firmly against the wooden beam, the wind tearing at their hair and shirts. Preparing to strap a new pulley around the yardarm, Crowleigh had the strap and pulley, a coil of rope, and a marlinespike hung about his neck. Hicks's face slid into a glower of concern as he whipped his head around, studying the sails. He mouthed something at Seamus, but the buffeting winds pinched his words like a pickpocket snatching trinkets.

The dread brewing in the pit of Seamus's stomach burned like rancid burgoo, and he barked upwards, "Furl the topmast! Reef—" The squall's invisible fist punched him from behind, his voice drowned by a short, quick rattle of thunder as the topmast and topsail tumbled in a ballooning tangle.

Heavens above! Seamus gripped the quarterdeck rail, his neck cramping from tipping back so far. He let out a low groan as Crowleigh and Hicks grabbed wildly at the tangle of plummeting ropes. *Hang tight—grab hold!* Locking his knees in anticipation, he almost cried out with relief as Hicks grasped two good handfuls of rope. Hicks's yell of alarm turned into a shriek of pain. Seamus winced, knowing that the momentum down the fibrous cables would be tearing the flesh from his palms, but Hicks held on. Crowleigh hit the water's surface with a wet crack of a splitting melon. The weight of the tackle around his neck instantly pulled him under, his white shirt billowing ghost-like for a fleeting moment before disappearing.

Christ Al-bloody-mighty! What an unholy mess! Sloughing the horror that coated his back the way a snake sheds old skin, Seamus burst into life. "All hands! A man overboard!"

Carpenter Hanson kicked over the half-filled water barrel, launching it into the ocean for the stricken man. Blight wrestled the helm, immediately spinning it down. Seamus braced for the change in momentum as the *Elias* pushed across the wind. Lashing the wooden wheel into this position, Blight thundered across the main deck to help the others lower the cutter. Seamus peered over the gunwale as half a dozen men flung themselves into the lowering rowboat. He scanned the wake's creaming arc as the *Elias* slowly circled, hoping—praying. *Come on, Crowleigh, man. Where are you?*

Straining against the oars, the rowers dragged the cutter past the stern towards where Crowleigh had fallen. For crying out loud! There was little hope of saving the poor wretch, though he knew none of his men would give up until they had exhausted themselves.

Hicks picked his way down the tangled rigging with slow, agonised movements. Roused from his cabin by the commotion, Dr Sykes inspected Hicks's shredded palms, the white, wet, shiny blisters bulging through the oozing blood. With strips of clean linen, Sykes bound the destroyed hands. Hicks cradled his clawed, quivering fingers to his chest, his sandy-whiskered face greyed with pain. He bowed his shoulders as he leaned heavily on the mizzenmast's trunk for support. Seamus empathised at the blazing blue pain that would be searing up

Hicks's arms. Rope burns—especially ones that deep—were pure agony.

"Bearing up, Hicks?" asked Seamus.

"Yes, sir," Hicks grunted through gnashing teeth.

Seamus turned his attention back to the ocean, his misery sinking as the cutter circled the empty surface. With sweat-stuck hair clinging to their cheeks and foreheads, the oarsmen reluctantly turned towards the *Elias*. Beside Seamus, Chittenden leaned his elbows on the gunwale. The showboating popinjay would pay for this! Seamus's muscles quivered with the heat of the rage running through him.

At the sight of the returning cutter, Chittenden snorted and bellowed, "Get back out there, you lazy sods. Find him!"

The anger simmering behind Seamus's ribcage tore through his core and erupted. "Damn it, Chittenden!" He rounded on the man, thrusting a finger skywards as the wind shook the broken topmast like a spindly twig. "Look what you've done! I *said* you were driving her too heavy! Now you've damaged my ship *and* cost me one of my men!"

"I also said we'd sail right by that rain—and we did," said Chittenden in a nonchalant drawl. He held up his palms. "A broken topmast is an unfortunate hazard of such a voyage."

"It's not worth the price of a man's life!"

The first mate blinked slowly, drawing himself up to his full height. "How many men have *you* lost at sea over the years? Hmm? No one aboard this ship was pressed into service. Crowleigh was here by his own volition—he knew the risks."

Cold-hearted bastard! Seamus flicked a look up into the tangled rigging, eerily devoid of sailors. Every man had come down to help with Crowleigh's rescue. He glared back at Chittenden. "Get up there, you incompetent fool! Clear that lot away before it blows to tatters, or I'll string you from the yardarm myself!"

Chittenden's smooth cheeks were pale, but he looked at

Seamus through half-lidded eyes and shrugged. "No fuss or bother. I'll soon secure that lot. Shan't take me long."

Seamus bunched his fist, the build-up of the punch swelling in his chest and back. The impudent sod had no idea just how close he was to earning a broken nose. Flexing the tension from his old injured wrist with a click, Seamus watched Chittenden begin his unhurried ascent up the rigging. He ordered Bosun to signal the cutter to return.

Turning at Carpenter Hanson's voice, Seamus spied him and young Hicks heading towards the mainmast. The carpenter's marlinespike was slung around his thick neck with a heavy coil of rope. A large knife sat in its sheath on his hip, and he chatted to young Hicks, equally equipped.

"Now's as good a time as any for you to learn the ropes, my boy. Up you go." Carpenter Hanson clapped young Hicks's back, and the youngster's throat swallowed thickly. Seamus followed his upward gaze to where Chittenden lay along the yard, trying to smother the loose sails with his long arms and legs. Every time the *Elias* pitched, Chittenden stopped shimmying and held tight.

"How'll we pick up the fallen mast?" squeaked young Hicks, his neck craning, his broken nose scrunching lopsidedly. "What is that—a hundred and fifty feet high?"

Seamus frowned at the topsail billowing messily. The tangle of ropes appeared to be knotting themselves angrily as they rode over the swells. Before Carpenter Hanson had a chance to reply, Seamus held up his hand to the two men. "One minute, please, gentlemen."

Hanson and young Hicks paused, turning expectantly. Seamus rubbed the slick of sweat from his top lip with his thumb and nodded at Lincoln. "Bosun, all hands aft."

"Aye, sir." Lincoln piped the order.

Seamus pointed threateningly at the pale blond head bobbing

along the yardarm and roared, "Except you, Chittenden. Stay up there and rectify that shameful disorder."

With the returned oarsmen gathered in an exhausted huddle, Seamus studied the mustered men. He rubbed a damp palm discretely down one thigh. "Men, are you satisfied that all has been done to save Colin Crowleigh?"

Carpenter Hanson stepped forward, the marlin spike swaying from the rope about his neck. "Sir, Crowleigh don't know how to swim. He was too heavily dressed." Soft murmurs of agreement rippled around.

Seamus stiffened his spine and pinched his lips. "Very well then. Smythe and young Hicks, bring up Crowleigh's chest. As captain, I'm answerable to the deceased man's effects. I'll hold an auction for his possessions. Bid what you will for them. I want nothing left that can be called his."

Smythe, a new ordinary seaman, was on that awkward verge of manhood where his round, un-whiskered cheeks betrayed him as a boy, but his blossoming confidence and fortitude hinted of the man he would become. That awful haircut did him no favour, though. The solid chunk of black fringe had the uncanny curve of a bowl about it. Nevertheless, Smythe responded immediately to Seamus's order, as did young Hicks.

Seamus fought back a grimace of guilt, and he squeezed his elbows tightly into his ribs. Crowleigh's life was barely out of his body, and here he was casting the last of him away. He rubbed a knuckle hard over his lips. Needs must when the devil drives. He coughed to clear the thickening in his throat. "And then I want all hands restoring this vessel to full working order."

He glanced around the sailors' grim-set faces. Several glowered at Chittenden up the mainmast, their faces as dark and ominous as the receding grey clouds.

SEVERAL WEEKS LATER, the *Elias* prepared to anchor in Cape Town's Table Bay, its cutters readied to go ashore for provisions. Seamus had given the children permission to be above with Miss Lissing, to see Table Mountain shrouded in its tablecloth of early morning mist.

Seamus hunched over his desk in the captain's lounge and shivered, chilled by a mild fever. He was recalculating their arrival in Sydney Town when Grace entered the lounge, carrying two pewter mugs. Stopping beside his chair, she offered him the steaming elderflower tea. Scooping both hands around the hot metal, Seamus inhaled the steam, disappointed that his blocked nose deprived him of the florally fragrance.

"How are you feeling today, my love?" asked Grace, perching on the arm of his chair, blowing her own tea.

Seamus slid one arm around her hip and rested his cheek against her breast. The white cotton was blissfully cool against his blazing skin. "Miserable. It's but a trifling sniffle," he assured her.

"You aren't alone in your misery." Grace widened her eyes. "Chittenden's in fine form today."

Wincing at her words, Seamus sipped the fragrant tea. The warm liquid soothed his scratchy gullet. Heavenly bliss. He did not wish his enjoyment spoiled by Grace's complaint about Chittenden, but he dutifully glanced at her.

"There's no jesting and enjoyment in the men these days," she protested.

Seamus tightened his brow and slid the half-empty pot beside the ledger on the desk. "True, but the men all work just a little harder and a little quicker under that dragon-green gaze of his." By Neptune, it galled him to give Chittenden any credit, but if they were to make up for lost time, the man's efficiency could not be overlooked.

The look on Grace's face told him she thought otherwise. "Only hastened by fire-breathing insults!" she quipped.

He curled his arm tighter around her hip. His dream of pushing the *Elias* to set a blistering time to Sydney Town had initially dissolved in disappointment, but now, he tapped the inky figures on the page before him. "By my calculations, we've made up that lost time. And in this new venture of ours, Dulcinea, time is money."

Grace thudded her pot of tea on his desk, the pale-yellow liquid slopping over her hand. She wiped it on her plum skirts. "Seamus, he's just threatened to flog Shelby Hicks for stacking wood on the deck. Is that not his duty? To bring the wood up from the hold for both galleys?"

Seamus's head pounded. "Unpleasant conduct aside, Chittenden is breaking no laws."

"No, but he's breaking the men's spirits. Where on earth did you find him?"

Seamus opened the desk drawer with a dry scrape and handed Grace the folded packet. The flap of the cracked seal yawned open. "He came with this reference. From the Duke of Berkshire."

"Are you acquainted with his lordship?" Grace inspected the letter's contents.

"Not personally. Admiral Baxter is, though. He assured me that Berkshire is a respectable man whose word is reliable."

Folding the paper, Grace tossed it back into the open drawer. "Hm! Clearly, his lordship is either a poor judge of character, or Chittenden hid his true colours from the man."

"I agree. Chittenden's a contemptible brute, but the quicker we arrive in New Holland, the quicker we can be relieved of him," Seamus reasoned. He closed his eyes as Grace's slim fingers brushed his hair back off his temple, her light touch relieving his thumping skull. He opened one eye as she asked another question.

"What of his insubordination to you? Surely he has broken the law there?"

The marrow of his bones ached with weariness. He turned to look at his wife's flushed face. "We run a much smaller crew on this packet, as you well know. To lock Chittenden up now just before we enter the westerlies will leave us another pair of hands short." He rubbed both hands over his face. "We're already two pairs down." He swallowed deeply, thinking of Colin Crowleigh lying on the bottom of the ocean, and of Toby Hicks's torn hands. "It doesn't make sense to take down another."

"Wouldn't you rather be a man short than put your trust in that waster? He's brought harm to our ship and to the men's morale."

"Hush, my heart. It doesn't help to have anyone hear of our discord with the man."

"But—"

Seamus halted her indignant splutter by pressing his finger to her mouth. "Do you really want to add hours to O'Malley's watch as second mate by taking an officer from him? We've long, cold, hard days ahead of us. O'Malley won't thank you for burdening him with the extra work." He slid his finger along her lips and traced the outline of her jaw. "I'll be the first to help Chittenden carry his trunk ashore in New Holland. He shan't be making his return journey with us. Let me handle his insubordination." Shoving his chair back, he drew her onto his lap and kissed the soft skin behind her ear. "And in the meanwhile—" Her skin pebbled against his lips. "Let's be thankful the children have kept to order."

Her breathy laugh hitched as he curled his hand around the curve of her hip and, kneading her soft flesh, shifted her higher. He might be temporarily deprived of that addictive scent of hers, but there was nothing wrong with his other senses. Her nails raked through the hair at his temples again and he closed his eyes in bliss. Her hands stopped, framing his face, and he opened his eyes. Mischief danced at the corners of her mouth, and his heart thudded. In broad daylight? Brazen little minx!

EMMA LOMBARD

"A feigned flogging won't bring the likes of Chittenden to order," she teased.

After circumventing Emily and Edwin's punishment, he had approached Grace with the caution of a lion circling a lioness with new cubs, careful to keep upwind of her ire. Her reward for him not harming the children had surprised and delighted him—and it was insatiable.

"Grace." The rasp in his voice had little to do with his fever. Hell's bells, had he known earlier in his parenting journey that a gentled fatherly hand would deliver such impassioned husbandly delights, he would have two unholy terrors on his hands. She wriggled her pert bottom in his lap, and he growled as his desire betrayed him. "Grace, we mustn't—"

At alarmed cries of warning outside, Seamus thudded his forehead against her collarbone. What now? Stealing a quick kiss, he nudged Grace off his lap and scraped back his chair. Striding from the lounge, he forced his heavy legs to look lively.

Despite the scenic view of the curved bay with its flat-topped mountain, Seamus's innards clenched at the large merchant ship looming on their leeward side. Her topgallant masts were neatly taken in as she bobbed peacefully at anchor, the American stars and stripes fluttering idly at her peak. Heavens! The current! It was drawing the *Elias* in too quickly. The *Elias*'s men worked frenetically to gather the sails.

"Let go the anchor!" Chittenden bellowed from the quarter-deck, his voice twanging with panic. Despite his order being obeyed immediately, the dropped anchor did nothing to slow their approach. Chittenden shrieked, "Damn the lot of you! Anchor's gone down foul. Pay out chain. Pay out chain!"

Seamus's heart dropped into his heels. By Neptune's forked trident! There was no time to let go the second anchor. The *Elias* drifted broadside towards the American vessel. Up on the quar-terdeck, the children's shrill screams mingled with the circling seagulls above. Grace tore up the stairs and, gathering the children into the circle of her arms, dragged them down to sit. Turning his attention back to the *Elias*, Seamus gripped the gunwale, his fingers biting into the wood.

"Collision! Larboard side!" he roared. The ship's bell, clanging in alarm, was accompanied by the shrill whistle of Bosun's pipe.

The splintering shudder reverberated through Seamus's legs as the *Elias* grated along the other ship's hull. He glared at the *Peacock*'s jib-boom passing between the *Elias*'s fore- and main-masts. Like a great scythe catching against shafts of wheat, the wooden beam severed their rigging. The larboard rail splintered as though struck by cannon shot. With a sharp, neat snap, the *Peacock* lost her martingale at the bow. A dozen sailors from both vessels stabbed fiercely at the gunwales with handspikes, pushing the vessels clear of one another. The collision slowed them and, as more anchor chain released, the *Elias* swung clear of the *Peacock*.

Sweet Christ in Heaven! Seamus's breath exploded from him as he realised that, besides tangled anchor chains, no great harm had come to either ship.

"Sir!" O'Malley's sharp retort came from behind.

Seamus glared over his shoulder.

O'Malley's freckles dissolved against his puce skin. "Has Chittenden's incompetence not reached its limits, Captain? Jaysus wept! His father should've wiped him off with a curtain." The second mate stared in dismay at the shredded dangling ropes above. His sleep-puffed eyes blinked against the bright daylight.

"It has, O'Malley. And I've reached mine too," said Seamus in a low growl. He bellowed for the second anchor to be let go. The satisfying rattle of dropping chain was a balm on his taut nerves. He bounded up the quarterdeck.

Grace drew Emily to her feet. Edwin's wide eyes darted around at the disarray.

"Is everyone unharmed?" Seamus puffed.

Drawing Emily into her side, Grace nodded. "Yes, we're well." She glanced towards the bow, frowning. "Can't say that about the *Elias,* though."

Seamus ran his hand over Edwin's fine blond hair and, gently tugging on his ear, plastered a smile to his lips. "But a little bump, my boy. Nothing to worry about." He arched one brow at Grace and Miss Lissing. "Please, take the children below while I attend this matter." He flicked his eyes over to Chittenden, and Grace nodded.

With his fury barely in check, Seamus headed across the white-scrubbed planks, his strides wide and perfectly balanced. Chittenden's neck flushed, but he set his shoulders and raised his nose at Seamus's approach.

"Chittenden!" Seamus barked, the heat rising from him prickling the skin beneath his tight collar. "What the devil are you playing at, man!"

With an all-too-familiar tut, Chittenden drawled, "Not my fault the anchor ran foul."

Did the bastard gain pleasure from his own ineptitude? Seamus snapped his teeth together, driving a spear of pain through his already thumping head. "For crying out loud, Chittenden, have a care, man! There's expediency, and then there's downright foolhardiness. Has the sun addled your mind?" A large blister bulged on Chittenden's nose like a pulsing oyster. He clearly was not coping with the subtropics, even in winter. Heaven help the man at the height of summer.

Sniffing, Chittenden rubbed his nose, and the bulging blister dented. "What creature can rest with his skin ablaze?" he grumbled.

"To your quarters immediately, Chittenden. And for Christ's sake, get some sleep." Seamus bit back a retort to tell him to go stick his head in a water barrel first.

Chittenden wove his fingers together and, turning his palms

outwards, cracked his knuckles before shrugging. "Don't mind if I do. Since it's the end of my watch anyhow."

Seamus's temper bubbled like an erupting volcano. Drawing on a lifetime of discipline, he allowed his heartbeat to slow and regulated his breathing so that when he gave his next orders, it was with complete control.

For the next three hours, under his calm instruction, the *Elias* gradually untangled from the *Peacock*. With professionalism restored, he disregarded the humiliation of being dragged halfway across the waterfront before a harbour full of ships. He brought them neatly to anchor, safely away from any other vessels. The decent thing to do now was to apologise to the captain of the *Peacock*. He intended to restock as quickly as possible and make a hasty escape, since he was undoubtedly the laughing-stock of the Cape Colony. Fire and damnation, how would he ever live down the shame?

Chapter Five

INDIAN OCEAN, 30 JUNE 1841

A week later, at the helm, Grace clasped the teak handles of the ship's wheel. With a steady pressure against her palms, she enjoyed how the *Elias* responded to the wind in her sails with as much delight as the children playing on her deck.

The late afternoon of the Early Dog Watch was Grace's favourite time of the day. It was the only time the children were free to make noise since all the crew were awake for their evening meal. Emily dragged Alby in a miniature wooden wagon. The playful clicking wooden wheels added to the children's excited chatter and laughter. Miss Lissing and Sally McGilney hovered about, vigilant as always.

She watched her husband lean over the brass binnacle. With a measured look, he studied the compass needle floating and levelling itself under the glass dome. Nodding in satisfaction, he snapped the binnacle lid closed. The *Elias*'s bow cut effortlessly through the large swells, and a fine mist of wave spray hung in the air.

Moving beside her, Seamus clasped his hands behind his back, with his knees and body swaying easily as though he were a part of the ship. From up here they could watch the children's antics on the deck below. He glanced up at the sails, and Grace caught the smirk pulling at his lips—yes, he was happy with what he saw. And so was she.

At the children's laughter, she looked down at Edwin, now valiantly trying to tug the wagon. His stubby arms quivered, and his feet slid helplessly against the tortoise's weight. As the *Elias*'s bow rode up a swell, the wagon rolled backwards, yanking Edwin off his feet. Clinging tenaciously to the handle, he scraped halfway across the deck on his stomach before letting go. Grace flinched. Flooded with an overwhelming desire to scoop up Edwin and chase after the runaway cart, she loosened her grip on the helm. No! Her duty this minute was to the ship.

Tightening her grip, she watched as Ben Blight stuck out his foot and stopped the wagon's uncontrolled careening. Miss Lissing scooped Edwin to his feet, and Sally dusted him down. Emily laughed at her brother's antics, and Grace chuckled with relief that Edwin's pouting lip drew back in a smile. Ben removed his foot, and the wagon rolled freely towards Edwin again on the downward side of the swell. Edwin snatched at the handle for another try. At Seamus's huff of brief laughter, Grace turned. His eyes were soft, and the smile crease on his cheek deepened. She loved watching him enjoy the children. The further they sailed from Cape Town, the lighter Seamus's mood had become after the *Elias*'s mishap with the *Peacock*.

"You know, Dulcinea." He sidled a step nearer. "I pinch myself daily waking up beside you on this ship." Seamus pressed his arm against hers. "Have I told you what an excellent sailor you are?"

Her wayward curls were escaping once again from their

kerchief prison and fluttering across her face. "A good commander knows how to bring out the best in his sailors."

Seamus dipped his chin, his voice low. "I will instruct you and teach you in the way you should go; I will counsel you with my loving eye on you."

"Psalm thirty-two?" she grinned.

"Verse eight." He winked. His smile faded. "Pity Chittenden doesn't adopt a similar integrity."

Grace scoffed. "He isn't even worth my disappointment." She smiled at Ben stopping before the helm.

Placing one hand on the wheel, he returned her grin, his teeth flashing white through his ruddy whiskers. "Afternoon, sir. Mrs F."

"Blight," greeted Seamus.

Grace handed him the helm. "Thank you for chocking the wagon down there." She waved at the children below. "You saved poor Alby a nasty visit down the rear hatch. I hope the children aren't being too noisy?"

Ben's deep laugh boomed. "No, no, Mrs F. The young'uns' frivolities remind the lads of their offspring at home. They're glad of the happy noise."

Patting Ben's arm appreciatively, she headed down to the children. Alongside the starboard rowboat, upside-down and battened on the skids, Grace paused as a peculiar sound cut through the children's laughter. A buffeting gust blew the noise away, but she stood still, waiting for the eddying wind to bring it back to her. There it was again!

Tilting her head side to side, she determined the origin beneath the upturned rowboat. Grace ducked to peer under. Stinking blasted seaweed! Chittenden! He lay on the pile of tarpaulins, his hands behind his head, his mouth slack—snoring!

Ha! Have you now, you idle wretch! Grace stood, blood pounding in her ears. She took several deep breaths to steady her thrashing heart, her mind working through the next few moments. After escaping consequence for all his other mishaps, she was damned if she would allow the bastard to get away with sleeping on duty. Glancing up at the helm, she beckoned Seamus. He waggled his brows and nodded, sidling down the stairs.

"You summoned, wife?" He smiled suggestively.

His curious blue eyes, warm with humour, cooled as she injected displeasure into her voice. "Seamus, it's Chittenden. He's asleep." She jabbed her finger at the upturned cutter. "This is a *shameful* dereliction of duty."

Seamus's chin dipped, and his lips drew tight. "You're correct. It is." He dove under the rowboat, and Chittenden's snoring ended in a snort and a yelp. Seamus unceremoniously dragged the disgraced officer into the open by his scruff.

The first mate's habitually pristine clothes were rumpled. Hatless, his diluted yellow hair whipped messily across his sunburned, peeling forehead. He shrugged against Seamus's grip. "Unhand me!" The red of his sunburnt ears deepened, and he swiped the trail of sleep-induced drool from his chin.

Grace folded her arms as Chittenden stilled, suddenly becoming aware of his surroundings.

Seamus's white-knuckled fists snatched Chittenden's shirt front. "Chittenden! You're neither man, nor boy, nor soldier, nor sailor! You couldn't hit water if you fell off the ship!" snarled Seamus. "When I ordered you to sleep, I did not mean *on watch*! I'm locking you in chains."

A tingling creep of sweat broke out across Grace's scalp— she had never seen Seamus so furious.

Chittenden smoothed back his ruffled hair. "Have you never seen a man sent mad by the fiery sun, Captain Fitzwilliam? It's not a pretty sight. I was simply seeking a moment's reprieve in the shade." A collection of sailors and shepherds gathered around. Chittenden peered superciliously down his long, straight nose. "I'm first mate," he snivelled. "You require me to command this ship."

If she had not seen that Chittenden was being perfectly serious, Grace would have laughed aloud. Instead, she watched Seamus's eyes narrow. "What makes you think I want a man who barely earns his salt at my helm?"

Chittenden scoffed. "*Your* helm? It's common knowledge you lost your fortune on government bonds. This ship only came to be because you swallowed your pride and used your *wife's* money." He snorted. "Just because *you* have no shame in letting a woman come to your rescue, what makes you think that this crew wants a female in charge?"

Grace thrust her hands on her hips. "You've let power go to your head, Chittenden. Only a weak or inexperienced officer uses belittlement to keep his men in line. So, which are you? Inexperienced—or weak?"

Chittenden laughed mockingly. "I'll not have a woman question me. As first mate, I deserve to be respected."

Seamus pointed an accusatory finger at Chittenden. "Well, as captain, I'll answer that. You're inexperienced *and* weak. I warrant you've spent your whole life trying to gain your father's approval. Which is why you wield your authority so poorly."

By Chittenden's blink of surprise, Grace knew Seamus had hit the right note.

Seamus grunted. "I'm still unsure if it's your ineptitude at sailing that broke my topmast and drove us into another ship, or whether it's a ploy to slow us down." Scratching his chin, he added, "If it's the latter, then that makes you your father's agent."

Chittenden scoffed, spraying spittle. "Pah! Speaking of naval ineptitude—your own naval disgrace sank you to become master of an unproven vessel." Chittenden's white teeth shone in the sunlight, his sneer crooked. "Besides, I haven't failed entirely. God knows I've been pushing this tub to her limits. There's still a chance we'll reach Sydney before the *Fireli*—" He broke off abruptly, his lashes drooping.

"The *Firelight*? Your father's ship!" said Seamus.

Seamus had told Grace how he hoped Chittenden's competition with his father would sharpen his decisions, but this was clearly not the case. It had proven disastrous. She inhaled a long breath to check her tirade of choice curses. Instead, she said, "Your dogged desire to better your father has resulted in dangerous actions. You've jeopardised not only this ship and her men but my family too."

Chittenden made a show of earnestly waving an arm at the gathered crowd. "Does this woman have the authority to put *your* lives in her hands?"

A tremble of doubt fluttered in Grace's chest as she saw some of the new men shuffle uncomfortably under her direct stare. A couple cleared their throats, their gazes sliding away. Others looked at Chittenden, nodding their heads with growing looks of regard.

Seamus snapped. "Shut your mouth, Chittenden, or I'll strip you of all rank."

"Ahh." Chittenden smiled judicially at the gatherers. "But we're heading into turbulent waters, gentlemen. Wouldn't you rather trust a *qualified* officer than the wife of a disgraced commander? What sort of a sailor do you imagine he has trained her to be?"

The question hung heavy and unanswered.

Grace studied the uneasy faces. Her heartbeat pounded in her ears, and her gut clenched, but she spoke with a confidence stoked by the fires of anger. "Captain Fitzwilliam handpicked each of you because you're the best. We *will* sail this ship safely to Sydney, but we can only do it with your help. Neither Captain Fitzwilliam nor I want to see our investment sunk to the bottom of the ocean through incompetent command."

O'Malley nodded and raised his voice. "Mrs F. is correct.

Only feeble-minded halfwits would fall prey to such silver-tongued nonsense. This man has no regard for yer welfare. He's already proven that with his heavy hand towards ye."

Toby added, "Hear, hear! I'd much rather put my trust in Mrs F. than in a lazy dog who can't even stay awake on a four-hour watch."

The crew's mumbles of agreement swelled. Grace discerned that Chittenden's sleeping on watch put everyone in mortal danger—it was the worst sin a sailor could commit.

"I don't much like being on watch, but you'll never catch me kipping on the job."

"Poncy bloody officer. Thinks just because 'e's got 'imself an education that 'e's better than us."

"Chuck the soft cock down the hold."

Seamus glared at the crowd for so long that some began to clear their throats, shuffling when his gaze flicked upon them. Wooden creaks and lapping waves filled the silence. Even Grace wished he would say something.

He inhaled deeply and announced, "Lucius Chittenden is no longer an officer on this ship."

Grace gasped as he gripped Toby's slim shoulder. Cradling his bandaged hands to his chest, Toby firmed his sandy chin as Seamus spun him to face the crowd. "I choose Toby Hicks. He's an active and intelligent sort. Plus, he knows this ship better than any man here. And now he's your first mate. Obey him as you would me and remember to call him Mr Hicks." Seamus swivelled his gaze from Grace back to the men. "Is anyone unclear about their duty?"

The crowd responded with instant rumbles. "No, sir."—"Perfectly clear, sir."

"Oh, and Mr Chittenden, your no longer holding rank isn't an invitation to slack off. I expect to see you at every muster, musket drill, and watch. Is that clear?"

Chittenden peered mulishly from beneath his snowy brows. "Aye, aye, *Captain*."

Seamus nodded curtly. "Carry on."

There was an instant explosion of movement. Grace shuffled closer to Seamus and Toby to make room for the passing men.

Seamus turned to Toby, his lips twisting wryly. "And *that*, Mr Hicks, is how one ends up in the officer's land of silver spoons and china teacups."

THAT NIGHT in the great cabin, Grace stirred as Seamus slid beneath the covers. She rolled over, her exploring hand finding his cool bare hip and pulling him closer. She eased her head onto his chest as his arm enveloped her back. His skin was cold, and she shivered.

"Where've you been?" she murmured sleepily.

Seamus kissed the top of her nightcap. "Taking some air. Go back to sleep, Dulcinea."

She tipped her head, opening one eye. "I'm awake. What is it?"

Seamus blew out his breath. "Chittenden. I can't be sure he hasn't been planted aboard the *Elias*."

Sitting up, she twisted and lit the lantern on the side table. "You believe him a spy?"

Stuffing his pillows behind his head, Seamus hummed as shadows danced across his tight, stubbled jaw. "I'm unsure what he is. After the debacle with Father Babcock aboard the *Clover*, I thought I'd have a better nose for the stink of betrayal. Babcock worked under a clandestine veil, but Chittenden shows no such reserve."

"What'll you do with him?" Grace stuffed a sleep-ruffled curl back under her cap.

He reached for another loose curl and twined the brown

strand around his finger. "Even if he isn't acting as his father's agent, he's still a sloppy sailor." Pulling the strings of her night-gown, he arched one brow suggestively. "It beggars belief how his haste to beat his father keeps slowing us down."

"He probably thinks if he arrives first that he'll have first pick of the wool loads." Grace rolled atop him, and her desire stirred as his skin warmed beneath her. He ran a cool hand under the hem of her shift, and her skin peppered as his touch trailed up her back.

"Utterly unnecessary since there are more than enough bales in Sydney Town to go around."

Dipping her head, she savoured the cool of his mouth against her sleepy warmth, his roving lips distracting her from all thoughts of wool bales. He was not a selfish lover, and she appreciated how he enjoyed the dalliance as well as the dance, but tonight was her turn to lead.

When she released him from the kiss, he added, "The whole reason we've embarked on this journey of madness is because the colony requires regular and reliable transport."

Grace's heart thudded with wanting. "Madness, you say?" she breathed.

"Sheer madness." He grinned, flipping her onto her back. Wrenching off his shirt, he dropped it to the floor. She admired his wide-shouldered torso. Trailing her fingers tantalisingly slowly down the warm skin of his belly, she undid the strings of his trousers and freed his hips of their captivity.

"Well, I don't plan on letting Gregory Chittenden beat us to Sydney Town." Wrapping her legs around his back, she sensed his quiver of restraint in his flanks, fully aware he could easily take control of the situation. He waited for her to give the next order. "I want *him* to be the one waiting behind *us* at Queen's Wharf." She cupped his buttocks, thrilled by his compliance as she drew him nearer. "Speaking of behinds—" A groan escaped her throat as he inhaled sharply.

Lucius Chittenden had almost ruined the *Elias*'s maiden voyage—he would blazing-well not ruin this moment with her husband. She pulled Seamus down, and he covered her mouth with his, firmly slamming the hatch on her thoughts of that wretched waster.

Chapter Six

INDIAN OCEAN, 20 JULY 1841

Seamus pinned the chart's curled edge flat, unfurling its expanse across his desk. Swaying oil lamps sprinkled a warm glow around the captain's lounge as four heads cast domed shadows over the outlines of landmasses. Glancing up at Grace, Hicks, and O'Malley, Seamus pointed to a tiny island. "We curved south-east past Tristan da Cunha ten days back. My current calculation puts us here." He slid his finger to the middle of the Indian Ocean—halfway between the tip of the Cape of Good Hope and the continent of New Holland.

Three intent faces peered earnestly at the spot on the map. Hicks's slim eyebrows arched beneath his golden mop, and he looked ruefully at Seamus. "And we're definitely not heading further south, sir?"

"No." Seamus shook his head. "We're skimming as near to the westerlies as I dare, making the best time possible—despite

Chittenden's efforts." His sentence finished heavily with a pang of resentment.

O'Malley's Irish accent broadened. "Do the icebergs trouble ye, sir? Extra men on watch'll solve the concern, will it not?"

Seamus inhaled through his nostrils. "Not *only* icebergs—the wild winds—and waves too. I'll not risk my ship, nor my family."

O'Malley dipped his head. "Aye, aye, sir."

Seamus had made up his mind. "It's better for business to arrive late, but in one piece, than to not arrive at all." He jolted at the sudden volley of fire outside. Of course, Bosun Lincoln had the men drilling with their muskets and pistols today.

"Thank you, gentlemen," said Seamus, rolling up the charts. He nodded in dismissal, turning to Grace when Hicks and O'Malley disappeared through the door. "Time to examine the state of our defences." Tying the roll with a leather binding, he slid it onto a shelf carved just for this purpose. He offered Grace his arm. "Care to join me, my heart?"

"I would." She snatched her woollen coat and tartan shawl from their hooks, accompanying him into the icy southern air. He grimaced, the lapels of his own coat pulled up high around his neck.

Up on the forecastle deck, Lincoln ordered, "Make ready!" His clean-shaven face was pinched with cold, and he pulled his woollen hat over his ears, thrusting his hands into his coat pockets.

Seamus frowned as Chittenden beckoned to Smythe. Unhooking the powder horn from his belt, Chittenden dropped it and kicked it over to the ordinary seaman.

"Fill that up, Smythe, and hurry up about it. You're slower than a week in prison." The white whirls of Chittenden's words curled around his head. Without hesitation, Smythe scooped up the powder horn and scurried down the main hatchway like a rat that had unexpectedly escaped from its feline tormentor.

Arrogant bastard! Seamus seethed. Grace's grip on his bicep tremored, and he realised she had seen it too. Unfolding Grace's arm from his, he said, "Wait here. I'll sort out that firebrand, once and for all."

Striding towards the bow, he stamped some warmth into his feet. None of the men firing their weapons were wearing gloves. Their fingers must have been near dropping off with the cold. Nearing the forecastle deck, he barked, "Chittenden!"

Chittenden jolted and swung around. His musket swung wide and he fumbled, juggling the weapon like a court jester. Seeing the wooden stock slip from his grasp, Seamus sucked in an icy breath. By Neptune's forked trident—the fool!

The iron barrel struck the deck, exploding in a flash of sparks and smoke as it discharged.

The impact stopped Seamus in his tracks as though a yardarm had swung down and crashed into his chest. Fire and damnation, was he shot? It should have hurt like hellfire, but the numbness spreading across his chest made no sense. He was still standing, so it could not be too dire, could it?

He turned towards Grace. In an instant, he was transported back to the apple orchard during the duel with Silverton. She had the same wide-eyed look of horror on her face when she had believed him shot, and she pressed towards him now in the same time-stretched manner as though the air were thick with slush. Last time, she had reached him, crushing the breath from his lungs; this time, she was out of reach, yet something else crushed his breath. He stumbled. By Neptune, he had not lost his footing like this since his first year as a midshipman. The white horses skimming the waves did not look angry enough to unbalance him. He patted his breastbone, surprised to find it warm and wet. The numbness gave way to a searing burn that burrowed through his chest like a glowing poker, and his knees crumpled, betraying him. Dulcinea! He should not have toiled so hard this journey—missed out on his children's laughter—on

Grace's companionship, her touch. Damn Chittenden for stealing precious time away from his family. He was not done being a husband, a father. Sweet Christ in Heaven, not yet. Not yet.

"SEAMUS!" Grace's brain thudded with every beat of her heart as she pounded across the planks. She stared down at her husband splayed on his back like a drunken sailor outside an alehouse. His cravat bobbed deeply as he gasped and swallowed air, his skin grey and waxen. He coughed wetly, and a sinister patch bloomed, darkening the blue of his coat.

"Dulcinea! I'm dying." His eyes rolled back.

Oh, Lord in Heaven. No! No! No! This was not happening. Dropping to her knees, she clawed at his cravat. Though his gasps for air were not from his necktie strangling him, she still cursed. Her wretched fingers were so cold. She fumbled with the knot. Damn you! Biting off her glove, she loosened the cravat's knot and wadded the cotton fabric against the seeping hole. The saliva in her mouth dried as the bunched linen quickly turned red. Searing bands of panic squeezed her ribcage like the tentacles of a giant squid.

Toby and O'Malley dropped beside her. Snatching her head around, she snapped, "Fetch Dr Sykes. Hurry!"

Seamus groaned, clawing at her hand pressing on his chest. Oh, dear Lord! His top lip glistened, his skin ashen like an early-morning hearth. How could he perspire so? It was freezing. There was so much blood! Too much! She need not be a physician to know he was gravely wounded. Panting, she ignored the hot slick on her hands and pressed harder to plug the life-force leaking from her husband's chest.

Billy dropped opposite her, covering her shaking hands with his. They were warmer than the bloodied cloth in her palms.

"Billy!" The icy air burned the back of her throat with each gulping breath.

"I'm here now, flower. 'Tis all right," soothed Billy. He glanced up at the gathering crowd. "Help me carry him to the lounge." He looked at Grace, and it was as though his wide brown eyes could see straight into her screaming mind. Grace bit back a sob as Billy nodded. "Keep pressing down. Don't let go."

"I shan't." Grace grimaced against the stony panic pulling her down. A basket of hands scooped Seamus up, and despite his long groan of pain, she gripped the bloody compress harder. "You shall *not* die on my watch, Seamus Fitzwilliam!" she muttered under her breath.

From the corner of her eye, Chittenden's white hair flashed in the sunlight. She whipped her head towards O'Malley. "Put that man in irons. Chain him to the hold."

"Oi!" objected Chittenden. "'Twas an accident. What fool startles a man handling a primed weapon?"

If Grace had not been so worried about Seamus, she would have smirked in satisfaction as O'Malley and Bosun Lincoln lunged at Chittenden.

Before the men slid Seamus onto the cleared chart table, Billy ran his hands along Seamus's back and held them up for inspection. No fresh blood.

Shelby Hicks hovered by the door, his wide shoulders filling the frame in a way his older brother's never did, though he carried the same unruffled compassion. "Carpenter Hanson's trick is to cauterise wounds with hot tar. Would you like me to fetch a jar of pitch, sir?"

Seamus's eyelids fluttered open, his forehead rucked in pain. "No one's branding me with hot tar," he growled.

He was awake! Grace did not let her relief, or the weight of her helplessness, interfere with her dexterity as she unbuttoned his coat.

Billy shook his head at Shelby. "That sailor's cure-all shan't help in this instance. You may go."

Shelby's face twisted in remorse, as though wishing he could do more, and he slunk back into the shadowed passage.

Out of impatience, Grace tore her husband's shirt open, scattering the buttons across the room like a handful of thrown pebbles.

Seamus gave a wheezy chuckle and raised his head to stare at his chest. "Heavens, Dulcinea. That was my favourite shirt. And you can't sew to save your life."

He might be jesting, but the unnatural size of his pupils and his flared nostrils spoke of his pain. Grace gently pressed his head back. "Hush, my love. We'll have you fixed in no time."

The red hole in his skin was no larger than a cigar burn, but it glared at her like a red-eyed cyclops staring up from Hell. The initial surge of bleeding had eased, and a lone crimson trickle leaked slowly down his ribs. A good sign, was it not? She covered the unsightly wound with a fresh wad.

Billy gently drew Grace's hand away, and lifting the edge of the bloodied cloth, he grunted. "There's no wound on your back to show the ball exited your body, sir."

"It's still in there?" piped Grace. Oh, good grief—could this be any worse?

Seamus sucked air between his clenched teeth. "Dig it out."

Billy scratched at his hairline with a bloodied thumb. "By the angle of entry, it'll be near your heart and lungs." He blew out a long, slow breath. "I daren't risk cutting it out, sir."

She stared at her husband's lips, moist with sweat but blissfully blood-free. "I see no pink froth at his lips."

Nodding curtly, Billy repacked the wound with several clean wads of linen. "It mightn't have nicked a lung, but it's still torn a path of destruction through him."

Seamus gripped Billy's wrist and groaned deeply. "Blasted Hell, Sykes. Easy does it."

"Sorry, sir," the physician apologised. "I'm nearly done poking and prodding."

Grace helped him roll Seamus as he bound his chest with long strips of towelling. Her husband's jaw locked, and he swallowed convulsively as she rolled him onto his back again. She stroked his forehead and lowered her lips to his ears. "That's it, my love. We're done. Rest easy."

Billy tipped a laudanum vial to Seamus's lips. "Once this takes effect, we'll move you to your berth, sir. You'll be more comfortable."

"Indeed. Less of a sight for the little ones," whispered Grace.

Seamus rolled his head. "Don't let them see me like this." He swallowed, but the motion stopped short. "Rather their last memory of me be a happy one."

A clouded image of Elias's stunned, open-eyed death mask flickered to Grace's mind—the v-shaped dent in his forehead weeping red. She was aware our Em and Eddy were plagued by the same nightmarish vision. Seamus was right, she could not let the children see him like this. Blinking hard, she shook her head. "Nonsense. There'll be plenty more memories. You'll see."

Did she sound convinced enough to ease his worry?

BY THE THIRD MORNING, Seamus's existing fever had worsened. Billy had vigilantly sat beside the berth for another day, swapping watch with Grace while she saw to her other duties with the children and the crew. Billy clapped his hand to a deep yawn that suddenly pulled his mouth open. Fighting her own sway of tiredness, Grace lifted the bandage's frayed edge. The dressing had stemmed the bleeding, and a dark, crusty scab was forming around the edges of the nasty perforation, the puffy skin angrily discoloured.

"It's becoming inflamed." Seamus's fiery flesh validated her claim.

Billy scrubbed his hands over his face, pushing his hair into an untidy hedgerow across his forehead. "It's a marvel he lasted the night." He took her hand, squeezing it.

Seamus's voice unexpectedly cut through the oppressive air in the cabin, and he gurgled deliriously. "Yes, sir, Admiral. All hands present."

"Please, Billy! There must be something you can do?" Grace gripped Billy's broad, hairy wrist. Desperation swelled and filled her chest like the foreboding waves before a storm. How could this be happening?

Billy's brown eyes were dark with distress. "I'm that sorry, flower. Truly I am." He patted her shoulder. "I'll wrap him up and give him laudanum. Keep him comfortable."

"But the children? What do I tell them?"

Billy eased his hand over her shoulder and squeezed. "Have them come say their goodbyes."

Grace snatched her shoulder away. "No! I can't just sit here and watch him die." She reached for her tartan shawl and oilskin. "I wish to return him to shore. As quickly as possible. We're only a few weeks away from New Holland."

"He doesn't have weeks, flower. Every hour now is a godsend."

"Do what you must, Billy. Keep him alive." Twirling the red plaid over her head, she headed out into the frigid early morning air. Despite its bite, she sucked in its freshness, her spirit reviving after the living nightmare of the recent long night. The *Elias* cut effortlessly through the large swells. Grace made straight for O'Malley at the helm.

His eyes widened as he stared at her blood-encrusted skirts. "How fares the captain, Mrs F.?" O'Malley's ginger freckles stood out against his pale skin.

"Alive..." The tremble in her voice betrayed her, and worry

flashed in his eyes. The cold breeze clawed at the edges of her headscarf like icy talons, and she shivered. "Full sails, Mr O'Malley." She firmed her voice with resolution and authority. "I'll take the helm."

The shadows of horror faded as the fire of determination warmed the inside of her belly. If Billy kept Seamus alive, she would get them to Sydney Town—even if it meant taking them into the strong westerlies further south.

Wee Granny Mac, the wizened shepherdess, approached, her sharp blue eyes intelligently roaming the open ocean before settling on Grace.

Grace nodded. "Good morning, Mrs Mac—"

"Wee Granny Mac'll do, dearie," said the old woman, peering from beneath the navy kerchief swathed about her head. Her accent was the softer brogue of the Scottish Lowlands, but her voice was loud and clear with no hint of frailty. "Never been married. I'm too far gone in ma years to care of rumours about me travelling without escort." She glared at Grace through her stony, rheumy eyes that had clearly seen a tough life. "Threatened to take the castrating knife to the last man who asked for ma hand."

Grace gave a feeble laugh. "How may I help you?"

The old woman smacked her lips and tapped an arthritic finger on Grace's chest. "Removed that ball from yer man yet?"

"No, it's too deep. Dr Sykes says he can't reach it."

"Aye, and a head's not just for growing hair—there should be a brain in there somewhere." One crooked finger tapped her grey temple. "Put men's heads together and it makes a fence. So, never ye mind about what he says. I've seen shot make its way through a sheep, only to come out the other side."

Grace blinked. "My husband isn't a sheep."

"I hope he isn't, daft creatures are as thick as a ship's hull. But flesh is flesh. That ball's likely created a fever that's bound to kill him, aye?" Wee Granny Mac scrunched her nose. "If ye want him to live, ye must rid him of it. If not, his future's as thin as yer eyebrows." Without waiting for Grace to respond, the diminutive woman hunched down the quarterdeck stairs, her gnarled knuckles white on the rail.

The bloody ignorance! The old crone thinking she knew better than an Oxford-trained physician. Pushing aside the Scotswoman's words of doom, Grace opened the binnacle and adjusted the helm down until the compass's oscillating needle pointed to where she wanted it. Snapping the binnacle shut, she fixed her eyes on the undulating horizon, allowing only thoughts of wind-filled sails and a cutting white wake to occupy her mind.

Chapter Seven

INDIAN OCEAN, 26 JULY 1841

After a long, fatiguing watch battling the helm in the blustery conditions, Grace resumed her place beside Seamus's sickbed. With her spirit temporarily dislocated by exhaustion, she wondered what level of weariness qualified as insanity. Oh, that her soul might wander off awhile, somewhere warm and peaceful where the cold did not have teeth, nor worry claws, someplace where the clocks had no hands. None of her bravery mattered when she was so tired. Sleep might eradicate the pain in her joints, but right now, even her hair hurt, and sleep was a luxury she could ill afford.

Racked by fever and delirium, Seamus's head lolled in a heavy stupor, and he was unable to drink unaided. She lifted his head while Billy poured a trickle of water between his lips. Most leaked from the corners of his slack mouth, saturating the pillow beneath his rancid, unwashed hair.

Damn that fool, Chittenden, straight to Hades! "Please, my love. Drink, for me."

The physician drew the water skin away. "'Tis no good, flower. He's too far gone."

Grace quailed. "He'll die without water!" She tried not to think about her husband's withered bladder. It had been two days since Sally had needed to change the sheets, though the cabin still smelled sharply of urine. The cloyingly sweet tendrils of death grew thicker around him each day like the prickly, scrambling branches of a bramble bush.

"Aye," agreed Billy. "Won't be long now." He slid his large hand across the back of her shoulders.

She jerked free of his gentle touch. "Poppycock! You've made no effort to believe he'll survive from the outset," she snapped. She recognised it was tiredness and desperation speaking, but she would not give up. It was unfair to speak to Billy so, but her dwindling well of energy was reserved for Seamus. Did her friend not grasp this? She snatched the water skin from him. Tough if he did not!

"Allow me." She was desperate enough to try anything. Sucking back a large mouthful of the brackish water, she placed her lips over Seamus's.

"What are you doing?" Billy asked, his voice pitching.

Grace forced the vital liquid into her husband's mouth, sealing it in with hers. A searing flash of memory lit the inside of her skull like a hurricane lamp—her mouth pressed over Elias's as she offered him her breath. The warm, liquorice-fragranced puff had leaked from her sweet boy, his chest stilled for eternity.

Seamus's protruding Adam's apple bobbed instinctively, and she mewled in relief. Straightening up, she locked eyes with the physician. "I'm doing what needs to be done."

"But—"

Billy hesitated as she took another deep pull on the water skin, her cheeks bulging. She snorted at him through her nose and bent to Seamus again. *There we go, my love. Take another.* She funnelled another mouthful into him in a slow trickle. He swallowed that mouthful too, and she rested her cheek against his withered one, whispering, "Come back to me, Seamus Alexander Fitzwilliam. I need you."

Goodness, surely her lot in life could not include losing a son *and* a husband? Could fate really be so cruel? She squeezed her eyes shut, prepared to make a deal with the Devil if it meant saving Seamus. *Please!*

By the sixth night, Grace knew he was dying. As much as she hated him moaning and whipping about, it was preferable to him now lying so deathly still and limp. His previous twist of delirium had thrown him onto his side, where he faced the bulkhead, away from her. She curled up behind him under the quilt, and it was as though she were lying alongside a smelting kiln.

"Don't you dare leave me. Hold on a little while longer. We're making good progress. We'll be in Sydney Town before you know it," she whispered.

Reluctant to touch him because every little movement caused him agony, she was also desperate to touch him—she *needed* to feel him. His dry, hot skin scared her, so she tentatively laid her hand on the fresh dressing that Billy had wrapped around his torso earlier. She gently stroked the linen, not daring to press any firmer for fear of hurting him. She hesitated. Risking a harder feel, she fingered a lump through the dressing. Was that the ball Wee Granny Mac had said might make an appearance?

Grace peeled back the bandage's edge. Seamus's wasted flesh pulled tightly over his ribs like the staves of a barrel. She tentatively ran her fingertips over a hard lump under the skin on his back. Good gracious! The hot, blackened swelling looked fit to burst. She hastily rolled off the berth and, snatching up the lantern, darted to Billy and Toby's cabin. She hammered on their door.

Billy answered, his day clothes rumpled, his hair nested. His sleepy eyes became instantly alert despite the late-night interruption. "Is it the captain?" His furrowed brow cut a deep line down his forehead.

"Yes. There's a lump on his back. It's black and bulging," said Grace without preamble. "Wee Granny Mac said the ball might push its way through."

He snatched up his leather holdall. "Only one way to find out."

He snipped off the bandages and squinted at the blackened lump on Seamus's bare back. His long fingers probed gently, and Seamus groaned. "It's tender for him," said Billy. "But I can feel it. Must've driven clean through his chest." He took a small step back. "I must cut it out."

Grace's jaw slackened. "You said it would kill him to cut him."

"Aye, but if we leave the ball in any longer, it'll *certainly* kill him. Cutting it out only has a *possibility* of killing him. Worth the risk, by my reckoning." He looked at Grace unwaveringly, and her thumping heart calmed under her friend's steady brown gaze.

She nodded.

Billy thrust open the mouth of his medicine bag and rummaged around. Finding what he was looking for, he held up a shiny scalpel. Grace's saliva dried, and she swallowed stickily. She knew all too well the feel of those shiny, sharp tools of his. The tip of her tongue probed the gap in her teeth where Billy had pulled her tooth, broken in an alehouse brawl. The sounds of the outside world faded as she focussed on her friend's deep voice.

"I must take measure of it." He feathered his fingers across Seamus's back. The lump moved under his fingers, the motion reviving Seamus, and he thrashed weakly against the sheet covering his legs, groaning in a voice tight with pain and delirium. Billy spoke through gritted teeth, "The ball's grinding against the bone of his shoulder." He flicked his head at Grace. "Sit atop him. Hold him steady."

Grace pinched her lips and clambered onto the lumpy feather mattress. Straddling Seamus, she pressed herself down, wrapping her arms around his skeletal frame. Old Bailey's bells! He was wasted to nothing!

She hissed through gritted teeth. "Do it—quickly!"

The lump was glossy and violet like the skin of a freshly harvested aubergine. Billy's calm recital broke through the pounding in her head. "Pull the skin tight. Press the blade down the centre. Hard and deep as it'll go."

Grace turned her head, fighting the wave of nausea rushing up the back of her throat. Seamus screeched, barely sounding human, then drooped limply beneath her.

She flinched as putrefying discharge sprayed the back of her hand as hot and thick as burgoo. Good grief—it smelled worse than rotting bilges! She lurched over the edge of the berth, the contents of her stomach scalding her gullet and splattering noisily at Billy's feet.

"Sorry," she gasped, wiping the vomit from her lips with her unsullied arm. She examined the wound cautiously, keeping her head back. Mustardy pus oozed from the raw slit.

The doctor scrunched his eyes and peered closer at the wound than Grace dared. "What's that dark matter?" she asked.

"Looks like a chunk of coat." He dug it out with the scalpel tip. The lump of cloth was infused with gelatinous gore and bone chips. "The ball likely pushed a bit of it in."

Grace grimaced. "Where's the ball?"

"I must keep digging."

Grace turned away again, unable to watch Billy tunnel into her husband's back. At least Seamus's deep stupefaction meant he did not suffer the physician's probing. A small mercy.

"Scalpel's slipping over the ball," he grunted. "It's too deep. I can't get beneath it."

"What about tweezers?" asked Grace.

He made a negative noise in the back of his throat. "I'm better off using my touch." With a bone-chilling shudder, Grace fixed her gaze to the planks above, trying valiantly not to envisage his finger sliding into her husband's living flesh.

"Got it!" he cried triumphantly.

Grace made the mistake of looking. The misshapen lead ball bulged from the cut and slicked down Seamus's pale skin, leaving a bloody trail. Billy withdrew his finger from Seamus's flesh, the wet sucking sound immediately followed by a surge of pus and dark foreign matter.

"By God! It's the wad!" The doctor gave a shaky laugh. He swiped his forearm across his forehead, his fingers slick and glistening in the dim lantern light.

Another breath of decay wafted up from Seamus's back, and Grace dry retched. "That must be the last of it, surely?" She sat up, still straddled over her husband's inert body. Good Lord, she had thought he looked lifeless before, but now— "Is he—dead?"

Billy reached a hand to Seamus's chest, his fingers matting the blond chest hairs with green and red gore. "No. His heart still beats." He dropped the deformed ball into the trough of the candlestick holder with a metallic clang. "I'm not yet done, flower. I've still to wash and stitch the wound."

Using half a bottle of neat whisky to wash away the last decaying fragments of wadding and mortification, Billy rinsed the offensiveness from his hands with the other half. Grace had watched her friend stitch plenty of flesh before, and it did not take him long to close the wound's mouth. He drew a fresh bandage from his medical bag. "Now all that's left is to wrap him up."

Still straddling him, Grace slid her arms under Seamus's armpits and drew him into a sitting position—a task once inconceivable on the giant man, now made terrifyingly easy. His forehead thumped onto her breastbone, and she pressed a kiss into his greasy, matted hair, not caring that the sour tang of him tingled the inside of her nostrils. Billy swiftly bandaged Seamus's chest, dressing the heavily scabbed front wound, as well as the newly stitched back incision. He helped Grace ease Seamus back onto the brown-stained pillow. No longer groaning or fighting against the fever, her husband lay like a corpse.

Had they pushed him too far? Grace slid wearily from the berth, falling heavily into the wooden chair beside it. Goodness gracious! She was shattered, her misery too great to even cry.

SEVERAL DAYS LATER, as Grace leaned over to infuse water into Seamus's mouth, his shaky hand reached for the back of her head. She jerked back.

"By Christ, that felt good," his voice rasped weakly. "More, if you please." He attempted a grey-tinged, lopsided grin.

"More water?"

"Yes, that too."

Was he on the mend? Did she dare hope? Grace sank her forehead to his, whispering, "I thought I'd lost you."

"I'm too stubborn to die, Dulcinea." His hand dropped heavily to the clean sheet. His face was thin and gaunt, though his eyes, while hollowed and bruised, were clear. The fever had clearly taken its toll on him. She kissed his sallow cheek, ignoring the miasmic vapours of his breath that brought back an unbidden memory of Silverton's stench.

"I'd never have forgiven you if you'd left me," she whispered, tears warming her cheeks.

"I'm here now." He wheezed. "I'm not leaving."

Grace closed her eyes, tempted never to open them again. The musty stink of her damp woollen skirts made her begrudgingly wake. She had slept in her clothes for several weeks, too exhausted to change after wrestling the *Elias* and tending to Seamus.

Speaking of battling the ship—"I must go. The helm is mine next watch."

"Sleep, Dulcinea. You're beyond weary."

The niggling worry that he would sink back into his fever spiked enough panic in her chest to speed up her heart. She shook her head and inhaled deeply, the surge of wakefulness clearing her foggy thoughts. While she had clung to the certainty of his recovery as tenaciously as the octopus had clung to Father Babcock's hand, she was not naïve enough to believe her husband's recuperation would be anything but slow and painful.

"I can't. Not yet. Soon." She could barely compose a complete sentence.

"By the feel of her, we're moving at a fair rate of knots. Where are we?"

Avoiding the answer, Grace rose and kissed his forehead. Of course the wind was bloody-well up. The dangerous squalling gusts that Seamus had so diligently avoided now tore at the sails —and it was all her doing. She murmured into his hair. "You concentrate on mending." Turning swiftly, she snatched her oilskin hanging on the hook by the door, shivering as she shrugged into the damp garment.

"Grace?"

She neatly sealed his questioning tone by closing the door behind her. Fastening the double row of buttons quickly before her fingers numbed, she made her way up to the quarterdeck, the oilskin hood her only protection from the whipping gales of sea spray. Glancing up into the rigging, she frowned at the smaller sails torn loose and flapping uselessly. Ducking her head as a particularly vicious gust of salty water stung her face, she stepped over to Toby at the helm.

"Afternoon, Toby." The icy wind made her front teeth ache.

She ran her warm tongue over them and took the helm from him. "How are your hands?"

He grunted and shook his head. "Keep her head up to the sea, Mrs F.," he said through gritted teeth clamped with cold. Water dripped from his sandy whiskers as though he had been doused with a bucket of it. "Wish this wretched wind would ease enough to allow a little more canvas to be spread."

Grace gripped the wooden handles to steady her dizzying fatigue and glared up at the grey billowing sky. If Toby could manage the helm with torn hands, she would persevere too. Sleep was not a risk she could afford; she must watch for the moment it became safer to lower more sail. "I'm determined to beat the *Firelight* to Sydney. This shall not all be in vain."

Toby swiped his bandaged knuckles down his face, his red-rimmed eyes blinking away the water. "The lads are equally determined. We've a mutual resolve to keep the *Elias* moving forward." He glanced down at her, the concern in his soft, grey eyes thawing the ice-chips of dread dangling from her nerve endings. "The colony's relying on us for the government goods, is it not? And Squatter Barclay for his shepherds?"

She pulled the hood of her oilskin further over her forehead. "Yes, but more pressing is the captain's health. Although Dr Sykes's ministrations have yielded some positive results, I'll rest easier once I have him ashore."

Despite the near overwhelm of responsibility, sheer grit kept her standing resolutely on the deck, enduring Neptune's thrashing. Was Seamus ever bowed by his duty like this? Did he rely as heavily on the men as she did? He always had such an air of steadfastness and complete control—did the sailors see this in her?

Chapter Eight

INDIAN OCEAN, 27 AUGUST 1841

L ying in his sickbed, Seamus sensed a shift in the air—
the wind had changed. Bosun Lincoln's muted bellow
outside blended with the howling wind. "Lower the
topsails! Hard beat to the windward."

Seamus pictured Bosun Lincoln holding the speaking
trumpet to his mouth, saltwater dripping from the rim, as the tiny
figures in the rigging burst into life. Soon the satisfying whumps
of lowered canvas filled the air, snapping taut in the wind, the
Elias instantly renewing her efforts in the water.

Grace lay fully clothed on the cot at the foot of his berth. She
had burst into the cabin in the dark hours of the morning and
collapsed there, boneless. Stirring from the sleep of the dead, she
smacked her lips and tongue stickily before even opening her
eyes. Half awake, she rose and drank straight from the water
carafe.

For pity's sake, she looked a mess! Her hair was a matted

nest, and she had lost weight. Her eyes were crazed red and raw, abused by saltwater and exhaustion.

"Thirsty, Dulcinea?"

Gasping as the last of the water drained from the carafe, she swiped her arm across her mouth. "Are you well?" she asked, pressing a cool hand to his forehead.

He loosely clasped her hand in his. She did not feel as tiny to his bony fingers these days. "Fuss not." He smiled, taking in her colourless face. "Have a care, my heart. You look terrible." He squeezed her fingers gently to let her know that his honesty was well-meant.

Grace's mouth curled, though her eyes remained dull. "I must eat and return to duty. We made good headway yesterday." She reached for his plate of left-over fish pie on the bedside table.

"Grace." His voice was soft and edged with concern. "You can't keep going like this."

She began to protest, but her full mouth prevented her. She chewed industriously, her chin firming.

He gave a small mirthless laugh. "Look at the two of us. Neither in any condition to sail our own ship." He fixed his gaze on her peeling lips, his own curling in a smile. "Hicks tells me we've made excellent progress under your command, *Captain*."

Grace swallowed, then snorted. "We'll lose all progress if I don't head back out."

Blaming tiredness for eroding her honied words and warm smiles, Seamus tipped his head. "I'm worried for you." Wariness fell across her eyes like a curtain. She shifted another mouthful of food into her cheek to interject, but he held up his hand. "I've seen sailors who've kept the deck night and day without rest. Eventually, even the strongest men succumbed to the wet, and cold, and exhaustion. Men who lost their hearing and eyesight, only to be put to bed, raving deliriously. I shan't permit you to do this to yourself." He paused a moment, indulging her petulant pout.

"We require all hands if we're to make good time to Sydney Town." She scraped the fork across the tin plate, sucking the prongs clean.

Seamus nodded. "I agree. Which is why I've had Chittenden released from the hold."

Florid blotches exploded across Grace's pale face, and she slammed the empty plate down. The fork bounced with a tinny clatter on the floor. "Pardon?"

"Dulcinea—"

She jammed her hands onto her hips, her bloodshot eyes widening. "Don't you *Dulcinea* me, Seamus! How can you entrust him with our ship?"

Seamus inhaled testily. "Because I can't sit by helplessly while you work your fingers to the bone. Chittenden may not be officer material, but he's a sufficiently capable seaman under a watchful eye."

"We require no help from the likes of *him*. It's a dangerous gamble, Seamus."

"I understand you don't like the man, but—"

"He shot you!"

Flinching, Seamus licked his lips. "An unfortunate accident. I'm not handing him command, Grace. I've ordered him released so he can help sail the ship."

"How long has Chittenden been on watch?" she asked curtly.

Glancing at the clock, Seamus replied, "You've been asleep twelve hours. He'll be coming off his second watch."

"Twelve hours! Why didn't you wake me?" Her indignation brought more colour to her cheeks.

Seeing her chin jut out, he quickly added, "I'm still the commander of this ship, Grace. My order is final." She blinked back tears with a look of betrayal that tore at his heart.

EMMA LOMBARD

"Suit yourself." Her voice wavered. "I'll be at the helm." Storming across the cabin, she slammed the door.

He flinched as the framed family portrait jumped and slipped sideways. With her thundering footsteps receding down the passage, Seamus reclined on the pillows, wincing as the stitches in his back pulled. Worse than the stitches was the painful path that the bullet had made through his chest. It ached perpetually and became an excruciating stabbing if he inadvertently coughed or sneezed. He still had no use of his left arm. His shoulder blade, chipped by the ball, was taking its time mending.

He closed his eyes and listened to the sounds of his ship. Voices of men on deck mingled with Emily's voice reciting times tables in the saloon. His frustration at not being able to leave his berth splayed like a razor-edged star in his gut. With a satisfied nod that at least the *Elias* was moving at a steady pace, he closed his eyes against the bone-deep grogginess and tried not to think of his wild-haired wife fighting her own battle of weariness.

Unable to sacrifice too much of his energy to his children's insatiable questions, he allowed them a five-minute visit a day to assure them he was alive and well. They were bearing up well enough under Miss Lissing and McGilney's care. If only he could care for his wife as such, he would not be submerged neck-deep in this cesspool of guilt.

Scuffling footsteps scraped on the deckhead above him, followed by bellows of indignant cries and a bone-chilling shriek. Grace? Seamus stretched his eyelids wide as a sickening, fleshy thud reverberated through the wooden hull. What, by Neptune's forked trident, was going on now? With gargantuan effort, he sat up and slid off the berth.

His knees buckled, and he leaned heavily on the bedside table to steady himself. Damn and blast, he was weaker than water. Using the furniture and walls as a crutch, he made slow, painful progress along the passageway leading to the main deck. Cursed Devil! It was as though someone was running him through with a red-hot cutlass! He gritted his teeth against crying out. Blinking against the brightness outside, he scowled in confusion.

Chittenden lay motionless on his back, his face misshapen as though a novice sculptor had been let loose with a chisel on a slab of marble. Several sailors circled Chittenden's prostrate form, and the ripple of anger in the air was tangible. Grace stood propped between Blight and O'Malley. Between the two flame-headed sailors, she appeared ghostly and her hands trembled but, other than that, she looked unharmed.

"What in fiery damnation is going on?" Seamus's voice cracked dryly, cut short by the pain shooting through him.

THAT BLOODY, bloody man! Working remnants of oily fish and pastry from inside her cheeks with her tongue, Grace burst into the pale sunshine. The cold air she sucked through her nostrils was a salve on her irritation. As riled as she was at Seamus's decision, she would not give Chittenden the satisfaction of seeing her blazing ire. Her heavy footsteps halted as young Smythe marched towards the ship's bow, his handspike shouldered like a musket. At the forecastle deck, he whirled on his heel, his uneven fringe blown flat by the wind as he marched smartly back towards her, looking very much like a sentry. His narrow eyes drooped when he spotted her, his round cheeks igniting.

She frowned. "Smythe? What are you up to?"

The young sailor halted stiffly before her, shoulders shrinking. "Being a marine, madam." Where was the confident, cocky young man who had boarded back in London?

"That's no musket." She jabbed a finger at the handspike over his shoulder. "Who tasked you with this fool's errand?"

"Mr Chittenden."

Bleeding bloody rats' tails! She took a slow, deep breath and carefully slid aside the irritation in her voice. "Resume your duties, Smythe."

"To take the helm from Blight?" Smythe's white-knuckled grip on the handspike eased.

"Yes, if that's where Bosun has you." Grace picked out each man on deck, searching for Bosun Lincoln. Why had he not put a stop to this lunacy? She rolled her shoulders. At this hour, he was likely partaking in the midday meal, and Chittenden was wretchedly-well exploiting the opportunity. She fixed her gaze onto her pale-haired target as she made her way up to the quarterdeck where Chittenden stood at the rail, hands clasped behind his back in perfect imitation of Seamus as he surveyed the activity below. Sucking a sharp breath through her nostrils, she called out, ensuring her voice was not too shrill. "Mr Chittenden? A word if you please."

With his customary swagger, Chittenden shuffled around.

Grace pointed at Smythe trading places with Ben at the helm. "What is the meaning of that?"

"That squint-eye's intellect is slowed by the Brummy blood in his veins. He was being ignorant and clumsy about his work. Has a wishbone where his spine should be." The smug man shrugged. "A little drilling works wonders to bring a sailor back to order."

Grace leaned back to allow the breeze to wash away his odour. His breath stank like one of Ben Blight's farts passed through a boiled onion. "Need I remind you—you no longer hold authority on this ship."

Chittenden sniggered, peering down his long, straight nose. "Captain Fitzwilliam might not think twice about putting his wife to work, but 'tis a dangerous thing. I'm not required to do *your* bidding. Captain freed me and ordered me to go about my duty. So, if you don't mind, *madam*—"

"Not so fast. The captain may have released you from your

bonds, but I hold authority on this watch." Grace cursed the warmth of her flush as she saw Chittenden's eyes roll at this female foible.

"I'll not be made a fool of by anything in petticoats!" His gaze roamed down the front of Grace's bodice, and this new scrutiny sent a shiver across her skin, reminding her of Silverton's oily interest in her. He sniffed sharply. "*I'm* the one who gives commands, especially to pretty ones like you." His look of curiosity tightened. "I must admit, you'd make a fine sight—dropping to your knees before me, you mealy-mouthed wagtail."

"I beg your pardon? You've not earned *one ounce* of my attention, you crotch flea!" Her palms prickled as they filled with blood, and she thrust her chin at him. "Remove yourself from my quarterdeck, or I'll have you removed." She dug her fingernails into her flesh as she turned to leave.

"You dare turn your back on me, woman!" He snatched her from behind, lifting her. He was a towering man, as tall as Seamus. She whipped her head back, her skull mashing his mouth and nose with a satisfying, gristly crunch. He gasped explosively. Stinking seaweed—that hurt! Sparks of light flashed behind her clenched eyelids. Fighting her instinct to lean forward and wriggle from his grip, she deployed the element of surprise by leaning back against him. Ha! *That* would show him.

Instead of dropping her, his grip tightened. He staggered, unbalanced, and slammed against the railing. Grace's stomach clenched and swooped. Blazing Hades! They were going over. Blue sky and spired masts filled Grace's vision as they tipped back. With nothing else to grab onto, she clung to Chittenden's arm still locked around her waist like an iron shackle. The shriek of terror exploding from the pit of her stomach was cut short as Chittenden slammed onto the main deck with a meaty thud. Her skull smashed into his face again, the crack of his head against the wooden planks like two billiard balls colliding.

The impact punched every sip of air from her lungs, and her

throat seized in panic. His body had offered little cushioning. His arm slid from her midriff, thudding to the deck. Her agony reignited the memory of the time she had toppled over the cannon during her intervention in Toby's flogging aboard the *Discerning* all those years back. And just as she had done then, she rolled to her hands and knees, her mouth working word- lessly. At least her bottom was covered this time. With a hissing suck, the damp, briny air filled her lungs like well-pumped bellows. Oh, sweet mercy!

Resting her head onto her bunched knuckles, she coughed, gasping like one of Edwin's newly hauled fish.

"Good God, Mrs F.! Are you injured?" Strong, warm hands grasped her from both sides, lifting her to her feet.

SEAMUS SAGGED HEAVILY against the bulkhead, his strength draining fast. He stared in horror at Grace. Still wheezing, his wife shook off Blight and O'Malley's hands and hurried over to him. She propped herself under his free arm. Heavens, he was as feeble as a filleted fish, and here was his wife, clearly winded by some altercation with that pale-haired bastard, coming to his aid. If he did not feel so grim, he might even feel a little emasculated, but just this minute, his desire to lie down overrode any other emotion.

Seamus glared at Chittenden. "Is he dead?"

Blight dropped to his haunches and placed a hand on the felled man's chest. He peered up from beneath his coppery thatched eyebrows, his lips twisting. "No, sir. He breathes." Blight's intense blue gaze shifted to Grace, his voice swelling with pride. "Watertight delivery, Mrs F.!"

"What by Neptune's forked trident is happening? Has every ounce of order left this ship?" Seamus frowned.

Chittenden gargled as though he had a mouthful of water.

Growling, Blight swiped his meaty finger through Chittenden's mashed mouth and flicked blood and bits of teeth onto the deck. Ungently, Blight nudged the senseless man onto his side with his knee, and a thick gloop of bloody mucous slid from the corner of Chittenden's mouth.

Blight rose and, wiping his bloody finger on his trousers, turned to Seamus. "This useless meat sack laid his hands upon Mrs F. She showed him what she thought of that!"

Seamus deepened his scowl. Trouble plagued his wife no matter where she went—thankfully, she had the wherewithal to kick it squarely in the vitals whenever it ventured too near.

Grace rubbed the back of her head, and when she lowered her hand, Seamus's already tender gut spasmed. "For crying out loud, you're bleeding!" His previous conviction about his wife's capabilities melted like a pat of butter on a sizzling skillet, the hot buttery oil slicking a path of worry through his innards.

Coughing again, she shook her head as she inhaled deeply through her nostrils. "A little egg is all. It's not grave."

Seamus flicked his head at Blight and growled. "Fetch Dr Sykes."

Blight hesitated. "For Mrs F. or Mr Chittenden?"

"Have him tend my wife first. Carry that incompetent lump to his berth."

"Aye, aye, sir. He's about as useful as a peg-legged Cook Phillips in an arse-kicking contest."

"No," countered Grace. "Chittenden needs more doctoring than me."

Seamus clenched his eyelids tight as a wave of dizziness clashed with the ship's undulating momentum. He pressed his free palm to the lattice-windowed bulkhead to steady himself. He barely had strength to stand, let alone challenge Grace's contradiction.

She shuffled beneath his arm, grunting under his weight. "Right, back to bed, Captain."

Hicks popped under his other arm, and they shuffled back down the passage. In the cabin, Grace dithered over him, withholding the details until he was settled with a sweetened pot of hot tea in his hands. She then told her tale.

"Blasted Hell!" Seamus snatched her hand, fighting the fist of anger punching the inside of his ribcage. "Not even a day out of irons, and he was back to humiliating my men."

Grace's thumb caressed the scar along his wrist. She dipped her chin. "That surprises you?"

"It shouldn't, but it does."

Grace continued her account, including Chittenden's grievous insult.

"He said *what*?" Seamus interrupted her flow with a splutter of outrage. Damnation! He grimaced, pressing an open palm to his chest to quell the piercing pain.

Grace took his empty mug, which had tipped in his loosened grip, and placed it on the table. Shushing, she gently eased him back against his pillows. "I shan't continue if you allow it to upset you."

Seamus opened his eyes. His breaths came fast and shallow through his nostrils. "Are you positive you aren't injured?" His already light head was nearly floating off his shoulders after her retelling.

Grace reached up, meekly rubbing the back of her head. "It's only a lump. My head is obviously harder than his face." She held her fingers up. "Look, it's barely bleeding anymore." She nibbled her top lip and swallowed deeply against the pain of her thumping headache. "I thought I'd killed him."

Seamus arched his brows at his petite wife. "It's not as though the bastard didn't have it coming, Dulcinea."

By Neptune's trident! How had he misjudged the man so poorly? He would like to blame his lack of judgement on the ravages of fever, but his error stemmed back long before then. His wife's fortitude against misadventure had saved not only his life but the ship too. So, why did it feel so wrong? Perhaps Chittenden was right. Realisation of the truth sent jagged-edged fissures through Seamus's soul. He was barely in control of his vessel, and certainly no longer in control of his world. His manhood was crumbling like dried clay beneath his feet. At least his father was no longer around to witness this failure.

There was a firm rap at the door.

"Enter," called Seamus.

Sykes's black doctoring bag preceded him through the doorway.

"Billy!" The smile that lit Grace's face faltered. "Is Mr Chittenden awake?"

Sykes's lowered lids hid his dark brown eyes. "The man's taken quite a knock." He slid the leather holdall onto the foot of the berth. He stepped over to Grace. "And so have you, by all accounts. May I examine you?"

Grace sat and ducked her chin as Sykes parted her brown curls. The decent-sized lump was divided by a jagged oozing cut. Seamus looked away as Sykes hummed. "Hmm, not too bad. Shan't need stitching."

Head still bowed, Grace peered at Seamus from the corner of her eye. "Told you it was only a bump."

Seamus made a noise of acknowledgment in the back of his throat. She had endured a violent altercation, while he was bedridden like a ninety-year-old man. He should be relieved she had barely a scratch, but a serpent of shame slithering through him lifted its head and hissed. She should be asking for some willow bark for the headache she undoubtedly sported, but that would be admitting she was hurt, and she was unlikely to do that. She took another sip of tea.

Busying himself in his bag, Sykes withdrew a linen swab and dabbed Grace's head. "Remarkable considering Chittenden's grievous injury."

Grace's head jerked up, her green eyes pooling with concern. "Will he live?"

Sykes folded the white cloth, now dappled with pink spots. "He's still knocked insensible. I fear blood will gather in his head and congest his brain." He shook his head, his lips pressed white. "I've seen this kind of invisible wound before. The patient can become fully recovered, only to succumb days later."

"So, it's mortal?" said Seamus, rubbing small circles on his temple to ease his own headache. He must ask Grace to log this event, even though the explanation would paint his incompetence for all to see. He wished he were at the helm, where the wind could whip away this noxious self-judgment and blow it far out to sea; instead, he lay here, stewing in his own self-pity.

"Unless by miracle or magic he is cured, then yes, I'm afraid it doesn't bode well," said Sykes.

Grace sucked in a quivering breath, and Seamus reached for her hand. This was not her burden to bear—he was her husband and captain, though Heavens knew he was barely strong enough to bear it himself. "You've done nothing wrong, Dulcinea."

Sykes slid his hand onto her shoulder. "Captain's right, flower. You defended yourself against a man who had no right laying hands upon you. There are witnesses aplenty."

Chapter Nine

SYDNEY TOWN, 30 SEPTEMBER 1841

"One hundred and thirty-nine days? Under the command of a woman?" Captain Appleby, harbour master of Port Jackson, blustered as he leaned back heavily in his chair in the crude, wooden harbour master's office at Queen's Wharf. It was the day after the *Elias* had arrived, and Grace sat opposite Appleby, with Toby standing just behind her shoulder. A prickle of irritation clawed its way across her scalp as the harbour master directed his question at Toby.

The only window in the room was propped open with a stick. The unfamiliar land-based smells pressing in were more grotesque than the ship's odours—the blood of butchered animals, the stench of excrement and unwashed bodies, and the sickly-sweet aroma of rum and bitter hops of beer wafting from alehouses. Though the alehouses were not all to blame for the stink of old beer. She coughed, crawling her gaze back to Appleby.

"We had planned on attempting the journey in fewer than one hundred days but—*circumstances*—dictated otherwise." She pursed her lips.

Appleby's forehead wrinkled deeply as he raised his sparse eyebrows. "Quite, quite, my dear." His was a placating tone Grace supposed he reserved for women. "I heard of your troubles."

"And what might those troubles be?" She slid her gaze sideways to Toby. He widened his eyes and minutely shook his head, his shoulders hunching.

"'Tisn't every day a woman skipper brings a fully laden packet ship into my harbour."

By the look of the harbour master, Grace doubted he was married. His clothes, rumpled and uncared for like hastily packed luggage, rode up the mound of his belly. The bulge told of a diet of ale rather than regular home-cooked meals, as did the smell of him.

Bristling with importance, Appleby asked, "Which of your men navigated through the heads? Treacherous bit of water that. Not for the faint-hearted."

Grace's cheeks warmed. "That would be me, sir. I had responsibility of the helm."

Appleby's potbelly jiggled as he laughed, and he slapped his knee. His laughter dribbled to a halt when he caught hold of her glower. Easing the handkerchief from his top pocket, he wiped the oily smirk from his lips. Her irritation spilled into anger. Condescending little worm! She stiffened her spine and shuffled forward in her seat.

From over her shoulder, Toby's voice came low and firm. "Mrs Fitzwilliam speaks the truth, sir."

"Mhmm." Appleby's left eyebrow dipped, and his lips tightened.

"Captain Fitzwilliam required tending." She inclined her head at the *Elias* docked outside the begrimed window. Steaming funnels and furled topmasts competed with swirls of squawking seagulls for lofty positions above the busy harbour. "I wasn't about to bob in the ocean awaiting a pilot when I could take the task to hand."

"That you did," placated Toby, stepping into view. Aiming his gaze at Appleby, his habitually soft, grey eyes hardened, his displeasure glinting like polished silver. "I've not had the pleasure of sailing with a finer commander than Mrs Fitzwilliam. Save the captain himself. He's done a fine job of teaching her the ropes. She's an excellent navigator too."

Appleby huffed through his nose. "And how is your husband, Mrs Fitzwilliam? Is he at the Rum Hospital?"

She frowned. "The Sydney Infirmary and Dispensary?"

"One and the same." Appleby ran his hand over his dishevelled brown hair. "Never catch *me* there. All those reeking vapours seeping into those walls. Of course, Captain Fitzwilliam might have enjoyed a visit to the Military Hospital had he still been in the Royal Navy..." Appleby's voice trailed away as Grace narrowed her eyes. His awkward attitude in engaging her in conversation cemented her notion that he was indeed *not* married. Had the blustering fool no sense of diplomacy?

"No, my husband is convalescing at home." Rallying to take charge of the conversation, Grace leaned her forearms on Appleby's desk and clasped her hands. "Do you doubt my account, Captain Appleby?"

The harbour master shrank back. "Loosen your corset laces, madam. The explanations flowing from your mouth can't be given breath without making a mockery of your husband." He scoffed. "What man allows his wife such liberties?"

All pomp and ceremony this one. She would show him. Grace rose, her barbed look harpooning him like a whale. "My account is true and accurate, sir. I've the testimony of many a witness, including Captain Fitzwilliam. Will you challenge *his* account too?"

Appleby turned over the ledger's cream page. "I've your husband's account before me." He tapped the inky loops. "Appears you were instrumental in the first mate's death aboard the *Elias*?"

Grace blinked. That was her account, written by her own hand. Though Appleby need not know this little detail. Despite Billy's postulation that Chittenden might awaken after his fall, he had not. Although she had not set out to kill the man, she carried the weight of his death like a yoke pressed into her nape. And, like any burden carried for too long, it became heavier with time. But she was not about to let this pontificating little man twist the knife of remorse any further.

Before she could respond, Toby dropped a heavy fist onto the desk and raised his voice. "Absolutely not, sir! 'Twas a terrible accident. Nothing more."

Appleby barely moved his head as he rolled his dark, brown eyes up. "An accident that afforded you a hefty promotion to first mate, did it not, Mr Hicks?"

"Mr Hicks was promoted before Mr Chittenden's demise," said Grace. "I alone affected the situation."

Toby shook his head. "Come now, Mrs F. 'Twas self-defence. Pure and simple."

Huffing through his nostrils, Appleby slammed the ledger shut. "Let's see what the magistrate makes of it."

Grace glared down coldly, and Appleby paled, his gaze sliding to the desk. "How thoughtless of me." Her tone dripped like honey off bread. "To burden you with circumstances you're unqualified to process."

Appleby's chin snapped up, his eyes narrowing.

She smiled sweetly. "As harbour master, I'm sure you're *swamped* with important tasks such as—counting chests of tea and such." She waved towards Toby. "Speaking of which, Mr Hicks has the *Elias*'s inventory. I'll leave him with you to undertake a full account of the goods in our hold."

She turned and winked at Toby. "Oh, and Mr Hicks, don't forget to declare Mrs Barclay's trunk of undergarments. I'd hate for any *important* officials to think we're sneaking ladies' drawers into the colony." She glanced back at Appleby, widening her comely smile. "I'm sure Squatter Barclay will understand your accounting of his wife's smalls." Turning regally, and ignoring Appleby's splutters of protest, she glided from the dingy office.

Stinking bloody seaweed! Self-important men like Appleby set her teeth on edge. She stormed over to William Wells' sandstone house, her scowl and hurry-footed bustling of skirts dividing people from her path like the pointed bow of a ship cutting the ocean. The Sailor's Homecoming publican had been more than happy to rent his house to them again. Grace estimated that the weekly rent they paid equalled two weeks' takings at his hotel. What sensible entrepreneur would not accept *that* offer? As before, he had no qualms with becoming a temporary resident in his own establishment. The neat little garden he had cultivated out back made for an equally agreeable tortoise residence.

With the heat of her anger tempered by the brisk walk, Grace halted in the wood-panelled entrance as Emily's voice trickled down the narrow staircase. Miss Lissing had transformed the extra bedchamber into a schoolroom, and Emily was reading out aloud. *Oliver Twist*—again.

Grace found Seamus convalescing in the sunny dayroom, the pleasant glow of the southern spring sun filtering through the arched windows, warming his fever-ravaged body. He lifted and rotated his left arm, wincing as he tried to raise it above his head. The chipped scapula, although now healing, restricted him from lifting it any higher than his shoulder. Billy was not optimistic it would improve either. With his shirt sleeve rolled up, Seamus's old knife-scar carved a prominent white line across his thin, pale wrist.

He dropped his arm when he caught sight of her sweeping in. She nodded at the scene of domesticity—depleted teacups and crumbs of fruitcake on side plates. Between William Wells' maid, Biddy, and Sally McGilney, her husband wanted for nothing in the food and drink department. Eyeing an extra slice of fruitcake on the tray, Grace broke off a corner, popping the dense spiced piece into her mouth. Mmm—heavily brandied, Biddy's secret ingredient. Raisins, orange peel, and walnuts in the moist cake tumbled about her mouth in a semi-sweet explosion, leaving that dark, boozy aftertaste she loved so much.

Seamus dipped his face, and Grace rose on her toes to kiss him. Unable to shave with his injury, he had grown out his whiskers. They prickled, and she did not care for the barrier they posed to their intimacy, preferring the warmth of his skin against hers. Running her fingernails lightly along his jawline, she offered, "Will you allow me to shave you?"

He jerked his head back, and his lips tightened, the line beside his mouth cutting deeply into his cheek. "I can still handle my own razor." His blue stare was hard and unblinking.

Grace slowly lowered her hand, and her décolletage warmed uncomfortably. "I didn't mean to imply you couldn't—" She folded her arms to keep them occupied. Gracious! She had hoped his bleak mood would lift once they came ashore. Confined to his berth, his stubbornness rivalled that of a donkey cornered by a wolf—defiantly staring down anyone who entered the cabin until the discomfort forced the unfortunate to leave him alone.

But she was having none of this now. Gentling her voice, she ran her hand down his whiskered cheek again. "I know how itchy you find whiskers. I only wish to make you more comfortable, my love." She turned to walk away. "But of course, if you don't—"

His cool-tipped fingers gripped her wrist. "Wait."

She swivelled slowly on the balls of her feet and took a breath before meeting his gaze.

Despite the grey rings of illness around his eyes, his boyish charm twinkled. "Shall I remove my shirt?"

Heartened by his attempted humour, Grace released her breath and bumped her hip into his. "Keep your clothes on, Captain. Some of us have a reputation to uphold." She sashayed from the room, exaggerating the sway of her skirts. "Wait here."

"You're shameless, Grace Fitzwilliam!" His laughter followed her from the room.

Returning with his shaving kit and a bowl of steaming water, she drew him onto the stool before the window. "Have a seat."

Lowering himself, the height of his gaze matched hers, and she swallowed deeply at the intensity of his stare. "Keep distracting me with that look and you risk a cut throat," she laughed, waving the lethal blade.

He took the razor from her, his gold-bristled lips twitching. "I'll save my adoration for *afterwards*." Hooking the end of the strop over the window latch, he pulled the leather strap tight and slowly and gently pulled the blade along it, realigning the fine metal edge.

"How are you faring today?" asked Grace, dipping the badger-hair brush into the warm water and agitating it across the bar of soap.

The blade, flashing silver in the sunlight as he held it up for inspection, wavered. "I'm bearing up well enough." He laid the razor on the tray with a metallic clink. "As long as I'm not forced to look in a mirror."

"Why not?" Grace shuffled him into the centre of the stool and draped a towel around his shoulders.

"Christ, Grace." The agony in his tone betrayed him. "I'm supposed to be responsible for the direction of my life, and our family, and I can't even blasted-well shave my own whiskers!" He squeezed his eyes shut and opened them slowly. They were piercing blue, and full of hurt. "You know I'm open to your wisdom and counsel, but I feel I've lost the final say on matters these days."

There was no accusation in his tone, but his words stung. "I never meant to undermine you." She hoped her tone was gentle enough not to provoke. "I was trying to be strong, for us both."

He ran his clawed fingers through his hair, ruffling the sleek surface. "That's the issue right there. My tail is quite down. I've lost the courage to suffer the consequences of my decisions. What kind of husband transfers his duty to his wife?"

Grace ground the bristles into the soap harder than was necessary. "Stop questioning yourself, Seamus. This isn't you." Nodding in satisfaction at the generous dollop of creamy foam on the brush head, she set about lathering him up. "Sharing what's rolling around in that head of yours with me isn't weak. Men of principle keep their word, even when it hurts. So, tell me what's bothering you. Please."

She worked the brush in small circles across his jaw, and he closed his eyes and twisted his lips around the foam. "How did I so sorely misjudge Chittenden?" His voice was barely a whisper.

She stopped the brush a moment before resuming the swirls. "You had an ultimatum. We both did. For the *Elias* to make good time to Sydney."

"Yes, but was I so fixated on our commercial endeavour that I was blind to the depth of Chittenden's ineptitude?"

Grace could not believe she was about to defend that tyrant, but her husband required assurance. "Lucius Chittenden wasn't all bad. As you rightly observed, despite his sharp tongue and iron fist, he jollied the men to perform at their best."

"Yet, in the same breath, he also damaged the ship."

"Over-eagerness isn't a sin. And besides, his recklessness didn't cause too much harm, did it?"

"He shot me!"

"It could well have been any other man who fumbled his weapon."

"What bothers me most is not being present to witness him turn on you."

Memories of the fall ignited Grace's guilt, and she nibbled the inside of her cheek silently. No! She sucked in her bottom lip in determination. Chittenden had attacked her as brazenly as Silverton had—*more so*, before witnesses! As confusing as this self-reproach was, she would not allow it to blow her life off course. She valiantly changed the topic. "A letter arrived today, from the Barclays. They've invited us to Barclay Hall." She stopped working the brush and studied him. "Are you up to travelling just yet?"

His sunken eyes swivelled to meet hers, and he smiled wanly. "In another week or two, perhaps."

Grace breathed in the fresh nutty scent of the walnut-oil shaving soap as she deposited the brush on the tray and picked up the blade. "I went to see Captain Appleby today." The flavour of that weaselly man's name on her tongue soured the cake's pleasant aftertaste.

"The harbour master?" Seamus spoke through barely moving lips as Grace eased the razor down his cheek, letting its sharpness and weight do the cutting in a whispering rasp.

"He questioned my account that I saw the *Elias* safely into his pox-ridden harbour." She swished the blade in the steaming water. "He couldn't fathom a woman capable of such a deed." Gently pulling his skin tight, she continued the downward scraping strokes.

"The man can't help his ignorance. There's not many a fellow who could manage what you did." The kindness in her husband's blue eyes eased the sting of Appleby's earlier insults.

She smiled warmly at his encouragement. "Well, I didn't do it alone. All hands executed their duties with the utmost diligence." Motioning him to close his mouth and pull his top lip tight over his teeth, she continued, "And Miss Lissing did a fine job of keeping the children otherwise engaged. Plus, I had Billy's help digging that ball out of you." She whisked the razor in the water bowl again.

Seamus scowled, stroking the middle of his chest. "That sawbones dug into my back like he was burrowing to China."

Grace kissed his cool, foamy lips, then tipped his chin up with one finger. "That *sawbones* saved your life. And I'll thank him for it for all my living days."

"What else did Appleby have to say? Did our manifest pass muster?"

Grace's hand trembled, and she withdrew the blade from Seamus's skin. "He had a rather strong opinion about my involvement with Chittenden's death."

"Let's cease wasting good breath on Chittenden, shall we?" Seamus curled his arm around her waist and drew her in.

Shrugging his arm off, she stepped back and tilted his chin up again. "I never cease thinking of the bastard," she said through gritted teeth.

He tried to lower his chin, but Grace pressed it up again. She dared not share Appleby's threat to take this matter to the magistrate. Her husband had enough to manage without concerning himself about that woman-hating bag of air. She had dealt with his kind for years—it was the price of womanhood.

He grasped her wrist and lowered his forehead to hers. His breath was warm and brandied from the cake. "You were protecting yourself, just as Blight taught you. Just as you always have."

"The responsibility still lies with me. Someone has to pay. Isn't that how justice works?" A sliver of doubt sliced through her chest like the cold blade of a cutlass. She had not *chosen* to take his life. Did that matter?

"Grace, if I'd witnessed him hurt you, I'd have put a pistol to his head myself. He received his comeuppance. *That* is how justice works." His eyes swivelled down. "Don't burden yourself with regret, my heart."

How could she *not* be plagued by regret? Seamus was right, that wretch Chittenden got what he deserved. But her actions were likely to have consequences on her family. And *that* was unbearable. She gently twisted her wrist from his fingers and swizzled the blade in the grey water with its whisker-hair flotsam. "Let me finish you off before the water cools too much. Head back."

There was a knock at the front door, and Grace tutted. Sally and Biddy were at the market. Grace listened for Miss Lissing's footsteps coming down the stairs. Nothing. The knock came again, louder. Sighing, she wiped the razor on the towel over Seamus's shoulder and laid it on the tray. "I'll answer it."

She was halfway through the front parlour when she heard the door open.

"Oh, Mr Hicks. What a pleasant surprise." Miss Lissing's voice was light and welcoming.

"Miss Lissing." Grace heard the tremor in Toby's voice, and she stilled to hear his words. "Care to join me at the cricket on Sunday?"

"Oh, I, um—"

"That is, unless you've already other plans—with other people—to go out—"

Grace clasped back a chuckle. Part of her wanted to turn away and offer them privacy, but another was intrigued by this unexpected turn of events. Curiosity won, and she pressed back against the wall.

"I love a good game of cricket, Mr Hicks," said Miss Lissing, laughing lightly. "My brothers were such bricks, teaching me how to bowl and bat. I scored a hat-trick once. They weren't too pleased about *that*."

Toby's shoes shuffled dryly on the sandstone steps. "That's a fine story." He cleared his throat. "If you wouldn't mind—please, call me Toby. Mr Hicks is my father. Not a man I need reminding of."

There was a small, uncomfortable silence that the governess broke. "Of course. Then, please, call me Erin."

"Splendid—wonderful—marvellous." Toby's voice cracked with excitement.

Grace's heart lifted at the sound of their voices, so naïve and unsure of one another, dancing around the possibilities.

"You boast quite a vocabulary," teased Miss Lissing. "You can impress me with more of your fine words on Sunday. Say eleven o'clock?"

Grace did not need to see Toby's face to know that it would be blazing like a forest fire under his sandy whiskers. She curled her arms around herself in a comforting hug, delighting in her friend's good fortune.

"Who's playing?" asked Miss Lissing.

"The 17th and 39th Regiments, I believe," replied Toby.

"Oh, the 39th?" Amusement lightened her tone. "I hear General Rollyson's quite a dashing fellow."

Toby cleared his throat with half a laugh. "Indeed. Attracts the ladies like moths to a candle—not that you're a moth— you're far too interesting and colourful to be a moth. You're—"

A soft kissing sound halted Toby's runaway speech, and Grace's eyebrows shot up. Oh, ho! Toby Hicks had himself a sweetheart, and a bold one at that. Grace headed back towards Seamus, heartened by this budding season of love. She wrapped her arms around her husband's clean-shaven neck from behind and pecked his cool, damp skin.

Perhaps Seamus was right. She had not killed Chittenden on purpose, and not a single man aboard the *Elias* questioned Chittenden's death. Now all she could pray for was that Appleby's threat was as empty as his head.

Chapter Ten

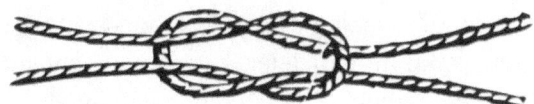

The semi-circular sandstone docks teemed with vessels and humanity. Outbound pinnaces, laden with boxes and barrels for holds, passed inbound vessels laden with goods for the colony. Grace smiled at the familiar brawny jack tars from HMS *Generous*—barefooted, in short-sleeved, open-necked jumpers, flashing hairy arms and tanned chests. A trio approached with rolling strides and devil-may-care attitudes. Grace grinned at their precariously balanced caps, marvelling how they did not fall off. A nostalgic pang fluttered in her chest at the memory of her time on HMS *Discerning*. Had she looked as young and carefree back then when Gilly found her outside the Two Chairmen alehouse? Probably not—she had been fleeing Silverton after all.

With efficient dispatch, Grace oversaw the loading of the Barclays' goods onto three bullock-drawn wagons lining the wooden dock beside the *Elias*. Toby ensured the remaining goods were whisked away to the government warehouses guarded by soldiers in red coats.

The brick-shaped leader of the bullock train approached Grace with an easy-going lope, his whip resting crookedly over his shoulder. Although his weight might be perceived by some as a weapon, she sensed Big Bob was not a violent man, as his waggling wiry-tendrilled eyebrows attested. She wafted away the frenzied swarm of buzzing flies. The horse and cattle muck littering the dock did little to deter the annoying creatures.

The dirt in the bullock-driver's smile creases darkened when he grinned as though someone had inked them there. Clearly, washing and grooming were not part of a bullocky's repertoire. Doffing his floppy leather hat at her, Big Bob gave a quick, sharp whistle. "Yabby!"

Nearby, the ugliest dog she had ever seen slunk low to the ground as it darted between the multitudes of bovine legs, narrowly avoiding being crushed by the impatient stamping hooves. Its rough, black fur with patches of grey and white had a blue sheen to it. The dog slipped under the large wagon wheels with lightning speed. Grace wondered how many times a day the bullocky's off-sider came close to being crushed to death with his dexterous dashing about. Seemingly unworried about any imminent mortality, the dog slunk up to its master's heel and sat, tongue lolling from its short snout with evident enjoyment.

"Bloody dog," grumbled Big Bob, shaking his head affectionately.

Grace capped her eyes against the bright sun as she peered up at his leathery face, lined and slightly yellowed like old ivory. "Yabby? Is that his name?"

"Yeah. Looked just like a yabby as a pup."

"What on earth is that?"

"Bloody ugliest freshwater crayfish this side of the Snowy River. Comes in blue, just like Yabby here." He fondled the dog's ears, and the dog's mouth drew back wider.

Grace pressed her lips in amusement at the huge man's propensity for swearing just as effectively as a sailor. "Thank you for escorting the shepherds to Gilly Downs."

"Happy to show 'em the way." He plonked his hat atop his greasy, grey-streaked hair. "They'll need to fend for themselves, mind. I'm no bloody maid, set for cookin' and carin'. They'll be safe enough if they stick with me. Takes me a day and a half to Gilly Downs—as opposed to half a day's journey by horse, that is. Always get there in the end. Glad of the company, though—the extra hands too. 'Tis a bloody lonely job this." He cocked his head over his shoulder. "A load as bloody big as that'll likely break a wheel or collapse the yoke. That slab of marble packs quite a weight." Big Bob turned his sunburned face back to Grace. "Least it's too heavy for them flamin' bushrangers to nick."

Catching sight of Grace's worried frown, he countered, "Bugger-all to worry about, not with so many men with guns. Of an evenin', we'll tie up with other bullockies. Them bloody rascals have the freshest news in all Sydney Town. There isn't a rough road, a ninnyhammer customer, or a new bloody arrival that isn't known to us drivers." His profanity oozed from him with the airy ease of a harmonica. Clearly in no hurry to be going, Big Bob rested the stock of his whip on the ground. He nudged his leather hat back further on his head, exposing a sweat-cleaned line high on his wide brow. "Is it true what them's sayin'—that you commanded that big, bloody ship all on your lonesome?"

Grace's cheeks warmed under his casual scrutiny. "Not quite by myself. The officers and hands made the job possible."

"But yous became captain? After your husband was shot by the first mate?"

"Well—yes—"

"Bloody oath, Lady Cap! You're no cornstalk." He widened

his eyes appreciatively. "And the men—thems all followed your orders?"

Grace hesitated. She was not about to add any more fuel to this fiery gossip. Besides, this storyteller would likely add his own kindling regardless of what she told him. "I'm no captain—my husband is alive and recovering well."

Clearly angling for more tasty morsels, Big Bob added, "Heard said you dug a bloody great ball of shot from the cap'n's chest with your bare hands?"

"My, my, news really does travel fast around here." She smiled. "Dr Sykes cut the ball from his back—with his scalpel and medicine chest to hand. It wasn't all bare-handed surgery."

Big Bill's wiry eyebrows rose in admiration. "You killed the bloody shooter then, single-handed?"

Grace turned the bullocky's phrase back on him. "Is that what you've heard said?" Her neck shrank into her shoulders at the reminder. Running her hand across the back of her head, she fingered the knotted scar on her scalp. "Mr Chittenden died after falling from the quarterdeck."

Big Bob guffawed and shuffled his worn leather boots in the dust. "Come on, Lady Cap, don't ruin it for me. The thought of you droppin' a seven-foot giant, with your hair blowin' behind yous, wailin' like a bloody banshee, makes for much more inter-estin' tellin'. That'd be a bloody sight for sore eyes. Isn't a soddin' man alive brave enough to face a woman in full fury. You're all bloody claws and teeth with your hissin' and spittin'."

"Good grief! Is that people's perception of me?" Grace could not help smiling at the man's open grin. Her gaze rested on Wee Granny Mac hunched patiently on the wagon. "I also credit Wee Granny Mac with my husband's survival."

Big Bob looked back at the tiny woman and clicked his tongue. "She'll be a bloody good sort to have on the station then. If she's half as good with sheep as she is with people, Squatter Barclay'll welcome her with open bloody arms."

"I'm sure he will," she concurred. "Could you please deliver this to Mrs Barclay?" Grace held out a sealed packet. "Tell her we'll be at Gilly Downs by month's end. Once I've tied up a few more loose ends in town."

The compact square of folded paper was dwarfed in his giant hand, but he tucked it safely inside his coat. "Callin' that bastard Chittenden a *loose end* seems fittin'." Big Bob's wide smile tapered. "Sounds like he got what he had comin'." He clenched his meaty fists, and his knuckles popped like small firecrackers. "This town's filled with enough mutineers, pick-pockets, and murderers. We don't need no overly ambitious toff like him deprivin' our humble colony of its supplies through his carelessness just 'cause he didn't take to you, Lady Cap."

Grace eyed the stranger, surprised by his ready belief in her sailoring skills. It took an exceptionally enlightened man to be so accepting of her position. Her affection for the rough traveller grew. Chittenden should count his lucky stars he was safely tucked away in Davy Jones's locker instead of at Big Bob's mercy.

With an affable grin that offered eternal reassurance, Big Bob flicked the brim of his hat. "Hooroo, Lady Cap. Best be on my way then. Come, Yabby, you bloody mongrel!"

Very few men respected her as an equal, but at least those who did appreciated her unequivocally. Had she just added this colourful character to her secret club of allies?

A COUPLE OF WEEKS LATER, Seamus sat with Grace in the decadent dining room of the newly built Barclay Hall, enjoying a final cup of tea with the Barclays before the day's chaos ensued. The four adults huddled down one end of the long, polished table that comfortably seated twenty. The head armchair looked deceptively dainty, though it bore Barclay's large frame well. Seamus shuffled back on the red velvet upholstery; the thick fabric, while perfectly comfortable now, was bound to become hot and itchy in the coming summer months.

The view through the white wooden French windows led across the wide veranda, past the old wooden cottage, and down the hill to the river cutting through the sheep run. It was the dry season, and clear water rippled across polished pebbles, like marbled birds' eggs nestled peacefully on the streambed. Barclay had mentioned that the water churned an angry brown in the wet season, spilling its banks with the same fury as molten magma topping the rim of a volcano. This was undoubtedly a land shaped by extremes—drought, flood, and blistering temperatures.

Seamus swivelled his gaze back to the dining room. The pale marble slab he had shipped over would be a tidy finish to the hearth. As warm as the weather was, a crackling fire would not go amiss to ease the ache plaguing his back. Since his fever, his body had tussled with the elements, and today the cooler morning air was winning. He was relieved that the rambunctious Barclay children ate in the children's dining room, a decadent delight in which Emily and Edwin happily immersed themselves. He wondered how long it would take the Barclay brood to grow to five. Mrs Barclay, unable to keep up with the demands of so many youngsters as well as assuming responsibility as mistress of the new grand house, had resorted to the services of wet nurses and nannies. As would he in her shoes!

Spitting out as many offspring as quickly as she had done meant Mrs Barclay was no longer the svelte young girl he had first met at the Governor's Ball, though this did not deter her husband's attention.

Rest and fresh air had expedited Seamus's recovery, and he hoped a short ride out to the nearby paddocks with Barclay this morning would limber up the twinge in his back. The copper-headed squatter shook open the week-old copy of *The Sydney Herald*, the broadsheets rustling like leaves scurrying in autumn.

"Well I never!" His flushing, ruddy face peered over the top of the paper. "You've caused quite a stir in the colony, Mrs Fitzwilliam."

"Me?" Grace's teacup paused halfway to her lips, which were pretty and pink again after being chapped by wind and salt for so long. She tilted her brown-curled head, settling the china cup back in its saucer with a soft clink.

Barclay broke out in a wide, toothy grin, coughing importantly before reading aloud. "The merchant ship *Elias*, famous for having been taken into Sydney Town by Mrs Grace Fitzwilliam, wife of the master, now lies at the foot of Queen's Wharf in Sydney Cove. The circumstances attending her voyage to New South Wales, and the heroic conduct of the master's wife, have earned widespread circulation through the newspapers, though some conflicting accounts and statements have found their way before the public."

Grace laughed lightly. "Isn't that the truth! You should hear Big Bob's version of the tale!"

Barclay continued the important missive. "On the voyage, Captain Fitzwilliam was accidentally shot and grievously wounded by one of the hands. Through the affliction of his wound, he became delirious, such that he was unable to give any orders or attend any duties appertaining to the ship. Mrs Fitzwilliam, with bravery beyond that of many men, coolly assumed command in order to ensure the safety of all souls, which included her two young children, a governess, and a maid-servant. Captain Fitzwilliam's leisure hours, previous to his being overtaken by his wounding, were employed in teaching his wife the science of navigation; and when her husband was no longer able to tend to his duty, she left his bedside at intervals and took the station he had rendered vacant on deck."

Grace peered at Seamus through her lowered eyelashes.

While his open-mindedness to allow her to learn the workings of a ship had played a heavy role in their latest adventure, his worst fear was coming true. Printed in black ink for the world to see were all his failings. He poured himself some more tea and swigged a large mouthful of the unsweetened black liquid, savouring the distraction of its tepid trail down his gullet.

The broadsheet rustled again as Barclay lifted it higher, squinting to read the tiny print. "The duties of Mrs Fitzwilliam were thus divided between the cares and attention her husband required, and the navigation of the vessel. When they reached the Heads at the harbour entrance to Sydney, she was warned of the danger the ship would encounter passing in, and was advised to lay off until they could secure a pilot. This she also refused to do, but, presumably on her acquired knowledge, she took the helm herself and steered the vessel safely into port. Witness our heroic country-woman, Grace Fitzwilliam—"

"*Our* country-woman?" interrupted Grace, confusion pinching her face.

Mrs Barclay leaned forward and patted her arm. "It's a compliment, Grace dear. They've taken you as one of their own. God knows this new little colony needs a few more heroes and heroines to balance out the scoundrels." Laughter rippled around the table.

"Spot on, lambkin." Barclay winked at his wife before continuing to read. "Witness our heroic country-woman, Grace Fitzwilliam, who, poor wife as she was, already overshadowed by the sacred primal sorrow of her sex, yet, with a strong will and stout heart, steered her husband's vessel, through storm and through calm, to Sydney Town."

Barclay folded the large sheets and slapped the publication beside his breakfast plate. "Bloody marvellous stuff!"

"Sounds more like the imaginings of a novel writer," said Grace, her cheeks pink with self-consciousness.

Seamus stared at the valley beyond the homestead again.

Dirty sheep blended in with the dry, crisp grass yet to be quenched by a decent downpour. The daft creatures would likely be spread as far as the tall scribbly gum tree that marked the start of Gilly Downs, an hour's ride away. A blackened, jagged lightning-scar had rived the trunk's top half in two like a poorly executed beheading. His manhood was similarly cleaved by hearing Grace's publicised accolades.

"Are they not the facts?" queried Mrs Barclay, her milky forehead rucking.

Grace sighed. "Yes, they are. But they sound more glamorous in print than they played out in real life."

His wife was right, of course. It *was* a heroically embellished account. At least the journalist had left out any mention of Chittenden's demise. The last thing Seamus wanted to add to his plate was a public reckoning about the death of his demoted first mate.

Chapter Eleven

Grace was delighted that in the month Miss Lissing had spent at Gilly Downs, she had pulled the eldest Barclay child from his unruly sibling rabble and turned him into a complicit little learner in the purpose-built schoolroom.

At the start of each school day, Miss Lissing drew a shiny-faced Noah Barclay into Emily and Edwin's lessons, as well as a reluctant ten-year-old Nevin Buchanan. Of a morning, the children learned Roman, French, and English history, broke down Latin syntax, worked on multiplication, and read poetry. Their afternoon routine consisted of planting potatoes, bringing in the cows for milking, turning the vegetable patch, splitting wood, and polishing the brass on the horse harnesses.

But today after lunch, the children, armed with fishing poles, burst onto the sweeping gravel circle outside the front of Barclay

Hall, bouncing and skipping like lambs in springtime, their unbuttoned coats flapping. The rabble tore through the old log cottage's yard on their way down to the creek, nearly colliding with Grace and Jim.

"Hey, you lot," Jim yelled. A pale cloud of dust swirled up around the children's well-worn boots as they halted. "Didn't Old Quill task ye with planting the rhubarb up at the big house?"

Aquilla Jacobs—Old Quill, as he was affectionately known in the district—had been a shepherd until afflicted with Barcoo rot. A simple scratch from an old dried tree branch on his ankle had festered into a deep, inflamed wound. This source of moisture in the dry heat had attracted hundreds of flies, and the inflammation had spread up his leg, resulting in half his calf wasting away. Jim had told Grace that Old Quill never ventured far from the homestead these days.

Nevin cracked a toothy grin. "Aw, uncle, Cook says she'll bake us a fish pie for supper if we can catch enough before sundown." He slung an arm around Edwin's shoulders. "Eddy here even has an extra pocket full of worms for his poor wee brother."

Grace smiled as Nevin winked at Eddy; the older boy's acknowledgment of his dead twin was a thoughtful touch, even if the rascal was using it to persuade his uncle into agreement.

Jim's lips pursed in readiness to spit out a reprimand at his black-haired nephew, so uncannily like him. Emily's blue eyes widened, and the corners of Edwin's mouth tugged down. Grace nudged her friend with her shoulder.

"Please, Jim. I'll help tend the garden. Our Em and Eddy love to fish. Besides, it'll give us a chance to catch up." A glowing affection filled her chest as his moon-shaped face transformed into his familiar, easy grin.

"Aye, be off, ye wee ruffians, afore I change my mind." Jim chuckled and nodded, and they swarmed down the rutted track, hooting and laughing. "And for the love of all that's holy, be sure to bring back some fish this time," he yelled after them. Shaking his head, he harrumphed. "Their poor fishing days have little to do with lack of fish in the creek."

Grace hooked her arm in his. "It'll do our Em and Eddy wonders to spend the afternoon splashing in the creek and climbing trees. I only hope the other boys don't take to sword fighting with sticks—our Em will trounce them!"

"She best be prepared to take as good as she gives. Nevin's a crack shot with his sling. While I've taught ma boy never to discharge stones at folk, it's never stopped him firing sheep droppings. They're too light to hurt, but they'll likely send the lass squealing off in disgust." Jim hooted with laughter and drew her up the hill to the shearing shed. "Come on, then. Best be seeing how our newest shepherdess is faring."

Upon Wee Granny Mac's arrival at Gilly Downs, Jim had taken one look at her wizened frame and, declaring she would not survive a day out in the harsh New South Wales bushland, had promptly engaged her as Old Quill's assistant to teach the new shepherds how to treat sick and wounded sheep.

Grace glanced at her long-time friend from the corner of her eye. He looked happy, his face still as round as she remembered, though browner. The harsh climate had deepened the lines around his eyes, and he was still clean-shaven, though the wiry hair at his temples was prematurely flecked with white against his black mop.

"You look well, Jim. How's farm life compared to ship life? Do you miss it?"

"Aye, a bit. Though I don't miss being permanently damp. And there's one thing about Cook—she knows how to fill a man's stomach." He patted his belly, which still looked as flat as the day she had met him. "Though truth be told, I miss having a berth that rolls with the waves. There's a certain comfort about it." He pulled one of his protruding ears. "And I miss the lads. The shepherds and shearers are grand, don't get me wrong. But there's nothing like the oath of the sea to bind men with the fiercest loyalty. 'Tisn't half as much sport tending a brainless flock of sheep either. Mother of saints—if sheep had two heads, they'd be twice as thick!"

"Do you regret your decision? To stay behind?"

Crinkling his nose, he shook his head. "I've no regrets. 'Twas the right choice. For Nevin. I've grown rather fond of the wee rascal, what with him being exactly like his da." Jim plucked a wayward stalk of straw from his trouser leg and twirled it in his fingers. "Don't know what kind of da I am, but he seems happy enough. Though he doesn't much like it when I tan his hide." He laughed. "He's a good lad. 'Tisn't too often I've to do that." He tossed the straw aside. "How are ye faring, lass? Ye've had a bit of a rough trot yerself with yer lad's passing." His brown eyes brimmed with the same kindness and compassion as always.

She smiled sadly. "Hasn't been easy." The deep ache of Elias's loss still dwelled inside. "But it has dwindled with time."

"Does it help ye to have the other wee laddie around as a reminder?" he asked gently.

She dipped her eyebrows in contemplation, then slid her gaze towards him, nodding. "I think it does. I suppose it's like you having a bit of Rory left behind in Nevin?"

"Aye, once it stops paining ye to look at them, there's a certain comfort in having them near."

"I've missed *you*, Jim."

He leaned his shoulder against hers. "Aye, and I you. Though, it doesn't sound like ye've been too poorly off without me." He quirked one eyebrow up. "Is it true ye beat yer first mate to a pulp with yer own wee hands?" Jim's face was open in expectation, and without judgement.

She shrugged.

"Crivens, lass!" A laugh burst from him, and he scrabbled his hand through his hair, spiking it up. "I well and truly corrupted ye all those years back, did I not? It'll be a brave man who dares take over yer ship again. Especially after the last one ended up looking like he'd run face-first into the business end of a bull."

Good grief! Where could she even begin to explain how it felt to kill a man? She had suffered terribly with guilt after Gilly had been killed by another, but Chittenden's death was by her hand alone. How come she had not felt this way after she had stabbed Silverton? With all that blood beside Highgate Pond, she had truly thought him dead, though ultimately, his death was not by her hand. Was it that Chittenden had not looked as grievously injured, or that she had not plotted to kill him as she had Silverton? Had Elias's death turned her sense of right and wrong on its head?

Jim's laugher, deep, rich, and full of life, faded into a silent frown. "What is it, lass?"

Shaking her head to clear her gloom, Grace laughed back. "Nothing." She smiled at his monkey-like face with its protruding ears. "Still no *Mrs* Buchanan on the horizon? Nevin's ten already. Hasn't he been without a mother long enough?"

Jim's bronzed face darkened, and he lowered his long, dark lashes. "Well—" He gave a tight cough.

Grace's heartbeat increased at his slow, shy grin. "Oh, Jim! *Is* there a special someone?" She gripped his firm, sinewed arm. "Who is she? A local girl? Someone from town? I want to know *everything*."

Jim rubbed the back of his head and laughed. "For the love of all that's holy, Mrs F., ye've not changed a bit. Still talking nineteen to the dozen—not letting a man squeeze a word in edgeways."

Grace clamped both lips between her teeth and widened her eyes. Despite her comical attempt to be silent, anticipation and curiosity needled her like the quills of a porcupine. He had better speak soon, or she would burst!

He rolled his eyes and chuckled. "Her name's Pearl—Pearl Clementine. She's a milkmaid. Works in Harris's Dairy." His smile softened. "Met her the first time Harris held a dance in his milking shed. Everyone in the district was invited, and Squatter Barclay was kind enough to let us go."

Unable to restrain herself, Grace blurted, "Did you dance with her?"

"Aye, nearly every dance."

"What does she look like?"

Jim tipped his head back and hummed. "Never thought to put her looks into words. I just see her as she is."

"Ugh! Give me *something*!"

"Och, I suppose she's about yay high." He raised his hand to his shoulder. "She's long brown hair that she keeps plaited in a thick rope down her back. I can all but circle her waist with ma hands—" Jim stopped abruptly, blushing.

Delighted that he had divulged this intimacy, Grace nodded in encouragement. "Go on."

His Adam's apple dipped. "She's the smoothest, softest cheeks, and her eyes are as large and brown as a dairy cow."

A dairy cow! Grace bit back a snort of laughter. It was kindly meant—she just hoped he never said it aloud to the poor lass. "How old is she?"

"Nineteen this past summer." Jim grinned. "She's a fine one indeed."

"And is she funny, or shy, or outspoken?"

"By all the holy saints, Mrs F., the Spanish Inquisition's probing wasn't half as relentless as yours." His laugher was warm and hearty, and he shook his head in mock exasperation. "If ye must know, she's a bonnie wee thing. She only has to bat those pretty brown eyes in my direction to send me heart skidding about my chest like an oiled piglet. Can scarce breathe when I'm near her."

"Oh, then perhaps she's no good for you after all." Her words tripped lightly, though she feigned a mask of earnestness.

"Why's that?" Jim's black eyebrows quivered.

"If you can't breathe around her, then she *must* be bad for your health."

"Och, away with ye!" Jim nudged her with his elbow.

With the joke up, she could not contain her smile. "Has Nevin met her?"

"Aye, he has. If he weren't a wee laddie, I'd have some competition on my hands. Boy's completely smitten. She doesn't help matters by sending him parcels of cakes and sweets along with the letters she sends me."

"I hope you write her back? You're an accomplished penman, you know?"

Jim scratched one eyebrow with his thumb. "I had a good teacher." He nudged nearer and winked. "I wrote her a poem, though not too clever, mind." Jim's ears turned beetroot red, and he shrugged. "She must have liked it well enough—she sent me a lock of her hair tied in a ribbon."

"She sounds *lovely*, Jim! If she's half as sweet as you've painted her, you'd best be making your move before some roaming swaggie sweeps her off her feet."

"No chance." Jim chuckled. "My Pearl favours creature comforts like a bed to sleep in and a firm roof above. She wouldn't be swayed by some wandering traveller."

"What of a dashing English soldier in his scarlet uniform then? He'd be able to keep her in that lifestyle."

Pressing his lips smugly, he shook his head. "She's not partial to soldiers, seeing her da's an ex-convict—though he's head dairyman at Harris's now." Some of the humour slipped from his voice.

"Sorry. I was only teasing," said Grace softly, relieved to see the wrinkled furrow in his forehead smooth out as she smiled. "I can see she makes you happy."

"Aye, that she does." He patted her hand in a consolatory gesture.

In the warm, dark shearing shed, a chorus of bleats greeted Grace as half a dozen sheep paced frantically alongside the wooden palisades, bug-eyed in panic. Stupid creatures, as sharp as a sock full of soup they were. The air was filled with dusty tones of sweet hay and a deep overlay of liquorice and freshly scythed grass—or the smell of prosperity, as Elijah liked to call it.

Grace recognised the three new shepherds from the *Elias* standing dutifully to attention before Old Quill. Each man was dressed alike: wide-brimmed hats, drab grey trousers tied at the ankles with string, and sweat-stained shirts, once white but now an indiscernible grey. Old Quill had a heavily fleeced ewe upended on its rump, compliantly docile in this peculiar position. He rifled through the patchy burr-riddled fleece with stiff-jointed fingers, crooked like knots in a twig. They were working hands, calloused and ingrained with dirt, with one black nail. Hands familiar with sewing gashes in flesh from dingo bites and pulling dead lambs from their mothers' bodies.

"Scab," he said matter-of-factly, gnashing his gums together.

Sliding her hand free from Jim's arm, Grace leaned in. The scraggly sheep was missing whole patches of wool, exposing wet patches of flesh—reeking, inflamed, and edged with mustard-green pus. Oh, the poor creature!

"Rubbed itself raw against trees and bushes," continued Old Quill.

"Aye," concurred Wee Granny Mac. "Wee beasties in the fleece send a sheep to an early grave, driven mad by the itch."

Grace winced and stroked the sheep's nose in sympathy. The animal flinched, eyes wide with agony as it tried to kick free. "How does it bear the pain?"

The walnut-faced woman cackled. "Dafties, the lot of 'em—can't scratch 'emselves and remember to eat at the same time."

"They are indeed." Old Quill wrestled the ewe back onto the base of its tail. It slumped, its eyes rolling, its muscles twitching spasmodically. "They'll die wool-blind if not shorn. They'll die if you don't dag and dip 'em. They'll also die wanderin' off into the bush, likely taken by dingoes." His yellowed, rheumy eyes glared up at the young shepherds. "'Tis your job to make sure the daft buggers don't indulge in any o' that."

"And how do we stop the scab?" asked the black-haired youth, his eyes glistening with intelligence and interest.

"Dipping the lot of 'em into a bath of tobacco and mercury a couple of times cures a flock. Though, this bag o' bones has given over to hysteria," said Old Quill, flipping the shuddering sheep back onto its feet. "'Tis too far gone for treatment." He nodded at the youngest shepherd. "Your first job's to put this poor creature out of its misery. Take it out back and butcher it. Then feed it to the dogs."

Grace sucked in a breath. Wee Granny Mac might have the stomach for such things, but she did not. "I think I'll head back to the house now. I promised Mrs Barclay I'd help her unpack the trunk of books and atlases I brought her."

Jim smiled and nodded. "Can ye wend yer way back alone? I must get on with docking and castrating the lambs."

Seamus's laughter swung her attention around. He was already in the outside pen helping Elijah. Through the gaps in the ironbark planks, Grace studied her husband a beat longer. Despite his coatless back, his dishevelled hair, and the bloody castration knife in his hand, he looked—happy. She knew he hated the idleness that had been forced upon him, but here, tasked with purpose, he was a man content. Not even the black carpet of sheep muck underfoot could deter him.

"Yes, thank you, Jim. I'll see you later." Grace slid an affectionate hand down her friend's arm, turning away from the young shepherd dragging the protesting sheep around the corner.

IN THE LIBRARY, Grace hesitated by the open door. Adelia stretched up on her toes to seat a thick leather volume on a high shelf. A second woman reached into the open trunk and handed her another book. Goodness, how long had it been? Four or five years? The ex-governor's daughter wore the same middle parting, with her plaits curled like a halo.

"Mrs Deas Thomson!" Grace rushed forward, her delight genuine.

The woman's severe hairstyle held no bearing on the kindness and joy now flooding her face. "Mrs Fitzwilliam, how lovely to see you again. Mrs Barclay has been filling me in on all your news." She grasped Grace's fingers, her wide hands warm and solid.

Grace inclined her head at the open trunk that offered an array of odours—musty, used books offset by the sharp inkiness of new ones. "Would you like a hand?"

"Yes, thank you." Adelia beamed. "When we're done, we can take some tea in the parlour."

"Ah, yes, a much more palatable task than the one Jim just offered," said Grace, handing Adelia a leather-bound atlas. "I'm not particularly squeamish, but after an intimate explanation of how to remove a lamb's privy parts, I declined."

Adelia's laughter still carried a trace of her youthful giggle. "I'm glad my days of docking and castration are over."

"Best that our Em's not about. She's a bit of a softie when it comes to animals," said Grace.

"*My* menagerie usually consume my day. It's a relief to have Edwin here to divert Noah's attention," said Adelia. Her sun-freckled friend clearly did not shy from rolling up her sleeves, despite the pretence of grandeur her new home presented.

"I'm glad my son is enjoying the company of another lad," said Grace. "I think he's missed it."

"Plus, you've the added task of being mistress of Barclay Hall now." Mrs Deas Thomson waved her hand, her short, square nails moving in an arc.

Above in the nursery, toy wheels thundered across the wooden floorboards, no doubt shiny and slippery in their newness. Ruth and Eve Barclay shared the common interest of tricycle riding, and their delighted shrieks and giggles mingled with Gideon's infantile squalls.

Adelia shook her head at the pressed ceiling, her loose, sandy bun wobbling. "Utter chaos! Can't blame Mr Barclay's escape to the shed today." The grin, showing off her neat white teeth, told that she would have it no other way. She ran her hand over her belly. "And now we've another little one arriving."

To Grace, the noise above was the music score of life she enjoyed the most—the cheerful unbridled symphony of happy children. She turned at the soft knock on the library door.

"Miss Lissing, come in." Grace slotted a book onto the almost full shelf above.

The governess entered with a newspaper tucked under her arm, her footsteps stuttering to a halt. "Oh, you've company. My apologies."

Mrs Deas Thomson waved her hand again. "Come in, dear. No need to stand on ceremony with me. I'm Mrs Deas Thomson."

Miss Lissing bobbed. "Pleasure to meet you." She licked her lips and tipped her head at Grace. "Begging your pardon, madam. Might I have a word?"

Grace rubbed her hands on her apron, shedding the dust of paper fibres from her fingertips. "Of course." She motioned to the brown leather chesterfield, and Miss Lissing perched on the settee edge. Grace sat opposite and smiled in expectation. The governess offered her the folded newspaper, and Grace wondered if it was the same paper that told of her account. Newspapers had a long lifespan on Gilly Downs. News of the world was passed around to those who could read until it became a tattered and besmeared knot of paper with which the shepherds started their campfires.

While she had no interest in news of England, it amused her how Seamus cherished his broadsheets. To him, they were treasure-troves of information—land for sale, lost or stolen items, horse auctions, and even the published lists of unclaimed letters still lying at the Post Office. She had not believed her husband to be an overly sentimental man until he professed that reading the names of familiar streets was almost as good as seeing the signs in person. However, this particular paper was local, and still in excellent condition.

"What am I looking at?" asked Grace.

Miss Lissing's long, slim finger pointed to a small printed advert on the front page. "This advertisement."

SEEKING BUSINESS PARTNER

Madame Eulalie Dubois—a pupil of Pierre Letellier, Member of the Academy—seeks an English Protestant lady, fully qualified to impart a sound English education, to join her in the management of her school.

Grace glanced up from the folded paper. The young governess's oval green eyes shone, and her slim hips wriggled closer to the edge of her seat like a sparrow on the verge of flight.

"And what's this to me?" Grace asked.

"I wrote to Madame Dubois before we left Sydney, enquiring

about *why* she was looking for a qualified teacher," said Miss Lissing.

Mrs Deas Thomson hummed. "Ah, yes, I'm well acquainted with Madame Dubois. She believes that while parents might be happy for their children to learn French from a real Parisienne, they're perhaps more comfortable entrusting the rest of their education to a reputable Englishwoman. It's a respectable position she's offering."

"Have you a reply?" asked Grace.

Miss Lissing's milky cheeks flushed, and her voice pitched. "Yes. Mr Singh, the trader who visited yesterday, delivered it. I know I'm in your employ, Mrs Fitzwilliam. And please be assured, your children's education is still my priority, but..." Her voice trailed off as her gaze flitted to the paper. "An opportunity like this rarely comes along. I had no intention of leaving you at the first chance or of setting roots in this far-off land." Her slim shoulders bunched. "Please believe me."

"I believe you." Grace nodded.

Miss Lissing's tight brow eased, and she pushed an auburn wave of hair back over her shoulder. "You know I strive to ensure your daughter receives an education that equals that of boys her age?"

"Indeed," concurred Grace. "It's that sentiment that secured your position. Too many women pay more attention to what they place *on* their heads rather than what they place *within*."

Drawn by the conversation, Adelia sat on the footstool. "Funny how the pubs in this town are so well supported while the library... *isn't*." Her gaze caressed the rows of books lining the library shelves.

Mrs Deas Thomson nodded. "Indeed. The English habits of our young country merely imitate the old one."

Grace crossed her ankles and shuffled back comfortably. "If you ask me, they'd do better if to avoid the priggish notions of Mother England altogether."

Adelia scraped a straggling wisp of golden hair off her fore-head and wrapped it neatly around the large bun. "Won't argue with you there, though most folk can't see past the transported convicts and penniless immigrants. Many believe the colony has a long way to go before it resembles anything of life in England."

Miss Lissing looked between them, head tilted. "Do the free settlers not wish to attain a higher class? In essence, what Madame Dubois is offering in her school?"

Adelia laughed. "You mean a *resemblance* of a higher class!"

"The good people of Sydney Town have much to learn before they can measure their success in this endeavour," countered Mrs Deas Thomson. "Though that's perhaps not a bad thing."

"No doubt they still have silly things to unlearn first," said Miss Lissing with an emphatic nod. "Such as the idea that boys deserve a higher quality of education than their female counterparts."

Mrs Deas Thomson's eyes widened, and she turned her head slowly towards Grace. "This girl has spirit. I like her."

Adelia rolled her shoulders and shifted on the footstool. "Pardon my forwardness, Miss Lissing, but have you the means for such a transaction? Madame Dubois is seeking a *business* partner. That typically requires a financial investment as well as the offer of service." She inclined her head towards Grace. "And aren't you still in Mrs Fitzwilliam's employ?"

Florid faced, Miss Lissing straightened up. "I am, but I respectfully tender my resignation." She folded the paper on her lap, then met Adelia's gaze. "My savings should be a sufficient deposit while I await the remainder of funds from Papa in London."

Grace recognised the same free-spirited passion she had discovered in herself as a young woman. She smiled kindly. "This is all very well, Miss Lissing, but our Em and Eddy are returning with me to England next month. I trust you'll help me find another suitable governess before then?"

Miss Lissing grabbed Grace's hand familiarly. "Indeed, madam! It'll be my pleasure to help you find my replacement."

Grace squeezed back and hummed, half in agreement and half in amusement. Just how much of *this* decision had been born of Seamus asking Toby to remain behind as his agent?

Chapter Twelve

S eamus glanced across the drawing room at Squatter Barclay standing before the fireplace. The lantern light picked highlights of pink out of the white, exquisitely veined marble mantel. The grazier's cravat hung loose around his neck, untied after the roast lamb, jacket potatoes, and green beans Cook had spoiled them with that evening. Barclay was explaining how, during the shearing season, neighbouring stations hired the shearing shed at Gilly Downs and, for a nominal fee, rented the extra space in his Sydney woolstore for their bales.

"Aren't they the competition?" Seamus enquired.

"Suppose they are." Barclay ran a hand contemplatively down his weather-worn cheek. Red hair and pale skin were no match for the harsh climate, the crow's feet around his eyes deep like plough furrows scratched into sun-baked soil, though his clear blue eyes glinted judiciously in the candlelight. "But we look after our own out here. There's plenty land to go around, and London's demand for wool is insatiable."

"I've always been wary of business crossing into personal territory."

"Doesn't do to make an enemy of one's neighbours in this remote part of the world. Not a season passes without fire, flood, or drought. Just last summer, we all rallied together to save Powell's property to the north. A bushfire swept through Madden Run, turning their pastures into a blazing hellfire."

The squatter shook his head at the memory. "Heat singed the hairs right off my hands. Crackling flames consumed trees like a demented demon. And the smell—" He cleared his throat and swallowed deeply. "Let's just say I lost my appetite for lamb roasts for months afterwards."

Seamus swiped his fist across his lips. "Christ, Barclay. I can only imagine. Fire is my greatest fear aboard the ship." He inhaled deeply, glad of the wall panels' woody scent, new and freshly oiled.

Barclay harrumphed. "Took sixty men pumping water from the well for twelve hours to save the main house and surrounding outbuildings. Wasn't anything to be done for the shepherds out in the bush. Madden Run lost four good men that day."

Seamus raised his snifter, the brandy shimmering golden brown. "May they rest in peace." He took a deep drink.

"Your new shipping office all in order?" asked Barclay.

"Indeed. The upper floor of Barclay & Co. Woolstore is the perfect home for the Elias Shipping Company. A perfect partnership in a perfect location at the quay."

Earlier today, Big Bob had loaded up Gilly Downs' final bales from the shearing shed onto his three wagons, ready for transport to Barclay's wool store at Semi-Circular Quay tomorrow. The other bales had been steadily transported to the warehouse during the year.

"Your man, Hicks, is as quick as they come," said Barclay.

Seamus hummed in agreement. "That man's nous for business is that of a bloodhound on a trail." In addition to Barclay's wool, Hicks had also secured contracts with three smaller stations, neighbours to Gilly Downs.

"It needs to be if you're to trust him as your agent while you're away to London again."

"Hicks's fealty to my family has stood the test of time. There's no finer man for the job. He's finalising the purchase of the *Quintus Roscius*—a passenger ship with a generous hold."

"Ah, yes. The second in the Elias Shipping Company's fleet."

Seamus's lips twitched in amusement. Two ships hardly constituted a fleet, but he appreciated Barclay's optimism. "Since you're planning on having enough wool to fill two ships in the near future, it made sense to capitalise on the opportunity." He rubbed his forefinger across his lips. "If I'm not mistaken, she's named after a first-century Roman, renowned for his great comedy."

"Indeed." Barclay's shoulders jiggled as he laughed. "Rather she be named after a comedic Roman actor than a Shakespearean tragedy like *Titus Andronicus*, I say."

Seamus inclined his head. "She's not half as pretty as the *Elias*, but she's watertight and solidly built. And Captain Robert Robertson's a fine commander."

"Robert Robertson?" Barclay arched one brow.

Seamus shrugged, a smile quivering on his lips. "Perhaps his mother was clean out of inspiration the day he was born?"

"Have you given any more thought about offering passage to immigrants? The shepherds you brought are marvellous, but I'll require many more to work the interior as Gilly Downs expands —and single women to balance them out."

"Yes. Grace and I have discussed this. The governor has called for practical sorts, who'll not shy from working the farms."

"Hear, hear!" Barclay raised his glass. "Afraid there's not much demand for gentle types like ladies' maids and milliners."

"I'll investigate further once I return to London. Grace's uncle, Admiral Baxter, no doubt has connections in the Colonial Office. And now I've the ship to accommodate it too."

"With the volume of souls these days desiring an escape from unemployment and starvation, you'll not struggle to fill a manifest." Barclay's wistful stare into the bottom of his empty glass did not look like that of a man wanting more brandy. He raised his gaze slowly, and Seamus's humour trickled away. "You're a good man and a fine friend, Fitzwilliam—and God knows I haven't my wife's penchant for idle gossip—but a rumour abounds that Captain Appleby has reported your first mate's death to the magistrate."

Seamus's stomach dropped like a ship down the back of a thirty-foot wave. By Neptune's forked trident! The quicker he could finish loading, the quicker he could depart. Hopefully, time and distance might erase his shameful smear from this town's memories. He circled his thumb around the rim of his glass, keeping a cool tone. "The man met his untimely demise through no fault of my crew."

One of Barclay's ruddy brows dipped. "It's not your crew you should be worried about. Appleby's clearly taken umbrage with your wife for some unfathomable reason."

Seamus shot to his feet, biting back a groan at the pinch in his back. He had been laid up for so long that his body was unused to a hard day's work and was now punishing him for it. "I've witnesses aplenty to assure the magistrate of my wife's innocence."

Patting his arm with a solid hand, Barclay said, "No doubt you have. Just thought you'd want to be armed with this knowledge."

Seamus threw back the rest of his brandy and dropped the heavy-bottomed glass on the side table with a wooden thud. "Takes a careless man to cross me, and an even more reckless one to cross my wife."

THE FOLLOWING MORNING, Seamus rose at dawn with the rest of the household. Leaving Grace to be fussed over by Mrs Barclay, he urged his own horse down to Big Bob's bullock train lining the narrow track alongside the creek. Emily followed on her pony with Edwin behind her on the saddle.

The three wagons disappeared and reappeared in the damp morning mist that clung to the stream's edges like a child clinging to the comfort of a mother's petticoats as though afraid of the rising red orb on the horizon. The rectangular bales—piled high, stamped with the Wooloongilly Downs name, and secured by a spiderweb of ropes—were a satisfying sight. On the driver's seat beside the giant bullocky, Miss Lissing sat upright and tightly corseted as usual, her tapestried travelling bag hugged to her chest. Grace had advised him of the governess's departure, and he was sorry to see her go. Anyone who could tame that eldest Barclay boy deserved a hefty dose of respect.

"Good morning, Miss Lissing." Seamus tipped his hat.

"Captain." She inclined her head, her auburn waves curling over her shoulder.

He nodded at Big Bob. "Ready?"

"Keepin' us company, Cap'n?" Big Bob pushed up the brim of his floppy leather hat with his whipstock. "You'll set a fairer pace on your own."

"Indeed," replied Seamus. "I'll escort my family ahead. See you in a few days?"

"Righto."

Noah and Nevin swarmed around the wagon, chatting excitedly and calling final farewells to their teacher, and to Emily and Edwin. Emily swivelled in her saddle, her breath white on her plump lips. "Oh, please, Cappy. May we ride with Miss Lissing?"

"No. I must return to town. I've business with Captain Appleby."

"*Please*, Cappy," implored Emily. "At least as far as the lightning tree?"

Seamus peered up the hill to Barclay House, glaringly white against the drought-crisped landscape. Grace was headed down the slope, a vision in her red tartan shawl. He could spot her in it anywhere. She twisted in her saddle to give Mrs Barclay one final enthusiastic wave. Turning back, she swiped her thumb below her eye and ducked her chin low.

"Please, Cappy." His daughter's voice brought him back to his current dilemma. Emily and Edwin had flourished with other children around. An extra hour to their journey was not too burdensome a price when it would keep that smile on his daughter's face. Grace reined up beside him and sniffed, and he offered her his handkerchief before taking a deep breath and turning to his daughter. "Very well. But only to the burnt tree. After that, we're moving ahead."

"Oh, thank you, Cappy!" Emily's white teeth split her face in a victorious grin, and Edwin jiggled in the saddle behind her.

A hand stroked his forearm, and he glanced at Grace's short-nailed fingers, the unsightly dents and ragged tears nearly grown out after the arduous voyage. "Thank you, for granting them a moment more with their friends."

Seamus chuckled. "Getting soft in my old age."

With the sharp crack of his whip, Big Bob set the cattle in forward motion, his dog nipping mercilessly at the cattle's heels. The bullocks bellowed in mournful objection, but they pulled dutifully, staggering sideways at the immense weight pulling against their shoulders, until the wagons began to clatter along. The dappled dog, obviously seeing the children as more creatures to be rounded, darted around them, nudging their legs and causing them to scurry forward and shriek with laughter.

"Don't forget us, Miss Lissing," implored Noah. His grimy

bare feet patted along beneath the fraying hem of his corduroys. A lone tear cleared a path down the boy's cheek, branded with Barclay freckles. "Will you write to us, Miss Lissing?"

"What d'ye want that for, ye mug?" Nevin scrunched his nose, nudging his friend with his elbow. "Then we'll have to write back. Ye know how much I hate writing!"

Scowling, Noah spun and landed a flesh-thudding punch on Nevin's arm. "No one's making you!"

Nevin laughed, rubbing his shoulder. "Ye punch like a lassie," he teased. Noah poked out his tongue. Despite their different stations, they were more like brothers.

As an only child, Seamus had never been punched in jest like that. He had missed out on the camaraderie he was now witnessing. As terrifying as Grace's delivery of the twins had been, he was glad for Emily's sake that she had a sibling.

"Och, lad," said Nevin, slinging his arm around the younger boy's shoulders. "Wouldn't ye rather fish with me, or fetch honey for Cook's damper instead o' sitting cramped at yer desk?"

"I'll fetch honey with you, Nevin," proposed Edwin eagerly.

Emily offered, "I'll write to you, Miss Lissing."

Seamus caught Miss Lissing looking down fondly at the duo scrambling to keep up with the creaking wagon, and at the two on horseback. How the devil did she follow what each was saying with them talking over one another like that? Heavens, he was looking forward to the peace and quiet of the open road.

With his head pounding, Seamus nudged his horse a little way ahead and beckoned Grace with his head. The two borrowed horses knew the track well, and they settled into a comfortable swaying gait as their hooves clattered across the wooden bridge.

Grace handed back his damp handkerchief. "I shall miss it here."

Tucking the folded linen square into his outer pocket, Seamus reached out a hand. She took it, her slim fingers chilled by the cold reins. He rubbed his thumb over her scarred knuckles, willing his heat into her. "You're freezing."

She sniffed, the tip of her nose red. "I'll warm up as soon as we're away from the stream. Look, the sun's up now."

Seamus glanced behind, narrowing his eyes as the last of the wagons loomed through the mist shrouding the low bridge. The wooden structure squeaked and shrieked at the metal-rimmed wheels cutting into her planks, sounding like the wide-winged fruit bats that filled the night skies about here. He swivelled around and eased his horse nearer to Grace's, his knee bumping against hers. "Were we alone, I'd have you join me in my saddle. You'd be warm in a jiffy." Her knowing giggle stirred his desire, and he squirmed in the saddle.

"Your poor horse! How would he see with my skirts flapping back over his head?"

The image of his wife straddling him, her hips rocking in rhythm with the horse's steady gait, exploded into his thoughts like gunpowder in a flash pan. He hummed at this unexpected, but not unwelcome, consideration. Rising in his stirrups, he adjusted his trouser legs. "Christ, Dulcinea. Bit early for such temptation, isn't it?" He glanced over his shoulder at the chaotic horde and then shook his head at her. "Especially when there's no chance of me making good on your devilish invitation."

She shrugged one shoulder slowly and twisted her lips, unsuccessfully holding back an impish smile. "You offered."

"To warm you, not *ravish* you." He grinned, the air cold on his teeth.

She made a high-pitched, nonchalant sound. "One and the same."

He had planned to share Barclay's news about Appleby's duplicitous plan to report her to the magistrate, but he did not want to spoil her good mood. No, he would deal with Appleby himself. Put the puffed-up cockerel in his place. If it was an assertive husband's word he was after, he would gladly deliver it.

The children followed the wagons for nearly two hours until they reached Gilly Downs' boundary. Seamus turned his horse's nose east towards town as Nevin and Noah bunched together beside the burnt gumtree waving and yelling out their final goodbyes.

Several long and dusty hours later, Seamus stabled the horses behind The Sailor's Homecoming and led his family down the lane, which had uninterrupted harbour views. His toes pinched tightly in the front of his boots as he made his way along the steep, narrow alley that would bring them out at the sandstone house. His heart lurched with fond familiarity at the *Elias*'s neatly furled sails. Perfect! Her hull sat satisfyingly low in the water. Once the bullocky arrived with the final load, she would be ready for departure.

He brought his gaze back to the world of narrow lanes. The rabbito had an impressive queue of customers waiting patiently while he skinned fresh rabbits as efficiently as pulling off a glove. A fruit and vegetable seller dragged his laden cart up the steep hill, head bowed in strain. Heavens! Why the devil did he not employ a horse or a donkey? As the greengrocer turned into another narrow laneway, Seamus realised that a large animal could not traverse the rabbit warrens of The Rocks.

The seller's booming voice swelled in the narrow lane like sails in a gale. "Peas, young and green! Come and get 'em. Lettuces, with hearts like heroes!"

Several shabby and weary-looking wives stepped from their darkened doorways, jingling coins in their apron pockets as they merged towards the vegetable cart. Their scowls and frowns morphed into girlish giggles as the charismatic greengrocer lavished them with compliments.

"Looking lovely as usual, Ada."

"Why, Beryl, you done somethin' new with your hair?"

"Nancy, m'darlin', a sight for my sore eyes, you are!"

Nearing the safety of their temporary home, Seamus allowed

his thoughts to wander back over the previous journey. Chitten-den's bloody face loomed before him, and like turning a page in a book, his thoughts slid from the dead sailor to the troublesome harbourmaster—a man about to hear a piece of his mind!

Climbing the sandstone steps of William Wells' house, Seamus shoved the door open, and Emily and Edwin squeezed past him, tearing up the stairs in a race. Where did they find the energy? At the jangling of horses' bridles and clopping hooves, Seamus glanced over his shoulder, instinctively scooping an arm around Grace's waist at the sight of the three mounted police. He frowned at the familiar green bloom of feathers sprouting from the leader's navy shako. Major Winfield!

About to dip his head in greeting, Seamus blinked in surprise as Winfield reined in his horse with a vicious tug. The white stal-lion's eyes widened, and he tossed his head to shake off the discomfort. The younger of the uniformed men slid from his saddle, handing the reins to his companion. The constable's one eye fixed on Grace, his other, a wet red slit in his face. The older constable stared at the ground, his discomfort fuelling Seamus's own.

Seamus's throat tightened. "May I help you, Major Winfield?"

Winfield held his gaze a moment more before pressing his lips and swinging his head towards Grace. "Mrs Fitzwilliam, you are hereby apprehended on a charge of manslaughter against one Lucius Chittenden, Esquire, aboard the British vessel, *Elias*."

Grace gasped, and Seamus drew her behind him, moving to the step's edge as the officer shuffled forward. Seamus slid on his mask of authority, and the man halted. The one-eyed scoundrel was barely old enough to grow whiskers—and he would not live long enough to attempt it if he laid a hand on Grace.

"Sweet Christ Almighty, Winfield, what's the meaning of this?" Seamus snarled.

Winfield's stallion flinched and stepped back. Ignoring Seamus, he continued addressing Grace. "By order of Judge Albert Porter, you shall remain in your residence under the guard of constables Herman and Morrison until you are presented before the court."

Grace's slim hand hooked around his arm, her fear quivering through the strength of her grip. "Seamus?"

He clamped her hand to his ribs with his elbow. They would have to tear off his arms before he let them take her. "Take heart, Dulcinea," he whispered from the corner of his mouth. He firmed his chin at Winfield. "Who's responsible for this madness?"

Winfield continued his pompous droning. "Judge Porter has afforded you this kindness because of Mr Deas Thomson's benevolence, who pleaded leniency on your behalf. However, should you attempt to leave your residence, you shall promptly, and without recourse, be remanded to Her Majesty's Gaol." He licked his lips and smacked his tongue. "Unless you wish to find yourself crammed in a single dormitory with the lowest female miscreants this town has to offer, I suggest you capitalise on Judge Porter's clemency."

Seamus sucked in a sharp breath. "Answer me, damn you! Who is responsible for this? Is it Appleby? He's so full of shit even his eyes are brown."

Winfield slid his reptilian gaze over to Seamus. "If I want your opinion, Captain, I'll ask your wife!"

Were it not for Grace's grip on his arm, he would have launched himself at the man. She grabbed his bicep in a double grip, her tug tweaking his injured shoulder. "Seamus. Don't."

Winfield snorted. "I see you've nothing to say in your defence, madam, and you're saying it rather loudly." His horse shuffled sideways and he yanked its head down. "You know, you're not totally useless, Mrs Fitzwilliam. You serve as a perfectly bad example to the citizens of this town."

Grace stiffened. "The only culture *you* own, Major, fits somewhere between a cockroach and those white globs in the corner of your mouth that tell of your thirst!"

Seamus inhaled sharply and glared down at his wife. What was she thinking? Provoking the lawman like this? He could not be prouder! He inclined his head at Winfield, silently challenging the man to better the insult.

Winfield scowled and wiped the corners of his mouth with his gloved thumb and forefinger. "All crimes committed at sea by the master or crew of a British ship can be tried before any Supreme Court in the colony. This crime is made such by English law, and the punishment fixed by English law." He nodded curtly, and the green plume flicked dismissively as he wrenched the reins to turn his horse.

THE FOLLOWING MORNING, Grace stared across the parlour at Maitland Locke, the defence lawyer Seamus had hired. Were it not for the man's grey hair, she might have thought him a child. He shuffled back in the wingback chair, and his brown leather shoes dangled a foot above the floor. She cared not a fig for the man's stature, instead leaning forward to make sense of the words he uttered in a startlingly deep voice. "You'll appear before the magistrate in the next couple of weeks."

So quickly? How could this be? There would barely be any time to think, let alone concoct a defence.

"The trial shouldn't take long. A half-hour at most—"

"Pardon?" Grace blinked. Good Lord! It took longer than that to don a corset and petticoats—not that she wore the former, instead preferring to breathe over vanity. In less time than it took to dress formally, her fate would be decided by a room full of strange men. "Why so hastily?"

Locke tilted his head, one brow arching. "Magistrate's a busy man. He'll have over a dozen cases to hear that day. Once Wilbur Rafter has presented the case against you, the witnesses will testify under oath, after which I'll cross-examine them. You'll have your chance to state your case."

Seamus grunted. "Rafter will have a devil of a time finding a single witness from the *Elias*. There's not a man aboard who would say a word against my wife."

"He's presenting your ship's books as evidence of the crime."

"Purported crime!" Grace's voice rose to a shrill. With Toby's hands still bound in bandages after his fall from the topmast, she had been the one to record Chittenden's death. Was there anything in her wording that might implicate her? Crushed by exhaustion at the time, her memory of it now was foggy.

Locke lowered his eyelids, his voice softening. "Apologies, madam. The *purported* crime."

Seamus burst from his seat. "Damn Appleby to Hell!" Gasping, he pressed his hand to his breastbone and rolled his injured shoulder. He glared down at the unruffled lawyer. "Christ, Locke! Tell me you've a solid case?"

There was a desperation in his voice Grace had not heard before. For goodness' sake! Her husband's worst enemy right now was his pain. He had always been her mainmast, solid and seated deep into the hold of her soul, but she feared this new fragility in him. Could he weather another storm?

The defence lawyer tugged the front of his cravat. "Captain, your testimony will certainly hold sway." He crossed his ankles and jiggled one foot as he craned his neck up. "But since you did not observe the event, I'm unsure whether Mr Rafter will even call you as a witness. All we have is your wife's account."

"Does that not suffice?" Grace scowled.

"Madam, you'll be presented before a jury of men, many of whom will not be happy to have their time wasted with the concerns of a—woman." The dip in Locke's voice confirmed he disagreed with this sentiment.

EMMA LOMBARD

Seamus lowered himself to the settee's edge, and she nudged alongside him. The ridges of his ribs pressed against her arm, but she curled her fingers into his, and he returned a grip that said he would not let go, no matter what.

"We'll be ready," Seamus said.

Locke shuffled forward on the settee until his feet touched the floor. He rose and bowed. "Do excuse me. I mustn't dally. Much to prepare."

Grace nodded mutely. What was there to say?

Seamus slid his fingers from hers and escorted the stunted man out. When he returned to the parlour, he stopped at the doorway, leaning his shoulder against the frame. Grace squeezed her fingers together in her lap until her knuckles popped. "Seamus, the children. I'll not have them kept prisoner in their own home."

He pinched the bridge of his nose and squeezed his eyes shut. "And I'll not have you kept prisoner either." Wincing, he stood upright. "Appleby's earned a proper dressing down! Who does that self-righteous idler think he is?"

"Seamus, wait. Don't risk it." She offered her hand, unable to hide the tremor. "Winfield and his men have already proven reckless. Remember the slaughter at Gilly Downs with the bushrangers? I want you to take the children to Miss Lissing. They can reside at the school—at least until this storm blows over. They'll be safer there."

Folding his long frame beside her, he nudged closer until their thighs pressed together. He nodded. "A worthy plan that will no doubt delight them."

"Precisely. They'll believe it a great adventure."

Plus, she would not put it past that green-feathered fiend to parade her through town in chains on her way to the courthouse —a sight she wished to spare her darlings.

136

Chapter Thirteen

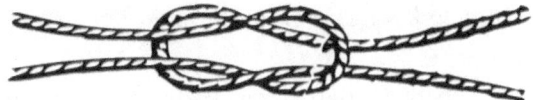

G race studied the courthouse's interior. Every surface
gleamed with polished wood—the panelled walls, the
judge's bench, the witness stand, and the prisoner
dock where she now stood. Behind the judge's bench, the royal
coat of arms announced, 'Dieu et mon droit'. *God and my right.*

Flaming Hades! It was hotter than a ship's head in the tropics
in here! Even with the high windows ajar, there was no breeze to
cut the stifling air of pressed bodies. Sweat trickled down her
lower back, and her thighs slicked together as she shifted her
weight from one leg to the other.

Wilbur Rafter, the Crown Prosecutor, was tall, his lanky
frame hidden beneath billowing black robes. Strands of snowy
wig-hair littered his shoulders. His pale, cat-like eyes burned into
Grace, and she averted her gaze to Judge Albert Porter, a stern
spectacled gentleman in a red robe and matching wig, who in

turn was peering over the rim of his gold wire-framed spectacles at the clerk reading out the charges.

Among the jury of twelve male landowners—stifling yawns and pulling at collars—Grace recognised only the foreman, Mr Potts. He and his wife had attended a dinner at Barclay Hall. Surely, he would not allow anything to befall her? The portly grazier dipped his head at her, and the knot of nervousness in her gut eased. The clerk's nasal drone brought her attention back to the charges.

"Grace Elizabeth Fitzwilliam is called upon and indicted for the manslaughter of one Lucius Roland Chittenden upon the high seas aboard the British vessel called the *Elias*, the property of Seamus Alexander Fitzwilliam, on the twenty-seventh of August 1841."

Judge Porter peered down his nose at her. "How do you plead, Mrs Fitzwilliam?"

Her tongue stuck to the roof of her mouth. "Not guilty, my lord."

The crowd buzzed. Her trial was clearly feeding the entertainment-starved inhabitants of this little town, though she did not welcome being their fodder.

The dark, ceiling-high panels closed in on her, and she squirmed, the manacles and chains clanging and slithering around her feet with a hiss of shame. Just as she had suspected, that bastard, Winfield, had insisted she be shackled on her transport here this morning. Seamus sat in the front row of the public gallery, and the muscle in his jaw flexed. Despite his displeasure, he looked magnificent in his neatly pressed, black wool suit. She drew strength from his calm.

Judge Porter glanced at his fob watch. "Luncheon approaches. Present your case—post haste, Mr Rafter."

Rafter rose fluidly. "My lord, Mr Chittenden was a dutiful officer with the weight of an irregular crew upon his shoulders. As confirmed by the ship's logs—and lauded by the broadsheets

—the captain, after his accidental injury, relinquished much of his duty to his wife, the accused. She was at the helm more than he. And as we all know, gentlemen"— Rafter pivoted neatly to face the jury—"the fairer sex is unable to sustain a man's job for any length of time."

Nearly all the heads nodded, and more than a few avoided Grace's eye.

Rafter sighed. "When a woman swoons and faints, is it not a gentleman's duty to prevent her from falling ungraciously to the floor and risking possible injury?"

The jury of men glanced at one another, nodding again. Grace's cheeks burned. Like a flock of sheep, the blazing lot of them! Did none own independent faculties?

Waving an airy hand at Grace, Rafter continued, "But in this case, when Mr Chittenden held Mrs Fitzwilliam as she staggered about a rolling deck, he found himself viciously attacked, and suffered the consequence of death." Rafter's feline gaze snapped onto her, and she raised her chin. Pressing his lips, Rafter turned and dipped his head, his tone simpering. "Thank you, my lord."

Judge Porter drew off his spectacles, and, with the gaping sleeve of his robe, began polishing them. "Your first witness, Mr Rafter?"

Rafter ran his finger down the cream sheet in his hands, frowning and humming. He flipped the page and scoured the second before stabbing his finger at it. "The Defence calls Mr Benjamin Blight."

Ben stepped into the witness stand, his thick, fiery whiskers neatly combed, his hair plastered to one side. He stood solemnly in the witness stand, his calloused right palm raised, the stump of his little finger as stiff as the others. Her red-whiskered friend swore the oath as sourly as though he had a lemon in his mouth, and he rolled his eyes away from Rafter. He caught Grace's eye and winked. At ease and unintimidated by the formal proceedings, Ben was the same kind-eyed man who had taken her under his wing as a newcomer on the *Discerning* and taught her how to defend herself. And, just like then, she felt safe in his hands.

Rafter stepped around the Prosecutor's desk and stopped before Ben. "Mr Blight, please tell the court what you witnessed of the interaction between Captain Fitzwilliam and Lucius Chittenden, in the matter pertaining to Shelby Hicks on the *Elias*'s main deck, on the tenth of May earlier this year?"

"I was up the foremast when I saw Mr Chittenden smack young Shelby Hicks about for sipping water. Captain Fitzwilliam called Mr Chittenden to him. 'Twas clear he was getting a talking to."

"Could you hear the nature of the conversation?"

"No. The wind was fair up. Didn't pay much mind to it till I heard the captain raise his voice that whatever he'd just said was an *order*."

"And Mr Chittenden complied?"

Ben pulled his chin whiskers. "After a beat. Flaunted a fair dose of defiance first."

"But Captain Fitzwilliam didn't take action against Mr Chittenden for this alleged disobedience?"

"No. Not that time, but—"

"Isn't it fair to say that by his own inaction, Captain Fitzwilliam himself didn't consider Mr Chittenden insubordinate?"

Ben's mouth tightened, and his tongue flicked between his lips. "Just saying as I saw it."

"Mr Blight, what's your position aboard the *Elias*?"

"Fore-topman."

"And how long have you been a sailor?"

"Some twenty years."

"And did you at any stage sit for the Examination in Seamanship, or in Navigation, at the Royal Naval College?"

Ben shook his head. "No, sir. Did all my learning on the ship.

Never had a mind to be an officer. I'm happy enough peddlin' me trade up the sheets."

"As an experienced sailor, how did *you* rate Mr Chittenden as first mate?"

Ben stiffened at Rafter's placating tone. "Any sailor worth his salt could tell he were no good. Couldn't keep a tight ship. He had her sails flapping about like my mam's petticoats on laundry day. He even ran us into an American merchantman off the Cape Colony. Plus, he was caught kipping on duty. What kind of an officer do you call *that*?" Ben's voice tightened, and he cocked his head.

With a voice dripping like melted lard, Rafter neatly side-stepped. "Allow *me* to ask the questions, sir." Clearing his throat with a wet cough, he continued, "To clarify, you *always* follow orders, to furl and unfurl sails—your area of expertise?"

Ben's nostrils flared as he inhaled. "Yes, sir. 'Tis why I followed Mr Chittenden's order to let out all the sails the day the topmast broke, even though there was a storm a-brewing."

"Is every man aboard not duty-bound to the vessel's safety?"

"Yes, sir. But—"

"Was it your place to decide the best course of action for sailing her?"

"No, sir. Though every sailor aboard knows the danger of a squall. We were in clear, open water with winds fit to whip us into the next week had the right sails been set."

Rafter's grey, wiry eyebrows arched. "Oh, so you'd studied the charts, had you? Determined that you had a clear run ahead of you?" He craned his long wrinkly neck forward, much like Emily's pet tortoise.

"No, sir. But I understand ships and know how they respond to sails. And I recognise a clear bit of ocean when I see it."

"You say your expertise lies in the sails, and that you knew the topmast would break, but your worry about reprimand from Mr Chittenden held you back from speaking out about it?"

Ben hesitated and ran his thumbnail across his whiskered mouth. Sweat glistened across the bridge of his nose as his gaze slid slowly from Grace back to Rafter. His protracted silence stretched time, the seconds marked by his twitching jaw muscles. "'Tisn't a man's place to question an officer."

Rafter let Ben's answer coat the room before taking two steps closer to the witness stand, his voice hardening. "Mr Blight, surely *your* duty towards the preservation of the ship and the souls aboard should have outweighed *any* other concerns?"

Bleeding rats' tails! Rafter had led her friend down his twisted passage of questions. Ben threaded his fingers and squeezed, his knuckle popping as though preparing to round a corner into a dark, unknown alley.

"Don't know what you mean."

Rafter obliged. "Is it fair to conclude that *your own* negligence of not speaking up contributed to the topmast breaking?"

"Oi! Steady up there!"

"But you *knowingly* allowed dangerous conditions to prevail." Rafter shook his head and tutted. "No wonder poor Mr Chittenden had a devil of a time keeping you all in line."

Locke jumped up. "My lord, the defence is rambling— without a question in sight!"

Judge Porter peered over the tops of his spectacles at Rafter, and harrumphed. "Have you another question, Mr Rafter?"

"Of course, my lord. Mr Blight, did you witness Mr Chittenden shooting Captain Fitzwilliam?"

Ben rolled his neck, releasing a gristly crack. "I did."

"Was it intentional?"

"'Tis the responsibility of every sailor to keep hold of his weapon."

"But did Mr Chittenden *purposely* point his musket at Captain Fitzwilliam and fire upon him?"

"No. The fool fumbled a primed musket. It fired when he dropped it."

"Was Mrs Fitzwilliam about?"

Ben hesitated and blinked. "Y-yes, but I don't see how that would have stopped his carelessness."

Rafter clasped his hands before him and inclined his head at the witness stand. "Would you agree that Mrs Fitzwilliam is a handsome woman?"

Ben's blue eyes widened and flicked from Seamus to Grace. The colour of his skin matched his whiskers. "Never had cause to look at her that way."

"Come now, Mr Blight, what man could resist those pink cheeks and dark curls?"

Locke's chair squealed on the wooden floor. "My lord! What is the meaning of this?"

"I was beginning to wonder the same, Mr Locke," agreed Judge Porter. He waved his gavel at Rafter. "Do get on with it, Mr Rafter."

Rafter nodded. "Mr Blight, has Mrs Fitzwilliam's presence ever distracted you from your duty?"

"No, sir! Never."

"Well then, you've a heartier constitution than most." The lanky lawyer cocked one eyebrow and smirked at the smattering of laughter. "Did you ever witness Mr Chittenden having his head turned by the captain's wife?"

Ben gave a watery laugh. "If anything, he abhorred her. Scarcely tolerated his subordinates, let alone a woman."

"So, she *was* a distraction to him?"

The smile slid from Ben's face. "Not the way you're implying."

"Whether lured by attraction or repelled by her temptation, it seems as though Mrs Fitzwilliam indeed caused disruption on deck."

"Just a bleeding minute—"

Rafter held up his hand. "Thank you, Mr Blight." He clasped his hands behind his back. "In your own words, please tell us of the altercation between Mrs Fitzwilliam and Mr Chittenden on the *Elias*'s quarterdeck on that fateful day."

Ben let out a low growl as his ginger eyebrows clashed together in a scowl. "I were coming off the forenoon watch. Had just handed the helm to Smythe when I heard Mrs F. shout near the quarterdeck rail. That bast—Chittenden—had her gripped from behind, causing her feet to dangle clear off the deck. He had *no place* manhandling a married woman like that! Quick smart, she whipped her head back—cracked him good 'n' proper on the snout—just like I taught her!" He beamed at Grace, pride blazing in his sharp blue eyes. "That soft-boiled egg toppled over the rail. My heart fair flew from me chest when I saw Mrs F. go over with him! I ran down to her. She was as stunned as any, falling from such a height. Though I knew she was as right as rain when she rolled off ol' Humpty Dumpty. She was fair shaken, but there isn't anyone tougher than our Mrs F."

The blanket of curiosity from the public gallery smothered Grace, and she shuffled further back in the stand, steadfastly returning the stare of the fidgety woman beside Seamus. He bowed his head and squeezed his eyes closed. Grace turned her frown on the testifying sailor. She knew he meant well, but this did not paint her in a pretty light. Hush, Ben, *please*.

Rafter's slow blink oozed smugness. "And what of Mr Chittenden?"

"Ha!" Ben scoffed. "Looked as though he'd kissed Thor's hammer. Had to scoop bits of teeth out to stop him choking on them. Though I was chary to offer him the service."

"Where was Captain Fitzwilliam during all this commotion?"

"In his sickbed. But he arrived soon after, half crippled. Demanded to know what in blazes was going on. Told him how Chittenden had attacked Mrs F. Captain took one look at the mangled man splayed on deck and ordered him to sickbay. Wouldn't have afforded the bleeding sod the luxury myself. But an order's an order." Ben's chest expanded with a satisfied breath.

"Thank you for your colourful account, Mr Blight. Your witness, Mr Locke."

MAITLAND LOCKE, Grace's defence lawyer, stood, his chair squeaking in protest. He did not look too dissimilar to Rafter in his robes and wig except that instead of salt-and-pepper-speckled whiskers, he sported a double chin and was a good head and shoulders shorter.

"Mr Blight, is it fair to say that Mr Chittenden's repeated insubordination was apparent for all aboard to see?"

How *did* such a deep voice come from such a little man? Grace wondered, not for the first time.

Ben's cheeks reddened like a shiny, over-ripe tomato. "My oath it was! Never seen the likes of it in my life. Had a devil-may-care attitude that weren't respectful towards the captain."

"And how was he towards the men?"

"Right mean bastard. Given half a chance, he'd whip a man like a horse with that crop of his." Ben rubbed the spot between his flaming brows with his forefinger. "Saw him smack young Smythe just for looking at him funny. Crowleigh didn't fare much better. A kick up the backside sent him head over heels down the main hatch. His crime—taking too long to shit in the head."

The courtroom erupted into a litany of sniggers and squirming bodies, and Judge Porter hammered his gavel on his bench. He peered down at the witness stand. "Mr Blight, do keep your language within respectable boundaries."

Ben nodded sheepishly, swallowing with a deep bob of his Adam's apple. "Aye, aye, sir."

The judge glanced back to the short lawyer. "Please proceed, Mr Locke."

Locke stepped towards Ben, his thin, grey brows raised in question. "Mr Blight, you mentioned you were up the foremast on the twenty-fifth of May, when the squall broke the topmast. What happened?"

"Mainmast's topsail snapped like a matchstick. Came tumbling down—with Toby Hicks and Colin Crowleigh in it. Gave me the fright of my life, seein' men dropping like that. Hicks managed to grab the ropes on his way down. Tore his hands up right proper."

The crowd gasped and hissed in sympathy. Clearly exploiting the wave of empathy rolling across the courtroom, Ben added, "He couldn't work with them for nearly a month afterwards. Though he fared better than Crowleigh."

"What happened to Mr Crowleigh?" said Locke, clasping his hands behind his back.

The sailor's cheeks drained above his whiskers. "One minute he was stood there, grinning like a squirrel with a new hoard of nuts, the next he slapped the water like a pistol shot."

"Was he retrieved from the ocean?"

"No, sir." Ben's voice hitched, and he swallowed deeply. "Lost for good. That one's squarely on Chittenden."

The crowd in the courtroom murmured in low, conspiring tones. Grace shifted her weight from one hip to the other, but she reconsidered as the iron manacles bit her ankles. She glanced over at Seamus. The line of his lips spelled a shift in his mood. He was hemmed in by a broad-shouldered gentleman to his right and the fidgeting woman to his left. Fanning herself in exaggerated waves, the woman's elbow knocked persistently into Seamus's arm. He looked fit to snatch the fan and snap it in two. Instead, his jaw muscle flinched, and he shuffled forward on the seat, leaning his elbows on his knees. Rafter's voice drew Grace back around.

"Mr Blight, did you hear what transpired between Mrs Fitzwilliam and Mr Chittenden on the day of the accident?"

Rafter pressed his knuckles on the table, unfolding himself. "My Lord, it is the jury's place to determine whether the nature of the incident was accidental or deliberate—*not* Mr Locke's."

Judge Porter's nostrils flared as he inhaled. "Adhere to the facts, Mr Locke."

Locke nodded. "Yes, my lord." He turned to Ben. "Did you hear what transpired between Mrs Fitzwilliam and Mr Chittenden *on that fateful day*?"

"No, sir. I was having words with Smythe as he took the helm."

"Did you *see* Mr Chittenden grab Mrs Fitzwilliam?"

"No, sir. He already had her clear off the deck by the time I looked over."

Maitland Locke narrowed his eyes. "How can you be sure he *didn't* have her in his grip to save her from stumbling over in the rough seas?"

Ben snorted. "I'm as sure as the sun'll rise in the morn. Mrs F. has as fine a pair of sea legs as any. That sun-baked blister was more prone to tumbling about! Ask any hand aboard."

"Thank you, Mr Blight," said Locke. "That is all." He turned respectfully towards Judge Porter. "I'm finished with this witness, my lord." He swept his black robes around the table's edge and sat with a squeak of wood.

Grace wondered whether anyone would replace the noisy chair.

Chapter Fourteen

Seamus placed his right hand on the Bible. Locke had doubted he would be called as a witness, but by Christ, he was more than ready to defend his wife. He glared at Appleby sitting at the end of a row in the gallery, arms folded. Pah! Bastard had a hide to be ranked captain with that rumpled mess he called a uniform. He looked like an unmade bed.

"Do you swear by Almighty God that the evidence you shall give will be the truth, the whole truth, and nothing but the truth? If so, please say 'I do'."

Seamus licked his lips. A whisky and water to wet his whistle would not go amiss about now. "I do." With practised poise, he swivelled his gaze from the ferrety clerk to Wilbur Rafter.

"Captain Fitzwilliam, would you be so kind as to give us your account of the water incident between Mr Chittenden and Mr Hicks."

"Mr Hicks was attempting a drink of water when Mr Chittenden slapped the ladle from the boy's hand before reprimanding him harshly."

"And how did you respond?"

"I explained to Mr Chittenden that drinking water aboard my ship isn't a punishable offence."

"And what was Mr Chittenden's response to this dressing down?"

"His obnoxiousness bordered on insubordination."

"Captain Fitzwilliam, why did you not discipline Mr Chittenden for this alleged insubordination?"

"The man was new aboard my vessel and unfamiliar with my ways. Having previously served with the Royal Navy, I knew he likely had rigid views about discipline. I reminded him that discipline aboard the *Elias* was Bosun Lincoln's privilege, and that he wasn't to take matters into his own hands. Although wholly unreasonable, his actions weren't illegal." Seamus ensured his words were clipped and succinct.

"How magnanimous of you, sir," drawled Rafter. His burst of arrogance was short-lived under Seamus's unyielding stare. Flushing, Rafter brought the questioning back to point. "Did you witness any more of Mr Chittenden's alleged heavy-handedness?"

"A couple of times, Chittenden kicked items over to my men. He never handed anything directly to them. Several of my crew served in the Royal Navy, where discipline is doled out as regularly as rum rations, so they wore Chittenden's reprimands admirably."

Rafter fortified his backbone and, planting his feet firmly, returned Seamus's fixed gaze. "Is it fair to say that had you firmer rules aboard your ship, you might have enforced a stricter regime of discipline on Mr Chittenden from the outset, and prevented this misfortune?"

"By Neptune, man! Are you blaming *me* for Chittenden's incompetence?"

"Would you have shown the man such leniency were you still in the Royal Navy?"

Flinching, Seamus scratched at the itchy streak of perspiration along his hairline. "The *Elias* isn't a Royal Naval vessel—"

Rafter cut him off. "Thank you, sir, for clarifying."

Seamus took in Grace's guilty flush. Back as far as their first days together on the *Discerning*, she had chided his unbending adherence to disciplining his men, and he begrudgingly bore her challenge to earn the men's respect rather than beat it into them. For the most part, it earned him the reputation of a fair and reasonable captain. Still, there had always been those who had exploited his leniency for weakness. Holburton, who should have been chained to the hold but instead orchestrated Grace's kidnapping onto O'Reilly's ship. Babcock, a known murderer whom he let loose among his crew and family. And now Chittenden. Blasted Hell, he should have stripped him of his rank at the first whiff of insubordination, then they could have avoided this whole sorry mess.

The stringy lawyer cocked his head. "Did you ascertain the backgrounds of all the sailors in your employ before bringing them aboard the *Elias*?"

"I did." Seamus lowered his voice, though Rafter did not respond to the edge in his tone. Cavalier bastard! Seamus took in a slow, deep breath to steady his drumming heartbeat.

"Including Lucius Chittenden?"

"Yes. He carried a letter of reference from the Duke of Berkshire."

"Did you verify that the duke was, in fact, acquainted with Mr Chittenden?"

"No," Seamus replied bluntly. At Rafter's incredulous rise of grey eyebrows, Seamus elaborated. "Mr Chittenden appeared only days before we sailed. Lacking time to validate the authenticity of that letter with the Duke of Berkshire himself, I verified it with Admiral Arthur Jameson Baxter, who confirmed his lordship's word was sound."

"So, by your own admission, sir, your lenient discipline and sloppy administration created disharmony aboard your ship from the very beginning?"

Locke's chair squeaked and scraped back noisily. "My lord, Captain Fitzwilliam isn't on trial here."

Judge Porter nodded sagely at Locke, then he turned to the tall, whiskered lawyer. "Mr Rafter, do refrain from treating Captain Fitzwilliam as the guilty party."

"Yes, my lord." Rafter's lips pressed thinly in his greying whiskers. "Captain, did you afford your wife the same level of discipline as the other souls aboard your ship?"

"I had no need. Her actions required no punishment."

"Come now, Captain, at best that's out-and-out favouritism— at worst, nepotism." He arced his arm through the air at the jurors. "Any man can deduce that."

Seamus grabbed the rail before him, the muscles in his thighs wound tight and ready to launch. "I disagree."

"Could you please give your account of that fateful day?"

"I was in my sickbed when roused by my wife's loud cry. Heading above to learn the cause, I discovered her being supported by my men. Chittenden lay upon the deck with his face stoved in."

"Was he deceased?"

"No. He lingered until around eleven the following morning, when he then expired."

Rafter swished the folds of his gown and sniffed loudly. "I've nothing further for this witness, my lord."

LOCKE ROSE and stepped towards Seamus, pressing his steepled fingers to his lips as though in thought. Capitalising on the moment of reprieve, Seamus closed his eyes and took in a long, slow breath. When he opened them again, Locke asked, "Captain Fitzwilliam, did you catch Mr Chittenden asleep on duty?"

"I did."

"And how did Mr Chittenden respond?"

Seamus smirked, and he gestured his clammy palms upwards. "Not much he could say after being caught in the act."

"And what did you do?"

Seamus straightened his spine, his voice unwavering. "I stripped him of his rank."

"Why not chain him in the hold? Is sleeping on duty not the most grievous sin?"

"The *Elias* runs with a lean crew. With the loss of young Crowleigh, and with Hicks injured, I couldn't afford to lose another pair of hands."

"I see. And after Mr Chittenden shot you—"

Rafter's lean frame unfolded in one smooth motion. "Objection, my lord! Witnesses have already confirmed the shooting was *not* intentional. Mr Locke's tone implies it was."

"I'll rephrase, my lord," said Locke. "Captain, during your recovery, what did you do when you discovered your wife had locked Mr Chittenden in the hold for his carelessness?"

"I ordered him free."

"Did you seek your wife's counsel on this matter first?"

The question was asked as respectfully as possible, though Seamus bit down on his molars at the snorts and sniggers from the overcrowded gallery. He clamped his arms to his flanks to stem the fresh prickle of sweat in his armpits and glowered around the courtroom, daring the culprits to make eye contact with him.

"Captain Fitzwilliam?" Locke's deep voice sharpened his attention.

"No, sir, I did not. My wife had spent weeks battling heavy seas, tending our children, and ministering my wounds. I could see she was exhausted. I calculated that even Mr Chittenden's most basic skills could give her a reprieve from the unrelenting conditions."

"Mr Rafter has accused you of favouritism and nepotism, but could you share with the jury what happened after your children were caught stealing tarts from the galley?"

Seamus fixed his gaze on Rafter. Ha! This would show him. Nodding at Locke, he elaborated, "They were made to publicly confess their crimes before both receiving six strokes to the bare posterior." He twisted his head and raked his gaze over the jury. "Of all the punishments meted out by me that voyage, my children bore the harshest."

Several jurors nodded, and others bowed their heads together in collaboration. There was a collective swell of whispers from the public gallery too. Seamus ran his palms down the thighs of his trousers and rotated his right wrist until it clicked.

"Was this beating made public?"

"No, sir, but not a soul aboard missed their screams that day." He panned around the public gallery, picking out his crew one by one—and was met by an emphatic nod from all.

"Thank you, Captain. Nothing further, my lord," Locke concluded, taking his squeaky seat again.

Seamus turned to Grace. Her chin was tight as she held back tears, and her breath came out in short puffs through her flaring nostrils. She had never looked prouder.

Chapter Fifteen

G race scratched a tickle behind her ear, ignoring the jangle of chains, and instead concentrated on Wilbur Rafter's heavy-lidded eyes. They narrowed as he stepped beside the large counsel table, his gravelly voice reaching her across the courtroom. "Mrs Fitzwilliam, could you please tell us of the events leading up to Mr Chittenden's alleged attempt to wrestle command of the *Elias* from you?"

Grace tilted her chin up. "Which time?" A shimmer of laughter rippled through the crowd. To any observer, Seamus's expression did not change, but Grace caught the tiny crinkle of approval in the corner of his left eye.

A shadow of annoyance quivered across Rafter's face, but before he could object, Grace released the press of her lips. "I reprimanded Mr Chittenden for continuing to assert an authority he did not possess."

"And what authority was this?"

"He had Mr Smythe aimlessly marching about with a hand-spike shouldered as a musket. He said this fool's errand was to bring Smythe back to order because he had been clumsy about his work. When I challenged Chittenden's authority, his conversation turned lewd, and he—propositioned me."

"Can you please tell us *precisely* what he said?"

Grace scrunched her nose at the judge. "It's not within keeping of Christian English, my lord." She silently cursed the blush that crept up her cheeks, but it earned her a look of sympathy from Judge Porter.

"Understood, Mrs Fitzwilliam." He cocked his head, almost in apology. "Nonetheless, I'd like to hear the truth."

Grace looked at Seamus for encouragement, pleased to have his unemotionally steadfast presence anchoring her in place. Her heartbeat rose as she repeated Chittenden's words. "He said he liked commanding attractive women, and that I'd make a pretty picture—dropping to my knees—like a wagtail."

The courtroom erupted, and Judge Porter pounded his gavel. "Silence! Silence, I say. If you wish to remain spectators in this court, you'll do so silently. If not, I'll have the lot of you removed. Is that clear?" Under the judge's baleful glare over the top of his spectacles, the people in the court settled quickly. No one wanted to miss out on what happened next. Judge Porter swung his sharp gaze over to Rafter, and with a gruff noise of consent he nodded. "Continue, please, Mr Rafter."

"And this remark, unheard by any other, is what caused you to lash out at Mr Chittenden?"

"He deserved a punch to the throat for that," said Grace, smarting. "But no—"

"Ah, so you admit to wishing him harm?"

"No! Just because I believe he deserved it doesn't mean I acted upon it."

"Mrs Fitzwilliam, I take it that you don't agree with Mr Chittenden's sentiments that a woman is incapable of commanding a ship?"

Grace squared her shoulders. "Certainly not."

"Isn't it intriguing then that, as soon as your husband regained his faculties, his first conscious action was to release Mr Chittenden and relieve you of this duty?"

Grace lowered her shoulders and wryly drew up the corner of her mouth. "*Intriguing* would not be my word choice."

"Clearly, Captain Fitzwilliam had no faith in your ability to keep his ship sailing under safe conditions if he—"

Seamus exploded from his seat in the public gallery. His face blanched, his lower eyelids tightened dangerously around his icy blue stare. "Shut your bone box, you pettifogger! I said no such thing. Cease putting words in my wife's mouth!"

Rafter's mouth dropped open. Loud hoots of laughter and gasps of astonishment rippled across the courtroom. Seamus clenched his fists, his chest heaving.

Judge Porter looked discomfited, like he had a bad case of piles that had suddenly flared. He banged his gavel furiously. "Hold your tongue, sir! Hold your tongue!" He matched Seamus's intimidating glower. "Captain Fitzwilliam, interrupt my court again, and I'll have you marched right out of that door." He jabbed his gavel towards the back of the courtroom.

The corners of Rafter's mouth tweaked up as he opened his palms towards the jury. "He won't even allow her to answer her own questions, so how can we believe he entrusted an entire ship to her? I'm done with this witness, my lord."

LOCKE SHUFFLED OFF HIS CHAIR, the leather soles of his shoes patting lightly as they dropped to the floor. His rucked brow would not have looked out of place beside a graveside. "Mrs Fitzwilliam, what happened after Mr Chittenden made his indecent proposal?"

"I ordered him off the quarterdeck, but he refused. As I

walked away—he grabbed me from behind, lifting me off my feet. He was far superior in strength and size."

Locke gripped the witness stand rail, his squat body leaning towards her, his voice tight. "Did you fear for your life, madam?"

The tension in the courtroom was as taut as a drawn bow with a nocked arrow quivering against the string, and Grace sensed the collective breath being held as everyone waited for her answer. It was moments like these that drew the entertainment-starved crowds to the courtrooms. Scenes would be recounted word for word around campfires and dinner tables for weeks to come.

"I was more angry than fearful. I had no notion what Mr Chittenden intended to do next. All I could think of were my own actions."

"Quite, quite." Locke, clearly playing for his audience, paused and gave Grace a long, mournful stare from beneath his puffy eyelids. It was only at Judge Porter's impatient cough that Locke blinked, his eyebrows furrowing into a mask of concern. "How on *earth* did you overcome this David and Goliath dilemma, Mrs Fitzwilliam?"

Grace flicked her gaze to Ben, who gave her a knowing smile. Keeping her face neutral, she said, "I protected myself against a man who took advantage of my husband's absence to attack me."

"And he did this in broad daylight? With all the watch as witnesses? Seems rather risky, wouldn't you agree?"

Grace shrugged. "There's no accounting for some folk's stupidity. One can't expect to find what God chose to omit."

The arrow loosed and the tension whooshed from the public spectators. Even more snickers peppered the courtroom. Judge Porter whipped around to try to pick out the perpetrators, but a sea of lamb-faced stares met his spectacled glower.

A thunderous crash shattered the silence, and Grace's irons

jangled as she jumped. Every head in the room swivelled to the rear door. Judge Porter's head snapped up sharply, his jowls wobbling as he glared at the two intruders. "What the devil is the meaning of this?"

Good Lord in Heaven! Grace clapped her hand to her mouth. Big Bob hauled in a petite man by the scruff of his neck. By the bullocky's flushed countenance and heavy-footed gait, it was clear he had not long stepped from the pub. The elfin man's eyes bulged.

"Halt the bloody wagons!" bellowed Big Bob. He dragged his victim forward, dumping him beside the counsel table. Spotting Grace in the prisoner dock, he grinned and wrenched off his sweat-stained hat. "Hooroo, Lady Cap!"

Judge Porter thundered, "Who in Heaven's name are you?"

Big Bob swayed, blinking and squinting. He bowed deeply, and greasy, grey strands of hair fell across his face. "Your majesty."

"I'm not a blasted king, you fool. Address me as 'my lord'." Judge Porter bristled. All traces of the earlier droopy tiredness around his eyes were replaced by a tight, narrow squint.

"Yes, your lord." The giant man straightened, then bowed again. "Big Bob, at ya service."

"*My* lord," corrected the judge testily.

"Yes, *your* lord." Big Bob swiped his hair back with one hand and jammed his hat under an armpit. "Buggered if I'm bowin' again—I'll bloody fall over!" He leaned one hand heavily on the counsel table.

"Mr Bob—Big—Mr—" The judge fumbled. "Sir! You're interrupting these proceedings. Leave my courtroom immediately, or I'll hold you in contempt."

"Uncross your trotters, your lord," slurred Big Bob. "Found this mongrel down The Sailor's Homecoming. Got talkin' about this whole bloody palaver." He slapped his thigh, raising a cloud of fine dust from his worn breeches. "Bloody oath! Reckon you'll want to hear what he has to say." He jabbed a thick finger, with a dirt-encrusted nail, into the slimmer man's ribs. The tidy gentleman grunted and flinched. "Gawn, tell 'em. Tell 'em what yous told me."

Judge Porter's patience snapped like a brittle twig. "Sheriff! Remove these two men at once!"

"Now, hold on a bloody minute," objected Big Bob. "May I rot in me tracks and die a dog's death if his story isn't worth listenin' to!" Seeing the burly sheriff approaching, the bullocky shot the judge a wild-eyed look.

Judge Porter's already flushed cheeks turned a deep purple, and he shifted in his seat. It had been a long day of sitting. For a moment, Grace thought the magistrate might deny Big Bob's request, but he slammed his gavel down to hush the court. He peered over the gold rim of his circular spectacles and pointed at the diminutive man with his gavel. "Who are you?"

The man's rake-thin frame and prematurely bowed shoulders were those of a man married to his writing bureau, though his suit was excellently cut. "Quintin Hartley, Sydney agent of Lloyds of London, underwriters of the *Elias*." Despite his undignified entrance, the man raised his chin and fixed his gaze on Judge Porter with the confident air of an equal.

What on earth had a gentleman of such esteem been doing drinking at The Sailor's Homecoming? Grace rubbed her red, raw wrist to ease the pressure of the heavy iron cuff. Then again, this little penal colony was hardly endowed with gentlemen's clubs. Even Seamus drank there on occasion, preferring the alehouse to any of the gin houses. Though Hartley was probably regretting his choice about now.

The judge removed his gold frames and rubbed his eyes with his thumb and forefinger. Sliding his spectacles back onto the bridge of his nose, he shook his wigged head. "A man of your standing should know better than to burst into my courtroom!"

"Apologies, my lord." Hartley scowled at Big Bob, who

stood docilely in the sheriff's grip even though one shrug of those powerful shoulders would easily free him. "This is not my typical *modus operandi*, my lord."

The reverberating gong of the clock at Hyde Park Barracks drowned out the clopping jostle of carriages outside. Twelve deep-throated chimes. Judge Porter snapped open the face of his pocket watch for the umpteenth time and grumbled under his breath.

The public clock was notoriously wrong, though Grace could not remember if it was twenty minutes too early or too late.

Clicking the watch latch closed, the judge ordered, "Speak swiftly, Mr Hartley. My tripe and onions grow cold."

"Yes, my lord." Hartley dipped his head at Grace. "Good afternoon, Mrs Fitzwilliam."

The panic of the unknown and the lung-crushing heat was a giddying combination, and Grace wished she were seated. She shuffled forward in the dock and drew her iron-wrung ankles together. Her breath quickened, and she nibbled the inside of her cheek.

"To my learned knowledge," began Hartley nasally, "never before has a gentlewoman been required to adopt command of such a sizeable and valuable vessel as the *Elias*, the delay or loss of which would have been substantial not only to her husband, but to Lloyds as well."

Good gracious! Grace sucked in a gasp of the thick, treacly air. Her worry had lain solely with getting Seamus safely to Sydney, and certainly not about tallying any bills on foreign shores.

Hartley was not done. "Every sailor accepts shipboard life as a dangerous occupation. My own investigation concludes that the incident with Mr Chittenden was just one such danger. He was not the only sailor to lose his life on that fateful voyage."

Grace's nails dug into her palms. Stinking bloody seaweed!

Had Big Bob's good intentions just sunk her—torn the hull out of her case?

The courtroom was silent, the crowd collectively leaning forward to hear Hartley's words. "Mrs Fitzwilliam, by your own talent and vigour, you affected command over the crew and influenced them with such conviction and faith that all were rendered dutiful to you. Hereby, I am authorised to present you with a gift of one thousand pounds for your efforts in commanding the vessel." Hartley turned to the judge. "Rest assured, my lord, Lloyds is *not* in the habit of plying murderers with monetary rewards."

Several heartbeats of silence filled the courtroom, then the crowd exploded in a riot of clapping, jeering, whistling, and foot stamping. They had come for a show, and by goodness had Quintin Hartley just delivered a spectacular *coup de grâce*.

Judge Porter sagged. It had been a long morning, and he looked long past the point of holding the rabble in contempt. His gavel repeatedly cracked until the hullaballoo hushed. "Mr Rafter. Mr Locke." He scowled over the rim of his glasses. "I'm done with this circus. Present your summaries now."

Wilbur Rafter glided around the counsel table and confronted the jury of stern-faced men. "A sailor's life isn't an easy one. We've heard how important it is that each and every member aboard a vessel, including the captain, fulfil his duty to its fullest, because dereliction of that duty can cost a man his life. But how is a disgruntled officer to remedy the injustice of an incompetent captain out on the open seas? If he resists, it's mutiny. Yet if he succeeds and takes the vessel, it's piracy. Or if he yields or is stripped of his rank, he endures risk to his own life under such incompetence. You may have heard of some of Mr Chittenden's missteps here today, but by her own account, and indeed that of Mr Hartley, Mrs Fitzwilliam was no feeble damsel who needed steadying on an undulating deck. And as Mr Blight attested, she employed the fighting skills he taught her—to *full* effect. She's not guilty of manslaughter—she is guilty of *murder*. Thank you."

Maitland Locke rose, looked earnestly at Grace sitting in the dock, and then swung his gaze to the jury. At least Big Bob's interruption had revived them from their heat-induced stupor. Twelve pairs of eyes were fervently fixed on the short lawyer.

"As witnessed today, Mrs Fitzwilliam has been highly complimented by the underwriters, who have shown their appreciation of her determined spirit and capable command. Any man who steps foot aboard a British vessel knows that if a sailor resists his commander, he resists the law, leaving mutiny or submission his only two choices. It's clear that Mr Chittenden resisted *both* of his commanders, and by refusing the route of submission, he chose mutiny. And the price for his folly? His life. Thank you." Locke tried to wriggle gently into the wooden chair to avoid the annoying squeak—to no avail.

It took the jury eight minutes to reach their verdict of not guilty.

Chapter Sixteen

Taking full advantage of her newfound freedom, Grace agreed to accompany Billy to the apothecary while he purchased the final supplies for the upcoming journey. He loped alongside, his lanky feet still too big for his body. His buoyant attitude had lured her here, not because he required any help buying supplies, but because a conversation with him renewed her confidence that there were still good people left in this world.

"Fine day for a walk, is it not, flower?" He grinned, exaggerating his already bouncy gait.

"More than fine." With her arm linked in his, she beamed as Emily and Edwin danced around them like maypole dancers. They had Madame's permission for a day trip out, but at this moment, Grace was regretting the decision. There was so much to prepare for the journey next week, and she did not have time for their childish proposition.

"Oh please, Mamam! It's what we both want. Isn't it Eddy?" Emily jarred her elbow into her younger brother's ribs, and Edwin grunted, half in agreement and half in pain.

Grace licked her thumb and wiped the smear of Biddy's plum jam from Edwin's cheek. Her son found the preserve's sugary sweetness as irresistible as she did. The bright morning light glinted off the cobbles of the narrow lanes, newly washed by the pre-dawn rain. The world appeared new and whole again.

"But you wouldn't see me for months and months if you did that." She licked the jam from her thumb, humming as she shook her head. "Hmm?"

Edwin swung his blond head towards her, a look of resolution pronouncing the bulge of his cherub cheeks. "We'll be with Miss Lissing the *whole* time."

Emily skipped backwards a few steps. "And when we break for the holidays, we can stay at Gilly Downs."

Grace frowned at the two eager faces, and she reached up to readjust a hairpin. Their suggestion had caused a headache that was slowly spreading to the roots of her teeth. "I'm unsure," she said uncertainly. "What say you, Billy?"

They halted outside a narrow shop-front with a door painted the blue of a high summer sky. The facade was emblazoned with hand-painted words in the same blue: *Apothecary.* It had an inviting feel about it. On the bench outside, two old women sat knitting and chatting, with their matching crocheted shawls and caps pulled down tightly.

Emily turned her persuasive head tilt towards Billy. "We'd much rather be at school with our friends than be stuck on the *Elias* again."

"Stuck, you say?" Billy folded his arms. "You're fortunate to have the opportunity to see the world."

"Oh, yes," agreed Emily. "We *are* thankful, but... but..." She lifted her chin, and Grace recognised the family trait. Her daughter squared her shoulders, trying—and succeeding—to mature her tone. "The benefits of staying at school in Sydney outweigh those of journeying back to London without a governess."

Stinking seaweed! She had a point. Decent governesses were few and far between in this town. No wonder Madame Dubois had been so keen to snatch Miss Lissing at the first opportunity. Though there was more chance of Grace being dragged behind the ship all the way to London than there was of her leaving her children behind.

"Do enlighten us of these benefits, Empem," said Billy, failing to suppress a smile.

Emily held up one hand, counting off the reasons on her fingers. "Learning French from Madame Dubois, performing in concerts, making new friends, and Christmas at Gilly Downs."

"And so we don't be killed by pirates!" piped in Edwin.

She hissed and aimed a kick at her brother before flicking the old ladies a guilty look. "Don't be daft, Eddy!"

Edwin scowled, his cherub cheeks puffing. "That's what *you* told me!"

Billy tapped Emily on the nose. "I've something for you, young lady." Digging deep into his trouser pocket, he withdrew a rectangular tin. The children's eyes widened. Billy shook it, rattling the contents enticingly as he nodded at the bench. "These boiled sweets are only for well-behaved children who sit quietly."

Emily and Edwin sat with a speed that made the two old ladies cluck in amusement. The lid of the sweet tin popped, and Billy handed it to Emily. He plucked a golden orb from the container with his long, elegant fingers and deposited it in his mouth with a wink. "Share with your brother. Your mama and I shan't be long."

Grace peered through the clean window, past the jars of herbs, spices, and tea beside the medicinal powders and tinctures, to the tall, dark figure behind the counter. Jeremiah Ravensdale, the colony's only apothecary.

Pushing open the blue door, she was greeted by the waft of powdered resins and ancient rooms. The bell above chimed, and Ravensdale turned, his hands stilling from their task of weighing dried ingredients on a brass scale. A sour-faced woman with a pert little hat stepped past Grace, a brown-papered parcel tucked possessively under her elbow.

Grace appreciated this shop with its ceiling-high shelves towering above. Each shelf held a row of jars or bottles identical to others in that row, each row housing a different shape or colour. Underneath, dozens of equally sized drawers were categorised with the same gold-and-black labels as the glassware. The extraordinary symmetry of the shelves offered her order and balance that had been missing these past few months. Grace inhaled the heady fragrances of spicy cinnamon blended with bitter cinchona bark.

"What ails, flower?" asked Billy, unfolding his list and glancing over at Ravensdale.

She peered up at his kind, brown eyes. "Oh, Billy. What am I to do? The children wish to stay at school, but Seamus wants me with him on the *Elias*." She stared miserably at her best friend. "I'm being split in two."

Billy's brows dipped, his face soft with fondness. "What says the captain?"

"He thinks that it's a wonderful opportunity for the children to remain behind. The climate. Miss Lissing's excellent education. The support the children will have from the Barclays, from Jim..."

"But?" Billy prompted.

"But what if something happens to one of them? They'll be stranded a million miles away, in need of—*me*." Her voice trailed away, and she pressed her tongue to the roof of her mouth to push away the tears that prickled her eyelids. Billy's gentle gaze did not help her cause, but she held it anyway. "I'm their mother. What good am I if I'm not here to comfort them and keep them safe?"

Billy slid his large hand over her shoulder and squeezed. "Grace, what happened to Elias was truly, truly awful, but 'twas an accident. You can't prevent your other children from experiencing life for fear something might befall them."

A tiny part of her marvelled that Billy had been able to draw straight to her main concern, but a more significant part flared angrily. "How do you know? How do *any* of us know?"

Unruffled by her outburst, Billy continued calmly, "Look how you've prevailed through life's hardships. Me too. I came close to death in Newgate, and you experienced a horror even worse than death, losing a child—but we've survived. God—"

Grace shrugged from his grasp. "Don't talk to me about God! He and I are not on talking terms."

Billy smiled kindly. "He's listening, flower. He knows your struggle."

She snatched up a sack of camomile tea and hiked it on her hip. "Please, Billy! If I wanted a sermon, I'd march myself up to Church Hill and have my pick of any number of preachers to lecture me on God's good grace." She dumped the sack of tea onto the countertop, the thump tipping over a small slate on a tri-legged stand. Scrunching her nose in apology at the apothecary, she righted the sign. *Tea leaf reading?*

"Good morning, madam."

She let out a breathy laugh and pointed to the sign. "I'm surprised to find a man of science invested in the art of divination."

Ravensdale cocked a dark eyebrow. "My old apothecary master reckoned there was no harm in learning the ancient ways. Would you like your leaves read? I'm just about to have a cup myself." He drew open the curtain behind him to reveal a young boy setting the table for tea. Steam curled from the teapot spout, and the youngster stuck his tongue out of the side of his mouth as he slid the patterned pot onto the table.

"Care to join me?" Ravensdale smiled serenely.

Grace winced at Billy. "Should I?"

Billy shrugged. "What's the harm?"

The closing curtains brushed against the back of her skirts as she turned in the small back room and perched on the chair the young boy had pulled out. Ravensdale lowered himself opposite her and folded his hands together. "Drink up. Then swirl the leaves, and put the saucer atop the cup, and flip it over."

Good grief, this was utter madness. Just how desperate was she for answers? She inhaled the soothing, smoky fragrance. Hmm, camomile. Billy had introduced her to it for its calming effects, though she loved it mostly because it tasted like baked apples. The delicate cup barely held more than a few mouthfuls, and as she swallowed the last, she did as she was bidden. A dribble of tea leaked from the upturned cup into the saucer.

"Face the cup's handle towards your heart."

Grace bit back a smirk of scepticism as she made her move.

"You're right-handed, so using your left hand, turn the cup clockwise three times."

She complied without hesitation this time.

"Now slide your saucer over to me."

Ravensdale turned the teacup right side up—it was dwarfed in his hand. "The leaves closest to the handle's edge represent your immediate future, and the leaves closer to the middle of the cup are your future further out," he explained, his words dribbling into silence as he studied the patterns in the cup.

Grace squirmed. What on earth would Seamus think if he found out she was dabbling in these ancient arts? The logician in him would scoff at the illusion of it all, and the zealot in him would scorn at the blasphemy. Surely, some answers would be better than no answers?

"I see lots of water—*lots* of water—like a vast journey."

A likely line that matched every inhabitant in this town!

"I see a heart," he droned.

Grace grabbed his hand and, tipping the cup towards her, peered into the speckled mess of stewed vegetation. Bleeding bloody rats' tails! A cold shiver ran down her neck as she spied the solid shape of a heart stuck to the cup's side. She released his hand and leaned back slowly.

The apothecary looked at her with steadfast patience, his eyebrows raised in silent question. Folding her arms, Grace scowled and nodded at him to continue.

"A heart means that there's love here, and much fun to be had."

Hmph, by whom?

"This is a poignant decision for you, but it's the right one. Stop thinking about it with your head. Start listening to it. Follow it with your heart."

Easier said than done.

"I see a seahorse as well. It's looking forward. You're being gently guided through life changes. Though you'll be able to envisage all aspects, so you'll be less likely to leave matters unattended. It'll require great patience, but all will come in divine timing."

Ravensdale looked up from the cup, and a flitter of uncertainty scurried beneath her ribs like an octopus seeking shelter under rocks. She folded her arm tightly across her chest, but then she dissolved her frown as Billy slid his hand across her shoulders again.

"All will be well, flower. Even if you haven't faith in the tea leaves, or in God at the moment, have faith in yourself. You know better than anyone that you're the last person to ever hurt your family. Certainly not intentionally. *Believe* that you're capable of making these decisions." Billy's breath puffed from his nostrils. "The Devil has you in his grip. If you let fear or indecision stop you, then he'll have won. Don't let that Hell-demon win this battle."

Billy was right. For the dozenth time that day, her decision swung in favour of accompanying Seamus. Even if she stayed behind, it was not as though the children would be with her every day. They were well settled at school now, and more importantly, *happy*. Echoes of her wedding vows taunted her: ... *and into your eyes that I smile each morning*. She had promised her husband this, and she meant it too. She took a long, deep breath. Right, decision made.

Chapter Seventeen

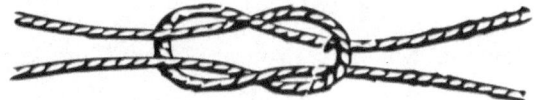

S eamus knocked on the door and stared at the hand-
painted sign—*Madame Eulalie Dubois, Headmistress.*
He hoisted the pile of books, bound with twine, onto his
other hip as he had done with his infants whenever his arm grew
weary. He had never managed to seat them on his hip as comfortably as Grace or McGilney did, despite his best efforts. He
stepped back and glanced down at his wife. Her mouth twitched
as she nibbled the inside of her lip.

Muffled footsteps paraded across the floor above as muted
voices and laughter filtered down the stairs. He caught Grace's
gaze drawing wistfully to the top landing, clearly hoping to catch
a glimpse of Emily or Edwin. Someone was butchering a clarinet
in the music room at the end of the hall. The building was
bursting with life and unharnessed potential, though the astrin-
gent chemicals and sour gases creeping under the closed door on
his left reeked the same as the science room in his own school.

He had never forgotten the thrill of using the burner lamp to perform experiments.

Leaning down, he whispered, "Reminds me of my own visit to the headmaster's as a youngster." He winked, relieved that his grin made her smile.

"Only once? I find *that* hard to believe." She smartly snapped her head forward as the brass knob turned with a squeak.

"Ah, Captain. Madame. You are here," greeted Madame Dubois, her thin, neat countenance so prim that a stiff breeze might topple her.

Seamus dipped his head. "Madame, you're looking splendid this morning."

The headmistress's prim glare transformed like summer clouds puffed by a warm breeze, and she patted her hair, her laugher light and high. No doubt emulating the latest Parisian fashion, the plaited twist of Madame Dubois's toffee-coloured bun looked more like a decadent twist of pastry in Mr Dortmund's bakery window than a hairstyle. Seamus's stomach growled.

"The children will be down shortly."

Seamus's gaze followed Grace's towards the empty stairs again. The large house was ideally suited for Madame's boarding school, with its numerous downstairs rooms making perfect classrooms and its upstairs bedchambers converted into dormitories. When he had brought the children here before Grace's trial, Madame had shown him the fully stocked library, and a drawing room where she said the students gathered in the evenings to play card and board games. She had also been quick to point out that the school even had servants' quarters, and a coach house with stables. The children had been promised that they could cultivate their own seedlings in the greenhouse out back, if they wished. It was the assurance that they would learn to play tennis on the court at the bottom of the garden that had won Edwin over; for Emily, it was permission for her tortoise, Alby, to live in the greenhouse.

The stairs creaked, and beside him, Grace gasped. With newly scrubbed red cheeks, Emily and Edwin grinned and waved. As though suddenly remembering herself, Emily jabbed Edwin in the ribs with her elbow, and they both dropped their hands. An air of happiness followed them down.

Madame Dubois's arm swept towards Seamus and Grace with the gracefulness of a ballerina. "Ah, Emily, Edwin—your parents are here."

Emily's blue gaze widened at the French schoolmistress as though the pronunciation of their names—*Emeely* and *Edween*— was a decadent treat. Boarding school, and the favourable climate here in New Holland, clearly agreed with them both. Look at them—fair sprouting up like weeds!

"Oh, Mamam! Cappy! Eddy and I are having a delightful time. Mamam, I know you're unhappy with us staying behind, but Miss Lissing has been a real brick."

The headmistress's elegant hands reached for the books. "Please, allow me, sir." Seamus handed them over, and she slid them into the bookcase near the door.

The colour drained from Grace's face, except for two high spots of red on her cheeks. Her smile did not reach her eyes. "What have you two been up to?"

Emily's two blonde plaits jiggled as she bounced on her toes. "I earned a distinction in needlework—for designing a cool summer dress. I can't *wait* to begin sewing it."

Seamus ruffled Edwin's soft, blond hair. "And you, my boy?"

Edwin beamed, his missing front tooth marring the perfect white row. "My teacher is Miss Butterfield. In the mornings, we sit in a circle, and she touches our heads with a peacock feather when she calls our names."

Emily rolled her eyes. "Ugh, the little ones are *so* fortunate.

They don't have to sit for *hours* practising handwriting—they hammer and saw wood instead. Miss Butterfield also draws maps and sends them into the garden to find hidden treasure."

Madame clasped her slender hands together. "Indeed. Miss Butterfield believes little ones learn better with their heads, hearts, *and* hands."

Edwin slid his hot little hand into Seamus's. "We even have our own veggie patch." He scrunched his button nose. "But it's not as big as the one at Gilly Downs."

Seamus looked down as Madame gave a mild hum of approval. "*Oui*, Matron Oberholzer uses only the freshest vegetables for meal preparation."

Emily nodded importantly. "Matron is from Austria. She speaks *no* English, and she can be a bit grumpy." Her blue eyes widened, and she snapped her head round to the headmistress.

Grace laughed lightly. "I'm sure I'd be grumpy too if I didn't understand what people were saying to me." She straightened the bow of Emily's plait and tweaked the curl at the end.

Emily waved her hand at the landing above. "The girls' dormitory has the most *wonderful* view over the bay."

Seamus bit back a chuckle at his daughter's skilful turn of conversation. *Deft save, young lady.* "Made any friends yet?"

"I have," gushed Emily. "Bunny!"

He laughed. "I meant a person, not another animal."

"Oh, no—her name's Mary Anne Tumbleton. I call her Bunny because she's timid and sweet—like a bunny. She likes me calling her that. We're both nine."

Tumbleton. The name swirled in Seamus's mind. Ah, yes, the family with the terrible tale attached—and unfortunately the latest talk of the town. The blessing of it meant that Grace's name no longer dripped from gossipy tongues.

Young Miss Tumbleton had been at Miss Harriet Barnes' school with her little sister Hattie. On that fateful day, little Hattie, feeling unwell, had gone to sickbay, where Miss Barnes accidentally gave her arsenic instead of magnesia. Tragically, the child had died. The authorities berated Miss Barnes for having arsenic in the sickbay, but her defence was that it was there as rat poison. Seamus did not blame the mother for removing her remaining child from Miss Barnes's care. It was struggle enough adjusting to Elias's accidental loss, though he had never once blamed the hackney driver.

Emily looked pleased with having a friend the same age. She would require the company if she began missing him and Grace. Seamus cleared his throat. "Right, children. Time to go. Must be aboard when the tide turns."

Emily and Edwin hesitated a heartbeat before grabbing their mother's waist together. Biting her bottom lip, Grace squeezed her eyes shut as a low hum escaped her throat. She bowed and buried her head between the two blond ones, gripping them like a sailor clinging to two rum kegs in a storm. Seamus swallowed the walnut paralysing his oesophagus.

"Oh, my darlings! I'll miss you horribly," Grace managed in a soft whisper, her voice catching.

"Me too, Mamam! But we'll see you soon," said Edwin with youthful enthusiasm.

Heavens, his son had no idea just how *long* their parting would be. Grace's hand spread across Edwin's broad back, her fingertips stroking rhythmically. Seamus knew that touch well. He had lain many a night, staring into the night in blissful contentment as her caresses lulled him over the edge of sleep.

He inhaled sharply at the notion that he would have her all to himself over the coming months, shame swiftly coating his glee into a hardened chrysalis of guilt. It was not as though he took pleasure in leaving the children behind. He was doing so at *their* request. As deep-seated as his desire had been to escape the horde of children at Barclay Hall, he was particularly fond of his two. By Neptune, he would miss them *tremendously*.

"I'll miss you too, Mamam." Emily planted a kiss on Grace's cheek.

Seamus ran Emily's glossy, golden plait through his hand as though it were a cat's tail. Just like her mother's hair, only tight braids could tame these ringlets. Their tresses were one of his favourite features about them both, and he stroked his daughter's woven hair again to commit the silken feel to memory.

Drawing a step back, Edwin stretched his hand out formally. "Goodbye, Cappy." Seamus took his son's small, slick hand and shook it. Not caring about Madame Dubois, he dropped to one knee and yanked his boy to him in a fierce embrace.

"Goodbye, my boy. Be good. And take care of your sister." It took all his effort to steady his voice.

Releasing Edwin, he scooped up Emily. Her grip around his neck pulled his hair ribbon loose, but just at this minute, he did not care. He closed his eyes and breathed in the clean, sweet scent of his daughter, with hints of chalk dust and ink. Savouring the squeeze of her arms, he pressed his cheek against her soft one. Christ, if they dragged this out too much longer, he would lose the battle against the rising tide of heartache in his chest.

Emily twisted her head, her velveteen lips warm and wet against his ear. "I promise I'll be brave. Just like you taught me."

Seamus chuckled and planted a kiss on her temple. "I know you will, my darling," he whispered back. "You're the bravest soul I know."

Emily guided his head around to murmur into his ear again. "Take care of Mamam, Cappy. She's not as brave as me, even though she pretends to be."

Beside him, Grace's face was pale and tight. Although she was not crying, her red-rimmed eyes deliberately studied the painting of a gigantic Saint Bernard at the foot of a staircase, upon which a little girl sat, with her arm slung comfortably around the great, shaggy beast.

Oh, Dulcinea! Let me end your misery quickly. He lowered

Emily to the plush hall runner. With a sudden pull that left his arms feeling desolately cold and empty, he turned to Grace and tucked her icy hand into the crook of his arm. Bidding the head-mistress farewell, he swiftly turned his wife out of the front door.

The children ran out to the landing, watching them descend the few steps to the street. "Bye, Mamam! Bye, Cappy!"

Turning briefly, Grace covered most of her crumpling face with her hand to blow Emily and Edwin kisses. She swung her head back sharply as the first tear spilled down her cheek. At the sound of the children's efforts to return the kisses, she swept her hand above her head in a show of catching them. Their sweet giggles rang out, cut short by the door's solid thud.

Grace's footsteps faltered, and Seamus gripped her hand tighter. "Oh goodness, Seamus! I don't think I can do this!"

Releasing her hand, he swept his arm around her slim back. "Of course you can, my heart. They'll be all right, as will we. It's a new and exciting chapter in their lives. You'll not deprive them of the adventure, will you?"

"No," she said meekly. "I know of the benefits, but it doesn't lessen the pain of our parting."

"It doesn't," he conceded. "But we'll bear it as we always have—*together*."

He helped her into her waiting carriage. For pity's sake, her misery was set to flood the interior. He gripped the window latch beside him, and the wooden rail juddered, biting every inch downwards. Blasted thing! Sucking in a lungful of hot air, he gathered the courage to face her. He leaned forward on his elbows, slowly running his index finger down the bridge of his nose before pinching the end in consideration.

"I'd understand your reluctance were we leaving them in an English boarding school, but here, they'll receive a decent education without all the *stifling devilment*, as you so eloquently put it, of a British institution."

She sniffed. He offered her his handkerchief, a smile, and

further words of comfort. "Without the likes of Chittenden to impede our journey, and with favourable winds, we can be to London and back in no time. The children will hardly have time to miss us."

"And what of *my* missing *them*?" Her voice thickened, and she pressed the handkerchief to her eyes.

"They'll be in good hands, Dulcinea. Between Madame Dubois, Miss Lissing, and Mrs Barclay, they'll not want for anything."

She swiped her eyes roughly, and a shadow of reluctance tightened her face.

He drew up one corner of his mouth. "You know my greatest fear is keeping you all safe aboard the ship."

"Oh, don't bloody belabour the point," she snapped. "I've heard it enough times over the years."

"Yes, Dulcinea, you have," he added softly to counter her flaring temper. "There's merit to my concern, as you well know."

"I know!" she snapped. "Gilly and the Fuegians. Bloody O'Reilly! Father Babcock, and now Chittenden." She clapped her hands to her face and sobbed until her cry ran silent, marked only by her jerking shoulders.

Oh, Dulcinea! The last time she had cried so pitifully was after Elias. Was it fair of him to tear her away from Emily and Edwin?

Sucking in a giant gasp, she dropped her hands to her lap, and white imprints of her fingers lingered on her wet cheeks. "I just can't leave them, Seamus. I can't! I *need* them."

"As I need you." He reached over to caress her cheek, but she flinched. He waited patiently, and she slowly drew back towards him like an iron rod to a magnet. She lowered her long lashes and sighed as he cupped her face. Leaning in, he whispered, "From this day it shall be only your name I cry out in the night—"

She opened her eyes and pressed his palm against her damp

cheek. "And into your eyes that I s-smile each morning." She hiccoughed.

He smiled. "My vows to you all those years ago run as true in my blood now as they did then. I desire you beside me each morning when I awake." Kissing her knuckles, he shifted over onto the bench beside her and curled his arm about her shoulders. "I'm a sailor, Grace. My life is at sea. You knew that from the moment you met me."

She slid her hand over his heart. It bucked and thumped wildly in his chest.

"I know, my love. You're an excellent mariner and a wonderful father. You've done wonders in both regards. But—"

Her hand slid to her lap, and Seamus's innards slithered loose as though drawn by an executioner's blade.

"I'd like to buy a house. In Sydney."

He breathed out a breathy laugh and loosened his arm around her shoulders. "Grand idea. Have our own home to stay in when we return."

"Yes." She drew the word out slowly and tightened her hand into a fist around the lapel of his coat. "Though I don't just want it to return to. I want it to live in. Now."

His chest expanded as he sucked in a breath and held it. "What the devil do you mean?" By Neptune's forked trident! He knew what she blasted-well meant, but he was determined to have her say it. Perhaps she would hear the absurdity of it once said out loud.

"I'm staying," she whispered.

"Dulcinea." He kept his voice soft, and she glanced warily at him. He shook his head. "I need you aboard."

Her gaze hardened defensively like the lioness she was, protecting her cubs. "I'm sorry. I'll not survive being so far from them."

He licked his lips and rolled his wrist twice, clicking it both times. "Then we shall bring them with us."

She shook her head, her breath juddering. "You saw how happy they are here. They've so many opportunities." Despite the sunny day outside, determination absorbed all colour and warmth from her eyes.

"Since when have the children had a say in our setting course?" The muscles and tendons running down his neck and across the tops of his shoulders bunched into a tight knot, pulling uncomfortably on his scar. Biting back a grunt, he added, "And what of your duty to *me*? To the *Elias*?"

She nibbled her thumbnail. He concentrated on the bendy spring of her nail between her teeth, and not the flood of guilt threatening to course up his throat and eject the contents of his stomach over the carriage floorboards.

"I've a duty to our children too, Seamus."

He whirled and thrust himself away from her, his back colliding with the carriage's side. "So, you'll leave me as easily as that?" The rise of guilt and anger soured into bitter bile in his craw.

"Damn you, Seamus Fitzwilliam! You believe this easy for me? I want to stay *for our children*, yet you act as though I'm tearing our marriage apart."

"You are!" He raked his fingers through his slicked-back hair, and his already loosened ribbon fell into his lap. Ungently yanking his hair into a tail, he tied it again. The carriage clattered to a halt, the springs swaying them both back and forth. He scowled at the forest of masts in the harbour. How in Heaven's name had they arrived so quickly?

"I'll be like all other sailors' wives, awaiting their husbands' return home," she countered heatedly, folding her arms.

"You belong by my side, now and always."

"Our children require a mother. I can't leave them behind. I just *can't*."

Damn and blast this devilment! Toying with the idea of punching the carriage roof and yelling at the driver to turn around, he hesitated as a symphony of ship's bells clanged eight times. Noon! The tide had turned. He could not delay the departure. He glanced back up the gangplank. Blight and O'Malley stood sentry at the top, waiting to pull it in. Both sailors peered down curiously, and Seamus caught the look that passed between them. By Neptune's trident! This tardy departure was squarely on him—or rather, his *wife*. He grasped her hand.

"Damnation, Grace!" he hissed. "Will you have me drag you aboard? Cause a scene?"

Her chin quivered, the dogged determination in her eyes fading to unfathomable sorrow. She tried to speak, but her words came out as agonised sounds jammed deep in her throat. The weight of his decision crushed his lungs as though someone had dropped a nine-pounder on him. "If we delay any longer, we'll miss the last of the February wool sales—there shan't be another until June. I've a contract to honour."

"Then don't delay." She cast her gaze into her lap.

Seven months, he rationalised. He could make the return voyage in seven months, perhaps six, if he steered the *Elias* further south below the Roaring Forties. Without Grace and the children aboard, he was prepared to risk the stronger winds and icebergs. He trusted the crew filling his decks. The hands would be dismayed to learn she would not be sailing with them. Perhaps the promise of a bonus two-months' pay if they returned the *Elias* to Sydney Town in anything under seven months might boost morale? As would the thrill of hazarding the Great Circle. Overriding the spear of jealousy piercing his chest, that the children would see Grace while he would not, was a tremor of excitement humming through him as tight as the stays on a mainsail. And with Hicks remaining behind as his agent, she would at least not be alone.

"I'll return as quickly as humanly possible," he promised, kissing her hand and committing the scent of her to mind. She leaned in, and he lowered his lips to meet hers, her kiss slow and lingering. "I love you. Farewell, Dulcinea."

"Goodbye, my love. Be safe," she whispered, her breath like warm apple.

With pupils magnified by tears, her Pacific-green gaze latched onto his soul. Christ, if he delayed a second more, his desire to keep her near would overwhelm his composure. It was already crashing against the inside of his ribs like a prisoner fighting the iron bars of a prison. He loosened his grip, and her fingers slid from his grasp gently, slowly, like a feather picked up by a breeze.

He slipped smartly from the carriage, his footsteps tapping the wooden gangplank like the beat of an executioner's drum. Oh, that it was a volley of rifle fire he faced instead of months without her. At least iron shot would kill this pain.

Chapter Eighteen

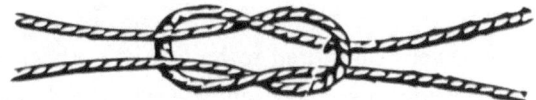

*CLIFFVIEW COTTAGE, DARLING POINT, 16
FEBRUARY 1842*

I n the empty bedchamber upstairs, Grace stared out the
window, its white-painted frame perfectly displaying the
bay's glistening blue expanse. The promontory cliffs of the
Heads coming into the harbour were a hazy grey in the distance.

Seamus was out there. Had his anger over her decision to
remain been usurped by his duty to the ship and his men? For his
sake, she hoped the hurt in his heart would not smoulder like a
slow-creeping peat fire, flameless from the outside, charring all
in its path. She wished she had explained the pain in her own
heart better. How the thought of leaving Emily and Edwin
squeezed her pulse to a standstill and took her back into the
colourless, lifeless years of her childhood nursery. She dared not
risk abandoning her children as she had been. Neither Mother
nor Father had loved her in a way that appeased her soul. It was
demanding enough accepting this pain in herself without trans-

forming it into the words Seamus needed to understand it. Stinking seaweed, she should have tried harder.

She had been in her new home a week now. Toby had seen a printed advertisement about the sale of Cliffview Cottage outside the post office. Enquiring after Marcus Turner, the previous owner, Toby had quickly made the purchase as Seamus's agent, fortunately before Mr Turner had begun selling any furnishings or *objets d'art*.

The Turners were rumoured to be travelling back to Europe after almost a decade of social exclusion had finally pushed Mrs Turner to breaking point. Marcus Turner was one of a new generation of local-born colonists. Despite his political achievements, his wealth, and his fashionable estate, his convict-stained origins stuck to him like tar. His long-suffering British wife had been tolerated as ladylike and amiable, but she was never called upon by the elite of Sydney's society. After years of struggling to be accepted, Mrs Turner had insisted the family leave.

It was the first home Grace could truly call her own, and she had an odd sensation that the cottage yearned to be filled with the squeals and laughter of a young family. Now, on the horizon, ships with sails in full bloom carried their hulks towards the docks or whisked them towards the open sea and the promise of adventure and profits. With practised watchfulness, Grace shifted her focus beyond the hazy, grey line where the ocean met the land to the clouds in the distance.

Goodness! It was almost impossible to believe that gales and cricket-ball-sized hailstones had battered the little colony just two days before. She had experienced worse, of course, when the *Discerning* had tipped in the storm, but it was a spectacular sight nonetheless. From this same window, she had watched the blue-and-gold blazes of lightning light up the harbour like a bonfire on Guy Fawkes Night. The angry, purple arc of clouds had swept across a vast tract of land, pelting hail and rain on the inhabitants and animals below.

GRACE ARISING

Her venture into town the day after the storm for supplies revealed tin roofs torn off as easily as fingernails, the collapsed roof of a warehouse at the docks brought down by the weight of the rain and hail, and a crumbled stone wall of the Presbyterian church up on Church Hill. Her healthy respect for the wind's power was laced with fear at the sight of giant gum trees torn from the hard, unforgiving ground, roots and all. The snapped and splintered remains of the ancient trunks probed the air like frayed ropes. At least the Cliffview Cottage had stood its ground. Gracious! What a nightmare it must have been for ships on the open ocean. Pushing aside the gloomy thought, she was thankful that today offered a glorious, clear-skied summer's day.

A hollow knock echoed from the entry hall down below. Jim Buchanan stood in the doorway, his leather slouch hat twisted in his hands, his face grey like ash in a cold hearth.

Her stomach swooped. "What's happened?"

Jim reached for her hand, his palm as rough as tree bark. "'Tis Squatter Barclay. He's been killed," he said thickly.

She squeezed his solid fingers as his words churned the dread in her stomach into a fizz of lightning that seared the marrow in her bones. A loud ringing filled her ears, competing with the hammering drum of her heartbeat. "How?"

"In the storm. He was checking on the shepherds. The branch of a gum broke—struck his head." Jim's bushy black brows drew into one as he swallowed deeply and concentrated on his boots.

Grace whimpered, clutching her hand to her stomach. "Oh, Lord! Adelia!" Her eyes stung with tears. "I must go to her. Today."

Jim blinked away his glassy stare and nodded. "Aye. I've already reported Squatter Barclay's passing to the authorities, and to the manager at Barclay & Co. I'll accompany ye, shall I?"

"Have you called on the undertaker? For a coffin?" The words tasted sour and unwelcome.

Jim shook his head and pulled at his protruding ear. "No

need. Dorian McDermott's handy enough with wood. He's already started the coffin." He ran his hand through his black thatch of hair. "I've called on the Reverend Blackwood. He'll be at Gilly Downs tomorrow."

She scraped her hands down the sides of her skirts and glanced back into the empty cottage. "Right. Yes. I—um—"

"I'll wait while ye pack a trunk."

"No. Sally can bring my things later. I'll fetch my shawl." Grace whirled in a flurry of skirts, and she took the stairs two at a time, her hem lifted high. The wool plaid was too hot to wear during the day, but she never left home without it. After nearly freezing to death beside a dying Gilly because of her foolhardy haste to leave the *Discerning* without adequate clothing, she chose to always be prepared.

Sally McGilney was heading down the hall with a wicker basket of dirty laundry perched on her hip like a tubby child. Upon hearing Grace's decision to stay in Sydney Town with the children, Sally had promptly dragged her trunk off the *Elias* before Ben and O'Malley had withdrawn the gangplank. Her housekeeper might not be as spirited as her brother, Gilly, but she was just as hard a worker, and as fiercely loyal to Grace. Billy was not granted the same reprieve. There had been no time for Seamus to secure the services of another surgeon, and Grace suffered his absence almost as much as her husband's. But this news of Adelia's tragedy trounced all self-pity.

"Oh, Sally! I've terrible news! Squatter Barclay has been involved in an accident."

Sally's dark brown eyes widened. "He hurt, marm?"

Grace pressed her forefinger beneath her nose to stem the burn of tears. "No. He was—killed."

Sally stiffened and gasped, the basket's contents disgorging onto the hall runner. "God 'ave mercy!" She hastily crossed herself. "How?"

"A falling branch. During the storm."

"Didn't much care for that bleedin' tempest." Sally scowled, her black brows rucking just as her brother's had. "Thought we was fair goin' to blow away!"

"I'm leaving for Gilly Downs—today. Will you follow with my trunk?"

"Course, marm." Sally bobbed.

Grace squeezed Sally's shoulder and headed into the bedchamber, her long skirts wrapping around her ankles with each hurried step. She yanked on her riding boots and snatched up her red tartan shawl. *Oh, Adelia, my friend. Hold steady. I'm coming!*

Stepping across the veranda with its wide cane chairs and blue-striped cushions, she looked across at the stables. The general factotum of Cliffview Cottage, Terry, a young lad in his early twenties, loped towards her with a grey dappled mare already saddled. Cliffview Cottage had come with two horses, both mares, mother and daughter: Star and Lunar, equally pleasant in disposition. Terry handed Grace Star's reins, and the horse's ears flickered at the sound of Lunar whinnying in protest at being left behind in the stable.

Grace ran a soothing hand down the horse's long neck. "It's all right Star, you'll see her soon enough."

The horses seemed to sense the riders' urgency, and they trotted along steadily. When they came to a part of the track wide enough to fit side by side, Jim pulled his horse even with Grace's. She turned, wanting to smile at her friend, but unable. He returned her sober look. She sat up more squarely in the saddle, searching for an opening in the conversation.

"Where's Squatter Barclay now?"

"Milady has him laid out in the parlour." Jim's tone was flat with sadness.

"Was he badly injured? Marked, I mean?"

"Not much. The branch clipped the back of his head. His neck took the brunt of it, his face untouched." Jim scowled.

"Crivens! Of all the ways to pass from this world, who'd have thought a wretched tree would become a widowmaker?"

A fresh tear trickled down Grace's cheek, and she swiped it with the back of her hand. She glanced at Jim, drawing comfort from his familiar round cheeks. "How's Mrs Barclay bearing up?"

He loosened his reins and licked his lips, his brown eyes darkening with concern. "Well enough."

"Hope this doesn't bring the babe on early." Grace urged Star on with an extra squeeze of her heels. She stared at the bushland without much focus as a fresh threat of tears squeezed her windpipe. She turned to Jim. "Tell me one of your stories. You've always been good at distracting me with them. It's not like you to be so quiet."

Jim quirked one eyebrow at her, his voice low. "Was being mindful of giving ye space to arrange yer thoughts."

"I don't *want* to arrange my thoughts." She sniffed, wiping her nose on her sleeve. "Tell me something that'll take my mind off this bloody wretched business. Like you did the first time I tarred the rigging on the *Discerning* and was scared witless. Remember?"

"Aye, I remember just fine." The hint of his roguish smile broke through his grey mask of worry. He scratched the black stubble on his chin with a dry rasp. "Hmm, what might I have for ye?" He adjusted his leather hat and pinched his nose, sniffing as he did so. "I've asked my Pearl to marry me."

The weight of sorrow in her chest took wing, and Grace offered him a genuine smile of delight. "Oh, Jim! How marvellous!"

He glanced bashfully from the corner of his eyes. "Aye, I took meself off to Harris's Dairy, new boots shined so as I could see me face in them. We walk out every Sunday, so my Pearl was waiting for me by the gate. I gave her the Luckenbooth brooch I'd had made by the silversmith in town."

Shifting the reins into one hand, Grace lifted the edge of the shawl to reveal her own gold brooch pinned to her chest. "Never leave home without mine."

"Ye'd think from my Pearl's carry-on that I'd given her the Crown Jewels."

"She's a lucky girl. You're a treasure in your own right."

The tips of his ears turned pink beneath the wide brim of his hat. "Och, away with ye."

"You've the gift of optimism, and an aptitude for happiness infused in every fibre of your being." Grace waggled a finger at him. "Your Pearl's a very fortunate lass."

Jim snorted. "Must remember to keep ma manliness on display every now and then. Stop folk think I've become a great, big dafty. Must keep swinging my axe to split wood, or hunting roo for supper to keep up appearances." His long-lashed eye winked.

"You needn't prove anything to anyone, Jim. You're a good sort, and others know it well enough. Everyone knows what you did for Nevin, giving up your freedom travelling the world to give your brother's child a good home. You're a jolly decent brick!"

Jim's broad shoulders jiggled as he laughed. "Try reminding the lad that next time I pin his arse down for lessons. Carries on like it's a punishment worse than death. Says 'tis a more honest day's work toiling with his hands than his mind. Can't fault his logic, but it pains me that he'll not expand his learning."

"This world needs people prepared to put their backs into it. Imagine the disaster if everyone sat about reading and writing all day. There'd be no crops grown, no houses built, no ships sailed."

"Aye," grumbled Jim. "Though it wouldn't hurt him to have a legible hand. His looks like a constipated beetle's scrabbled across the page."

As they approached a low branch, Jim tried to steer the stallion around. Pulling more firmly on the reins did little to sway the crabby steed, and Jim ducked to avoid being swept from his saddle. "Ye cursed mule of Satan!" he growled, kicking it in the ribs. The black beast swung its head around and tried to bite Jim's leg, but he pulled the horse's head down. It let out an indignant snort through its wide nostrils, spraying a fine mist of mucous across the path.

Grace would have laughed if she were not so worried that the wretched beast would turn at the sound of her giggle and try to bite her or Star. Edging the mare out of biting range, she asked, "Have you set a wedding date?"

"Aye, we—*had*." Jim pressed his lips. "But 'tisn't likely now, what with Squatter Barclay—"

Grace's voice pitched. "Just how soon were you planning to marry her?"

"We were soon to have a double wedding with Toby Hicks and Miss Lissing."

Grace reined her horse to a dead stop, a hot gush of breath escaping her mouth as she turned in her saddle. "Toby—and Miss Lissing—getting *married*?"

"Aye. He asked her the other week at the dance, and she agreed."

"Well I never! Neither mentioned a word about it." Gracious! The notion that she had been one of the last to find out stung a little. Then again, she had been rather preoccupied with her potential departure. Though who could stay cross with such happy news?

"Course, we'll have to wait a bit now. 'Til after the funeral," said Jim.

The heavy bushland opened into clearer open grassland, and with a familiar pang, Grace recognised the lightning-burnt gum tree that denoted the start of Gilly Downs' pastoral land. If the carpet of black-balled sheep droppings was not signal enough, the new, painted sign nailed to the tree left no doubt.

Welcome to Wooloongilly Downs
Proprietor: Elijah Barclay
1.5 miles to Barclay Hall
Any persons not calling upon the house,
or looking for honest work, will be shot.

Chapter Nineteen

WOOLOONGILLY DOWNS, 16 FEBRUARY 1842

Riding up the dusty track towards Barclay Hall, Grace thought the homestead appeared deceptively tranquil with its wide veranda and purple-flowered vine curling up the white-painted posts. She was surprised to see Adelia in the fenced vegetable patch, stabbing the earth with a fork. A mountainous, black-haired man worked the other end of the newly turned rows of soil, solid and silent. Adelia drove the implement deep into the dirt with a ferocity that drove the prongs right up to the hilt. At the approaching horses' clops, Adelia peered up from beneath her broad-brimmed sunhat. Jamming a hand on the small of her back, she stretched back, the mound of her belly arching.

Grace sprang from her horse and handed the reins to Jim. Pushing through the small, squeaky gate, she engulfed her friend in a tight, silent embrace. Adelia stiffened, holding her soiled leather gardening gloves out like wings to avoid dirtying Grace's dress.

Her friend's voice was thick. "I was doing all right—until you showed up." Her words whispered against the skin of Grace's neck. "It's unbearable, Grace."

She squeezed Adelia tighter. "I know it feels that way now, but I promise, it does become easier. You'll never forget him or stop missing him, but you'll bear it—in time."

"And what of now? I can't bear it. I'm not strong enough."

"You needn't endure it alone. I'm not going anywhere."

Adelia's spine sagged, and she clasped her hands in the small of Grace's back. "I feel so wretched unburdening myself on you when you've your own troubles to bear. I can't believe Captain Fitzwilliam departed without you."

Grace drew back and gave her friend a long, hard look. "He'll return when he returns."

Adelia lowered her arms, her tightly pressed lips unable to stop her chin from quivering, or her hazel eyes from filling with tears. Grace nodded gently in understanding. Her friend was coping remarkably. No doubt her unwavering sense of fatalism helped her face her husband's death with stoic calm. Adelia's years working the land of this sunburnt country had hardened her from the simpering city girl she had once been—though Grace understood how the tiniest touch of compassion was the quickest way to unravel that stoicism.

"Don't mind me." She patted Adelia's solid back. "I'm here to say hello to these two mucky mischiefs." On an upturned wheelbarrow near the fence, Ruth and Eve giggled, taking turns to spin the home-made wooden wheel. "Hello, you two!" She ruffled their soft, ginger locks.

Squinting up against the day's brightness, the two sisters grinned at her. Ruth waved. "Hello, Aunty Grace. Where's Emily?" Two pairs of blue eyes peered around curiously.

"Back in town, my darlings. At school."

Smiling at the disappointed droop of their shoulders, Grace turned at the sound of metal prongs thudding into the sun-baked soil. At the other end of the garden, power quivered off the stranger's broad shoulders as he wielded the garden fork into the compact earth.

"Right then," said Grace brightly. "Need a hand?" She waved at the rows of healthy plants of various sizes and shades of green. Tendrils of pea vines curled past the twine and up the wooden posts jabbed into the earth. Frilly carrot tops and tall corn stalks waved and rustled in the breeze. Grace's eyes widened at the enormous, bright green lettuce heads partnered in an adjacent row with spiky-topped onions. To be honest, the last thing she wanted was to be bent over back-breaking work after so many hours in the saddle, but perhaps it might work the stiffness from her muscles.

"Thank you," whispered Adelia softly. "I can't afford my hands to be idle. I was going mad with grief sitting quietly indoors with only my thoughts for company." She waved a gloved hand at the big house. "Mr Barclay's in there too."

"I understand completely," said Grace, retrieving a hoe that lay beside the wheelbarrow. "Oi, you two. Go pick those caterpillars off the lettuce heads before they chew through the hearts." The two youngsters slid off the barrow, eyes wide with glee.

Grace smiled at the simplicity of their enjoyment, and she turned to her friend. "What are we planting?"

"Marrows," said Adelia, nodding towards the rows of seedlings sprouting from wooden boxes near the fence. "But those weeds by the tomatoes want pulling first."

A dog barked in the distance, and Grace glanced at the nearest hilly pasture. Jim strode purposefully towards a large flock of sheep—straight back to work for him too then. His high whistles and short, sharp commands caused the black dog to dart around the panicked creatures, driving them up the hill towards a wooden holding enclosure beside the shearing shed.

Grace's gaze slid over to the crouching form of the giant, whose enormous hands now pried the tiny green shoots from another box with such refined gentleness, almost cradling the new plants as though they were infants, before carefully inserting them into the earth. At the touch of Adelia's hand on her arm, she turned.

"That's Mr Shyling. He's a shepherd."

"A shepherd? Planting marrows?"

A weary smile pulled at Adelia's lips, and she leaned in. "I'll tell you about him later."

Grace nodded. "Right, those weeds shan't pull themselves."

Laying down the hoe, she crouched and grasped a weed, its leaves soft in her hand. Pulling carefully to not snap it at its roots, Grace felt it give as it released its hold on the ground, and she blinked against the puff of dust.

With the vegetable garden newly turned and weeded, and the marrow seedlings planted and watered, and with her hands chaffed red from the garden implements, Grace could no longer delay going into the parlour. Elijah Barclay lay on a long trestle table. She had never had a problem being alone in a room with the man when he was alive; his solid, welcoming presence had always put her at ease. Only a few steps in, she stopped and slapped her hand to her nose. Lord above, she had smelt death before, but never emanating from a friend. The hot weather was clearly not conducive to a long lying-out.

Grace coughed and swallowed back bitter bile. She stared at Elijah, mottled grey and lifeless, as Adelia stroked the coarse red hairs on his arm, tracing over the knots of scar tissue and hard scabs on his knuckles. Jim was right, his face was unmarred, and Grace was relieved for the small mercy. But oh, how her heart ached for her friend and for the loss of a good man.

At the funeral the next day, Grace walked arm in arm with Adelia to the little graveyard on the downward slope behind the shearing shed. The procession followed behind the neat, white-painted coffin. Jim and five shepherds carried the coffin across their broad shoulders. Four white wooden crosses already inhabited the fenced-off graveyard: Rory Buchanan, a couple of shepherds who had died of fever, and an itinerant shearer who Jim said had slipped with the shears, cutting through the artery between his thumb and forefinger and bleeding to death.

Perfect. Grace wondered if it was appropriate to use this adjective to describe Elijah's funeral, or if just the mere thought of thinking of a funeral in such terms would have her hauled before the gates of Hades. It seemed a lifetime ago since she had buttoned up the front of her black mourning dress, determined to make Elias's funeral a celebration of the life her son had lived, and not the life he had lost.

Earlier this morning, she had pinned a golden wattle flower to Adelia's chest and one to hers. "Golden like the sunshine, and warm like Elijah's happiness."

Father Blackwood smiled at her across Elijah's coffin. He was rotund, bald and sweaty, but his gentle eyes filled with compassion that did not portray sorrow. He was a familiar fixture at all Gilly Downs weddings, christenings, and funerals, called in from Sydney Town to help bless the life events of the souls that inhabited this remote piece of the earth. And he was always ready with just the right words.

"Everyone leaves something behind when they die, be it a painting, a handsewn garment, or a garden full of flowers. We must live our lives so that when we touch something, it changes from the way it was into something we can leave behind. Elijah Barclay has touched us, in our hearts, and left us with his love. When we look at the love his wife and children have for him, we see him there, in their love for him, and in their love for one another."

He uttered other sentiments, but none branded Grace's soul like these. She dutifully sang *Amazing Grace*, just as she had at Gilly's rocky graveside in Port Famine all those years back, the words automatically forming in her mouth from a lifetime of repetition. But it was the sight of dozens of fuzzy orbs of golden wattles raining down on the coffin that she would remember forever. The children had gathered the flowers, and now, with a shower of tiny yellow blooms, Elijah's coffin was coated in a sweet scent that reminded her of vanilla bark.

"A penny for yer thoughts." Jim Buchanan's voice edged into her contemplation like a welcome hug. "What has ye smiling so prettily there, lass?"

"Wattles." She widened her smile.

"Och, aye. 'Tis a grand gesture. I think the bairns took their lead from that bonnie wee flower upon yer chest." He nodded at the furry head of flowers pinned under her collar.

Grace soaked up the warmth in his familiar brown gaze. "I wanted to remember today with none of the numbness. I don't want to be sad. I used to be afraid that if I remembered Elias, it would hurt too much, so I held on to those memories." She turned to Jim, peering at him earnestly. "But Jim, my heart is so full of memories it's bursting at the seams. They don't belong inside. They're meant to be freed and shared. I want to remember my boy, talk about him. Eddy does it with such ease. I want that same comfort." She glanced over at Adelia hanging from Victor Shyling's arm. "We must all keep Squatter Barclay's memories alive."

Jim coughed and swiped his thumb under his eyelid to catch the falling tear. He pressed his fist to his mouth, taking quaking breaths. He blinked. The tears spilled, and he let them. "Crivens, ye're the bravest lass I know."

She caught the tear about to drip off his chin and, studying the moistened tip of her finger, curled it into a protective fist. "That means a lot to me, Jim. Thank you."

Jim roughly scoured his hand down his face, his eyes framed with long damp eyelashes still clumped by residual tears. "They say God only gives yer what ye can manage, aye? I couldn't have watched ye grieve yer lad without it tearing me to shreds."

"I've made my peace with it," said Grace with a nostalgic smile.

Jim shook his head firmly, his straight black hair flicking over his wide ears. "Ye've more forgiveness in yer little finger than I have in my whole being. I wouldn't be able to give God that much after all He's put you through."

Grace glanced down at the coffin again. "I was blessed with a husband able to share the weight of it with me." She looked up, his brown eyes clear in the bright sunshine. "And friends, like you, who are like honey in a bitter cup of tea." She squeezed his elbow. "Excuse me. I must accompany Mrs Barclay back to the house."

Walking around the gaping hole in the earth, Grace looped her arm through Adelia's. The dark-haired shepherd respectfully stepped away. Her friend's breath quivered as she leaned in. "Mr Barclay is the first family interred here, but he shan't be the last. I'm determined to stay on at Gilly Downs."

Grace squeezed her arm and smiled. "There'll be plenty of time to sort that out later. Come on, let's head to the shade of the house."

In the parlour, neighbouring graziers paid their respects, sitting and drinking tea or sherry and eating Cook's tomato sandwiches and sponge cake. It was a stiff and formal affair, but up at the shearing shed, the shepherds, station hands, and servants of Gilly Downs celebrated their master's life in style with plenty of food, drink, and dancing—full of life, just the way it should be. Grace smiled at a particularly loud, drunken yodel that screeched across the valley, drowning out the confident, bright tune of a violin.

She gripped the sherry bottle tighter as she replenished Mr Potts' glass. "I must thank you for your part in my acquittal, Mr Potts."

The flush-faced grazier dipped his head. "Pity your new free-dom's been marred by this dastardly business."

A dribble of sticky sherry ran down the glass neck and over her fingers. "On the contrary, sir. I'm thankful to have the liberty to attend my friend in her time of need."

A horse neighed outside the open window, and Grace drew the crisp lace curtain aside with one finger to inspect the late arrival. She frowned as three horses approached, their hooves disturbing the carriage circle's newly raked gravel. A smartly dressed man, more suitably attired for a business meeting than a funeral, was accompanied by two constables. Neatly dismount-ing, the man unstrapped a leather case from his saddle, his head sweeping in a slow arc across the valley. What on earth was he looking at? The two constables tethered their horses to the hitching post.

Grace glanced at Adelia perched on the settee edge beside Mrs Deas Thomson, nodding mutely at the awkward attempts of well-wishers. She would do anything to see her friend in a perfectly practical cotton work dress, reeking of sweat, damp wool, and sheep dung, rather than in these wretched widow's weeds.

Potts peered over Grace's shoulder, his hot sherry-breath brushing her cheek. "Ah, Charles Long, Commissioner of Crown Lands. Probably come to pay his respects."

At a sharp knock, Grace opened the front door and smiled in welcome at the stranger. He was neat and compact, with a bristly row of whiskers above his top lip that reminded her of Surgeon Beynon from the *Discerning*, except Long's were speckled with grey. All that was missing were the round spectacles. "Mr Long? I'm Mrs Fitzwilliam, a friend of the family. Do come in."

Long blinked in surprise, then bowed. "Your servant, madam."

She gestured towards Adelia. "Mrs Barclay is receiving condolences on the settee."

"Condolences?"

Grace hesitated. "Yes. Squatter Barclay has passed. An accident in the recent storm."

Long inhaled a deep breath that swelled his chest. "Ah, an utter tragedy of which I was unaware."

Skirts rustled beside her as Adelia and Mrs Deas Thomson stepped up.

"Mr Long," greeted Mrs Deas Thomson. "Have you come to pay your respects?"

"No, madam. I'm here on business." Long inclined his head. "Squatter Barclay would have been expecting me—I sent a letter a month back. I was unaware of his misfortune."

Mrs Deas Thomson scooped her hand beneath Adelia's elbow. "Adelia, dear, this is Mr Long, the new Commissioner of Crown Lands."

The wan smile plastered to Adelia's face faltered. "Commissioner, welcome to Wooloongilly Downs."

Long pulled at his cream collar edged with dirt and sweat. "My sympathies for your loss, madam." He motioned to the two constables. "My escorts, Constable Herman and Constable Dwyer."

Grace swallowed deeply. Bleeding bloody rats' tails. It was the one-eyed constable who had kept her prisoner in her own home. If the man recognised her, he did not let it show, but his presence unsettled her. Why did the commissioner require an escort? Protection on the ride over, perhaps?

Long's eyes hooded with remorse. "Deepest apologies for the inopportune timing. Had I known of your circumstances, I would have postponed my arrival."

Mrs Deas Thomson tightly clasped her hands before her. "I hope that's true, Commissioner. I can only imagine Mr Deas Thomson's response to his land commissioners harassing grieving widows."

Long drew his shoulders down, his bristly whiskers

stretching in a tight line. "Of course not, madam. I shall take my leave—"

Adelia swept a hand over her forehead and squeezed her eyes shut. "No, no. You're here now. Please, step into the library." She turned, calling over her shoulder, "My maid will see your constables receive refreshments."

The open library windows let in a pleasant breeze fragranced by dry grass and minty eucalyptus. Adelia sank into Elijah's chair behind the desk, and Grace stood beside her, one hand settling on her shoulder. Mrs Deas Thomson lowered herself into the chair opposite Adelia.

Commissioner Long peered out through the open windows at the valley of Gilly Downs with its wooden bridge crossing the creek. His roving inspection scoured the lay of the land, and his eyes flicked perceptively. "There have been some improvements since the last commissioner's visit." He pointed to the new log huts clustered around their own bulging vegetable patches. "What are those over there?"

"That's where the new shepherds and their families live," said Adelia.

"Married quarters, eh?" Long's eyelids narrowed, and he nodded approvingly. "I'll require a closer look at those."

Adelia's shoulders stiffened. "Of course."

"Everything going well on the grazing front?" he inquired casually.

"Yes." Adelia's tone was clipped, but she elaborated, "We've made improvements to the sheep wash down there in the creek."

Long's head swung away again, humming as he strained his chin towards the crude wooden structure of fences and ramps running in one end of the creek and out further along. "Must have a bit of a look at that too."

Grace inclined her head. "I'm sure the station manager, Mr Buchanan, will happily show you around." Jim's voice echoed in her head. *Typical toff, pushing yer stuck-up nose where it doesn't belong.* She adjusted her smile into a pout of interest. "Had the previous commissioner seen the men's quarters?"

Long regarded Grace shrewdly. "No, but I assume that's it across the valley?" He pointed to the long dormitory hut. "Where's the station manager's hut? I must have missed it."

Adelia's chin lifted. "It's the old homestead below. Mr Barclay didn't deem it necessary to build another hut when there was a perfectly good cabin to be used."

The commissioner gave the non-committal blink of a consummate professional, without a hint of admiration or disapproval. Grace thought his performance before the Colonial Secretary's wife was commendable, and it made him as hard to read as a book of bloody braille!

Mrs Deas Thomson leaned forward. "Mrs Barclay has guests awaiting, Commissioner. I must ask you to state your business."

"I beg your pardon, madam, for diving into the impersonal world of business and finance at such a time." Long lowered himself into the chair beside Mrs Deas Thomson and ran his forefinger across the length of his whiskered top lip. He looked at Adelia. "You were acquainted with Commissioner Gordon, my predecessor?"

"Indeed. He dined with us on many occasions."

"Then you know it's my duty to prevent unauthorised occupation of Crown land?"

"Mr Barclay had his affairs in ship-shape order with Commissioner Gordon. I've the grazier's licence to Gilly Downs to prove it."

Long hummed as he lifted his case onto his lap. Unbuckling the strap, he lifted the leather flap to expose neatly segmented rows inside. With a crisp crinkling, he withdrew a piece of paper and laid it on the desk. He flipped the flap closed and lowered the case to his feet. His long finger, with an arthritically bent tip, tapped the paper. "This licence gives permission for these ten thousand acres of Crown land to be occupied and worked."

Adelia pulled a matching piece of paper from the top drawer. "I'm aware. I have my copy."

"Madam, the licence was issued to *Squatter Barclay*—not to the station itself."

"He left all to me in his will."

"That may be so, madam, but he didn't own this land. It belongs to the Crown. He was simply leasing it."

Adelia's slim brows drew together. "I beg to differ, sir. I have the title deed authorised by Commissioner Gordon himself."

Long's bushy whiskers twitched. "It's an unauthorised document with no legal standing. Crown land can't be privately owned."

Adelia blanched. "But Mr Barclay paid a considerable sum to Commissioner Gordon for the purchase of the five acres upon which Barclay Hall sits. You can confirm this with Mr Gordon."

Grace widened her eyes at Mrs Deas Thomson. "Is this true? The land can't be privately owned?"

Mrs Deas Thomson's brow crumpled. "It is, but therein lies a deeper problem." She bowed her head and took in a deep breath. "Mr Gordon duped several squatters in this regard."

Gasping, Grace squeezed Adelia's shoulder and shot Mrs Deas Thomson a stern look. "And just *what* is your husband doing about this scoundrel?"

Before she could answer, Commissioner Long's fingers drummed the desk like a snare drum. "Unfortunately, there is little the Colonial Secretary can do, since the crook has absconded to India."

Adelia huffed through her nose. "Very well. Then transfer the licence into my name. Or do you require a new lease? I'd be happy to sign one."

Mrs Deas Thomson's face fell, and her shoulders slumped. "Oh, my dear, a woman can't be granted a licence."

Adelia's smooth-skinned face, marred only by the dark rings beneath her eyes, was set in a mask of serenity. Through the intimacy of their friendship, Grace caught the slight flare of her nostrils and tremor in her hands, minor signs lost on the uninitiated man opposite.

Adelia clasped her hands before her on the desk. "Commissioner Long, I'm more than qualified to run Gilly Downs. My knowledge matches that of Mr Barclay." She scraped back her chair and retrieved a hefty ledger from the bookshelf. She thumbed it open and spun it around to face the commissioner.

"We've sold all the wool from the last season, and here"— she slid out a writing-filled sheet of paper from the back of the ledger—"is a contract for the next consignment of wool to be shipped to London with the Elias Shipping Company." She stabbed a cracked finger, ingrained with earth and hard work, at a row of numbers. "Those figures show Wooloongilly Downs' tidy profit last year. If it's the proceeds of assessment of stock you're here to collect, then rest assured because I have those ready for you."

Long's intelligent gaze darted about the ledger's double-page spread. "These are indeed impressive figures. However, your knowledge isn't in question, madam." His tone of neutrality was beginning to irritate Grace. "The government—"

Adelia's eyes narrowed, and she slapped her palms on the desk, her calloused fingers fanning across the yellowed licence.

"*The government*"—she pronounced the word as though it were a dose of quinine in her mouth—"is full of corrupt bastards like Gordon who steal from hard-working citizens. *The government* takes its disproportionate share of rent money from us squatters, but is quick to neglect our welfare out here. Despite the insecurity of tenure constantly hanging over our head, my husband and I had enough faith to invest our own money to make improvements to this godforsaken land." She waved her hand around the plush library, her voice rising a notch above conversation level. "We had no help from *the government* with the logistics of getting our wool to the docks, or even securing transport to London. This we managed thanks to other brave entrepreneurial souls like the Fitzwilliams. And despite all this, I'm *still* prepared to face the drought, ticks, wild dogs, noxious plants, fluke and footrot, all of which try to kill my only source of income on a daily basis!"

Good gracious, if Adelia's outburst shocked the commissioner, he did a splendid job of hiding it. Grace folded her arms.

Adelia shuffled to the edge of her seat, her voice rising to a screech. "So, forgive me for not being as sympathetic to *the government*'s poxy bloody laws that seem designed to crush the hope and spirit of every back-country squatter who has the misfortune to call this country home!" Her voice cracked on the last word, and she panted hard as though she had just run up from the creek at full tilt.

Mrs Deas Thomson rose and came around the desk. "Oh, my dear, it's not Commissioner Long's fault." She slid her arm across Adelia's shoulders, bringing her head down to meet hers. "It's the wretched law."

Wordlessly, Commissioner Long reached down for his case again. With the same unhurried motion, he opened the flap and withdrew a second document. Grace clenched her molars. The man was so dry he made a sheep's salt lick look like an ice block. Stinking seaweed, his professional control reminded her so much of Seamus's ability to remain calm under fire—a quality that exasperated her beyond belief, especially when she wanted him to flare up and fight back.

His grey eyes hardened like lumps of charred coal, though he affected a tone of sympathy. "You make a valid case, madam, but unfortunately, as Mrs Deas Thomson has stated, the law is the law." He slid the crisp piece of paper across the desk with his arthritic finger. "You're hereby given ninety days to vacate this land, including your livestock. After ninety days, said livestock will be considered unlicensed and shall be confiscated and made Crown property. Perhaps your station manager can negotiate a good price for your sheep with the new grazier?"

Grace thrust her hands on her hips. "Hold a minute! What sort of a man evicts a new widow from her home—especially one whose proceeds keep the likes of *you* in employ!"

Long slowly raised one shoulder. "I like to think I'm a gracious man, and in light of your acquaintance with Mrs Deas Thomson, ninety days is thirty more than I normally grant." His knobbed fingers fumbled with the buckle of his bag, and he rose smoothly. "I shan't keep you from your guests any longer, Mrs Barclay. I can see myself out."

Grace cut Adelia's indignant squeak short with a cry of her own. Ha! Blasted official was as useful as a wet piece of toast! Now she bloody-well knew why he travelled with a police escort —to save him being shot by vexed graziers!

Chapter Twenty

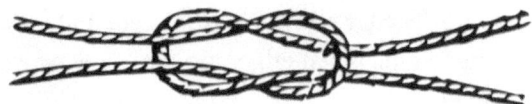

VERSAILLES, FRANCE, 8 *MAY* 1842

S eamus frowned at the crunch of coal grit between his molars and aimed towards the thrumming pulse of the firebox and billowing funnels of the two leading engines. Grinding his teeth, he shuffled through the throng of second-class passengers, all jostling to fill the open-topped wagons. The engines' snorts and hisses disappeared as he gripped the brass handrail and swung himself into the first-class carriage. Christ, it was no less crowded in here! Sidling along the narrow, carpeted passageway, he glanced into each cabin, frowning at the press of humanity that barely offered one seat, let alone four.

He sucked in his belly as he squeezed past a waif-thin Parisienne in an immaculate sapphire satin gown. "Excuse me, Madame." He tipped his hat.

The first-class damsel squeaked and, stepping up on her toes, pressed her back against the wood panelling. She blushed, her gloved hands fondling the red ruby dangling at her throat. Her sweet scent curled up his nostrils, and he sucked deeply at the heady fragrance. By Neptune's trident, she smelled like Grace— all lavender powder and femininity. He shivered, his flesh puckering in a wave of desire. Of all the vivid dreams he had of his wife, her scent was the one thing missing. He glanced over his shoulder with a ludicrous hope that Grace was just behind him. His heart hitched a beat—only his three companions followed. The aged droop of Baxter's brow and the red spider veins on his cheeks had softened his naval edge, though his eyes were as alert and caring as ever.

As though transformed by an artist's paintbrush, the woman's tight brow softened into a pique of interest as a second gentleman stepped past. Max Delisle, assistant to the British Undersecretary of State for the Colonies, and cousin of one of Baxter's war-time acquaintances, flashed his white teeth at her. Billy Sykes also sidled past her, tipping his pale straw boater, his grin equally charming.

With little patience for such female foibles, especially ones that only twisted his longing for Grace, Seamus frowned—if he did not find them a seat soon, they would blazing-well stand all the way to Paris! He sucked in a breath of annoyance, and oil- and coal-scented steam clung wetly to the inside of his nostrils. The last cabin was empty and, snorting in triumph, he grinned back at his fellow travellers. "In here!"

The private compartment would give him and Delisle a chance to finalise the details of his newest endeavour. With the *Elias* well run and with favourable winds, he had made the wool sales in plenty of time. Having already secured the services of Captain Harry McKay, master of the Elias Shipping Company's newest packet, *Saviour of the Seas*, he was set to add the immigrant trade to his shipping fleet. Goods were not the only commodity in high demand in New Holland—people were too, especially single women.

Sliding onto the maroon upholstered bench, Seamus pressed

his shoulder against the soot-streaked window and expectantly glanced around. Baxter barrelled in after Delisle and Sykes. Baxter and Delisle deposited their hats on the racks above and settled on the opposite bench. Sykes dropped beside Seamus and nudged the brim of his boater higher.

A piercing steam whistle announced their departure, and Seamus pressed his forehead to the cool glass as the conductors locked the outer carriage doors with a reassuring thud. Good! No further bodies to press their way into the packed compartment.

Already headed to Paris on government business, Delisle had invited Seamus, Baxter, and Sykes to join him. While this detour delayed Seamus's return to Grace by a couple of months, Baxter had persuaded him that having Delisle's ear in London was even more effective than having that of the Colonial Secretary himself. Just as servants were blindly made privy to the sauciest scandals of society through their invisibility, so were underling government clerks, especially those with personal ties to French statesmen. Young Delisle was visionary, believing that cordiality with the French freed Britain's diplomatic hand in other parts of the world.

In honour of king Louis Philippe I's saints day, the summer-long public celebration included waterworks and fireworks in the gardens of the Palace of Versailles. Delisle had insisted they go, and he'd insisted they stay until the last fountain stopped playing.

"What a magnificent day!" Baxter dropped beside Delisle, puffing like the loud engines outside, his face flushed from the brisk walk to Versailles-Rive Gauche Station.

"Breathtaking, indeed, sir," Seamus replied.

Delisle rubbed his hands together. "The Latona fountain with the golden frogs is utterly charming, is it not? It's marvellous how the water dances in time with the orchestra."

"I preferred the statues—*magnificent* works of art." Baxter harrumphed, and his double chin jumped with the cough as he waggled his grey eyebrows at Seamus. "Hmm, wouldn't mind one or two of those pieces back at Wallace House."

"Indeed, sir." Seamus nodded, glancing past his sun-pinkened reflection in the window to the countryside rolling by. With the sun dipping below the horizon, the long shadows of late afternoon disappeared, and the silhouettes of buildings and trees flicked past quicker in the dark. "We're making good speed."

"God bless the advances of industry, hey, my boy?" Baxter patted Seamus's knee.

Beside Seamus, Sykes frowned. "Nothing wrong with a horse and carriage. This train is all smoke and noise—like a great iron dragon gobbling up humans."

Flicking the sides of his jacket back and leaning forward, Baxter chuckled. "Come now, Dr Sykes. I'd have thought a scientific man like yourself would embrace the advancements of engineering. Would you rather we remain in the dark ages?"

Sykes's black bushy brows tightened. "Man was not intended to travel at such speeds. Rather reckless and dangerous, if you ask me."

Smiling as the skin on Sykes's hand tightened in a fist, Seamus assured him, "We're moving no faster than a horse at full gallop."

"I'd rather canter than gallop. I'd also prefer holding my own reins." Sykes adjusted his boater further back on his head. "It bodes well that the *Saviour of the Seas* relies on wind power rather than on steam."

Delisle undid his coat buttons and wriggled back comfortably. "The passengers might thank you for a more expedient migration across the oceans, Dr Sykes. It might negate the plague of the sea appearing in unholy numbers." He scrunched up his nose.

Sykes extended his legs, crossing his ankles. "The plague of the sea is the least of the immigrant's worries, sir. Typhus fevers hold greater concern." He raised both palms upwards. "Though I shall affect a thorough screening of all passengers before embarkation."

Rubbing the tip of his nose, Delisle sniffed. "Colonial society's welcome of immigrant ships has been more than a little prickly of late. Even the earlier convicts attracted less critique."

"Dr Sykes's presence aboard should allay all concerns," said Seamus. "These women and children are simply escaping the punitive circumstances of poverty. Most should arrive familiar with hard labour and come bearing spades of grit."

"Hear, hear," boomed Baxter. He tapped Sykes's shoe with his own. "Though it'll require more than medical skill to gauge the moral temperament and cleanliness of those wretched creatures."

"A challenge gladly accepted." Sykes dipped his chin.

Seamus was confident having an experienced surgeon along for the voyage would ensure the immigrants' health. Captain McKay's wife had also assured him she would secure the women's comfort and protection. "If the *Saviour*'s departure is delayed, the Elias Shipping Company will provide additional food, so the passengers don't expend their own supplies before even leaving England's shores."

Delisle grunted. "A generous offer, Fitzwilliam. Few private immigration entrepreneurs make such concession."

Seamus clicked his wrist. "No point in the investment if the commodity arrives unfit for duty—or worse still, dead." He stretched out his legs and nodded at Sykes. "The *Saviour* shouldn't be that far behind the *Elias*'s arrival in Sydney Town. Unless she's caught in the doldrums, of course. You'll be in fine hands under Captain McKay's command."

The train's lulling motion sedated his sun-drenched body, and he drooped against the window in companionable silence while Delisle and Baxter prattled on about the virtue and validity of Benjamin Morrell's discovery of New South Greenland. He rubbed his face briskly to revive himself. Ha! They were sitting inside an engineering marvel! He might even find Sykes's mistrust of the mechanical amusing were he not so distracted by thoughts of Grace.

The ache of missing her impaled him like a lance. Christ knew he had made a miserable companion all these months —likely something his crew would not thank him for. Had he predicted how miserable life would be without his wife by his side, he would have worked harder on his persuasion to bring her along. Sykes's cough drew him from his thoughts.

"Mrs F. would delight in the music and palace gardens."

"Indeed," agreed Seamus. "Now knowing their true splendour, I must bring her here when she next returns to London." *If* she ever returned to London.

This would be the last time he sailed without her. Heavens knew how he would coax her along the next time but, by Neptune, he would not relent until she did. The bilious roll in his gut that had struck when he stepped from the carriage at Semi-Circular Quay had not abated this entire time. He had not enjoyed a meal since.

He frowned at Baxter and Delisle, their circular debate irking him. Who the devil cared whether some American sealing captain had or had not spotted land so far south? It was hardly a viable shipping route anyway. Ignoring them, he pressed his lips and turned back to Sykes. "You've known Grace longer than I, perhaps you can shed some light on how to untangle that wilful knot of hers? Persuade her along next time." He was not in the habit of discussing the state of his marriage, though if there was anyone with whom he consulted about such matters, it was Dr Sykes.

Sykes cocked his head. "I'm but a doctor, sir. You're the mariner with the skill for untangling ropes."

Seamus laughed. "Snarled rigging is easier to untangle than my wife's reasoning."

Sykes offered a half smile. "Tell me, sir, what's it like when you're lost at sea after a storm?"

"At first, one has no idea where one is," admitted Seamus wryly. "The ship could be miles off course."

"Have you ever doubted your navigation skills would lead you to safety, and ultimately bring you home?"

"Not for a minute."

"Then perhaps you might invest in that same faith to navigate your life. You're simply caught in a storm, but it'll pass, just as all of life's struggles pass. You've endured many a storm." Sykes's soothing tone eased Seamus's annoyance.

He rolled his wrist and flexed his fingers as it clicked again. "It's easier navigating one's own ship than finding another lost at sea. We're on passing ships, my wife and I."

"I'm no expert in such matters, sir, but I reckon it takes a sturdy soul to love, and an even sturdier one to love after it has been damaged," said Sykes. He leaned closer, lowering his voice. "Together, you and Mrs F. have survived the worst torture a soul can endure—the loss of a child. If you'd taken her from Emily and Edwin, she'd have fought you till the day you both dropped with fatigue. Half the challenge for her is the pushback. It always has been." He huffed through his nose, his lips turning up in a gentle smile. "You gave her the freedom to sail her own course. When she's spent, she'll come back to her homeport—to you—to rest. As she always does."

Sykes was taking a courageous gamble to air these opinions out loud, especially since they were not his grievances to bear. Then again, he had asked for the man's view. Releasing the air from his lungs, Seamus slumped against the backrest. He massaged his scarred wrist and laughed lightly. "How has an affirmed bachelor, such as yourself, become so wise in the ways of love?" He frowned at the dark panelling, focussing on the dim light of the oil lamps throwing warbling shadows. The longer he stared, the wider the arcs became, like a ship in heavier seas before an impending storm. How could a carriage set on iron rails create such sway?

Sykes clasped his fingers comfortably in his lap. "I've sat beside enough death beds to know regret when I see it. The wisdom comes not from me, but from others who realised too little too late. I—"

The carriage lurched violently, slamming the back of Seamus's head into the panel behind. The air thickened with a fantastical drag of time, the carriage nose tipping up as Delisle dived forward. His mouth, gaping with the start of a scream, was silenced as it smashed into Seamus's chest with a pulpy, fleshy thud and a sharp crack. Blasted Hell! Was that the man's neck? A second jolt pressed him back into his seat. Heaven help, they were tipping up! Screeches and crunches of metal ricocheted through the carriage like the big guns' echoing retorts during a broadside as a second, then third violent lurch cracked his head against the window and threw Delisle off him. With the suddenness of its beginning, the mayhem ended. Seamus's initial relief at the standstill morphed into a flooded panic of breathlessness and disorientation. How could he be lying on his back but still be seated? A lone female wail led other voices in a crescendo of screams.

Gasping, he gripped his chest, afraid to look down in case Delisle's head had torn open his old scar. For pity's sake—the billows of smoke, angry hisses of steam, and screams of death belonged in the midst of battle, not on a leisurely Sunday train ride through the blasted French countryside. Finding no blood or fragments of bone beneath his tentatively probing fingertips, he coughed, then sucked in a gasp of the sooty air. One oil lamp still burned, spreading fragmented light across the cabin at odd angles. The bench opposite him—or rather, above him—was empty. Baxter! Delisle!

A low groan beside him drew his gaze across. Delisle lay across Sykes's lap, his face looking like it had met the full brunt of an iron skillet. Blood pasted his brown hair to his forehead, above which the white of skull flashed through the red-lipped wound. Delisle's nose was a purple, misshapen mess, his eyes coated shut by the blood. Seamus patted the young man's thigh, blinking in confusion at the man's extra pair of skewed legs. Sweet Christ in Heaven, they were Baxter's legs!

"Baxter?" Seamus croaked.

The old man's torso hung limply through the smashed hallway window. Dreadful moans mingled with the ping and creak of buckled metal settling. Seamus drew his feet onto the cushioned bench with a grunt and, clinging to the hat rack with tingling fingers, balanced on the awkwardly angled seat. It was as though his shoes were soled with lead. A flicker in the corner of his eye drew his attention to the cracked window beneath him. Shit! Their carriage perched atop the mountain of twisted engines and carriages, and shadows of men scurried up, scrambling to the peak. Far below, glowing dots of burning coals fanned out as far as he could see. The smell of hot iron, dirty coal smoke, and roasting flesh reawakened the nerves in his fingers and toes. Fire! The piercing shrieks of agony swelled into cries for help.

He drove his heel into the cracked glass, and it splintered with a sharp tinkling. "Delisle. Get up, man! Get out." Seamus grabbed Delisle's collar and thrust him towards the opening.

Delisle swiped his sleeve across his eyes and blinked thickly through his clotted lashes. "Jesus, Fitzwilliam! What happened?"

"We've derailed. Move, before the fire takes hold."

Delisle swayed dangerously. Heaven help, he would be no use helping carry Baxter out. At least the clerk was ambulatory, even if a little wobbly. Seamus calculated the admiral's position, scowling at Baxter's immobile, black-trousered rump. By Heavens, the man was quite a size these days. He would undoubtedly require Sykes's help. Seamus peered down at the smashed window. Would Baxter even fit? And if he did, could he manage him to the bottom of this mangled mess? A cold slick of realisation coated his nape. Grace would never forgive him if he could not swear he had done his utmost to save Baxter. She also would not thank *him* for dying in the process.

Black, streaked arms reached through the window, accompanied by garbled French yelling.

"Delisle, step down," ordered Seamus. "They have hold of you."

Delisle blinked, his puffy eyes mere slits that would likely be swelled shut before he reached the ground. Seamus's stomach clenched as he released his grip on the man's slim wrist, and Delisle sank into the scrabbling hands.

"Sykes! Help me!" Seamus bellowed, grabbing the admiral's belted waist and heaving. Sweet Heavens, he was wedged tight. Was he even alive? Thickening clouds of smoke billowed up from the pyre below. Coughing, Seamus grabbed Baxter with both hands and, steadying one foot on the window frame, strained back. He roared as the pain in his sternum nearly cleaved him in two. "Come on, you bastard!" Gasping, he released his grip and stumbled back, clamping his arms across the searing agony in his chest.

Sykes clambered across the seats and grabbed Baxter's waist. With a strength that belied his size, he scraped the old man back through the narrow window. Seamus winced as Baxter's clothes and skin snagged on the jagged glass. With a loud grunt, the doctor bent his knees and slung Baxter over his shoulder.

"I have him," he hissed through gritted teeth. Easing through the window with Baxter, Sykes flicked his head, gesturing for Seamus to follow. Ignoring the tug of jagged glass on his own skin, Seamus lowered himself to the upturned side of the carriage below and followed Sykes's bobbing straw hat down through the twisted sheets of metal and splintered wood panels. Smoke filled his lungs and burned his eyes, and coughing sent fresh throbs through his chest.

On firm ground, Sykes sprinted over to a clearing where uniformed railway guards attended the injured. Laying Baxter down as gently as possible, Sykes turned and disappeared back into the impossibly hot, billowing inferno.

"Sykes! No! Get back here," hollered Seamus.

Beside him, Delisle, almost blinded by his swollen eyelids, was clearly not yet ready to collapse either. He helped Seamus drag Baxter further up the embankment. With his hands on his hips, Seamus sucked shallow breaths through clenched teeth, each one snagging on a pinch of pain. He peered up at the colossal, blazing heap of carriages piled above the two engines—fire and damnation! It was a blessed miracle they were alive.

High up, two young men clung desperately to the ruins of a shattered carriage. One found footing against a carriage wheel and disengaged himself from the tangle. The other fell, arms and legs windmilling—swallowed up by the lapping tongues of flame. The wind swirled around the burning carriages like a wolf circling its prey, and the fanned flames flared in defiant response. Seamus wanted to cover his ears against the renewed shrieks of burning passengers. Instead, he dropped to his knees beside Baxter and shook the man's shoulders.

"Sir, wake up. Wake up!"

The admiral lay on his back, arms dropped to his sides. Barring a couple of nicks on his forehead, his mask of serenity could almost be of a man in prayer. Seamus ran his hands over the mound of Baxter's belly, reaching around his hips to his back. No blood. Shuffling down, he patted the two splayed legs. No apparent breaks. Why the devil was he not rousing? Scrambling on his hands and knees back up to Baxter's head, Seamus dropped his ear to the admiral's chest. Above the roar of panic, a woman's shrieks, shrill and deafening, doused any chance of him hearing a heartbeat. *Christ Almighty, hush up, will you!* He glared around at the culprit.

A woman in a veiled bonnet flailed as she pivoted back and

forth at the hips, her legs pinned between two carriages. She writhed in agony, calling, screeching, pleading for help. A crowd of villagers and passengers surged forward, only to be beaten back by the furnace raging around her. Several of the younger men tried again—and failed. The fire lapped closer, and the woman raised her arms and eyes heavenwards, her cries dying to silence. She lowered her hands and covered her face as the flames flicked higher. Seamus stared in horror as the inferno slowly consumed her dress and white scarf. *Sweet mercy! Someone end her suffering!* Her veil and bonnet blackened as, immovable and without uttering a cry, she surrendered to Hell. How was Sykes to survive that?

A hand gripped his shoulder, and he jerked towards it with a sob. Delisle's swollen face was a mask of grief. "Devilishly sorry, Fitzwilliam. Looks like the Admiral's cruise is up."

"No!" Seamus wrenched Baxter's shirtfront open and buried his ear in the curly grey chest hair. Squeezing his eyes shut and pressing his hand to his other ear, he held his breath—listening—waiting. The Admiral smelled familiar, woody tobacco mingled with clean sweat, remnants of their day of pleasure in the hot sun. It could not be. This man he had known for a lifetime, a man who had saved his life *twice*, could not be gone. Behind Seamus's eyelids, the flashes of flames became flashes of musket fire—of Baxter up on the pirate's quarterdeck with a smoking rifle that had felled Seamus's attacker—of the ringing in his right ear and puff of gunpowder curling over his shoulder as Baxter stopped Silverton's advance at the duel. This new silence in Baxter's chest, more terrifying than any attack Seamus had ever faced, turned the blood in his veins into a thousand silver shards.

Nothing.

No breath.

No beat.

Nothing.

He fell heavily to his buttocks and sunk his head in his

hands, his fingers snagging on singed clumps of hair. Deep gasps burst from the pit of his lungs and punched the inside of his bruised sternum. *Admiral, forgive me!*

A tin cup appeared before his bowed face. Water! He glanced up as a young peasant woman with a blue kerchief thrust the tin at him again. He threw it back in three gulps. Heavens, he could devour a bucketful right now! A uniformed train guard scurried past. Seamus rose and, snatching the official's arm, fired off in furious French, "Where's the water? Why aren't you dousing the fire?" He jabbed a finger at the woman's water bucket.

The soot-streaked guard shrugged. "There's none available, sir."

The young woman approached. "I brought this from the village well." She averted her gaze from the fiery wreckage. "It's all I have."

Seamus urgently scanned the towering inferno. Where the devil was Sykes? The firelight's macabre glow lit the pale faces pressed up against the windows, hands clawing ineffectually against the glass. The guilt of their demise threatened to crush the precious little bits of air he managed to suck into his bruised chest. He should be up there, saving them. A waft of smoke taunted him, and he coughed. By Neptune's forked trident! He gripped his chest. Even if he could navigate the fire, his injury rendered him absolutely bloody useless! The flames flickered higher than the top carriage, and he turned his back.

In all his thirty-nine years on earth, he had never experienced such helplessness as he did right now. A blackened man approached with a burned sack slung over his shoulders, the fabric dangling in burnt tatters like tobacco leaves hung to dry. The trembling firelight flickered across two charred legs. Sweet merciful Christ! It was a woman, her leathery flesh dark like smoked hams in a butcher's window. Thank Heavens she was not awake with burns like those. He glanced at the man. *Sykes!*

Sykes's hat, still perched on his head, was blackened and

knocked at a jaunty angle. The wide whites of his eyes glowed in the firelight, and his tears, bleeding away the toxic ash, cut two pale streaks down his cheeks. He looked like a man possessed. He lowered his latest charge to the ground with trembling arms, then twirled towards the chaos again. Seamus held out a hand that caught his friend across the chest.

Swaying, Sykes attempted to press Seamus's hand aside. "Just one more." His words slurred wearily into one another.

Gesturing for the blue-scarfed villager to hand him another cup of water, Seamus pressed his hand more firmly against Sykes's chest. "You've done well, my friend." He swallowed the thick sludge of ash and saliva. What he would not do for another slug of water! The tin cup trembled in his hand as he held it out to his ship's surgeon. "It's enough."

"I don't fear the fire." Sykes blinked slowly, black sludge bulging in the corners of his eyes.

"It's enough," repeated Seamus.

The doctor's arms slumped to his side, the water ignored.

Seamus stared silently at the female victim beside Baxter. With a churning twist in his gut, his breath caught in his raw throat at the red glint of ruby embedded in the melted flesh. He sank beside the admiral, resting his palm over the place where one of the most generous and valiant hearts had beaten. What a pitiful end for a decorated naval officer.

Oh, Dulcinea, my heart! The pain in his bruised chest was nothing compared to the thought of penning the admiral's demise to Grace. Her receiving this news without him there to comfort her was tantamount to cruelty. It would be kinder to withhold it and deliver it in person. This decided it—no more delays—it was time to return home.

Chapter Twenty-One

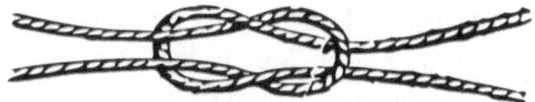

WOOLOONGILLY DOWNS, 1 JUNE 1842

Grace's life settled into the predictable routine of early mornings and a hard day's labour, always followed by a hot, hearty meal before collapsing into a clean, soft bed. The days at Gilly Downs comfortably passed into weeks, easing the ache of missing Seamus.

One cloudless Sunday morning, Grace convinced Adelia to rest. With her pregnancy extending before her, Adelia dug her fingers into her back and groaned as she sank into a white wicker chair on the wide veranda. Soaking up the winter sun, Grace's gaze followed the four Barclay children as they squealed and ran around kicking the sheep's bladder ball. The youngsters' short and uncoordinated legs made for a haphazard game. Unperturbed by their lack of coordination, the four children landed in a tumble of giggles as they wrestled for possession of the ball.

Grace smiled at Gideon's efforts. Despite being disadvantaged by his size, the red-headed lad showed more tenacity, successfully wresting the ball from his older siblings. They were too young to understand the implication of their father's passing, but would they remember him? Grace's concern wavered into sorrow—the child inside Adelia would grow up without even a memory of their father.

Closing her eyes, she wished for Seamus's nearness, her soul needing him like a parched creature craving water. This time away from him was unbearable enough without imagining it being the eternity Adelia was facing. The bush's foreign cacophony pressed in around—a rodent's shrill shriek cut short, the sharp chi-chi of galahs in the towering gum beside the house. A rough, warm hand curled in hers, and she opened her eyes.

Adelia's lips curled, but the smile did not reach her eyes, her silent stare glazed with grief and exhaustion. She had only wept once, after the wake and that wretched commissioner's miserable news. Adelia had allowed Grace to lead her by the hand and slip a nightgown over her head, and she curled up tightly in her arms. Adelia wept, wetting the front of Grace's nightgown with hot agonising gasps of despair. As the night surged forward, Adelia's sobbing had subsided, but Grace had remained wide-eyed and intertwined with her friend as she finally slept.

Now, Grace lowered the sewing basket to the veranda floor, withdrawing her embroidery and the watercolour of the *Elias* anchored before Table Mountain Billy had painted. She studied the ship's sails and held the yellow thread against the watercolour. A fortuitous match! Stitching the painted image to life on the blank mesh of linen stretched over the embroidery hoop was more challenging than she had imagined, but by goodness, she was determined to make a success of it. She would surprise Seamus with it when he returned. She smiled, her husband filling her mind with every stitch, the essence of his presence growing as the *Elias*'s hull took shape in her hands. It was oddly comforting.

Adelia arranged her own embroidery in her lap, her blonde

hair carelessly scraped back and fastened loosely with a ribbon. Her shrunken appetite pronounced the bulge of her midriff more than ever.

The Barclay children moved into the gum tree's dappled shade at the edge of the garden, trying out their new swing Victor Shyling had just hung. The hulking shepherd loped over to help Old Quill dig the drainage ditch along the vegetable patch's outer edge. Victor glanced over at the swing a couple of times, his lips curled in satisfaction.

Adelia sucked in a quivering breath. "Did I ever tell you that Mr Shyling delivered my dear Mr Barclay's last words?"

"He was *there*?" All vestiges of doziness slipped from Grace's body like a silk shroud slithering to the floor, and she shuffled upright.

"Yes. Mr Barclay's message was, 'Tell her she's the best thing that ever happened to me. Tell her not to be consumed by this, but continue to love me through our children.'" Her soft smile wavered. "Mr Shyling brought him back to Barclay Hall." Adelia hesitated. "It wasn't instant, you know? The branch broke his neck, but he remained conscious out there awhile." Her voice withered away on the light breeze. Grace sat motionless, her silence encouraging her friend to continue. "He made Mr Shyling promise to bring him home to me, and to—to look after the children and me. He's a good man."

"He's a shepherd, isn't he?"

"He was a wealthy landowner and sheep farmer in New Zealand."

"He *was*?"

"Only until the British Government voided the sale of land made by the local tribes to all settlers. He lost everything."

Grace harrumphed. "*That* sounds startlingly familiar!" Like bloody Land Commissioners manipulating the law for their own dastardly schemes.

"His eldest daughter died on the voyage over from England.

His youngest succumbed to pertussis, and his wife to tuberculosis. When he also lost his land, he left New Zealand with just the clothes on his back."

Grace clasped a hand to her chest. "How utterly tragic for a man's life to go so wrong."

"Indeed. He came to Australia looking for a life of simplicity, a life of little responsibility. Mr Barclay found him standing outside the old warehouse at Queen's Wharf, head and shoulders taller than everyone else. Recognising a gentleman down on his luck, Mr Barclay struck up a conversation with him. He knew right away that he wanted Mr Shyling's expertise on Gilly Downs. Offered him a job on the spot, though Mr Shyling declined the proposal of manager and settled for being a shepherd."

"Why's he always in the garden then? Shouldn't he be out in the pastures?"

"He's not left my side since bringing Mr Barclay home. He seems intent on keeping his word," said Adelia huskily. "It's a comfort having him about, knowing Mr Barclay trusted him. He barely says two words, but he's always there when I look for him."

Grace squeezed Adelia's hand, then resumed her sewing. Who was she to deprive a grieving widow of comfort, even were it in the hands of another man? Hopefully, a sliver of happy gossip might distract her friend. "Have you heard—Toby and Miss Lissing are to be married?"

Adelia's needle stopped halfway through the meshed material, and her head shot up. Supremely adept in needlework, she was stitching a portrait of Elijah from memory. The wavering orange thread in her needle captured just one of the rich arrays of coppery colours in his fiery thatch of hair.

"I hadn't. What a wonderful surprise."

"Ow! Stinking seaweed!" Grace flinched as she stabbed herself. She sucked the red dot's coppery tang as she dug for her thimble in the basket. Fitting the metal dome snugly over her wounded index finger, she added, "And you know about Jim Buchanan and the girl from the dairy?"

"I do." The smile panning across Adelia's face did not quite reach her soft hazel eyes. Sleepless nights had painted dark rings under her eyelids and extinguished the fire in the gold flecks. "Nevin told me one morning when he brought in the milk urn."

"They're planning a dual wedding." Grace reached for her half-finished cup of tea. Ugh, cold tea! Vile. Grimacing, she slid the cup back on the saucer with a loud clink.

"Wonders will never cease," said Adelia. "Have they set a date?"

Grace shook her head, carefully gauging the authenticity of Adelia's enthusiasm. The last thing she wished was to flaunt too much good news before her widowed friend. "Not that I know."

With an undisputable smile tugging at the corners of her mouth, Adelia bent her head and resumed sewing. Not two stitches in, she dropped her hands to her lap and gasped, jerking upright as though someone had lit a fire under her.

Grace's heart hitched as she stared. Was it the babe? "What's the matter?" Dumping her sewing atop the basket, she leaned forward and gripped Adelia's bony wrist.

Adelia's almond eyes, which only moments before were flat and bloodshot, sparkled. "We should have their wedding *here*— at Gilly Downs. God knows I could do with the diversion. What more delightful distraction is there than planning nuptials?" Excitement edged her voice.

Grace laughed nervously, regarding her friend with a long hard look. By the bells of old Bailey! She was being perfectly serious. "I suppose that's possible. Though you'll have to put the offer to Jim and Toby."

"Of course, of course. I wouldn't want to force their hand, but I can't imagine any reason for them to refuse, can you?" Adelia chuckled.

Grace stared contemplatively at the swaying canopy of tall gums in the distance. A wedding would be lovely. Had she sailed with Seamus, she would have missed the happy occasion. Perhaps this would help her find purpose in her impossible decision to remain behind after all. Blinking, she turned back to her friend's eager face. "Not a one."

Nevin approached on his daily pilgrimage from the vegetable patch to the kitchen, weighed down by a basket laden with tomatoes, skin stretched shining over the ripe, plump flesh. Grace's stomach growled in anticipation at the thought of Cook turning the pulpy fruit into her famous fragranced tomato soup. The youngster exited the kitchen, the empty basket swinging from one hand. Adelia waved him over.

"Morning, missus." Nevin flashed his white teeth. He was the picture of health. His skin kissed golden by the sun, his arms and legs sturdy from labour, and his carefree attitude inherited from his uncle, he was living confirmation that Grace had made the right decision to give Emily and Edwin a chance to bloom in this clime.

"Nevin, have your uncle come up to the house, will you?" said Adelia.

His gaze flicked to Adelia's untouched slice of lemon cake on the table. "Aye. He's just finished re-roofing the shed."

After the storm early in the year, the shepherds had found twisted roof sheets over a mile away. With everyone in town also requiring repairs, there had been a shortage of iron sheeting. This last delivery had arrived only yesterday.

Adelia held out her cake plate. "Take it. Be sure to finish it before you reach the shed." She winked.

"Ta ever so much!" Nevin beamed, scooping up the cake with long, dusty fingers. He darted off before slowing himself with a skip that bought him more time to enjoy his cake.

Little Gideon thumped up the steps, his round face red as a beet. He snatched Adelia's teacup and, draining the dregs, licked the perspiration and tea from his top lip. Wiping his nose with his arm, he tugged at Adelia's skirts. "Up, Mama."

Abandoning her sewing, Adelia swung the child onto her lap and straddled him over her bump. "Ooo, you sweaty little sugar-lump."

Happier with his higher vantage point, Gideon stuck his thumb in his mouth and slid his hand up the back of Adelia's neck, twirling the tumbled-down strands of her blonde hair through his chubby fingers.

"I doubt the babe appreciates this sweetness and light sitting on his head." Grace shook Gideon's soft, pudgy knee. A dozen black sheep droppings rolled from his pocket, scattering across the newly swept veranda.

"Gideon Levi Barclay. How many times must I say it? No. Hoarding. Sheep poo!" Adelia nuzzled her son's neck.

The little boy scrunched his shoulders, squealing in delight. "Raisins!"

"Sheep poo," repeated Adelia, laughing.

Grace grimaced. "Oh, my. Does he—*eat* them?"

Adelia arched one slim eyebrow. "Do you really want the answer to that?"

Giggling, Grace shook her head. "No. It's no worse than when I found Eddy with half an earthworm in his fist. I didn't even ask where the other half was." She gave her friend's belly a wary glance from the corner of her eye. "I'd feel much better if you'd leave the heavy lifting to others."

"Stop being such an old maid." Adelia's words carried no sting as she sank back in the chair.

Grace was relieved. The startled flame of panic in her friend's eyes, of needing to find the next chore or duty to fill the minutes of her day, had dimmed a little further today.

Jim ambled across the crushed-stone carriage circle, his sweat-stained leather hat scrunched in one hand, the other sunk deep into his pocket. Stopping at the veranda's bottom step, he wrenched his hand from his pocket and grasped the floppy brim of his hat in a double grip.

"No need to look so worried, Mr Buchanan," assured Adelia. She waved her arm. "Please, step up into the shade."

"Thank you, milady." The thick leather soles of his boots left dusty footprints up the steps.

"No, no. My thanks to you for the wonderful job you're doing to keep Gilly Downs running."

A wavering half smile, half frown flickered across his face, and he shrugged. "'Tis the least I can do after all you and Squatter Barclay have done for my boy and me." He loosened his grip on his well-worn hat.

"He's a fine boy, your Nevin," said Adelia. "Not afraid of hard work or to get his hands dirty. We're lucky to have him here on Gilly Downs—to have you both."

Jim's wide ears reddened, and he cleared his throat. "Thank you, milady."

"I've heard of the wonderful news of your engagement. Congratulations."

Jim's sweat-pebbled brow drew tight, and he locked his gaze on Grace. Ha! If looks could kill. She bit her bottom lip and waggled her eyebrows at him. Let him believe it was she who had spilled the good tidings to Adelia rather than Nevin.

With his frown not fully dissolved, he turned red-faced to Adelia. "Thank you, kindly."

"Could I tempt you to have your wedding on Gilly Downs?"

Jim's mouth slackened, and he stepped back like someone had pushed him. His fingernails rasped against the shadow of his whiskers.

At his hesitation, Grace added, "Did Pearl not say she desired a country wedding?"

"Aye. 'Tis only we'd planned to share our wedding day with Hicks and Miss Lissing. We're having the wedding at a wee kirk on Church Hill—even if 'tis the ugliest one in Christendom." He cleared his throat again. "As kindly meant as yer offer is, milady, I'll not forsake my friend."

"Jim." Grace rose and took his square, rough hand. "Mrs Barclay's offer is to you *both*."

"Crivens! I don't know what to say." Jim rubbed his nose, his lips twitching, his brown eyes a blank stare. He might be able to talk the legs off an iron pot, but Grace knew he liked to mull over serious considerations one thought at a time. She believed it a vice. He considered it a blessing—said it kept things much simpler in his mind.

Adelia's cheeks pinkened. "Perhaps you'd also like to speak to Pearl about it?"

Jim's eyes narrowed, and he nodded slowly.

Adelia swallowed convulsively. "I know how hard Squatter Barclay's passing has been on everyone. A wedding will do wonders for everyone's spirits, wouldn't you agree?"

Jim's brown eyes warmed, and he tipped his head. "That it would."

"You're welcome to travel into town, to ask Mr Hicks's opinion on the matter," said Adelia.

"Most generous of ye, milady, but I'll not be leaving ye alone at a time like this."

Grace wiggled his hand. "I'll go." She swung her head towards Adelia. "If that's all right with you?" Her innards squeezed like a sheet being pulled through a mangle on wash day. Her guilt at leaving her friend alone on the vast property wrestled with her obligations in town, though it was not so bad with Jim remaining. "I must present myself to the new office— see how Toby's faring. Our new ship, *Quintus Roscius*, should have arrived by now too."

Grace's words halted as Adelia arched eyebrows knowingly. "And to see our Em and Eddy?"

Grace lowered her shoulders. "Yes, that too."

Her friend's face softened with understanding. "You aren't a prisoner here, Grace dear."

She reached for Adelia's hand. "I'll have Toby engage Maitland Locke's services again. There *must* be some legal concession that will allow you to remain in your own home."

And if there was none, she would bleeding-well fight for one.

Chapter Twenty-Two

Seamus stood at the ship's bow, hands clasped behind his back, watching the gradual break of day. The first grey veins stretching along the eastern horizon threw indistinct streaks of light upon the surface of the deep. Over the years, he had heard much of the sunrise ashore, and normally, nothing compared to the sunrise at sea. No interference of birdsong or the wakening hum of humanity. No interruption of trees, hilltops, spires, or roofs deflecting the first beams that gave the day life. Except today, the grey ocean's boundlessness and unknown depth compounded his loneliness. Below, a dolphin's sleek form cut the water a few feet beneath the surface, its colour indefinable in the dull morning light. For just a moment, the world was colourless.

The air still had a slight nip to it, and he tipped his head back, eyes closed with reminiscence, waiting for the sun's warmth to caress his face.

With no other family in London, Seamus had put into motion that, once Admiral Baxter's estate was settled, Wallace House in Mayfair would be sold. After all, Grace had no sentimental attachment to her old childhood home. He recalled the outpouring of grief at Baxter's death, the blurry sea of mourners filling Westminster Cathedral's pews—so many in uniform, so many unfamiliar. In the chaos of it all, the depth of these strangers' grief for the man, who was like a father to him, affirmed how revered and respected he was by his officers and men. Seamus had stood by, sadness pulling at his shoulders like the straps of a knapsack filled with rocks, as Max Delisle made introductions to the Earl of so-and-so, and Duke blah-blah the Third, and Viscount somebody, the multitude of black suits and dresses blurring together. Only Admiral Courtney's lamenting the loss of a fine officer piqued his interest. Courtney—Seamus's Royal Navy mentor and friend—belonged in a world he understood. Only he understood the loss of a fellow officer.

Heaven help him—the hardest was yet to come, informing Grace that her beloved Uncle Farfar had been taken from this world in such a brutal manner. The man had survived wars, for Christ's sake, yet it was a pleasure ride that took him. The whole dastardly affair was grossly unjust.

"Sail ho! Off the larboard bow."

The cry from above drew him from his thoughts, and he lifted his spyglass, instantly spotting the two masts of a brigantine in the distance. With this steady breeze, she would be alongside soon enough. Her decks were filled with men whose curiosity had lured them above. By their dress and features, Seamus deduced they were traders of some sort.

The other ship's master hailed the *Elias* in Portuguese, but when Seamus did not answer, he tried again in English. "Ship ahoy!"

Seamus balanced, wide-legged, at the bow. "Hulloa! What ship is that, pray?"

The dark-haired captain snatched his cocked hat as the wind whipped it off his head. "The merchantman, *Santa Catarina*, from Portuguese Mozambique, bound for Portuguese Guinea. Where are you from?"

Seamus's boom rode across the swells. "The *Elias*, from London, bound for New Holland, twenty-two days out."

"What's news?" The Portuguese master clamped his tri-peaked hat with his elbow.

"No news. What's news?" asked Seamus in return.

"A packet, picked up in Cape Town. Addressed to you, sir."

What luck! Seamus pressed his thighs against the gunwales, barely believing his good fortune. Despite their delayed departure, he had been bitterly disappointed to receive no packets from home. Considering he had promised Grace a blistering return, it was illogical to believe she would bother to send a letter after him. But now, these wholesome tidings were just what he required.

Seamus ordered Smythe and young Hicks into the cutter, sending Captain dos Santos a flagon of his best Duroc cognac. After the sailors returned with the packet, Seamus raised his hand at dos Santos in farewell. The *Santa Catarina* filed away, leaving the *Elias* to resume her ploughing through the waters, and Seamus to enjoy his delivery.

He glanced down at his daughter's neat, straight lines with their perfect punctuation, wishing for a fleeting moment that they were Grace's exquisite penmanship instead. A tumorous pustule of ingratitude soured the back of his throat. What the devil was he bemoaning? He should be thankful for *any* news from home, and that the *Elias* continued her course without mischance.

Surrounded by an empty ocean, he wanted nothing more than to allow Emily's letter to momentarily carry him away to another time and place. His desire to be with his family surged through his veins as he withdrew the compact note. The wind and currents, dragging him across the distance to Grace at a respectable fifteen knots, were still too blasted slow for his liking. The strong breeze rustled the tissue-thin sheets as he unfolded the letter.

He conjured Emily's voice, her cleanly clipped words that rushed together when excited. For pity's sake, was he even remembering her tone correctly? No wonder he could barely remember Elias's infantile squeak after all this time. He often tried to picture Elias growing up alongside his brother, but in his dreams, his boy was forever immortalised in infancy—round-faced and mop-headed. He missed him—every day. It had taken all his willpower to eradicate the memory of Elias's broken body —a babe on the verge of boyhood. Some days, he was even thankful to have had that ray of hope and sunshine in his life, if only to enjoy for one season. On days like today, his gratitude was less benevolent.

Come on, Fitzwilliam. Shake off these morbs! With a jerk of his head, he inhaled the briny, buffeting wind and scoured the top of the page. His melancholy faded as the daylight brightened and he absorbed the words on the page.

Dubois House, Sydney, New South Wales, 26 January 1842

To my dearest Cappy,

Miss Lissing has been kind enough to let me use her fancy paper. I've even been allowed to sit in the library to write! School is simply marvellous. Mme Dubois is prim and proper, even more than Miss Lissing, and she expects only the most excellent etiquette from us. We are all given daily marks for our decorum, and I received the highest marks with Mme Dubois presenting me with a Certificate for the Highest Conduct and Manners. Mme Dubois says that Eddy still has a way to go in the manners department. He is now as tall as my shoulder.

We have a thick textbook from which we learn about the different branches of Scientific Arts, but I prefer Uncle Hicks's scientific lessons. His explaining the mathematical reasons for hauling ropes aboard the ship, then allowing us to practice said principles on the ropes, was far less boring than learning these theories from the written word alone. Don't tell Miss Lissing this.

Some of the girls did not take kindly to me receiving my Certificate for the Highest Conduct and Manners, especially that wicked Lily Bell. She thinks she's so much better than the rest of us just because she's Squire Bell's daughter. She said you left Mamam, Eddy, and I behind in the penal colony because we're stinking immigrants, and that you didn't want us anymore. I was so tempted to deliver her a nose-ender, just as Mamam did to Tommy Holburton, and I really would have had I not just received my Certificate. So instead, Eddy put a fat wolf spider in her bed.

Lily Bell almost burst her stays. She ripped off her slipper and swatted it. And oh, Cappy, you'll never guess what happened! The spider had a million spiderlings hanging about it—they filled the bed and spilled onto the floor!

Seamus's chuckle whipped away on the wind. Had Emily been stood before him, he would probably offer her a censorious scowl, but reading her sheer delight at these antics filled him with a cheeriness that had been missing all these months. By Neptune's trident, it would be marvellous to hear those giggles again. Turning to the letter's second page, he read on.

Even if I were afraid of spiders (though I am not), it would have been worth it to see Miss Hoity-Toity wet her drawers. I laughed so hard that I almost wet my own! Miss Lissing let Lily Bell sleep in sickbay all by herself for the rest of term because the ninny refused to sleep in her bed. Thanks to Eddy, I'm now a heroine to the girls in my dormitory. They are so thankful to be rid of Lily Bell that I know that they will not rat on me. So, my Certificate for the Highest Conduct and Manners is safe.

We spent our end-of-term break at Gilly Downs. Matron

*Oberholzer promised to care for Alby when I'm away. He likes
her because she brings him kitchen scraps. It was so hot last
Sunday that after lunch, everyone from Barclay Hall went
down to the watering hole for a swim—even Mrs Barclay!
Ruthie told me that the stork will soon bring her another new
brother or sister. I'm sure this is untrue. I've seen plenty of
kookaburras, galahs, and rainbow lorikeets, but not one stork.
Besides, storks have no hands, so how would they carry a
babe?*

*I think Big Bob the bullocky will bring the child, or maybe
Mr Singh, the trader—he always has the most interesting
goodies in his wagon. Nevin thinks Mrs Barclay has the babe
in her pouch, like a kangaroo. Perhaps this is true because you
can even see it sticking out.*

Oh, Cappy, how I miss you. Come back soon.
Your faithful and obedient daughter,
Emily Elizabeth Fitzwilliam

Carefully folding the tissue paper and slipping it back into its
envelope, Seamus smiled. His daughter's happiness was undeni-
able. If only she had mentioned more about her mother.

O'Malley drew alongside his shoulder. "News from home,
sir?"

Seamus nodded, unable to keep the smile from his lips.
"Yes, from Emily. Little rascal and her brother are up to no
good."

The first mate chuckled. "If those are the tales she's prepared
to share, imagine their *true* mischief."

Seamus scoured his fingers across his mouth and cheeks, his
unshaven stubble rasping. He owed the man an apology for
earlier. O'Malley had come to him to advise that two of the
water barrels in the hold had spoiled and were the culprit of the
latest outbreak of the squirts. It was hardly the man's fault. So, it
was wholly unbecoming of him as the master to accuse the man

of allowing the spoiled water to be served. Rancid water was a curse of every ship.

Seamus clasped his hands behind his back. "Apologies for earlier, O'Malley."

The Irishman waved his long-fingered hand. "Consider it forgotten, sir.

The tension in his wrist clicked. "I had no cause to take my frustration out on you." Regret burned the lining of Seamus's stomach, and he smirked. "Doesn't bear thinking what it must be like living with such an angry imp."

"'Tis understandable, sir. Ye lost a good friend."

"It's not just Admiral Baxter." Seamus rolled his neck, and it cracked. As first lieutenant aboard the *Discerning*, he had prided himself as a fair commander. One who kept a tight ship through order and discipline. Then a fiery Grace Baxter had barged her way into his life in spectacular fashion. Her challenging his authority had unbalanced his strict sense of the world, but ultimately it had made him a better leader of men. How was he now a worse captain in her absence? Was his dependency on her a weakness? Christ! He had hoped that his sacrifice, to journey without her, would at least prove he could still stand on his own two blasted feet. How come it felt as though he was failing?

"If 'tis yer wife yer worried about"—O'Malley scratched the back of his coppery head—"that spirited lass is capable of holding the fort till ye get back." He flashed a row of white teeth.

Seamus appreciated his first mate's attempts to cheer him up. The feeling was short-lived. "It's that spirit of hers that worries me."

"Surely ye trust her, sir?"

Seamus thumped the flat top of the gunwale with his fist. "Yes, of course I blasted-well trust her. It's—" He paused. Damnation, he had done it again! He had the emotional range of a teaspoon, and his men were paying the price. He took in a sharp breath of the briny air. His mood was not about to miraculously improve, and since O'Malley had no magic tonic either, he was damned if he would stand here all day long apologising to his subordinate. "Excuse me." Turning sharply, he strode away.

Heavens, what he would do for a five-mile stretch of coastline to walk off this attack of the collywobbles.

Chapter Twenty-Three

hile Maitland Locke had not yet found a permanent legal solution to Adelia's leasing woes, he had at least earned her another ninety days at Barclay Hall while he tackled the ridiculous law. Grace pushed aside the awareness that the end to this extension was rapidly drawing nearer, and she blew warm breath into her cupped palms, the precious warm air escaping through her fingers in whorls. For a land notorious for its blistering summers, it had a decent bite in winter. She inhaled the cold morning air—*rain*. Of all bloody days!

The native birds' songs might not be as pretty as those in England, but they hummed with life, contrasting against the sun-crazed yard around Jim's log cabin, the cracks in the dry earth gasping for water. Grace nodded in approval at the surroundings, the crispy winter brown made appealing by its current wedding adornment. The new surrounding veranda Jim and Nevin had added to their cottage a year back was a hive of activity.

Long trestle tables were laid in neat rows in the yard, and Grace flicked snow-white cloths along their tops with efficient snaps born of years making beds. She stepped back, envisaging the tables groaning with Cook's delectable fare. Thank goodness the plague of flies died out at this time of year. In summertime, their numbers were sufficient to pick up a roast chicken and carry it off! With hands on her hips, she rotated slowly, absorbing the merriment.

Elsie McDermott hammered out a toe-tapping tune on the old piano tucked in the corner of the wide veranda. Her dark-haired husband, Dorian, flashed her a cheeky Irish grin as he accompanied her on his fiddle, practising for the long night ahead. If the pre-wedding festivity was an indication of what was to come, the inhabitants of Gilly Downs were in for a crapulous evening. Grace made note not to be too swept up in the revelry and have cause for regret in the morn. The younger children shrieked like gulls at the harbour as they scurried around, getting under her feet, but she was in no scolding mood—not today.

A young station-hand adjusted the bolt of white cotton on his shoulder as Victor, sans barrel or box for height, drooped the train of material across the veranda's facade. Afric, one of the nursery maids, issued strict instructions. Unperturbed by the petite woman's bossing, the black-haired giant smiled down indulgently. Clodagh, the other nursery maid, was cleaning windows while keeping half an eye on the children. Grace chuckled under her breath at the memory of the original glassless holes that had left Adelia horrified upon her arrival at Gilly Downs as a new bride.

A whinnying horse drew Grace's gaze along the dirt track leading up from the creek. The black-robed priest wrestled his gelding. It pulled eagerly at its bit, straining towards the smell of the other horses. Sliding from his saddle and looping the reins over the fence rail, the heavy clergyman patted his riding coat off. He grinned in greeting as Jim Buchanan bounded through the pretty arch of plaited twigs, thick with olive-green foliage curving over the gateway.

"Good day, Father Blackwood. Made it in one piece?"

"Good morrow to you too, Mr Buchanan. Mrs Fitzwilliam." The clergyman pushed his round spectacles up, to little effect as they slid down his shiny skin. "A good day to be married?"

"Aye, Father," chortled Jim. "As good as it gets."

Father Blackwood cast his gaze around the activity and scratched along the inside of his collar. "You have the old place looking quite cheerful."

"Many hands, and all that."

Jim led Grace and Father Blackwood under the decorated arch, and around Old Quill balanced atop a chair on his gammy leg. The old man reached for the horseshoe wound with white ribbon that Wee Granny Mac held aloft with gnarled fingers.

"Now mind ye don't hang it upside down, or ye'll tip out all the luck." The old woman scowled, smacking her gums. "Don't want it knocking the good Father here on the head."

Old Quill grumbled, "Now, Grizzie, just because ya've twisted my will to eat ya rabbit food with my meat, don't give ya licence to tell me how to hammer in a nail. Had my hand to carpentry since before ya was born."

"Aye, and what was it like apprenticing with Jesus, then?" She growled, "And don't call me that soft-headed name, or I'll slice yer tongue out and serve it to ye cold for breakfast!"

Grace and her two companions stopped, and they all glanced at the old couple. Theirs was an unconventional relationship. To see them together, anyone would think that their scowls and gruff conversation was a result of an inherent dislike for one another. But this could not be further from the truth.

Father Blackwood clasped his hands solemnly. "Old Quill, I

EMMA LOMBARD

hear you've allowed Wee Granny Mac to take up residence in your hut?"

The wizened old man lowered his arms and shook his hands as though to encourage blood flow. "You've heard right, Father."

The priest coughed politely. "Perhaps I can help you remedy your lack of marital vows once I'm done with Mr Buchanan and Mr Hicks?"

Inhaling a wheezy breath, Old Quill widened his eyes and shook his head in warning. "Tread lightly, Father."

Wee Granny Mac stepped uncomfortably near to Father Blackwood, her neck angled back awkwardly as she poked him in the chest. "I don't need to be marrit to the auld beggar to know he's the one I want to annoy for the rest of ma days. Wouldn't do it even if his arse were dipped in diamonds," she declared with supreme Scottish hard-headedness. "Mention it again and I'll have the castrating knife to yer bollocks when ye next sleep—priest or no priest."

Grace bit back a laugh as Father Blackwood stumbled back, wide eyed.

Old Quill chuckled. "I tried to warn ya."

Both Wee Granny Mac and Old Quill had lived lives with very little tenderness, and they lived only by what they knew. Grace was amused that Wee Granny Mac's daily threats to disembowel or poison Old Quill were her way of letting him know she cared about him. She was sure the old woman would not bother him in such a manner were it not so. It was also apparent the unfortunate Father Blackwood was unfamiliar with being addressed in such a manner, and he looked like a shiver searching for a spine to run up and down.

The priest bristled and inclined his head sharply. "Perhaps another time then?"

"Aye." Wee Granny Mac sucked her lips between her gums. "Perhaps when all ma teeth grow back, hm?"

Grace glanced around at the laughing over by the woodshed.

Four shepherds were fashioning wooden benches from split logs, their hammers knocking in rhythmic unison. One said something unintelligible, and they all burst into spirited laughter again.

Digging his hands into his coat pocket, and with his cheeks colouring further, Father Blackwood turned his attention back to Jim. "Been a trifle nippy."

"Aye, it has been." Jim snatched out a hand, grabbing Noah Barclay's arm just in time to prevent the four-year-old from tearing headlong into one of the shepherds' wives, heavily laden with two glass vases bursting with native flowers. "Steady up, laddie! You and yer friend." He stabbed a finger at Noah and Edwin. "Help Nevin take Father Blackwood's horse to the stables. Then get yerselves up to the main house and help him bring down the rum and ale casks from the storehouse. Roll them carefully, mind, I want no breakaway barrels taking someone's legs from under them."

Grace suspected that the casks could all be loaded on a wagon and brought down in one trip, but the hard job would keep the lads out of mischief and feeling like they were a part of the special day. Their flushing faces confirmed her theory.

With a jaunty swagger of importance, Nevin led the horse and duo up the hill towards Barclay Hall. The two youngsters' self-control dissolved into a scuffled run as they elbowed one another for the lead, their loud yells of laughter echoing across the valley.

Grace eyed the clergyman's red flush easing around his collar. "Father, why don't I take you up to the big house for some refreshments?"

"Jolly good." The clergyman stared at the hill and exhaled a breath of resignation. "Right then, let's go."

On the way up, they passed Toby driving the wagon laden with a pile of straw Grace had requested. Her idea was to tie the straw in bundles and create an aisle of hay twists from the arch to the veranda. Grace nibbled her lip—she only hoped Jim had understood what she meant. Knowing him, he would lay a path of loose straw and call it done. She swallowed back a laugh.

Toby raised his leather hat and beamed through his sandy whiskers. "Glad to see you've arrived safe and sound, Father Blackwood."

The priest attempted a reply, but it came out as a wheezy grunt.

In the kitchen building, Cook instructed Emily and Ruth on how to lay out small damper balls on tin trays. The sight of the clammy, breathless clergyman had Cook flurry around the table, wiping her floury hands on her apron.

"Why Father Blackwood, you don't 'alf look parched." She took from his arm the coat he had removed halfway up the hill.

Grace winced. Thankfully, he was too flustered to notice the white handprints Cook left on the dark material. The poor man must suffer terribly in summer.

"Take a seat on the bench outside," Cook fussed. "I'll bring you some gum blossom cordial. Much better than boring old lemonade. Just made a fresh batch for the wedding."

"Thank you, Cook," panted Father Blackwood.

Flaming Hades! The heat of the kitchen was worse than the inside of a gold smelter. Grace wanted nothing more than to scurry back into the cooler air outside. Cook was a saint for enduring such conditions! Neither Emily nor Ruth seemed too bothered either.

Grace sniffed appreciatively. "Oh, Cook, is that goose?"

The heat-induced glow on the flat-faced woman's cheeks darkened, and she giggled. "'Tis."

"Explains why yon gander is causing such a racket." Blackwood's head peered around the corner, and he waved at the grey fowl wandering around the yard, its neck stretched long and its feet pigeon-toed as it waddled around honking forlornly.

Grace turned to the sound of pouring liquid. Cook offered her a glass of cloudy cordial. "Ham was prepared earlier. There's a

lovely block of stilton, and we've got the damper dough ready."
She nodded her capped head at the trays of dough balls. "Cakes
are made too." She proudly pointed at two white marzipan
squares on the sideboard—simple, matching cakes with pink and
red roses piped along the top edge.

Grace took a deep drink and rolled the bitter-sweet flavour
around her tongue. "A feast fit for Queen Victoria herself."

LATER THAT AFTERNOON, Grace smiled as Jim and Toby stood
together on the wide veranda, coats pressed, boots polished, and
hair brushed. The two brides had decided on simple matching
gowns without veils, but each groom only had eyes for his own
bride.

Father Blackwood picked up his Bible and stepped before
the two couples. The calmer activity clearly suited him better,
and his cleanly shaven face was unflushed and hopeful. "Well,
friends, hundreds of people are marrying all around the world
today, but none in such a singularly spectacular place. As we
proceed, let us be aware that around us are two of the most
precious gifts of all, water and love. And it looks as though
we'll soon have an abundance of *both* here this afternoon." A
ripple of laughter rumbled across the crowd, and like a wooden
barrel rolling across the deck, a rumble of far-off thunder
agreed. Grace eyed the brewing storm clouds on the horizon
that had teased all day without a drop, now darkening
ominously.

The clergyman's round cheeks glowed as he looked at the
bridal couples. "Dearly beloved—"

The gander loudly interjected, honking and flapping its
wings. The crowd laughed again, and Nevin darted towards the
offender, shooing it off in squawking protest. With all distrac-
tions dispensed with, Father Blackwood finished the ceremony

in the serious, undulating tone synonymous with men of the cloth.

Sinking back into her chair with happiness, Grace never took her eyes off Jim's and Toby's faces. Jim, a Scot through and through, and her first friend aboard the *Discerning*, whose large, brown eyes had twinkled mischievously as he horrified her with untrue expectations of a sailor's life. She had been so naïve back then, so trusting of him, but even after all this time, that trust had never faded. Except now, that twinkle in his eye was no longer hers to own. It belonged wholeheartedly to Pearl, and she was glad to give it over.

Toby spoke his vows as gently as always. Her sweet dear friend who, despite life's hardships, had never allowed his kindness to be bruised. Grace had been blessed with a lifetime of his thoughtfulness, which she did not mind sharing now with the new Mrs Hicks.

Both brides glowed with happiness. Pearl Buchanan, with a white satin ribbon woven through her thick brown hair, wore the braid curled around her head like a crown. Her high-set forehead led down to her beautiful brown eyes that matched Jim's impish spark. A true match, those two! Erin Hicks, normally so undaunted by anything, could barely get the words out through her tears, and Toby looked as though he could not love her more for it.

Grace grinned at her two friends sheepishly kissing their new brides to a round of foot stamping and applause. She bit back a groan as large, heavy drops plopped in the dirt, creating little puffs of dust and quenching the parched, sandy hues into a damp, rich brown. Stinking seaweed! Here it came.

The pattering rain fell heavier, and Jim and Toby nodded briefly at one another before darting into the increasing deluge. Taking their lead, the other shepherds and station hands ran into the pelting cloudburst to save the decorated tables and drag the benches onto the wide veranda. As inconvenient as it was, Grace knew the rain was a welcome sight to Jim, who had been uneasily watching the dry weather wither the vegetation and lap up the waterholes. And just at this minute, neither he nor Toby seemed to mind a jot that their carefully combed hair and best coats were soaked.

The updrafts caused by the downpour swirled clouds of mist across the veranda, lifting the edges of tablecloths and blowing over vases of flowers. Wedding guests yelled, some in wonder, some in dismay, as they scrambled to pin down errant tablecloths and rectify toppled unlit candlesticks. Sensing the growing despair, Grace waved at Dorian and Elsie McDermott to strike up a tune.

She grabbed Old Quill's leathery hand. "May I have this dance, sir?"

The old man's rheumy eyes sparked, and he drew her in, his hand fitting expertly in the small of her back. He led her around the veranda in a lively, limping step, laughing and bumping into her as more revellers joined in. Good gracious, the man could truly dance. The other guests clapped and stamped their feet in encouragement. The mood swelled with the steam rising off the backs of soaked coats as the dancing pace picked up with whoops and hollers.

In competition with the piano and the fiddle, the rain drummed louder on the tin roof. Grace glanced over Old Quill's shoulder. Dozens of slim waterfalls poured from the corrugated tin roof and splattered into muddy puddles below. The decorative straw twists lining the aisle grew limp, and a couple toppled over, sprawling in the mud like scattered pick-up sticks. The tablecloths, already besmirched by a layer of dust, turned from a brilliant white into a damp, murky grey. So much for all that preparation.

Old Quill inhaled heartily. "By God, there's nothing like the smell of wet clay and clean rock."

Grace nodded; the cool air was indeed refreshing. The lone

gander waddled from under the wagon, honking in protest at the deluge for its interruption of his search. Oh, the pitiful thing. She knew the ache of missing her mate. With her spirits drooping, she palmed Old Quill off to Wee Granny Mac. The old woman's fierce scowl let him know that this was a one-time occurrence, and that he had better not have any high ideas about asking her for another. Unperturbed, the old man drew her into his sinewy arms with a gummy grin.

Grace surveyed the crowd on the veranda, their faces fading fast in the premature shadow brought about by the storm. Candles would be useless with this wind—perhaps she should scrounge Jim's lanterns from inside? She spotted Victor, a head above the crowd, leaning contentedly against the wooden corner pillar, smiling gently at the revelry.

Adelia walked over to him and stood, unspeaking at first, with her arms crossed over her swollen belly. The broad-shouldered shepherd shuffled upright, his eyes flicking down at Adelia's upswept hair before fixing themselves on his shoes. Adelia smiled and leaned towards him as she spoke. The tall shepherd broke out in a shy but strikingly handsome smile. The man's white teeth were large and straight against his inky whiskers, and he boldly met Adelia's eye. Adelia's eyebrows rose in silent question, and he held out his hand to her. Smiling charmingly, she took it.

Grace frowned as, instead of leading her into the melee of joyful dancers, Victor led Adelia into the cottage. Where on earth were they going? Perhaps they had thought to fetch lanterns too? She did not wish to be upset with Adelia, but a prickle of discomfort raked down her neck at the sight of her newly widowed friend cavorting with a virtual stranger, and in her condition! Averting her eyes in disapproval, Grace glanced around the reception and realised that—despite the rain, and discounting Adelia's current moral dilemma—the Buchanan-

Hicks wedding had indeed lifted the morale of Wooloongilly Downs. Just as planned.

The shadows deepened, and when Adelia and Victor did not emerge with the lanterns, Grace stepped into the cottage on a mission. The central room was just as she remembered, with the rectangular table that doubled as the kitchen bench. The open back door showed the path leading to the kitchen building. The brick mouth of the coal-fired oven yawned open as Cook withdrew the freshly baked damper. She shuffled along the muddy path into the cottage and dropped the cloth-covered tin tray onto the table with a clatter, blowing her fingertips. The smell of hot bread was heavenly, and Grace's earlier loss of appetite reversed at the sight of the mound of sliced roasted goose, succulent and white with a trim of golden perfection. Cook already had three lanterns lit.

Grace reached for the handle of one. "Can you spare a lantern or two? The candles keep blowing over in the wind."

"O' course! As mighty fine as a bonfire would be about now, we don't want Mr Buchanan's home to be the kindling of such."

Grace glanced around the tiny cottage. The door to the bedchamber on the left was closed, as was the parlour door to the right. "Have you seen Mrs Barclay?" she asked lightly.

Cook nodded at the parlour door. "Milady's in there with Mr Shyling and Father Blackwood. Likely enjoying a minute of peace." She waved at the swirling mass of bodies outside the window. "Such merriment's not conducive to a woman in her advanced state."

Grace lifted the lantern. "You're quite right. I'll just pop my head in. See how she's faring." She gripped the brass knob and leaned her head towards the murmur of voices behind the door.

"… I now pronounce you man and wife." Father Blackwood's baritone voice carried clearly through the thin wood.

What on earth? Grace squeezed the door handle harder and,

forgoing a knock, she swung it open. Bleeding bloody rats' tails! Victor's shoulders were rounded, and his lips were on Adelia's!

Adelia's head jerked back, and she peered around Victor's broad arm. "Oh, Grace! I didn't hear you knock." Her milky cheeks flushed, and she took a step back.

Grace glared at Father Blackwood as he closed his Bible. How could he be so calm? The mistress of the homestead had just kissed a blasted shepherd in his presence, and here he was looking all righteous and smug about it. In the far corner, two new young station hands stood witness, leather hats screwed in hand. The look on their faces reminded Grace of the time Seamus had burst into her cabin aboard the *Discerning* and found Jim and Toby keeping her company.

"What is this?" asked Grace in a tight voice.

Victor swung his head slowly from Grace to Father Black-wood, and then to Adelia. "Perhaps you might like a moment alone with Mrs Fitzwilliam?"

Adelia ran her slim hand down his coat sleeve in an unsettlingly familiar gesture. "Yes, thank you." She nodded at the priest. "And thank you, Father."

Blackwood smiled and inclined his head. "God bless you both." He flicked his head at the two youngsters. "Come on, you two."

Just as Jim and Toby had escaped in a hurry, these two shepherds scurried eagerly through the open door. As Victor and the priest walked past, Grace pressed her back to the wall, her shoulder bumping a picture of pressed flowers. The door closed with a quiet click. Besides the festivity's muted tones outside, only the tick of the mantle clock sounded. Grace looked anywhere other than her friend's eyes. The lace curtains were new and, while not entirely white, were at least not the colour of tobacco spit anymore. The floors, smoothed and polished, no longer threatened to spit splinters into any unsuspecting socked feet. Along the mantle, Jim had lined small framed portraits of his family. The vase of orange, candle-like banksia blooms smacked of Pearl's touch.

"Grace?"

She dragged her gaze over to her friend and stared, unblinking.

"Allow me to explain." Adelia's voice was small.

Indignation rose like bile in Grace's throat, and she swallowed hard to avoid choking on her next words. "A bit bloody late, isn't it? Sounds like the deed is done."

Adelia tipped her chin up, a look of resolution firmly affixed. "Grace—"

Grace shook her head, and a scathing laugh escaped her lips. "Adelia! Your husband isn't yet a handful of months gone. This isn't proper."

Adelia smiled sadly. "You're right, my friend. It's not proper that I lost my husband. It's not proper that my children will grow up without their father. It's not proper that the Crown won't grant me a grazing licence."

"You don't know that for sure yet," said Grace sharply. "Mr Locke is yet to advise what the Colonial Secretary's take is on the matter." She lowered the lantern to a side table and thrust her hands onto her hips.

Adelia sighed. "I'm not holding my breath on that." She folded her arms. "You heard what Commissioner Long said about the lease belonging to my husband. Even Mrs Deas Thomson conceded it's the law. I doubt I'll be granted another stay of execution either."

Grace scoffed. "I don't recall the commissioner ordering you to marry the first man to come along. Adelia! You hardly know him, and he's as poor as a church mouse."

Adelia lowered her eyes, her neck and face pinkening uncomfortably.

Good! At least she looked suitably ashamed. And so she bloody should, cavorting about like a blasted harlot! Grace gasped and gripped the armchair's back, her fingers sinking into the padded upholstery. "Good grief! You didn't—did you —*betray* your husband?"

The gold flecks in Adelia's eyes sparked with fury. "It wasn't like that!" She scrubbed the trickle of tears from her cheeks. "I don't care that Mr Shyling isn't backed by a wealthy family. Mr Barclay wasn't either—he had my father's backing, remember? I'm a wealthy woman in my own right now with the success of Gilly Downs and the Woolstore. I need no financial saviour."

"You can't possibly love him after—after—such a short time." Her own judgement slapped her back a step, and she glared at her friend's stomach, her eyes widening. "Is that—"

"For crying out loud, Grace! No! It's Mr Barclay's. Mr Shyling can't have children. He was kicked by a horse as a child."

She folded her arms. "I thought you said he lost his two daughters?"

"They were his wife's children. She was a widow when he married her."

"Oh." Grace struggled to keep the criticism from her voice. "So the man has a penchant for wealthy widows, does he?"

Adelia ran her hand over the swell of her belly and firmed her chin. "Grace, I've an eviction notice with my name on it that, in a matter of weeks, will leave my children and me homeless. *I* asked Victor for *his name*, so that I may renew the grazing licence on Gilly Downs."

"Why didn't you tell me?"

"I couldn't risk you talking me out of it. I've done what needs to be done. For my children's sake. For Gilly Downs. Please don't judge me too harshly for it." Reaching for Grace's hand, she stared into her soul. "The scandal of a hasty marriage will soon disappear into obscurity, but Mr Barclay's legacy shall live on. I'll make it so."

The warmth of friendship enveloped Grace like one of

Seamus's fiery hugs on a frosty winter's night and slowed the thudding heartbeat in her ears. As shockingly expedient as this marriage was, she understood the reasoning behind it. Some of her own hasty decisions had moulded the life she had now, including the wretched loneliness that currently suffocated her each night in her empty marriage bed. At least her situation was only temporary. Seamus would return, unlike poor Elijah.

Her friend was about to become the most topical woman in the colony. The least she could do was leave the judgment up to God and the gossipy gums. "Oh, my sweet friend, a thousand apologies for thinking the worst of you. I've made a real hash of our friendship, haven't I?" She curled her arms around her fearless friend and squeezed her tightly. The babe bucked and kicked between them, and they both laughed. Grace broke away, rubbing the hard mound. "Sorry, little one."

Adelia hesitated, her red-rimmed eyes sliding down. "I'm rather relieved there'll be no more after this one. My children are such a blessing, but—" Her gaze rose slowly. "I'm tired, Grace."

The final flicker of anger in Grace's gut fizzled out like a campfire in the rain, replaced by the powerful punch of memory of her exhaustion after birth—her new babes drawing on her own life-force for sustenance—the endless nights of pacing and patting. Not to mention the ruinous effect on her body. And she had only birthed three offspring. This was Adelia's fifth! Goodness knew no one ever spoke of the leakage below with every sneeze or laugh. The notion of adding the mantle of grief into the mix did not bear thinking about.

She squeezed her friend's fingers. "I understand."

Chapter Twenty-Four

OFF CAPE COLONY COAST, AFRICA, 7 *JULY* 1842

Heading down the passageway past the captain's lounge, Seamus peered through the diamond lead-paned glass at Smythe slinking the short distance down the gangway from the deckhouse cabin to the galley, his oilskinned shoulders hunched against the cold, driving rain. The swirling black cloud rolling towards them darkened the heavens, and the heavy sulphurous odour preceding the electrical storm stung the lining of his nostrils. The sky's cold, angry mood matched that of the heavy, ugly sea. The shiver running down the back of Seamus's legs had little to do with the biting wind he predicted would invade his clothing once he stepped outside.

Smythe scurried across the decks awash with seawater, his footsteps light in anticipation of the hot, sweet tea no doubt awaiting him in Cook Woodhouse's deckhouse galley. The seaman's wet plastered head materialised from the galley door a few minutes later, the tin pot in one hand, and a tin plate filled with a sea biscuit and large chunk of cold salt beef—the only meal possible in such rough conditions—in the other.

Seamus gasped. Oh, what he would give for a plate piled high with baked hake and steaming, boiled potatoes saturated in a golden butter-and-parsley sauce! And the stove's warmth in the saloon. Current conditions forbade all luxury to enjoy either of those right now.

Outside, with his shoulder braced against the galley's outer wall, Smythe waited for a break in the swells before thrusting towards the deckhouse cabin door only a few steps away. Seamus's gut swooped as the *Elias*'s bow lifted, scooping a great wave of seawater over her deck. Smythe's black-haired head and slim shoulders disappeared beneath the churning swirl of water. Blasted Hell—all he needed now was a man overboard. Especially not that lad, who, out of Chittenden's shadow, was proving an excellent mariner.

The bow dipped on the downward swell, sending the water forward again, and Seamus gripped the door's brass knob, searching the receding wave. A movement beside the cutter caught his attention—oh, thank Heavens! Smythe, having landed on his buttocks, shook the water from his hair. He still held the tin mug and plate, but his chunk of salt beef rolled towards the starboard drainage scupper—a hole that effectively carried it and the wave of water from the deck. Rather the meal than the man.

The seaman peered into his tin pot and, with a comical shrug, upended the briny contents onto the deck. He staggered to his feet and, tucking his now empty plate under his arm, grinned and shook a fist at the helmsman above. There was no trait more necessary aboard a ship than a sense of humour, and this man now owned that and more. Seamus thrust open the door.

Smythe's humorous smirk morphed into an open-mouth laugh. "Here comes the Cape of Storms!" The youngster had grown out his whiskers, which lent him a look of maturity that matched his restored confidence.

Blight's deep-timbered laugh came from above. "You'll not be grinning so hard once you've had a smell of Hell, my lad."

Blight was not wrong. A storm around the Cape of Good Hope was no laughing matter. If his time with sailors had taught him anything, it was to maintain a habitual good humour about things, though Seamus knew he was doing a wretchedly poor job of that right now. He inhaled sharply and, resolving to do better, fixed his grin as he watched Smythe stride back to the deckhouse cabin without food. Every sailor knew better than to ask Cook Woodhouse for a second helping if his allowance had already been doled out. Though the others would not suffer the man to go without—all would turn a little from their own pots to fill up his, dividing the loss among themselves. His crew were good like that.

Up on the quarterdeck, Seamus took the helm from Blight and gave O'Malley the order to haul down and clew up. O'Malley's bellow echoed across the deck and up into the rigging. Young Hicks did not hesitate, scrambling up the mainmast rigging with the swiftness and dexterity of a young man in his prime, his thick flanks and shoulders making light work of it. Blight also scampered up the foremast to help the men to make all snug.

The sea rose ominously, and the *Elias*'s sleek bow plunged into the angry grey mass, punching up a huge plume of saltwater and foam that threatened to wash everything overboard.

Seamus's arms ached. The ship laboured and strained against the gale's howl as he found himself in opposition to Mother Nature—again. As usual, she shrieked furiously at his efforts to thwart her power. As though to prove her point, she threw a wall of needling hail at him, slicing his knuckles and cheeks with dozens of lacerations.

Night fell prematurely, dark and gloomy, with torrents of rain falling in blinding sheets, obscuring their position. The incessant booms of thunder were like war drums of the gods, forewarning of death and destruction. The lightning's vivid flashes illuminated the churning murky sky, adding to his disorientation in the icy storm. Ah, so this was how Mother Nature wished to play? Very well. He was not about to blasted-well become the sport of her wild billows. With numbed hands, he renewed his efforts at the helm.

A little before midnight, the vigilant leeward lookouts came alive, a bright flash of lightning revealing their animated gestures at the ragged coastline. An icy trail slithered through Seamus's gut. By Neptune's forked trident, it was barely a mile distant! They should be much further from the African shore. Heavens knew how far off course they had been blown. This rocky shore could be any number of landfalls along the wild and desolate coastline of the Cape Colony. Or perhaps one of the treacherous islands offshore? None of which offered favourable odds of survival. The wind whipped off his oilskin hood, and persistent, cold trickles triumphantly broke through the barrier of his collar, stealing the heat of his skin. He gasped at the cold, sucking in a spray of tangy saltwater.

Beside him, Blight helped wrestle the wooden wheel. The ache in Seamus's cold leaden arms froze at the panic in Blight's voice. "Wind's driving us straight to shore, sir."

"I have eyes, Blight!" he snapped. A squall whipped his hair about, seemingly determined to tear it out by the roots. He had to get the weight carried as low as possible, or this wind would tip them. Drawing up his wool-lined hood, he leaned towards Blight, bawling his orders to make himself heard against the tempest's fury.

"Aye, sir." Blight tucked his chin and vanished into the sideways rain.

Seamus tightened his gloved hands on the helm's handles, watching the shoreline loom more prominent and darker with each white flash. The cold gnawed at his injured right wrist like a fox crunching through week-old rabbit bones. Heavens, at least he was afforded the luxury of gloves Blight had brought him earlier. The men in the rigging worked barehanded because, without a sure grip, they would slip and fall to their deaths. There was no doubt it was a young man's game—one he was no longer at liberty to play. He glared at the wildly rocking masts, ignoring the watery loosening of his knees as young Hicks's lean figure eased along the yardarm.

With a slow, controlled breath, he focussed on the hands at the bow dropping the larboard and starboard bowers into the shallow water. A hot squirt of triumph warmed his back as the *Elias* jerked tight under the anchor cables. With death-defying skill, Carpenter Hanson and Shelby Hicks orchestrated the lowering of the topgallant masts to the deck.

At the end of the watch, O'Malley took the helm, and Seamus joined Cook Woodhouse in the galley deckhouse. He rubbed his numbed, chapped hands close to the iron stovetop, clenching his teeth against the agony of life creeping back into his fingers. The fire in the stove's belly crackled, the hot air in the small room oppressive after the icy outdoors. Seamus peered into the nearest bubbling copper. Flakes of tealeaves swirled and stewed in the boiling water. The tea slopped around, but the deep sides prevented it sloshing over. The heady aromas of tea and hot chocolate reminded him of a tea shop on the high street. All that was missing were the currant buns—and Grace.

"Liberal doses of treacle tonight, Cook Woodhouse. The men will thank you for it," said Seamus.

"Sir, allow me to serve supper in your cabin," said the rotund cook.

Seamus shook his head. "Not necessary. We're all stretched thin in this weather. I'll take my sustenance swiftly and be on my way." The pots, pans, and ladles hanging on hooks from the bulkhead bonged together with the same inharmonious din as Emily and Edwin's spontaneous brass band with pots and pans back home. Seamus scowled as an iron cauldron gonged against his head. Damn and blast this lousy weather!

Woodhouse cringed. "Tea or hot chocolate, sir?"

Seamus rubbed the throbbing egg on his scalp. "Tea. Please." He took the offered enamelled pot and bit back a grimace, the heat cutting his palms as though the smooth surface were layered with blades. He blew on the steaming liquid and sipped, wincing as a hot trail blazed down his gullet. Oh, sweet Heavens. The warmth. The earthy flavour turned exotic with sugariness. Simply divine! He dunked his raisin hardtack into his tea to soften it.

Blight and young Hicks stepped into the galley, their eyes red-rimmed, their hair plastered to their foreheads. The two men were equally broad-shouldered and filled the tiny galley. At the sight of Seamus, they hesitated and nodded at him in unison. "Evenin', sir."

"Gentlemen." He breathed in the thick, warm moisture curling from his pot. "Can't imagine any sailor who'd prefer their rum ration over a hot pot tonight, would you?"

"Indeed, sir. The rum only warms awhile," agreed Woodhouse, ladling out steaming brown cocoa into two pots. "Here, lads, warm yer gizzards with this."

"I'd pitch my rum to the dogs any day for a pot o' this honey, Cook Woodhouse!" Young Hicks laughed, his shaven cheeks bright red with cold. His grey eyes sparked with a confidence his older brother had lacked at his age. "Hmm, if this isn't the finest-tasting chocolate I've ever had, may God strike me down this instant."

"Aah," sighed Blight, smacking his lips beneath his fiery whiskers. "Beacon of light at the end of a long, dreary watch. Oh God, and sweeter than my missus's tits!"

"Blight!" Seamus barked. "Do you forget your place? I'll not have my supper ruined by such indecent talk."

Blight's chapped fingers tightened around the handle of the

mug, and he drew his shoulders back. "Apologies, Captain. Permission to leave, sir?"

Christ Almighty! It would be unfair to cast the man out in the cold again so soon, especially at the expense of his own frayed temper. Slugging back his rapidly cooling tea in three large mouthfuls, Seamus grabbed a lump of hard cheese. "No. Stay." He would rather be alone anyway, and he was anticipating climbing into his berth. He only hoped tonight he would be granted the sleep of the dead, and not be taunted by dreams of Grace.

In his cabin, he peeled off his dripping oilskin and hooked it beside the row of damp shirts and trousers hanging over the rope strung along the bulkhead. The garments chaffed against the planks as the ship heaved and pitched in the clammy gloom. Stripping off his shirt and trousers, he wrung them out, the salt-water splattering the planks. He was familiar with the miserable routine endured by everyone, himself included. The air was so wet and heavy he could taste it over the treacly remnants of the molasses-sweetened tea.

With palms still prickling with warmth from the scalding pewter pot, he squeezed the line of drying trousers. Selecting the least-damp pair, he forced his legs into the freezing leg holes, sucking in a hiss as the cold fabric slid over his nether. By Neptune's forked trident! Good thing he had no desire to sire any more children. Nothing would be left in working order with these temperatures!

He clambered into his berth and drew several layers of blankets and the heavy embroidered bedspread over him. All that was missing was Grace's warm backside wiggling into him. His teeth chattered as he thawed. Closing his eyes, he imagined the warmth of her in his arms. As he stroked the empty, icy sheet beside him, the exhaustion and homesickness balled in his chest and exploded through his fist. He hammered the mattress with repeated whumps until his bruised chest ached and he was no longer cold. Panting, he rammed his hand behind his head and scowled up into the blackness.

For pity's sake, this blasted journey could not end soon enough!

Seamus woke with a jerk. It was one of those falling dreams, where he awoke as he was about to hit the ground. His tongue felt too fat for his mouth, and he considered braving the cold for a drink of water. The hull jerked again, and he sprang upright. He rubbed his face, his mind instantly alert to the sound and movement of his ship. A pale, grey light stuck to the outside of the porthole.

What devilment? Had one of the anchor cables parted? He shuffled off his berth and snatched up his oilskin. Sucking in a breath to brace for the cold, he shrugged into the heavy wet coat and snapped the cabin door closed behind him.

The icy lashings of rain battered the lead-paned glass, and he clenched his molars as he stepped into the squall. Lurching towards the bow where several sailors gathered, he eyed the one remaining anchor cable. Damn and blast, he was right!

"Do you reckon she'll hold, Captain?" Young Hicks's wide, grey eyes barely masked his fear.

"Pray she does, Mr Hicks. The safety of this entire ship depends on that one small bower anchor." He squinted into the driving rain and hail, trying to get a measure of the nearby daggers of rock. The sea still ran mountainous, and the Elias was close enough to shore for him to hear the breakers crashing furiously.

By eight o'clock, the blackened clouds lightened to an unpromisingly drab grey as the sunlight valiantly fought to burn its way through. Heaven help, there was no sign of the gale abating, and the Elias was dragging her lone anchor, the current drawing them towards the rollers.

O'Malley headed over with a look that clearly showed he had come to the same realisation. Before his first mate had a chance to speak, Seamus gave the order. "Cut the anchor, Mr O'Malley. I'll run her as close to shore as possible."

His first mate's wind-reddened cheeks paled, highlighting his freckles, and he bellowed against the wind, "But Captain, we'll be dashed upon the rocks—"

"We might," hollered Seamus. "But the ship's no longer an object of consideration. The men are. We must put our energy into the preservation of human life." Seamus spoke with such decision that the knot of fear in his stomach eased a little. A hard choice, but the right one. "I'll run her as near the coast as possible," he yelled again. "It's the best chance of escape."

Ignoring O'Malley's wide-eyed panic, he roared, "Cut the anchor, O'Malley!"

The officer responded instantly, scampering towards the bow and bellowing orders. Seamus stepped up to the helm and readied himself for when the ship became his to command again. O'Malley dashed back and butted up beside him. Snatching the tangle of sodden rope at his feet, with a few expert twirls, he lashed himself to the wooden wheel, his hands melding beside Seamus's on the helm.

"We'll run her straight onto that sandy stretch, between those rocks," said Seamus.

"W-what if we miss the beach, sir?" O'Malley squalled.

"Not even the strongest swimmer can hope to gain the shore from this distance. We can't afford to miss it, O'Malley."

With the anchor no longer holding her to the seabed, the Elias shifted beneath Seamus's feet. Squinting through the driving rain, he glared at the immense waves swelling in the shallows before curling and crashing ashore.

"Jaysus, Captain! Behind us!" yelled O'Malley through gritted teeth.

Seamus whipped around, roaring as the grey wave pounded the Elias's stern like a sledgehammer smashing against a thick, wooden pile. Folding his arms around the helm, he clenched his eyes and mouth tight against the assaulting seawater, grinding his back teeth through the agony. Having O'Malley beside him was a tiny glimmer of comfort in this swirling Hell.

As soon as the wave rolled over the Elias, Seamus blinked the stinging saltwater from his eyes and searched the deck. Christ on the cross! The cutters were gone—swept clear in the blink of an eye, leaving the cutter skids as clean as a newly shaven chin. The chicken coop's splintered shell washed awkwardly against the gunwale near the stern, the rowboats' shattered boards floating nearby. Three miserable chickens floated among them, wet through and frightened witless at their sudden change of surroundings. The dark grey wave that had caused the chaos rolled on towards the shore without a care of the damage it had wreaked.

A bedraggled Smythe and young Hicks crawled from under the wreckage of the chicken coop. Young Hicks's nose bore a new red slash across the bridge, and it sat at an even odder angle than before. Smythe's narrow eyes winced as he yanked a wooden splinter impaled in his cheek, the intense cold immediately stemming the blood flow.

"Cursed devilry!" swore Seamus. He shook his head—it was hopeless. The time had come. "Mr O'Malley, muster all hands."

The men gathered before the helm, fighting the bucking deck to lean in closer to hear him.

"Gentlemen, we're going to ground. We've lost the cutters. Do what you must to lash together spars and barrels. Save yourselves."

Men scrambled in an uncoordinated, undisciplined mess. Through blue flashes of lightning, Seamus fixed his eyes to the shore, and the storm inhaled his wail as though sucking out his soul.

The Elias's hull bit into the sandy bar with a bone-juddering crunch like a giant chewing on rocks, the jolt so forceful it hurled every man violently to the deck. Sailors struggled to right themselves, some slower than others. Another wave lifted the Elias, smashing her upon the sandy seabed with another show of strength that knocked them all down like skittles. Confusion and alarm broke out on the lilting deck.

Seamus hung limply from his bindings against the helm, the rope cutting painfully into his still-tender sternum. His feet kicked the air as he tried to find secure footing on the slippery planks. O'Malley had untied himself and was lying across the wooden box that housed the helm's steering mechanism, his arms dangling as he struggled to untie Seamus's binds.

The icy rain stiffened and hampered Seamus's fingers. Sweet merciful Heaven, they had rolled broadside against the sandy ocean floor. The Elias's half-masts almost swept the water's thrashing surface. He stared in horror as Cook Woodhouse was dragged from the deck in a terrifying sweep of foam. Smythe floundered in the tangle of ropes and sails, in danger of slipping from the mainmast's trunk into the relentless swells below. Above the roaring water and howling wind came the even louder shrieks of the poor souls already plunged into the icy ocean, piteously invoking Heaven for help. Blight hung over a heavily leaning capstan, gripping young Hicks's outstretched arm. The youngster's thrashing feet kicked out at the raging sea below, his blond head flicking up at Blight in panic.

Seamus roared, "Hold him fast, Blight!" Toby Hicks had saved Grace on numerous occasions. He could not let his younger brother succumb—not like this, and not without attempting rescue. Was this how it would end? Oh, Grace! She would never forgive him. And there would be no chance to remedy their rift if he blasted-well died now.

The rope about his chest tugged once then fell mercifully free. Seamus nodded at O'Malley as he re-sheathed his knife. Young Hicks's shriek roused Seamus, and he gripped O'Malley's hand, allowing himself to be hauled up onto the helm housing. He grunted, the bruised cartilage in his chest aching in objection.

The pulse of pain darting through his arm weakened his grip. Thank Heavens for O'Malley's firm clasp.

Another frigid wave washed over his exposed position, and he gasped in pain, his limbs so benumbed he almost lost his grip on the housing. He stared into the yawing abyss of waters ready to receive him. His oilskin! He must shed it or risk being pulled under by the weight of it. Without it, he hazarded a death of cold. The decision was not difficult—he shrugged the waterlogged garment from his shoulders and pointed at young Hicks.

"I m-must help him."

Behind him on the narrow box, O'Malley's steaming reply curled over his shoulder. "Blight's a strong man, sir. He has Hicks. We must make our own way."

Seamus's breath juddered, and he gripped his chest to stem the pain. "Go ahead. I require a minute. Must catch my b-breath." The cold reduced his words to the erratic pizzicato plucks of a novice viola player.

"Then we'll w-wait together," stammered O'Malley.

As the minutes ticked past, the sufferers' sobs and moans became hushed. The creaking planks and the hostile rumble of waves filled the awful silence. The lashing raindrops dwindled, and the golden orbs of light cut tenaciously through the thick bank of cloud. A hollow crack deep in the ship's bowels sent an instinctive quiver of fear across Seamus's nape and renewed the straggling survivors' cries. He stared back at O'Malley, who nodded, tight-lipped and grey with worry, the seasoned sailor in him also knowing that the leaning masts' timbers were threatening to resign themselves to the white rolling sea. If they collapsed, they would splinter the deck into kindling. O'Malley squeezed his eyes tightly against the inevitable plunge into the icy water.

Seamus cast one last look around. Heavens above! His voice rang out with the strength and clarity mastered by his years on the sea. "Look!" He pointed to the fallen mizzenmast nearest to them. "The masts! They've made a bridge to shore. O'Malley, we must move, or the c-cold'll get us."

In confirmation, another freezing wave washed over Seamus, gnawing mercilessly at his energy. The timber of the masts and the battered hull quivered, groaning under the remorseless surf, sounding out the certain death that awaited him if he remained aboard. As Seamus shifted around to gauge the distance to the fallen mizzenmast, a hot trill coursed up his spine as young Hicks slipped from Blight's grip, his blond head disappearing beneath the froth near the foremast. Damn this whole cursed wreck!

A large wave crashed over the beached hull, knocking Seamus off his precarious perch. In the water, and with his eyes fixed on young Hicks's bobbing head, Seamus pulled himself along with powerful strokes, each movement like a donkey-kick to the chest. He reached the mainmast and, taking a deep breath, plunged beneath the frigid water. The tangle of ropes groped for his kicking legs, but he burst up the other side with a roar, the stabbing cold slicing into his skull. He lashed out again, swimming towards the foremast where young Hicks struggled to haul himself onto the mast's trunk. The youngster's strength was failing, and despite his own fatigue, Seamus renewed his kicking. Swimming up to Hicks, Seamus slung his own arm over the thick trunk and snatched the youngster's collar. Poor lad was wide-eyed and mute with exhaustion.

"Get up, Hicks," growled Seamus as he tried to shove him up onto the mast. Hicks pulled upwards, his legs windmilling before he splashed back down into the water again. Reaching beneath the freezing water, Seamus grabbed the back of Hicks's breeches. With a herculean strength, he hauled him up, but it was not far enough, and the young man fell back with a gurgling cry. Damn and blast, he was too heavy! Why could he not be a lean whippet like his brother?

An arm reached from above. Blight! The topman's fiery hair

was plastered to his skull, the long locks parting around his face like orange curtains. By Heavens, he could kiss that ugly mug right now! Seamus snarled at Blight through his locked jaw. "Save him! I owe his brother a life."

"Mrs F.'ll never forgive me if I don't save you, sir!" Blight roared.

"It's an order, Blight. Take Hicks. Now."

Blight swore and nodded, counting out loud. "One, two, three!" Yanking the spluttering youngster clear of the water, he draped him over the mast. Hicks hung gasping and clinging to the wooden trunk like a limpet.

Blight's fingers, hooked into a frozen claw, reached down. "You next, sir."

"Get him to shore!" Seamus ordered.

With his ruddy-whiskered face contorted into a twist of agony and guilt, Blight snatched Hicks's collar and dragged the struggling youngster along the mast. "Stay put, Captain. I'll be back!" he yelled.

Seamus's breath curled in the cold air, and a sob caught in his throat as Grace materialised beside him, her billowing white cotton skirts like spectres encircling him.

"Hello, husband." Her warm voice filled the glacial chamber in his chest.

His teeth clenched so tightly that he did not think it possible to pry them apart. Cold water was the cruellest thief, stealing warmth when it did not even require it. "G-Grace. What are you doing?"

Her light laugh carried off like a light summer breeze. "Not freezing my tail off like a brass monkey that's for sure."

"Oh, my brave and darling Dulcinea. Even in the grimmest of situations, you still have the capacity to astound and humour me." He kissed her forehead, and she looked up at him with a tenderness that almost burst his heart.

"Do you recall what day it is?" Her plump, pink lips

tweaked up.

Oh, what he would do to taste them! He scrunched his brow in concentration, his mind slowed by the cold. A blurry image came to mind, and he remembered his last journal entry.

"Em-mily's birthday. Ten years old t-today," he stuttered.

One perfectly arched eyebrow rose, and she scoffed lightly. "You've chosen a rather curious way to celebrate." She wrapped her arms around his back, burying her soft face against his neck. Her warmth flowed into his core where it took shelter with his remaining heat, and his jaw no longer painfully hammered his teeth together, the intense cutting pain dissipating. This was what Heaven must feel like.

His own voice rumbled in his ears. "Remind me to laugh when it's all over."

She tilted her chin up, tightening her arm around his neck, and drew her face to his. Her warm breath blew the cold ache from his bones as her scent of lavender and liquorice, of sweet breast milk, and that unmistakable feminine scent of her came to him—finally, after all these months.

"I haven't the strength to lift you, my heart." Seamus's voice tightened with grief.

"I shan't let go," she murmured, the corners of her pretty mouth lifting.

A distant part of his mind sparked at the mortal danger, but he was unafraid. With the world raging around him, he held the intensity of his wife's green gaze and allowed her to pour into his unshielded soul. She smiled as his torment eased. Her golden skin shone serenely as another ray of sunshine broke through from the heavens, illuminating her in the soft morning light. The sunlit wisps of brown and gold and red in her hair arched like an auburn halo around her head.

Seamus drew her to his lips and breathed her in. "I'll cherish and honour you through this life. And into the next." He closed his eyes and let the eternity of her love wash over him.

Chapter Twenty-Five

A soft knock at the door brought Grace instantly awake, the mother in her alert to noises that did not belong in the night.

"Mrs Fitzwilliam!" Victor's whisper was laced with urgency. "Are you awake, madam?"

Throwing back the covers, Grace's bare feet connected with the smooth polished floor, as icy and unforgiving as a frozen pond, and she jerked them up. Sliding them into her wool-lined house-slippers, she snatched open the door and was met by Victor's pale face, drawn with worry beneath his black whiskers. He lifted the lantern higher.

"It's Adelia," Victor whispered. "She says the babe's coming. She's in a bad way." Grace doubted the shepherd had much experience with childbirth, but still, her heart lurched in her chest. She had helped Billy set plenty of broken bones and stitch torn flesh, but other than her own, she had no practice in child-birth either.

A slow, low wail filtered through the hallway, and Victor's mouth turned down, his nested brows drawing together. "Will you come? Please."

"It's all right," Grace assured, slipping into her nightgown. "All that hullabaloo shows she's still in good spirits."

In the bedchamber, Adelia's golden-nested head swivelled on the bank of pillows. "Oh, Grace!" Her feet were flat against the sheets, legs arched like a grasshopper. Tendrils of pale hair clung to her forehead. "Something's wrong!" She gnashed her teeth, groaning against another quickening, her clenched fists threatening to tear the sheets. Collapsing back on the pillows, she swung her panicked hazel gaze to Grace.

"I'm here now," Grace assured, wiping back the sweat-soaked strands from her friend's forehead. "All's well." She flicked her wrist at Victor hovering rigidly near the door. "Fetch Wee Granny Mac, won't you?"

The man span with such haste his shoulder crashed into the door frame, and he disappeared into the blackened hallway with a grunt.

Adelia grimaced and reddened again. She dug her heels into the bed, her swollen body rocking side to side before sagging into a damp, limp heap. "I wish Mr Barclay were here," she wailed. "He'd know what to do."

It was true. Elijah had not only been present, but active at each of his children's births. First and foremost a farmer, he had been a practical man with few sensibilities. He had told Grace that delivering his children was no more an untoward task than aiding ewes during lambing. This was the first Adelia was birthing without him. No wonder her dear friend was so distressed.

"It should be his ruddy head between my knees, welcoming

our little one into the world," Adelia wailed. "It's how it's always been!"

"I'm here." Worrying that she fell woefully short of her friend's expectations, Grace pressed her hands onto the swollen belly, thinking back to her own births. She had not been aware of any of her babe's movements during the pains. Were they supposed to move? She strained to recall Billy's advice. In answer, the child beneath her palms heaved. Oh, thank goodness! Grace swallowed the jagged peach-pit of nervousness and smiled brightly.

A soft tap at the door revealed Wee Granny Mac in her drab, brown dress, her head tied in a beige kerchief. Her tiny leather boots shuffled over to the bed. With eyes bright and alert, she nodded at Adelia as her knobbed fingers unbuttoned her cuffs and rolled her sleeves above the elbows.

Wee Granny Mac glared at Victor and, jabbing a leather bundle at him, ordered, "Fetch more sheets, and a bowl of hot water. Then scrub ma instruments with lye soap. In boiling water —as hot as yer hands can bear. Rinse 'em well, and be sure to dry 'em with a clean cloth. Want no trace of sheep about 'em, aye?"

The silent giant lumbered from the room, looking relieved at having a practical task to hand.

The old woman clambered onto the wide bed. "Let's have a wee peek." Her gnarled fingers expertly examined Adelia's stomach. "The wean isn't head down, but 'tisn't lying sideward either." Her arm reached beneath Adelia's amniotic-soaked, blood-smeared shift, and with a satisfied harrumph, she leaned back. "Yer nearly there, lassie." She patted Adelia's knee as though patting a sheep. "'Tis anyone's guess as to which bit pops out first."

Victor returned, his thick arms laden with all the ordered items. He carefully placed the water bowl down without spilling any and piled the clean sheets beside it. Wee Granny Mac took the instruments bundled in a clean cloth and unhurriedly laid them on the bedside table, metal chinking as she set each item side by side.

Victor backed towards the door. Grace felt sorry for him. Adelia's suffering was not even his fault—he had not planted this child within her, and he was clearly discomfited by his wife's pain.

Wee Granny Mac twisted her neck and barked, "You own a pen, Shyling?"

Victor's back bumped against the door frame, and he frowned. "A p-pen?"

"Aye, best be getting back to it afore the station manager notices ye're missing!"

Grace gasped, and she injected admonishment into her tone. "Wee Granny Mac!"

The burly shepherd cleared his throat. "Oh, right," he muttered, gripping the brass doorknob. "I'll be in the library should you require anything."

Wee Granny Mac snorted as the door thumped closed, and Grace helped her pile clean sheets under Adelia just as she released another eerie moan. She crushed Grace's hand, puffing and hissing sharp breaths through pursed lips. Flailing heavily against the pillows, she snapped her teeth audibly. "If Mr Barclay were here, I'd tear off his bollocks for leaving me!"

Grace patted Adelia's white-clenched knuckles, disheartened how inadequate the gesture felt to appease her friend's pain and fear. If only Billy were here with a handy dose of laudanum.

Tears welled in Adelia's bloodshot eyes. "This is different to the other times. I'm dying!"

"Not on my watch," said Wee Granny Mac crustily, patting Adelia on the knee again. She looked at Grace and bobbed her scarfed head towards the newly scrubbed implements. "Pass me those scissors." She crooned gruffly as another quickening gripped Adelia. "Och, not long now, lassie. Yer doing grand."

Grace handed over a gleaming pair of scissors. "These ones?"

"Aye." Wee Granny Mac took the implement and ducked beneath Adelia's shift. Adelia screeched in pain, scrambling back against the pillows. She laid a withering glare on the old woman, who reappeared and dropped the bloody-tipped scissors beside her on the bed. "Needed a wee bit more room to move. We have a foot now—all wee toes accounted."

A new tightening drew Adelia's anger away from the tiny Scottish woman, and she roared, digging her heels into the bed and sliding down the pillows like a slow-moving avalanche. Wee Granny Mac inclined her head at Grace. "Can't have her wiggling about like this. Take a firm grip of her from behind. Pin her as ye would a sheep in a stand, so she doesn't move."

Grace clambered behind Adelia, whispering apologies, and hauled her into a sitting position. She pressed a kiss against her friend's moist hairline, remembering the smell of salt-scented birth-waters, perspiration, and blood from her own births. Adelia lolled heavily against her shoulder, and Grace tucked a damp strand of hair behind her friend's ear. "Nearly there, my friend. Nearly there."

Adelia shook her head fretfully, red-cheeked and exhausted, before straining hard once again.

From behind the makeshift screen of nightdress spread across Adelia's knees, Wee Granny Mac grumbled to herself. "Up the leg we go—ah—'tis a laddie." The old woman closed her eyes, her hands skilfully probing inside and out. She grunted in frustration. "Wee rascal's knee is tucked beneath his chin." She glanced sharply at Grace. "Here comes another pain. I've hold of the wean's ankle. Hold her steady, lass—don't want to lose ma grip!"

Adelia arched back so hard that Grace had flashes of her breastbone caving in, but she held her friend firmly, sharing her laboured breathing. "Come now. You can do it."

Wee Granny Mac let out a triumphant whoop. "Ha! *Both* legs! One decent push ought to do it."

"I can't," gasped Adelia miserably. "It's tearing me in two."

"Nonsense!" snapped Wee Granny Mac. "Ye've done this time aplenty to know this is it. Cheery lass."

Adelia scowled mutinously at the unsympathetic old woman, her growl of objection building as another tightening began. The veins on Adelia's neck bulged huge and red, and her growl turned into a deep-pitted roar. Unconcerned with the evil looks being cast her way, Wee Granny Mac ducked her head behind the shift again. Adelia's war cry ended abruptly, and her chin slumped to her panting chest. She reached up an arm and gripped the back of Grace's head. "Oh, please. Tell me it's out!"

Wee Granny Mac's weatherworn face popped up as casually as a neighbour nipping her head through the door. "Just awaiting his wee head."

"Pull it out!" retorted Adelia.

"No lass, that'd snap his wee neck as sure as a hangman's noose." The old woman sucked her lips between her gums and chewed down in concentration. "I'll help ye ease his chin out. Aye, here's another one. Give it all ye have, lass."

Adelia took a deep breath, and her whole frame shook with the effort, her low, even keening suddenly ending in a grunt. She slumped limply against Grace, panting hard.

Wee Granny Mac's wrinkles creased deeply in a celebratory grin. "Ye did it, lass! 'Tis a braw laddie. He's a bit on the wee side but—"

As though to prove to his mother that he was indeed a braw laddie, the babe let out a high-pitched wail that gurgled at first but cleared into a lung-splitting howl of objection as Wee Granny Mac indelicately scooped his mouth clear of mucous and blood. With age-old efficiency, the old shepherdess wiped down the squalling infant with a damp cloth and soft tufts of wool, free of dirty burred ends, but rich and slick with lanolin. She swaddled the tiny boy and handed the whimpering bundle to Adelia.

Leaning Adelia back onto the pillows, Grace stretched her cramped legs and wiggled her right foot to shake some feeling back into it. She stroked the bald scalp above the little face that scowled as though its owner was angry at the world. "He's so like the others. Do you have a name?"

Adelia tilted her head back, eyes glazed with exhaustion. "Mr Barclay wanted Moses." She hesitated, chin quivering. "I'm naming him Moses Elijah—after his papa."

Grace smiled. "How fortunate Master Moses chose today to arrive. He shares our Em's birthday. I'll postpone my return to town a few more days."

"Oh, no, Grace. I've the nursery maids to help. And Victor too. I know you must return Em and Eddy to school."

Leaning down, Grace pressed a kiss to her friend's damp cheek. "I've also to reopen the shipping office. Don't want Seamus hearing that I shut up shop *ad infinitum* to allow his agent to be wed."

"I hope he returns soon."

"So do I."

"I'm glad you're here." Adelia slung the bundled babe over her shoulder. "You saw me through the early days of my marriage to Mr Barclay. It feels right that you're here for the start of this one too."

Chapter Twenty-Six

I n the Elias Shipping Company office above Barclay & Co. Woolstore, Grace smiled at Toby, the intelligent gentleman before her catching her off guard. How dapper he looked in his new three-piece suit! Familial pride warmed her décolletage. And how far he had risen from that scrawny cook's boy on the *Discerning*, whose backside she had sought to preserve all those years ago. Now, *he* was the dependable one.

She peered through the grimy window, looking down on Semi-Circular Quay. The curved stone quay accommodated a forest of masts of nearly thirty merchantmen loading or offloading goods, the colony's life-source. An assortment of figures scurried about, pushing, pulling, heaving—carrying the motion of life on the busy dock.

Grace scanned around the room, nodding in satisfaction at Toby's attempt to have the shipping office resemble the professional space of a reputable company. Pity about the stink. The

cloying reek of lanolin from the Woolstore below was tantamount to shoving her nose into a sheep and sucking in a deep
breath. The enormous oil painting hanging on the wall opposite
the window was another of Billy's creations. The *Elias* was
rounding the Cape Horn in a storm, and he had brought the ship
to life in the fierce clutches of mountainous green seas and
bruised, swirling clouds. She stared at the two tiny figures
aboard—her and Seamus. *Oh, husband, do hurry home!* The
ache of missing him was a gaping chasm these days.

This painting was her second favourite piece—after the
family portrait, of course—especially since she had given up on
that wretched needlework. Clothes she could manage, and even a
quilt, but she just did *not* have the patience to count out all those
blasted stitches. At least she had provided Adelia with a good
laugh. The back of her unfinished embroidery looked more like a
surgeon's butchery under cannon fire than a work of feminine
finesse.

The two bulky cabinets housed an assortment of shelves,
stacked high with piles of bound paperwork. Some of the pigeon
holes were filled with loose sheaths, and the deeper shelves
held leather-bound ledgers. She winced at Toby's chaotic filing
system—a complete contrast to Seamus's symmetrical one in his
library.

"I know it doesn't look it, Mrs F., but there's a system to that
mess, I assure you." Toby's glance darted from the piles of
paperwork to her.

She tutted lightly. "I've no doubt in your clerical abilities,
Toby." She sauntered across the new rug and ran her finger along
the desk's bevelled edge, behind which hung the Union Jack and
a framed Queen Victoria.

"The new desk is marvellous."

"Courtesy of K. S. Wong, the Chinese cabinet maker."

"Ah, yes, I've heard of him. He specialises in cheaper lines
of furniture, doesn't he?" She trailed her fingertips along the

upright chair back tucked the other side of the desk. "Hmm, his quality rivals European design. I must pay him a visit. See if he has any pieces for Cliffview Cottage."

"I could escort you to his shop, if you like?" offered Toby.

"Let's sit and chat awhile, shall we?" Grace lowered herself into the straight-backed chair.

"Wouldn't you prefer to try out the new armchair?" A dark flush slashed high across his cheekbones as he gestured towards the finely carved, leather-seated armchair.

"No." She absently fiddled with the Luckenbooth brooch on her chest. "You're this company's agent. That seat is yours." Seeing his hesitation, she smiled warmly. "How is your lovely wife?"

Toby grinned like a youngster who had just won a toffee apple at a fair. "She's marvellous, thank you for asking. Madame Dubois has no issue with Erin remaining a co-owner of Dubois House even though she's married now. In fact, she says it lends the school a respectable air to have two married women at the helm."

"I hadn't realised there was a *Monsieur* Dubois?"

Toby hummed and tapped his lips. "I believe he's what one might call… a character of convenience."

"Ah, the illusion of a husband can work wonders in this town." Restless, she rose and peered through the window again, scouring the ships in the harbour and straining to catch sight of the ones coming in from the ocean. A group of seamen on one of the smaller vessels formed a human chain from the deck, up the metal ladder hanging over the quayside, along which they passed kegs and wooden boxes. A highly polished binnacle on a Royal Naval brig gleamed gold in the bright sunlight. Bleeding rats' tails—none were the *Elias*. She turned and feigned a casual air. "Speaking of husbands—isn't the *Elias* due any day now? Is there any word of her whereabouts?"

Toby's pale brows knitted together. "No. I thought Captain

Fitzwilliam might've sent word after he arrived in London. Perhaps he secured a quicker-than-expected turnaround? No point in sending a letter he'd only beat home."

"Perhaps." A cold slide of disappointment slithered down the back of her legs. Three solid taps on the door reverberated through the floorboards, and she raised her eyebrows at Toby. Could it be? No, why would Seamus knock?

Toby rose and swung the door open.

Appleby! What on earth did this stewed fruit want? He was as welcome as a mouthful of ulcers. The man blinked unapologetically at her over Toby's shoulder. He slid his hat off slowly, ruffling his wiry hair. "Madam." His waste barely flinched in a bow.

"Captain Appleby. How may I be of service?" Toby asked stiffly. "Mrs Fitzwilliam and I are in a meeting."

Grace was impressed by the tone of authority in Toby's voice. Clearly, Appleby heard it too, and he straightened his hunched shoulders, harrumphing. "I wish to speak to the commander, not the cabin boy."

His awkward pause and lack of eye contact sent a charged shimmer of worry across her scalp. She was certain neither she nor Toby would have given him any cause to question the Elias Shipping Company's operation. Besides, the man was so lazy that he only breathed because he had to. There was no way he had the skill or patience to find fault in their ledgers.

"Any news you have for me, sir, or this company can be spoken before Mr Hicks. He is the company agent after all," said Grace.

The harbour master raised his wobbly jowl and withdrew a folded broadsheet from beneath his arm. "I come bearing— news." He rotated his wrist, turning his hat in circles.

Toby took the paper and glanced at it briefly. His head swung around, his grey eyes wide and filled with alarm.

"What is it?" Grace shot to her feet.

In a couple of strides, Toby was by her side, his hand cupping her elbow. He guided her around the desk to the leather armchair. "Have a seat, Mrs F."

Her watery knees collapsed, and she sat heavily, the red leather cushion exhaling a hiss. "Toby, you're scaring me. What is it? Is it Seamus?" Her heartbeat thumped powerfully against the tight band of headache across her brow. She sat so still that she could have been made of marble—she certainly felt as cold.

Toby laid the broadsheet before her, and she lifted it, her gaze skittering across the tiny black script. The words blurred in a watery strain, and she blinked to clear her vision. She stopped on the square-shaped article in the top left-hand corner. Fear drove an icy spear down the hollow of her spine, impaling her to her seat.

MISSING SHIP

Hope has been abandoned of the missing merchant ship Elias. *The vessel, which was going from London to Sydney, was last seen by the Portuguese merchantman* Santa Catarina *just off the Cape of Good Hope in July last. The* Elias *was likely caught in the violent storm that swept the Cape shortly after she was last sighted. The ship was listed to load wool at Sydney for London and was then expected to load cargo, including 45,000 gallons of spirits and 250 barrels of gunpowder, in London for Sydney. The vessel is posted at Lloyds as missing, and it is thought that the ship has foundered with all hands. The* Elias *was in command of Captain S. A. Fitzwilliam, a native of the United Kingdom.*

Grace's stomach heaved, and a squirt of bitter bile flooded her mouth. *No!* She tore the sheet in half, but the words *foundered with all hands* still taunted her from the torn, feathered edge. She mentally ticked the names of her friends as though they were mustered before her. Ben Blight. O'Malley. Billy Sykes. Shelby Hicks. Black spots danced before her eyes, and she crushed the thin paper in her fist and tossed it across the desk.

"No! No! No!" She glared at the crumpled paper, slowly unfurling itself like a damaged moth trying to take flight. She slammed her palm onto the twitching ball.

Appleby cleared his throat. "The *Elias* is one of four ships reported lost during that storm."

The floor tipped, and Grace dug her fingers into the desk, her nails biting into the maroon leather inlay. Oh, Lord, please no! She wanted nothing more than to sink to the floor and release the primal howl building in her chest, but she was damned if she would parade her terror before Appleby. She glared at the harbour master, who still hovered and still turned his hat.

"How long have you known?" Toby's demand held little regard that he was addressing a ranked superior.

Who could blame him? That consumptive air-waster had just delivered news of his brother's demise. Oh, Toby!

Appleby gave another phlegmy cough. "On the fourth of July, *Santa Catarina* had already rounded the Cape on her way north to Portuguese Guinea when she crossed paths with the *Elias*. The two captains hailed one another, and Captain dos Santos delivered a packet to Captain Fitzwilliam." Appleby swiped his face with his handkerchief again.

Grace swallowed the iron ball in her throat, forcing her voice to stay strong. "Please, sit. Tell it all."

Toby's hand remained heavy and warm on her shoulder as the harbour master waddled over to the chair opposite. He sat with a long-winded sigh, as though relieved to be off his feet, and placed his hat on his knees.

"Upon Captain dos Santos' return to Cape Town a month later, he was surprised to learn that the *Elias* had not docked to restock supplies or run repairs. When he heard news of the storm, he established, with reasonable certainty, that his was the last ship to have contact with the *Elias*." Appleby's gaze fixed on the painting of the ship whose name had just left his lips. He shuffled straighter in his chair and pulled at the cravat at his throat. "Captain dos Santos sent a letter to London as well as Sydney Town with the hope that either port might have news of the *Elias*'s whereabouts. His letter arrived yesterday." Appleby wiped a palm down his thigh, leaving a dark smear on the navy fabric. "By all accounts, she's been missing seventy-seven days."

Seventy-seven days! How had she not known? Not sensed anything? Grace stared at Appleby who, having come to the end of his news, picked at his thumbnail in the silence.

Toby spoke first. "Thank you for the information, Captain. I trust you'll keep us abreast of further news?"

Appleby's bounce from his seat did little to hide his desire to vacate the shipping office with expediency. "Quite right. You'll be the first to know. Good day to you both." He banged the door shut, his heavy footsteps thundering down the outer stairs.

Grace sagged like a windless sail, and Toby grabbed her hand.

"Let's not presume the worst," he said. "The *Elias* was barely due back. There's no cause for alarm. If Captain Appleby had given us this news seventy-seven days past her *arrival date*, we might be forgiven for worrying. Have faith, Mrs F., Captain Fitzwilliam will be on our doorstep demanding an accounting of our profits before we know it." He handed her a white hand-kerchief.

Grace touched her wet cheek. How long had the tears been falling? Had she begun crying with Appleby still about? She took a deep, fortifying breath and looked into her friend's face. Good gracious, he looked so youthful with his optimism. His smile widened, and the deepened creases around his eyes trans-formed into an air of maturity and strength. She squeezed his hands tighter, trying to draw some of that strength into her.

"It's so difficult, not even knowing where they are or if they're injured." Grace sniffed loudly, her breath juddering. "You must be so worried about Shelby."

"Fretting won't hurry them home."

"You're right. We must keep busy. Keep a purpose about us."

Toby patted her hand. "You've fortitude enough to bear up until more news arrives, Mrs F."

Grace drew back her shoulders and swiped the handkerchief under her nose again. "Indeed. I'm no good at moping." She stared down at the shiny desktop with its uneven pattern of ink stains. Her nails had cut little crescents in the leather inlay. She frowned, drawing her raging thoughts to order. "I'll write to him —to Seamus—and send the letters to all corners of the globe— until someone brings news of him."

Toby nodded. "That's a fair start. Will you tell the children?"

"No." Her heart sank below her stomach at the thought of Emily's and Edwin's faces hearing the news. Telling them their brother had passed had been an excruciating experience, but now they were older and acutely aware how permanent death was. She would not subject them to such misery. Not without certainty. "As you said, fretting won't hurry them home. Our Em and Eddy are occupied well enough at school." Goodness knew every fibre of her being wanted to clasp her children to her chest and never let go, but that was selfishness speaking. She pressed a brave smile to her lips. "Last I spoke to our Em, she gushed about excursions to the beach and sailing regattas with her fellow boarders. Seems cruel to drag them away from such merriment."

"I wish there was a tonic for relieving your suffering." Toby lowered his chin, his soft grey gaze covering her in kindness. "Or a way for me to bear more of your suffering."

"You've enough to bear with your brother." She gripped his fingers. "Seamus is alive."

"How can you be so sure?"

Grace tapped her chest. "I can still feel him, in here." She swallowed. "I can't explain it. The strength of it is so real. I know without a shadow of a doubt he isn't gone." She withdrew her hand from his grip, their palms slicking apart. "Let me begin that letter. I'll feel better talking to him."

She opened the drawer with a dry scrape and dropped a clump of tidy white sheets to her left. She slid one sheet before her, and, picking up the goose-feather quill, she dipped the spearheaded nib into the inkwell and tapped off the excess drops.

Elias Shipping Company, Sydney Town, New Holland, 19
September 1842

My love,

I have had news of your disappearance. I refuse to believe you are gone, despite the opinion of many that you are. Dare I hope that you have only lost your rudder and been blown off course? Or perhaps been blown so far south that the pack ice has hold of you? Are you shored up on a desolate beach somewhere, running repairs to the Elias *after the ferocious storm you encountered?*

Wherever you are, my love, I refuse to believe anything other than the fact that you are alive and well, albeit perhaps a little soggy and battered. I feel your soul still entwined with mine. I know you are not dead.

I shall send dozens of copies of this letter with every ship, in every direction, with the eternal hope that one shall reach you. You need not worry that word of your disappearance has me fretting. I am bearing up well with Toby's support.

I trust you will send word at your earliest convenience, but until then, I shall say a prayer every morning and every evening for you. I know I vowed to cherish and honour you through this life and into the next, but I am not ready to keep that vow just yet.

Return to me, Seamus Fitzwilliam. I need you.

Your ever-loving wife,
Grace Elizabeth Fitzwilliam

Her hand ached, the tips of her two fingers and thumb, holding the quill, stained black. There, first letter done! She would write fifty, a hundred, a *thousand* more—if that many ships came this way. She would spread word to every captain, master, first mate, and lieutenant of every ship headed across the world. One of these letters would reach Seamus. There simply was no alternative.

Chapter Twenty-Seven

A couple of weeks later, bent over her letter-writing, Grace perked up at the pie-seller's cries filtering up from the quay below. "Fresh-baked pasties. Come get 'em while they're 'ot!" She dropped the inky pen with a clunk and arched her spine over the chairback, stretching out the stiffness of her repetitive task. Beside her, a neat tower of white packets teetered. Ten letters written that morn—only two more to meet today's quota.

"Fancy a pastie, Mrs F.?" Toby rose from his chair and withdrew a brass watch from his fob pocket. "I'm popping down to fetch myself one."

Food held little interest these days, but since she had only sipped a cup of tea for breakfast and had eaten no supper last night, a low growl in her stomach answered for her. "That would be lovely, thank you."

Toby rammed on his tweed cap. "Back in a jiffy."

A few minutes later, he burst through the shipping-office door, two paper-wrapped pasties balanced in one hand. At his energetic spurt across the room, Grace laughed. "You seem rather keen to tuck into your meat pie."

Toby slid the aromatic packets onto the desk, his voice cracking in excitement. "The *Saviour* is here!"

Grace smiled at his enthusiasm. "Those must be quite some pasties to bring back the Lord."

Toby's wide grin split his sandy whiskers. He shook his head. "No. The *Saviour of the Seas*. An immigrant ship."

"Are you expecting delivery of another wife I don't know about?" she teased. Grace's smile wavered as a cold trickle of doubt slid down her spine. "Has your affection for Mrs Hicks already cooled?" Hearing Toby's account of his new wife was the one lone flower of joy on her withered vine of misery these days.

"Not at all." He snatched up her hand, his fingers toasty from the pasties. "The pilots are all atwitter about the *Saviour*'s arrival. Apparently, she's one of Captain Fitzwilliam's new ships."

Grace launched her to her feet, the chair-back tipping and thudding behind her. "Seamus is here?"

The golden whiskers on Toby's top lip firmed, and he gripped her fingers tighter. The light in his grey eyes cooled. "I didn't say that."

The worry Toby's news had set free fluttered down like a flock of iron birds, curling her shoulders again under their unbearable weight. "Oh," she said in a small voice.

"But I believe Billy Sykes is aboard—as surgeon to the passengers."

Grace blinked. Billy? How could Billy be aboard, but not Seamus? Why were they not together? She rolled her shoulders back. Only one way to find out. Tugging Toby's hand, she cocked her head towards the door. "Come on then. Let's see if it's true."

Grace tied her bonnet and led the way down the stairs to the busy quay. Clambering onto an empty crate, she folded her arms tightly, her eyes fixed to the approaching brig's two square-rigged masts. Aboard, the sailors scurried about, preparing the gangplank and mooring lines.

The captain stood on the quarterdeck with, Grace presumed, his wife by his side. On the main deck, an assortment of females in varying states of health and spirits pressed eagerly against the gunwales, some waving at the men's enthusiastic calls below, others standing as watchful and wary as Grace. With the gangplank lowered, a surge of bodies purged themselves onto the quay. Some looked perfectly respectable, in plain but complete complements of clothing. Dark-eyed, dishevelled mothers dragged gaggles of small children ashore. Grace squeezed her upper arms, her attention drawn to a tight huddle of females dressed in matching drab linen frocks, each carrying an identical locked wooden box. Her heart plummeted, and she gripped Toby's shoulder. "Good Lord, Toby! They're only young girls."

Toby patted her hand. "Likely orphans, Mrs F."

A black-uniformed immigration officer bellowed, "Fare-paying passengers, this way to the drays. Take your belongings with you. Ain't no servants to carry your bags here." He pointed to a hollow, empty warehouse. "Fare-assisted passengers, this way for processing. That's it. Keep it moving. Follow the crowd."

A curious mob gathered on the quay to scrutinise the new arrivals. This was nothing new. She had seen it before, the scene not much changed since she first stepped foot on King's Warf years back with Seamus, and our Em but a babe. The only difference now was instead of a weathered, wooden wharf with scattered buildings along the foreshore, there now stood the impressive semi-circular stone quay and towering warehouses. But the mix of inhabitants was unchanged. Lecherous men looking for a young bride, respectable graziers and merchantmen appraising the women like livestock, business owners looking for healthy employees and even wives, the drunken whores spying potential rivals in the new arrivals, and the plain old idlers who had nothing better to do with their time than ogle unfortunates. There was an equal call of men's and women's voices above the dock's standard workings.

"Ain't no easier work than flat on your backs, girls! Madame Chastity White, at your service."

"We don't want no clumsy-ankle, thick-waisted bags fillin' our men's beds. Away, the lot o' yous!"

"Stinkin' bloody papists! Nothin' better than workhouse sweepings is wot you are!"

Distracted by a movement at the top of the gangplank, Grace gasped. Her fingers clawed into Toby's shoulder as she shook him. Stretching onto her tiptoes, she waved. "Billy! Over here!"

Her friend's dark head towered above the press of women as he carved his way towards her. She wanted to jump down and run to him, but she was afraid to lose sight of his wide grin. He raised his black hat, waving it as he flicked his hair aside with a toss of his head. Oh, how she had missed that silly fringe!

Tucking his hat under his elbow, Billy grabbed Toby's hand in a double grip. "Sweet Mary mother, you're a sight for sore eyes, Hicks!" He turned to Grace, and she launched at him, gripping his neck as though she meant never to let go again.

"Oh, Billy!" she choked.

"Now then, flower." He hummed into her hair, his solid arms enveloping her in a hug that restored some hope and happiness to her heart.

He stank of rotten eggs, but she did not care. He was here! She drew back, gripping his solid, wide hands, determined to hold onto him as long as he allowed. She dipped her face, and hot tears dripped from her chin. She laughed, her breath catching in a hiccough. "Your fingers—they're yellow."

Billy chuckled with an apologetic grin. "Been making

sulphur ointment for patients plagued with itching," he explained. "I'm a bit ripe on the nose."

"I could do with a liberal dose of your valerian root tincture." She shivered as he ran his hand gently down her arm.

His black eyebrows furrowed. "You not sleeping well, flower?"

"Not since news of the *Elias*'s disappearance."

Billy's fingers crushed hers, his tanned face blanching to the colour of sun-bleached driftwood. "She's not here? She was supposed to arrive before us."

Chewing the inside of her cheek, Grace shook her head. "Missing one hundred days now. Last seen north of the Cape of Good Hope."

Billy ripped one hand away and scoured his fingers through his hair, grabbing a fistful. "Good God! If she's wrecked anywhere along that coastline, then we sailed clean past her."

"You weren't to know," she said gently.

Toby gripped Billy's bicep. "Ocean's a vast expanse to search for one small ship. Captain dos Santos—the last to see the *Elias*—did his best sending word on to us here."

Grace's chin quivered. "Oh Billy, it was so strained between us when the captain left. I couldn't leave the children. I'm sorry there was no time to bid you farewell."

Billy helped her down from the crate and tucked her arm snugly in his elbow. His black mop, in desperate need of a trim, flopped over his forehead. "Now flower, remember the prophecy of the tea leaves—you'll require great patience. Everything will come in divine timing."

"But what if it doesn't?" she snapped, instantly regretting her sharp tone. She inhaled and swallowed, gentling her words. "What if he never comes back?"

What more was there to say? Seamus was gone. The warmth in her cheeks cooled. She placed her palms against Billy's chest, his pounding heart beating reassuringly through the cotton shirt.

Billy tilted his head back and, blinking up at the sky, puffed his cheeks out as he released a slow breath. He regarded her with that patience born from years as a physician—attentive, listening.

Unease wriggled through her belly like an eel in the mud. She tugged the lapels of his coat. "What is it?"

He pressed her hands to his chest. "There's a time in life for sunshine, and a time for wintery greys. Today is one of those days." She clawed her fingers into balls beneath his palms, and he gripped them tighter. "Flower, I bear terrible news. About the admiral."

The light about her dimmed, and she staggered a step back, her heel banging into the crate. Billy held on tightly, as though determined to keep hold of her until the light returned. Her stomach cramped. "What about him?"

"Did news of the train derailment in Versailles reach the broadsheets here?"

She shook her head and whimpered. "Not that I saw. Was he aboard?"

"Yes, we both were. Captain Fitzwilliam too."

Her blood ran cold, her breath quickening. He scooped an arm around her back, drawing her near, as if to absorb her imminent pain.

"Captain Fitzwilliam was unharmed. As was I," he assured.

"And Uncle Farfar?"

"I'm sorry, Grace. He didn't survive."

She blinked, dry-eyed. Could she pretend as though he had not spoken? Not delivered this heartbreak?

Billy continued. "The admiral was an extraordinary man— one of the finest."

"I don't understand. How did you and Seamus walk away unscathed, but he didn't?"

Billy bowed his head. "I'd rather spare you the details." He cupped her cheek in his wide palm, his words gentle and low. "But if you wish to hear them—"

Toby's interest in steam engines for their ships had resulted in many an hour of discussion recently. She had heard enough of blowing boilers and exploding fireboxes to know of their danger. She pressed her forehead against the solidness of Billy's chest and shook her head. "No. Not right now."

She clung to him, his crush blanketing her in a promise of protection. She would stand here all day if she could—just the two of them, alone, away from the world's disasters, and not caring about the crowd. Good grief, she really did not wish to know whether Uncle Farfar was boiled or burned alive.

Raising her chin, she asked softly, "Did he suffer?"

The dark-brown flicker of worry in his eyes hardened, and he shook his head emphatically, his black fringe swinging. "Absolutely not. It was instant."

Oh, thank the Lord! A ball of saliva squelched down her tight throat. She tried hard not to picture Uncle Farfar's body cold and alone in a coffin. It was a ridiculous notion to imagine him so, when she wholeheartedly believed him to be in Heaven—with Elias. Except, this left her alone, truly alone. Although she had not seen him in years, he was the last of her family. Was she now the matriarch? Did this make her an orphan? It certainly made her feel like one. Though, if what Billy said was true, the admiral would have been blissfully unaware of his impending death. Given a choice, she would opt for a death like that too. But not just yet. She still had too much life to live, and a husband to find.

Grace squeezed her eyes shut, warm tears building behind her eyelids. "I know I haven't seen him in years, but to know he's now gone... I miss him," she whispered, an ocean of tears bleeding down her cheeks.

"I know, flower, I know. May I accompany you back to the office?" Billy offered. "Or perhaps home, wherever that is these days?"

Quelling her fragility, she squared her shoulders and, gritting her back teeth, sniffed. "No need, Toby's here. You've your hands full with this lot." She waved over the crowd of women streaming into the high-roofed warehouse.

Toby's chuckle was mirthless. "God help your dealing with the new customs officer, Holloway. Right nuisance, he is. He placed the *Marigold* under quarantine last week, citing an outbreak of cholera. Bastard won't let anyone off until that grandiose government medical officer, White, gives them a clean bill of health to disembark. Her captain's declared her disease-free. 'Twas simply a particularly rough voyage that affected a larger number of souls with the plague of the sea."

"Best I go offer Holloway assurance that all passengers aboard the *Saviour* are clean." He stroked the back of Grace's hand. "Shall I pop by later with something to ease your distress?"

She raised her chin. "I'm not so much distressed as—as *determined*." She bobbed her head.

"To do what exactly?" asked Billy, one eyebrow cocked.

"I'm penning letters to Seamus with the hopes one shall reach him." Giving him one last squeeze, she slid her hand from his arm and nodded at Toby. "Best return to them."

"Aye, aye, Mrs F.," said Toby, winking. Grace appreciated his attempted levity. He tucked her hand into his elbow. "Let's hasten before our furry foe scurries down from the rafters for a taste of our pies."

Chapter Twenty-Eight

Summer arrived early, and with a vengeance, bringing with it wretched flies—and no news. Grace tramped along the cobbled street towards Semi-Circular Quay, the skirts of her light cotton dress swishing furiously. Emily's dress design from school was a godsend, and Grace had pilfered the pattern to sew herself three new summer frocks. No heavy fabrics or layers of petticoats would stifle her, thank you very much.

She had hoped a walk might clear her mind, but the thumping beat in her heels coursed through her hips, up her backbone, and crashed into the base of her skull. The repetitive impact jarred her teeth, intensifying her headache. The lure of the Elias Shipping Company's cooler interior drew her closer.

The tang of hot metal from the iron foundry stuck in her craw. On the street outside the ironworks, Big Bob's span of black bullocks stood patiently as he threw a rope over the towering cargo to his sidekick on the other side of the wagon.

"Why, if 'tisn't the bloody wonderous Lady Cap herself." The towering driver beamed.

Yabby slunk from beneath the wagon, his mottled grey-and-white ears flattened, tail wagging, and whining with pleasure. Grace held out her hand, and his speckled muzzle nuzzled into her palm. She had no idea how old the dog was, but he showed no signs of slowing down. Tongue lolling, he still looked thoroughly pleased with himself as he tipped his head for a better scratch behind the ear.

"Where are you off to today?" Grace tried to gauge the lumps and boxes on the wagon.

"Gilly Downs," boomed Big Bob, catching the snake of flying rope. His strong, thick fingers worked nimbly to wind the rope around the wagon's side beam, and he yanked it hard to tighten the slack before tossing it back over. "Victor Shylin's ordered himself some monstrous new contraption for balin' wool. Though 'tis in a million bloody bits right now."

"Ah yes, that must be their new iron-screw wool press." Her lips twitched in amusement at Big Bob's amazement.

He gaped. "How the flamin' Hell d'ya know that?"

She tilted her head. "Mrs Shyling told me they'd ordered it in her last letter."

Big Bob laughed. "Bloody oath, Lady Cap, you don't 'alf get about, do ya?" He shuffled along the wagon as the rope came flying over again. Gently kneeing Yabby out of the way, he growled affectionately, "Git away, ya bloody bag o' fleas."

With one last quick lick of Grace's hand, Yabby slunk alongside the bullocks, causing a disorderly raucous of bellows and nervous hoof thuds.

"D'ya hear of that great, big, bloody wreck off the Lord Howe's Island a few weeks back?"

Grace wiped her wet palm down her hip and shook her head. "Where's that?"

"'Tis an island east of here." He smiled indulgently. "Good for provisions—you know, water, meat, vegetables—but also muttonbird feathers for mattresses." The teamster rubbed his hands together with a dry rasp and leaned against the wagon's side. "Heard it from a sailor brimming with a good yarn an' happy to share it with anyone who'd listen."

Grace dug her thumb into her temple, and the thumping behind her eye eased momentarily. Big Bob's stance matched that of a man equally happy to share the yarn. Would it be rude to excuse herself and dash off? Just like his dog, his age was indeterminate. Despite grizzled grey hairs speckling his whiskers, his flat back and broad shoulders spelled a man still in his prime.

"Them island settlers witnessed the wreck 'emselves. Bloody travesty."

Grace rolled the stiffness from her neck, offering a half-interested smile. Bleeding rats' tails. Looked like she was in for the full serving.

"A double-masted brigantine was fetching fresh water and supplies, when a devilishly strong southerly current and winds blew the poor bloody bastard bang into an outer reef! Would ya believe she managed to steer between the reefs? Made it to deeper water too! Nothing no one could do with an injured hull, though, and she was soon guzzling water like 'twas cheap gin. They was forced to abandon ship."

Grace tightened her brow. "Were all souls saved?"

"Bloody oath, they were! They'd be too afeard to die. Wouldn't put it past that cantankerous bloody potato-eater of a pirate to chase 'em into the depths of Hell and drag 'em back aboard."

"Ah, yes. A ship is a captain's kingdom for him to command.

Some are crueller task-masters than others." Grace patted the driver's arm, releasing a puff of dust. "Please, excuse me. I must be off."

"Righto, Lady Cap. Just be thankful O'Reilly's lot are stuck out there and not 'ere in town. Them lot'll be in a fightin' mood with that reward hangin' over their heads."

O'Reilly? Grace stilled and stared, unblinking. Realisation rattled through her brain like a tumbling topmast, her heart trying to tear itself from her chest. A cold wave of panic washed over her at the thought of the Irish woman's twisted face only a few hundred miles away. So many years had passed since O'Reilly's son, Tibbot, had kidnapped her off the *Discerning*. But even the passage of time did not lessen the dread constricting her lungs.

Tying the final knot on the wagon, Big Bob took hold of the taut rope and shook it hard. The wagon rocked and creaked, but the load held fast. "By that seadog's easy accounting, he couldn't have known about the sizeable bounty on O'Reilly's head. Wouldn't have spilled his tale so bloody freely if he did."

Grace gripped the wagon's rough wooden sideboard, concentrating hard on keeping her feet anchored to the ground. How on earth was O'Reilly still alive, given her chosen vocation? Would Tommy Holburton still be aboard after all this time? Traitorous bastard!

When Grace did not move, Big Bob wrenched off his sweat-stained leather hat and swiped his arm across his glistening forehead. Ramming the tattered hat back on, his lips quirked, and not missing a beat, he continued, "Half o' Sydney Town'd gladly paddle across with bare hands for half a chance at that big, bloody prize. That murderous lot's stranded without another vessel. Doubt they'll make capture easy though. Only the bravest or most foolish'll try."

Grace swallowed a bitter ball of bile and flashed her teeth at him. "Speaking of paddling, I *really* must be off."

Dipping his head, Big Bob touched the brim of his hat. "Right you are, Lady Cap. Hooroo, then."

GRACE SWUNG OPEN the shipping office door, and Toby's head jerked up. "Mrs F.?" He rose, blinking in surprise at her sudden arrival. "Is all well? You look a bit peaky."

"A trifling headache. I'll be better once I've had some water." She aimed, stiff-necked, for the drinks cabinet. A crystal carafe of water stood near Seamus's spirits—he habitually liked a splash of water in his whisky. Sliding her eyes away from the untouched bottle of golden liquid, Grace drank deeply. In this devilish heat, even tepid water was an indulgence. Moisture teased her lips for the first time in hours, and she gasped as the last of the liquid slid down her throat. Recharging her glass, she headed over to Toby's desk.

She lowered herself into the chair opposite and, snatching up a folded broadsheet, fanned herself. The cool air on her skin quelled the heat of her alarm too. She smiled nonchalantly. "Toby, what do you know of the Lord Howe's Island?"

Toby's curious grey gaze fixed on her as he shrugged. "It's about four hundred nautical miles northeast of here. Not that far considering the distances we've sailed together."

Grace narrowed her eyes. Four hundred nautical miles meant about five days' sailing aboard a small boat. With favourable weather, of course.

Toby waved one hand, palm up. "Not much on that wild isle. Only a small settlement with a handful of people who trade goods with the whalers for fresh provisions." He smiled that gentle smile that had endeared him to her all those years ago. "A trader's heading out there in the next day or two. If it's a stealthy escape you're after, Mrs F., I can always squirrel you away in a hessian sack and add you to the pile of oat bags aboard the *Drover.*"

Despite her thumping head, Grace laughed. "My creaky old bones wouldn't be up to curling inside a burlap sack these days."

He winked. "Nonsense, Mrs F., you're as spritely as the day we met."

Rising, Grace folded her arms across her chest and sauntered to the open window, hoping to catch the sea breeze. She propped her bottom on the sill, her gaze lingering on her friend. "Hmm, the first day we met—what's that—sixteen, seventeen years ago?"

"Doesn't feel more than a blink of an eye." His lips turned up kindly.

"Any news from Captain Appleby today?" Her voice pitched in hope.

Running his lean fingers down his golden whiskers, Toby shook his head. "Nothing to report."

Grace nodded matter-of-factly. She was done sitting about waiting for government officials—especially *that* one. While her visits to Gilly Downs, plus her care of the children and the shipping company, had kept her occupied well enough for over a year, she had to do more. Never one for sitting idle, she resolved to act—today. She had a plan, albeit a risky one. But by goodness, when had that ever stopped her?

She took a deep breath, hoping that a warbling voice would not reveal her deceit. "I'm heading to Gilly Downs for a couple of weeks." Pointing below, she added, "Big Bob's headed there today. I'll travel with him."

Toby's brows drew up, but he nodded, his face calm with acceptance.

Good! Her regular trips to Gilly Downs meant no alarm would be raised. She could head to the island and be back without raising suspicions. Her impulsiveness had landed her in a few pickles over the years, but this was different. She knew the risk she was taking. Seamus was quite particular about the degree of loyalty and protection he expected from his employees, especially where she was concerned, but what Toby and Billy did not know would not hurt them.

Her gaze landed on the locked metal-banded trunk housing the company's private papers and valuables. Clarity sliced through her thumping headache like beams of sunlight. She ambled over to the desk, taking care not to appear too eager. "I'll require some coins—for Big Bob's services."

"Of course." Toby wrenched the narrow centre drawer open and handed her a slender brass key.

Grace unlocked the trunk, the mildly rusted hinges objecting with a screech to being opened. A segmented tray filled with letters and documents lay atop, but what hid on the trunk's bottom interested her most. She lifted out the insert and shifted a tidy pile of bound papers to the side. Aha! Reaching for the soft leather pouch in the back corner, she winced as the pebble-sized contents clinked like glass marbles. The leather pouch contained a single ruby, an emerald, and a diamond. Upon their departure on the *Clover*, with Seamus commissioned to complete his hydrographic survey of the coastline of Tierra del Fuego, Uncle Farfar had quietly slipped her the pouch of gems.

His voice echoed from the past. "Don't want you finding yourself in need on the other side of the world, with me power-less to help. These will be able to buy you into or out of most situations. Though do this old man a favour, poppet, and don't land yourself in any pickles."

This jolly-well qualified as a pickle! A stab of guilt jabbed her ribs at sneaking the gems so secretively. They were all that remained of the substantial bag of stones Uncle Farfar had given her. Seamus's financial disasters had put paid to the rest. Had she not kept the three most sizable stones separate in an effort not to keep all the wealth in one spot, for safety's sake, Silverton and Hamilton's meddling with Seamus's finances would have cost her the lot. Leaning over the trunk and feigning rummaging, she shoved the pouch down her cleavage. She lifted out a smaller, locked chest and slid it onto the desk.

Toby handed her a second key, and she opened the box of banknotes and coins. Withdrawing a selection of golds and silvers, she locked the tiny chest and returned it to the trunk. Gripping the lid to close it, she hesitated. The pistol Seamus kept in the trunk for easy access lay nestled in its velvet-lined case, the barrel's spotless gleam luring her interest like a magpie. She glanced over her shoulder at Toby. With his back to her, he bowed his head over the ledger, reconciling receipts for the carpenter's expenses from the *Quintus Roscius*. Shoving the bag of shot down her cleavage atop the gems, she snatched the pistol and tucked it into the top of her stocking.

Dropping the trunk lid and locking it, Grace rose quickly and shook her skirts into place. Depositing the key beside the ledger, she steadied herself as her resolve slipped. Poppycock! She could do this. She took a deep breath in and released it slowly.

Offering a silent apology for the deceit, she smiled at Toby as he glanced up from his writing. "Farewell, then," she said simply, reaching for her shawl.

"Take care, Mrs F. Give my regards to Mr Shyling."

Grace headed downstairs with her shawl draped over one arm. On the quay outside, the chaotic morning crowd swelled. Glad of her plain plum skirt, she blended into the thronging mass, with none paying heed to her elbowing her way through. Making her way around the semi-circular walkway, she ardently scoured the berthed ships and boats. Stinking seaweed! Looking for a single-masted cutter in this forest of crucifixes was near impossible. A small squeak of defeat escaped her throat. A red-coated marine approached, his gaze fixed intently on her.

She softened her smile and dipped her chin as she touched his arm. "Excuse me, sir. Do you happen to know which is the *Drover*?"

The lanky young marine's shoes snapped to a halt, his mouth pressed into a firm line. "No, madam, I do not," he responded formally. "Good day to you," he dismissed, resuming his brisk march.

Blazing Hades! She would have to turn on that shameless charm that amused her husband and worked wonders on other men. A grizzled, whiskered fisherman sidled up to her, his rancid clothes in tatters. "I'll tell you wot one's the *Drover*." He flashed a row of yellow and brown teeth that would need a family reunion to complete the set.

Dear Lord Almighty, his hot, fishy breath was as offensive as Mad Mahlon's! Grace recoiled back two steps. Widening her stance to propel off in a hurry if required, she narrowed her eyes. "Can you point her out?"

The fisherman ran his tongue over his teeth in slow contemplation before sucking loudly. "Reckons I can—for a coin or two."

The weasel was probably lying, hoping to make enough for a night's drinking. Then again, he might not be. Not trusting him to not have pickpocketing as a side business, Grace shifted her weight from one foot to the other, the pistol's bulk comforting against her thigh. Squeezing her fist full of coins, she let her shawl slip over her hand. Angling one hip towards him, and smiling as demurely as his eye-watering odour allowed, she discretely fished among the coins. Grasping one, she waved it before the fisherman's face.

His bloodshot, yellowed eyes fixed eagerly on the coin until he noticed the hole punched in the centre of the silver Spanish dollar. He rolled his eyes. "Pah! 'Tisn't even a real coin that!"

He was right. The colonial holey dollar had been demonetised several years back, but she was damned if she would waste good coin on the likes of him. "It's still a bit of silver that can be sold," she teased.

The fisherman licked his lips, his thick tongue white with thirst, then he tossed his head like a stubborn gelding. "Deal!"

His cracked fingers and grime-encrusted nails snatched at the silver dollar, but she whipped back quicker. "Take me to her. Once I confirm she's the one, I'll give you your coin."

Hacking, the fisherman spat, his brown spittle splattering at her feet like perforated fish guts. "You'd better not be two tonnes of horse muck in a five-pound sack!" He sniffed and wiped a globule of phlegm from his lip with his wrist. Turning, he flicked his head. Fancy how when a pretty smile failed to sharpen a man's will to help, the promise of silver always did. Simple creatures, they.

He stopped before a nondescript, mid-sized cutter. "That's her." He held out a palm, his scarred fingers the product of a lifetime of hard and ungentle work.

A squat, square-headed man stepped from the cutter's gangplank onto the quay.

"Excuse me," said Grace. "Is this the *Drover*?"

"'Tis indeed." The man's Cornish accent was a long way from home. He squinted against the sun, the weathered lines scrunching into a face only a mother could love. "Who's asking?"

"Oh—I—er—" she spluttered.

The fisherman gave an impatient cough, and she thrust the coin into his waiting hand. She turned back to the bandy-legged man still looking expectantly at her. "I'm looking for passage over to the Lord Howe's Island," she explained. "I hear you're headed there?"

The seaman's unkempt eyebrows dipped suspiciously. The Luckenbooth brooch on her chest clearly caught his eye, but Grace slung her tartan shawl over her shoulder. It was far too hot to be shrouding herself in wool, but it served its purpose to block his roving gaze. "I'm Mrs Haller," she lied. "Are you the master of this fine vessel?"

"Indeed, I am, madam." He bowed. "Captain John Andrews, at your service." He was a pleasant enough fellow, but his eyes were clouded with scepticism. "What's a fine lady doing heading all the way out to whaling country?"

"Visiting my brother. I can pay." She opened her palm to reveal five gold sovereigns.

The corner of Andrews' mouth turned down as he studied the coins. His hesitation did not bode well. Fumbling beneath her tartan wrap, Grace withdrew the gem pouch. Keeping her hands hidden, and with a quick tug of the strings, she opened the bag. Rummaging with her forefinger, she withdrew the smallest gem. She slid the pouch safely back into place and pinched a green stone the size of a pea between her thumb and forefinger.

Captain Andrews' eyes widened, and he snorted. "Well, put me on a horse and call me a donkey walloper! That's one fine jewel you have there, missus."

"My brother's at the trading settlement," continued Grace. "He—"

Captain Andrews held up his hand. "Mrs Haller, I've no doubt you've quite a tale, and not a word of it true. But those coins and a gem that size serve their purpose. They'll buy you passage—and a bit of silence too."

Grace blinked once, then twice, before pressing her mouth into a loose smile of thanks.

Pocketing the emerald inside his coat breast, Captain Andrews waved at the gangplank. "Welcome aboard the *Drover*, Mrs Haller. Happy to give up my berth to such a fine paying customer. Doubt it'll be up to standard, but…" He shrugged, almost apologetically.

"When's departure?" she asked, stepping onto the boat's deck. It was considerably smaller than any other vessel she had sailed on before. It seemed strange standing on a deck with only a single mast to peer up, the tree trunk blooming white sails instead of green leaves. The boat was not new, but it was apparent Captain Andrews kept her clean and orderly. The earthy smell of dry oats mingled with the familiar scents of wood and tar.

"Within the half hour," he said, smiling as her eyebrows rose in surprise. "No need to delay. We've all our cargo, crew—and *passenger*—aboard."

Captain Andrews showed her to his cabin below. By the *Elias*'s measure, the cabin at the stern was nothing more than an enlarged storage cupboard. The curtained berth was built above two deep drawers, the narrow desk barely wide enough to accommodate the wooden chair under it.

"Perfect," said Grace pleasantly. "Thank you for inconveniencing yourself. How long do you expect the journey to take?"

"Five or six days, weather depending."

Ha! Her calculations had been exact. "I'll remain below for the duration. I shan't be in your way." She was sure there would be opportunity to go above, but the fewer people who knew of her voyage, the better. It was up to Captain Andrews to explain to his lot why he was sleeping wherever he ended up sleeping. Hopefully, the emerald in his pocket would help him concoct a plausible enough story.

When put to scale in the tiny cabin, Captain Andrews was the perfect-sized man. Overhead, light from the dingiest whale-oil lantern colonised the murkiness of the vault with ghostly shapes.

If he was surprised by her declaration to remain out of sight, he hid it well. "If you feel queasy below, you can—"

"I shan't," she assured him, giving him a toothy grin.

He rubbed his nape. "Very well. I'll bring you two meals a day. Won't be much more than bread and salt beef. But the tea'll be hot."

"It's adequate, thank you, Captain."

She did not expect plain sailing, kind winds, or gentle waves, but the smaller vessel rolled and pitched much more heavily in the rough seas than any of the larger ships she had sailed. In the cabin, a little larger than a hearse, Grace lay squeezed into the coffin-like berth. Despite the surety in her bones that the water-tight vessel would safely deliver her to her destination, the baking summer sun beating down on the deckhead above painted visions of burning pyres. Clasping her slick fingers across her belly, she closed her eyes, determined to endure this roasting as nobly as Joan of Arc at the stake. For the first time in her seafaring life, she yearned to set foot on solid ground again.

Chapter Twenty-Nine

THE LORD HOWE'S ISLAND, NORTHEAST OF NEW HOLLAND, 26 NOVEMBER 1842

Grace sheltered in the palm tree shade, back from the strip of white sand, overlooking the azure lagoon. The island was impossibly pretty. The inlet, hemmed in by the outer reef, was as smooth as a lake. Wind-bent palm-tree trunks, topped with heads of greenery like oversized, tattered parasols, lined the sand. Across the bay towered two domed rocky monoliths.

The *Drover* was anchored just offshore, her crew tirelessly ferrying bags of oats across on the rowboat and shouldering them up the beach to a waiting horse—and *sleigh*? She spied the state of the rough track through the trees. Ah, too uneven to use a wheeled wagon—not unless the island's inhabitants intended to spend their days repairing broken spokes and axles. Rather ingenious.

Not yet topping the palm trees, the early morning sun cast

long shadows on the crystalline sand. The horse's powerful rump swayed as it patiently shifted its weight from one hoof to the other—then again, that might be her see-sawing equilibrium, not yet settled from the *Drover*'s short but tumultuous journey. Grace squinted along the bay of the curved lagoon, studying an anchored whaler. Indecision swayed her still-rocking brain like the gimballed compass of a binnacle. Was she ready to face O'Reilly after all this time? Could she step within a hundred yards of the mercenary without being shot by Jonas or Tibbot? Would O'Reilly bother to help her? Of course she would—this was not charity, it was commerce.

A man holding the horse's reins threw curious glances at her. Right, these questions would not answer themselves! She took a deep breath and stepped from the veil of the trees, her boots sinking into the fine pale sand.

"Good morning, sir," smiled Grace.

The man ripped his holey felt hat off, exposing a greasy mop of brown unbrushed hair that matched his unkempt whiskers. "Morning, ma'am." His face was deeply browned by the sun and lined, but his hazel eyes were clear. By the lean shape of him, Grace figured him younger than his face revealed.

"I'm Mrs Haller. And you are?"

Momentarily panicked by her forwardness, his gaze flicked over her as though she had a contagious disease. "Thomas Andrews."

"Any relation to Captain Andrews of the *Drover*?" She waved a hand at the cutter that bobbed much higher in the water now with most of her cargo unloaded.

Andrews nodded. "He's my brother." He paused, his gaze fixing more readily. "What brings you to our remote little island, Mrs Haller?"

"I... um... heard of the recent shipwreck. I... er... realised that they might be... acquaintances of mine. From a while back." It was easier to work with some semblance of the truth. Cursed

Hades! Why must she be such a terrible liar? No wonder Captain Andrews had not believed *her* brother lived on the island. She brushed her hot cheek with the back of her knuckles, then twirled one of her wayward curls. Perhaps he might think her high colour rouge?

"*Them*?" His wiry brows dipped. "That lot aren't"—he hesitated—"*your* kind," he finished diplomatically.

"Are they still here?" she asked, ignoring his sceptical frown.

Three sailors dumped more sacks of oats onto the wooden sleigh. The horse stamped its hoof, its mane juddering and sending up a buzzing swarm of flies that immediately settled back down on the creature's shiny pelt.

Thomas Andrews turned his attention back to Grace and narrowed his eyes. "They are. They're camping with the whalers further up the beach. Wouldn't recommend the likes of you mingling with that lot."

Trickles of sweat tickled her cleavage, but she tightened her shawl and caught the white flash of a tent in the tree line further along the beach. Half a dozen men barrelled from the trees, bare-chested and barefooted. Hollering and hooting, they dove into the clear water, splashing and wrestling like children.

Inclining her head and smiling with a confidence mastered from living aboard a ship full of men, she said, "Thank you for your word of caution, Mr Andrews. But as I said before, they aren't strangers to me."

Andrews hunched one shoulder up to his ear. "Very well, but should you seek refuge, I live with my wife and daughter up the track." He cocked his head at the well-trodden track snaking between the forest of palms and lush vegetation. "Our humble abode might be thatched with palm fronds, but it's cool, comfortable, and dry. My wife would cherish your company."

"My business shan't take long. I've already arranged return passage with Captain Andrews."

"Oh, he's not departing today, Mrs Haller." He tugged his

whiskers. "My brother always spends the night. Have him bring you up to the house when you're done."

Grace tried for a polite smile, though her gut clenched at the sight of the men frolicking in the shallows. Squinting against the bright sand's glare, she blinked her watery eyes, searching for any familiar figures. Bleeding rats' tails! They were too far away.

"Perhaps," she replied, non-committedly.

As she made her way along the stretch of sand, the palm tree shadows retreated higher up the beach. All but two of the men were out of the water now, their buttocks denting the white sand as they awaited the rising rays to dry themselves. On the passing palm trunks, marbled geckos lingered like stone gargoyles waiting for the early morning warmth to reach them too.

With her shoes slowing, she approached a familiar black-haired man. His wet hair hung in limp curls against his shoulders, his bronzed back patterned with white lash scars. Those well-defined shoulders and narrow waist spelled the physique of a sailor. He tipped his head back, laughing at something his companion had said. The familiar snigger froze Grace's feet as though the sand were suddenly pack-ice. There was no mistaking that strong-jawed profile—Tibbot *bloody* O'Reilly.

He fixed his leer on her for one beat—two beats—three beats.

"Jaysus!" He leapt to his feet in one spring, hanging on to the soggy tops of his breeches. The edge in his voice brought the other men to their feet. "Jaysus!" he repeated.

His agitation gave Grace a small thrill of pleasure, and she raised her chin at the two other men wading in from the sea. Her heart retreated to her spine at the one flat face she had hoped never to lay eyes on again. Tommy Holburton!

"You know that one?" asked the man behind Tibbot with the sing-song voice of a Caribbean local.

"As I live and breathe—Miss Maggot!" Tommy Holburton's gaze burned into her skin, taking in her empty hands.

Grace raised her open palms to him. Even had she wanted to step towards them, her feet were not cooperating just this instant. Standing still was probably wisest.

"What ye doin' here?" growled Tibbot.

It was clear she owned the surprise. Best use it to her advantage. "Tibbot O'Reilly," she drawled, crossing her arms. She wrapped her palms over her biceps and hoped to goodness the men would not see her tremors. Projecting her voice to hide the quiver, she said, "Fancy meeting you here."

"What ye want?" Tibbot glanced over his shoulder. The five men behind him crowded in, and when he turned back to Grace, his hardened glare liquified her thigh bones.

"I've come to pay your mother a visit." Stinking seaweed, her nerves made her sound like she was inviting the bloody Queen to tea. She curled her fingers into fists and dug them into her armpits. Might as well continue the pretence. "Is she in?"

"Don't know," sneered Tibbot. "Me balls are hairy, not crystal."

The men shifted, their bare feet sinking into the soft sand as they flicked glances at the encampment, their varying degrees of curiosity and fear all the answer she required. Tendrils of smoke from several small campfires filtered up through the green-fronded canopy.

"Would you care to announce me?" said Grace formally. "I would have brought a calling card, but—" Patting her skirts, she shrugged and twisted her lips wryly. "Appears I left it at home."

Several of the men spoke at once.

"Jesus, Tibbot! She's off her chump asking for Herself, bald-faced as she pleases," said Tommy.

"How d'you know Herself?" one of the men demanded, his sunburned face looking like he had bobbed for apples in boiling oil.

"Who *is* she?" Tibbot's Caribbean accomplice jabbed him in the back, his aquamarine, almond-shaped eyes squinting over Tibbot's shoulder.

Tibbot whirled on the man, snarling. "None of your feckin' business, Sunday! Want Herself knowing yer stickin' yer nose in her affairs?"

Sunday scowled and hissed as though Tibbot had thrown hot water on him. "Why'd you speak my name in front of her?" His cheeks greyed, the worry in his luminescent eyes sparking between terror and annoyance.

A short, pock-faced man gripped Tibbot's shoulder. "Jesus wept! She's the one wot Herself took off that navy boat a few years back."

"Shut up, tree stump," said Tibbot, rolling his eyes and shrugging off the man's hand. He barked, "Sunday! Go fetch O'Reilly. Tell her she has a visitor."

"Fetch her yerself," snapped Sunday. "I'll not be the one to lead her into no trap."

Sunday studied the shadows of the dense vegetation with a look of such calculation that Grace wondered if he expected an army to burst forth and sweep down the idyllic beach.

"I'm alone," she assured, stretching her arms to the side.

"Brazen hussy, don't look armed." Tommy smirked. "Knowing 'er kind, she's all skirts and no drawers."

Ha! Let him keep thinking that. Grace circled slowly, her arms held high. Old Bailey's bells! If stupid were a fruit, this island would be an orchard.

"D'ya trust her?" lisped a runt with ribs visible through his leathery skin.

"Course I don't blazin' trust her!" Tibbot snarled, his tone tainted with the threat of violence. "She's come seeking vengeance."

"She's *one* woman. We could easily take her," a voice sniggered from the back of the crowd.

"Take 'er 'ome to warm our beds tonight, hey lads?" Tommy's threat was laced with the promise of cruelty and anticipation of enjoyment.

The lisping whippet laughed. "I seen uglier, but I had to pay admission."

Grace lifted her chin at the same time Tibbot shouted, "Shurrup! The lot of ya. I need to think."

She sighed impatiently. "Will one of you fetch her, or will you continue mincing about like a bunch of dandies?"

Ominous growls of protest burst from the men, but no one stepped past Tibbot towards her. She watched as Tibbot turned on his men, her patience simmering on the edge of boiling over, her nerves buzzing with uncertainty. If he did not get on with it, she would march up to the encampment herself—not an ideal prospect. At least here on the beach she was in sight of Captain Andrews' crew.

"Watch her—don't touch her!" Tibbot commanded.

Grace took several steps away from them and plopped unceremoniously on her bottom at the water's edge. Her legs were barely holding her up, and sitting brought relief. It also bought her a chance to draw the pistol from her stocking. In one deft motion, she slid her shawl from her shoulders and freed the weapon, laying both in her lap.

She tucked a loose strand of hair behind her ear and cast a carefree glance over her shoulder. "I'll wait here then, shall I?" She needed them to lose interest in her so she could ease the bag of shot from her bodice.

Tibbot marched off, solid-footed. The tense watchfulness in the men's shoulders softened. Having eliminated herself as a threat, Grace slid out the shot pouch and buried it beneath her plaid. She glanced out at the exquisite vista of blues and greens of sky and crystal-clear waters. Were her skin not trying to crawl off her bones, she might have enjoyed the view. With tiny and careful movements, she loaded the pistol within the folds of wool, glancing over her shoulder with a feigned huff of boredom.

She stared up the beach, and her stomach almost leapt out of her throat at O'Reilly's square form strutting across the sand. Little wisps of sand kicked out before her like puffs of smoke.

The Irish mercenary was thicker set than the last time Grace had seen her. Her hair, greyer, was severely tied back, revealing the hard, aged contours of her ragged face. The tell-tale cigar jutted from between her clamped teeth as she wheezed her way towards Grace. What had not changed was the shrewd intelligence that glimmered in those beady grey eyes, which at this moment were unnervingly pinned on her. Tibbot tailed respectfully behind, and Grace spotted the knife handle protruding from the waist of his breeches.

O'Reilly flicked her wrist, and Tibbot stepped over to the others. A broad-brimmed slouch hat shadowed the guarded distrust on O'Reilly's scarred face. Her scarlet silk shirt, rolled over her elbows in deference to the hot weather, exposed her wrinkled tattoos. Glancing at Grace down the crooked crag of her nose, O'Reilly snorted, then she plonked beside her, groaning like a stretching dog.

"I tell ya somethin' for nothin', *mo chara*," O'Reilly puffed without preamble. "Gettin' old is a feckin' awful job. Wouldn't recommend it." Her stern face smiled, almost pleasantly. "'Tis mighty fine to see ya again, Mrs Fitzwilliam."

Grace stared dispassionately as the disconnected reality of what she was doing drew her from her body. It was as though she were above their two forms on the beach, looking down. Blinking and swallowing hard, she forced herself to acknowledge her acquaintance. "O'Reilly."

"Now, Tibbot Mac says ye've business with me?" O'Reilly's beady gaze slid to Grace's lap and froze as she spotted the pistol muzzle facing her. The old crone burst out laughing, her voice grating like rusted metal. Her cigar tumbled, and she fumbled it against her chest, cursing. "By all the holy saints, did those brainless eejits not even check ye for weapons? Jaysus, if the lot of 'em were a banquet, they'd be the apple in the suckling's mouth—all decoration and not much use!"

Despite the situation's gravity, Grace's lips twitched in amusement.

O'Reilly shook her head. "Mary and Joseph, I'm too old for this shite." She stuck the cigar back between her thick, moist lips and sucked deeply. "Would ye at least let me finish my last whiff afore ye put a ball in my gut?" Her smoky words curled around her head.

Grace tightened her grip on the pistol and licked her dry lips —a neat gin would work wonders to cut the drought in her mouth. "This isn't for you." She glanced back at the gang of men milling out of earshot—at least she hoped they were out of earshot. "It's for protection—from them."

O'Reilly's thin, grey brows rose, furrowing the three jagged scars across her forehead. "Well then, if ye aren't here to shoot me, what are ye here for?"

"To engage your services." Grace bit the inside of her lip to stop herself from jumping up and bolting back down the beach.

The old woman arched her back, and an unhealthy popping crackled across her shoulders. Sucking deeply on her cigar, O'Reilly's gaze wandered out to the whaler ship anchored offshore, her rasp filled with curiosity. "What's it ye're after, *mo chara*?"

"My husband is missing, caught in a storm off the west African coast. I want you to find him and bring him home to me." Grace's voice hitched, and she swallowed deeply to stem the threat of tears. Not here! Not before *her*.

O'Reilly huffed a double plume of smoke from her nostrils. "How d'ye even know he's alive?"

Grace relaxed her grip on the pistol. "I just do."

"It'd best be a powerful certainty, *mo chara*." O'Reilly

hacked a phlegmy cough. "To have me scour the African coast-line for a lone wreck—without knowing for sure that the ship's not at the bottom of Davy Jones's locker."

"You happened upon *me* in the archipelago maze," countered Grace.

"Ye're away with the fairies, ye are!" O'Reilly chuckled. She dropped her humorous smirk and sat silently, her only motion the occasional suck on her cigar as the trail of smoke dissolved on the gentle breeze. She sighed. "Ye realise I'm without a ship?"

"Surely it's not beyond you to steal one?"

"Ye wouldn't pick me as a sentimental type, but I miss my *Annabelle*. She weren't a beauty, but she was faithful." There was an odd catch in O'Reilly's voice. She cleared her throat with a sharp bark and flicked cigar ash from her shirt front. "Even with another ship—task like that don't come cheap." She champed down on the cigar's soggy end.

"I have these." Grace freed the gem pouch and tossed it at O'Reilly.

With surprisingly quick reflexes, O'Reilly caught it one-handed. Her knobbed fingers fondled the pouch's contents with an expert touch.

Upending the two gems into her palm, O'Reilly tried to whistle past her cigar, but it came out like a rush of breathless air. She seemed suitably impressed by the sizeable ruby and diamond.

"A start, to cover upfront expenses," said Grace.

"'Tis a pretty sight indeed." O'Reilly's arthritic forefinger fiddled with the jewels. She swung her head to Grace, lips pressed. "Not altogether sure I want the job. I've enough money set aside to leave this life. Was plannin' on berthin' the *Annabelle* in the tropics on an island like this. Enjoy what days I 'ave left bakin' in the sun."

"Please!" Grace did not care that her desperation slid out in her voice. "You've a reward of two thousand pounds on your head—"

O'Reilly stiffened, her head whipping around. "So you've come to take us in... by yourself? Jaysus, you always were a plucky little thing." She threw her head back, cackling.

"No, but I'll match that sum if you return Seamus to me."

O'Reilly's gaze lowered to the golden-hearted Luckenbooth brooch, her pupils flaring in recognition.

Grace's soul plummeted to her feet. She slid her palm over the brooch, hiding it from O'Reilly's greedy gaze. "No. Not that."

"I've money aplenty, but that pretty little trinket still has my eye."

Grace hesitated. Would Seamus forgive her? She licked her lips. It was a fair exchange—a lump of metal for her flesh-and-blood husband. Surely Glenna Fitzwilliam would want her brooch used to save her son—her only child? But if Seamus was truly gone, she would have little else to remember him by. Grace slid her face into an expressionless mask of clay. "No."

The old woman's scarred brow rucked, then she shrugged and drew up her knees to rise. "Suit yerself, *mo chara*. Ye've more to lose than me."

"No, wait!" With fingers trembling, Grace unclasped the pin and offered it wordlessly.

O'Reilly took the brooch with a nod and pinned it to her own chest. She stretched out one leg, rubbing her knee with a gnarled hand. "I've been on this dot of an island a month now. I'd be lyin' if I said I haven't been bored near out of my skull. I'm not cut out for whilin' my days away lookin' pretty on a beach. I'll be happier ending my days at sea." She pulled the cigar stub from her mouth and ground it into the sand, her steely eyes glowing with the promise of adventure. "I guess, *mo chara*, that means we've an agreement." O'Reilly offered her a liver-spotted hand, and Grace snatched it before she changed her mind, wincing at her grinding knucklebones.

O'Reilly flicked her head at the whaler ship. "I'll start by makin' Cap'n Carole of that there whaler an offer for his tub. Though the bastard'll no doubt charge me the earth. He's so tight he owes himself money." She chortled hoarsely. "'Tis meant to be if you ask me."

"What is?" asked Grace, studying the plain whaler swinging idly at anchor. There was nothing remarkable about the vessel.

"That ship's named *Belle*. My *Annabelle*'s delivered me her child of providence."

Grace rose and tucked the primed pistol into the waist of her skirt. Dusting the sand off her bottom, she turned to O'Reilly. "Very well then, I'll leave you to it."

Rolling onto all fours, O'Reilly stood with a long groan. Tucking the gems into the waist of her trousers, she turned without a word and headed back to the encampment.

Back near where the *Drover* was anchored, Captain Andrews waved his hat at Grace's approach, his stunted, bow-legged shadow mimicking the motion.

"Glad to see you back in one piece, Mrs Haller. Had my doubts."

"I'm perfectly well, thank you, Captain."

Captain Andrews cocked his head at the trail. Sniffing and rubbing his nose, he asked, "Joining us? You're welcome to fill your belly with Mrs Andrews' roast muttonbird, and my brother's ale. Get well settled for the night."

"I was extended the kind invitation earlier." She strained a smile. Right this minute, feigning social politeness with strangers was the last thing she desired. "If you don't mind, Captain, I'm not up to airing etiquette. And you were correct. That lot"—she pointed up the beach—"are indeed a dangerous crowd. I daren't chance staying longer than necessary. Could we sail this afternoon?" She did not trust Tommy Holburton not to fulfil his threat —goodness knew he had tried enough times before.

Captain Andrews frowned. "My men'll not thank you for the trouble."

"Might a gold sovereign in each palm persuade them?"

Humming, he rubbed his hand over his lips. "A gold sovereign or two might satisfy a deckhand, but 'tis not worth cutting short a visit with my brother."

Grace peered down at him. He might be small in stature, but he was still a proud man, clearly not prepared to forgo family duty for a few gold coins. She liked that about him. Rubbing the fabric of her skirt between her thumb and forefinger, she pondered. Time to appeal to the entrepreneur in him. "Captain Andrews, my name's not Haller. It's Fitzwilliam."

The captain took a step back and tipped the brim of his hat up. "Eh? As in Fitzwilliam of the Elias Shipping Company?"

"Yes."

"Blood and blisters! Why—how come—" His bronzed skin turned a sickly yellow.

She held up her palm. "Let me stop you there, Captain. I've a proposition for you." She waited a beat, gauging his interest. "The Elias Shipping Company imports goods into the colony. And you've a trading vessel to distribute such goods. What say you to a ten per cent discount?"

Andrews fiddled with his ear, his tongue toying with the corner of his mouth. "Thirty per cent."

"Fifteen, and first pick of the hold."

"Done." He nodded smugly.

Good. A small price to pay for a spot of her own company in the *Drover*'s baking cabin, and a heart full of hope.

Chapter Thirty

WOOLOONGILLY DOWNS, 28 *AUGUST* 1843

Waiting for news of Seamus was both a penance and a gift, the torture of his absence sweetened by the thought of touching him again. Filling her mind with the sound of his voice affirmed Grace's love for him, no matter the distance of miles or time between them, but was it proof enough he was alive? At night, in the cool stillness of her empty bed, her fingers craved the warm, smooth touch of the Luckenbooth brooch. Since her wedding, it had been a constant comfort she could reach for whenever the pain of missing him became too much. But now, even that was gone.

Drawn back to Gilly Downs by the distraction of preparations for the new shearing season, Grace welcomed the exhaustion that enveloped her in a deep, soundless sleep. Life at the homestead was a welcome diversion, the squabbling rabble of Barclay children a lot unto their own. Victor and Adelia had taken full advantage of Land Commissioner Long's glowing report of their highly lucrative sheep station, the Colonial Secretary not hesitating to renew the grazing licence and grant permission for the Shylings to reside at Barclay Hall.

Early grievances aside, Grace now accepted Victor Shyling for a true gentleman. Despite his quiet mannerisms, when he spoke, it was with a respectable dignity that she was irritatingly drawn to. How could such a giant harbour such gentleness? It was as plain as the nose on her face that he was as madly smitten with Adelia as she with him.

Excusing himself after breakfast one morning, Victor stooped to kiss Adelia's cheek. "I'm off. Heading out to Dorian McDermott in the northwest paddock. Been a bit of trouble with wild dogs lately." His voice was deep but tender, and his eyes sparkled adoringly. "See you tomorrow evening?"

Handsome devil! Grace thought.

Adelia's cheeks pinkened, and she squeezed his small finger, the thick digit almost filling her hand. "I look forward to it."

Grace nibbled her top lip to hide her amusement. Good grief, that current between them was like a spark of blue lightning across the room. There was no denying it, their attraction was palpable, and she was thrilled.

Victor's full black whiskers should have been intimidating, but newly combed and trimmed, they gentled him instead. Were they as soft as they looked? Seamus's growth was always sparse and prickly.

The giant grazier bowed. "Good day, Mrs Fitzwilliam."

His clacking boots faded into the day's sounds, and Adelia whirled in her seat like an excited schoolgirl. "Oh, Grace! Is he not absolutely wonderful?"

Grace nodded, her heavy bun wobbling. "He's a wonder."

"And haven't the children taken to him?" Adelia squirmed, shuffling closer.

"They have."

Only last week, with Emily and Edwin here for their midterm break, Victor took Edwin, Noah, and Nevin further along the creek to teach them how to hunt with his rifle. Emily had begged to join them, and Victor had agreed after Grace's nod of approval. The four youngsters hurried after the great, ambling man, taking two or three steps for every one of his. Victor permitted Nevin to carry the rifle, and the boy strutted importantly, not giving way to the weight of the weapon upon his shoulder. Noah's rosy cheeks glowed like the setting sun, overjoyed at being allowed to hunt. Elijah had only allowed the children to shoot at targets nailed to trees.

"And he's so knowledgeable about the station," Adelia gushed. "Took him no time at all to grasp the running of it."

"It's clear why Elijah placed such value in his counsel," Grace agreed.

"And oh, Grace, *in bed*! The man's—he's—" A violent blush drowned Adelia's sun-baked freckles.

Grace chuckled. "Hmm, I think even your *toes* are blushing right now."

Placing her hand on her chest, Adelia bit her bottom lip and slid her eyes away. "My toes have indeed blushed with the things he's done to them. You saw him last week, shearing without a shirt. You must know what I mean."

Grace's cheeks warmed. Dear Lord Almighty, had she seen him! She had barely been able to peel her eyes from his sinewed back that rippled with even the tiniest movement. Despite being fed a steady diet of shirtless seamen over the years, simply laying eyes upon a shirtless Victor Shyling made her feel like a gambler laying down Seamus's heart as her stake. The whole scene was far too reminiscent of that scoundrel Alby Church, with his honed arm muscles and tapered waist.

Perhaps it was because Seamus had been away so long, all decorous thoughts about her husband slid from the polite space in her mind and plunged over a primal cliff. Visions of a half-naked Victor Shyling did not help one bloody bit! She wanted

Seamus's touch, needed him to take her roughly, nibble her neck, grip her face, and kiss her deeply. Her longing throbbed uncomfortably below her pelvic bone. She crossed her legs.

Adelia's girlish shyness slid into seriousness as she met Grace's gaze. "I now truly understand the wonders you explained all those years ago when you schooled me in the ways of the boudoir." She hesitated as though holding back the anticipation of words bubbling inside. "I thought Mr Barclay remarkable. He was so sweet and gentle. But with Mr Shyling—" The soft skin at Adelia's throat sucked in as she inhaled. "I *feel* his kisses in the pit of my stomach. His touch prickles my skin like I'm too close to the fire. He makes me feel so *alive*, so… *safe*."

Smiling knowingly at the mesmerised glaze in her friend's eyes, Grace ignored the lance of jealousy piercing her gut. "I know what you mean." She patted Adelia's tight fist on the table.

"I love him, Grace."

"How so?"

The gold flecks in Adelia's eyes ignited. "How do *you* know you love Seamus? Is it that you can't stop thinking of him night and day? That you want to be with him every minute?"

Grace stilled as she regarded her friend. She knew all too well what it meant. How many nights had she dreamt of—*craved* —Seamus's touch on her skin? Not just his intimacy beside her, but his passion on her and in her, promising himself to her for eternity.

Adelia's nostrils flared. "Is it not love when I awake, and the world is light, and I forget that I ever suffered sorrow? Is it not love that giddies my insides, and gives me hope that I can achieve anything with him by my side?"

Good Lord above, she really was in love with him! Grace's solid resolve—of believing Seamus was not lost—cracked, doubt drilling its way through her core as though she were made of talc. Her throat constricted, and silent tears dripped off her chin. What if she never saw him again? How could she carry on?

Should she return to London? That held even less appeal now with Uncle Farfar gone.

The whites of Adelia's eyes widened, and she snatched Grace's fingers. "Oh, Grace dear. I'm sorry. How insensitive of me. Have you news of Seamus?"

Sniffing, Grace shook her head. "Not yet—but soon." She rose stiff-backed with a resolve not to cry any further. "Just popping to the privy. Those three cups of tea have gone right through me."

In the outhouse, Grace held her breath against the sharp ammonia tang of urine and the stench of well-fermented faeces while she arranged her skirts in the narrow confines. Her elbows bumped against the rough plywood walls, and she hissed as a needled splinter jabbed into the soft flesh above her elbow. Stinking seaweed! Pinching the offending shard, she yanked it out and rubbed the stinging hole.

There was an inordinate number of blasted flies about, especially in here. Dozens of dried insect carcasses, dead grass fragments, and clumps of mud crunched and crumbled underfoot. Her throat squeezed, and she gagged. At least aboard a ship, the soil washed away in the ocean and was not left to stew in the heat.

At the pounding of galloping hooves on the gravel road, she peered through an oval knothole. It was bright outside compared to the ablution box's dim interior, and it took a moment for her eyes to adjust.

A hatted man, bent low over the horse's neck, pressed it faster up the hill towards Barclay Hall. There was an urgency about him that sent her heart plummeting to her knees. Toby? Grace's gut twisted, instantly fermenting the lamb's liver and toast she had ingested at breakfast. With her legs threatening to drop her back onto the reeking hole behind her, she gripped the metal latch. Was it news about Seamus?

Grace lifted the bar, and the rickety door swung open with a painful shriek. She tore towards the dirt track, and Toby swung his horse towards her. He yanked the reins and dismounted before the horse completed its halt. Bolting towards her, he dropped the reins in the dust. The horse drooped its head, nostrils flaring, breath puffing in and out with the uneven sound of great bellows. Poor creature was near a state of collapse.

Toby swayed before her. The dust congealing in the creases of his eyes and the corners of his mouth had turned to mud with his perspiration. He withdrew a small ivory envelope from his inside pocket, crushed and ingrained with the dirt born of many a passing hand. Grace did not recognise the crest in the red glob of wax, nor the long wobbly handwriting beneath the wrap of string. It leaned the wrong way to be Seamus's.

Toby puffed. His whiskers, greyed by the fine talc of dust, hid the press of his lips.

"Is it—?" She stopped. Would saying it out loud disprove the reality?

Thrusting his hands onto his hips, Toby shook out one leg, then the other. His breathing was slowing, but his chest still heaved. As though suddenly remembering himself, he blinked and took a step back. "Perhaps you'd like a moment to yourself?" He swallowed, and his Adam's apple bobbed dryly.

"Stay. I want you near." She picked at the knot of twine, rubbing her fingertips together to shed the coarse fibres. It was the same twine that had bound the parcel containing the dress Gilly had given her aboard the *Discerning*. Did this package contain an equal delight? The outer sheet unfolded, and a hard metal object slid into her palm. Bleeding rats' tails! Her Luckenbooth brooch. What did this mean? Had O'Reilly failed? Was this the old hag's way of telling her Seamus was dead? Inside the packet were two clean, creamy notes, both neatly folded. Her fingers trembled as she opened the first.

Mo chara,

News of your husband, as agreed. All endeavours to discover Captain Fitzwilliam's whereabouts and return the information to you as swiftly as possible were made. Still, by the nature of my business, the luxury of speed must sometimes be sacrificed for the sake of stealth.

As fate would have it, your husband's first mate is the one responsible for my current wretched demise! He learned I was making enquiries about town and set out after me. Bastard put a ball in my gut before I had chance to explain.

I write to you from my death bed, and since I've not enough life left to enjoy the spoils, consider yourself free of debt for this service. I also consider myself cleared of debt for stealing you from your ship and delivering you to Silverton. You might perhaps be thinking that old age and gangrene have softened my wit, but you would be mistaken. This final deed of generosity is repentance for the sinful life I've led. I've made my peace. I did say I wanted to end my days at sea, did I not? At least I have that.

You've a will and a spirit to match my own. I saw this in you the first time we met. We've both fires in our bellies to rival any man; only, unlike you, I was cursed with empty pockets, and a face like a sack of spuds.

I return to you your brooch. I'll not leave it to Tibbot Mac. The greedy moocher will sell it in a heartbeat, and piss away the proceeds on the next whore to cross his path. Would be a pity to see such a fine piece dressing up some dock doxy.

For what it's worth, my blessings go with you, mo chara.

G.O.

Grace wanted to hurl the letter in the dust. Was Seamus alive or not? Curse O'Reilly and her wretched games. She thrust the read letter at Toby and wrenched open the second letter. The clicks, chirps, and buzzes in the surrounding dry foliage faded as she stared at the familiar looping handwriting. The inky lines snaked across the page in a blur—what if it was his last-ever letter to her? She would only have one chance to read his final words. She tipped her head back. The high, blue winter sky was unmarred by cloud or bird. Would this be the colour she remembered forever before the world as she knew it ended? Breathing in the eucalyptus's minty scent, she lowered her chin and read.

Cape Town, Cape Colony, 19 April 1843

My darling Dulcinea,

I hope this, my third letter to you in as many months, has reached you safely. Knowing of the fickleness of packets, I shall include all the details of my trials again, so that you might have solace in knowing what transpired. Let me hasten to assure you that I am quite well, although rather embittered that my return journey to you has been so inconveniently delayed.

The Elias *was caught in a storm off the Cape of Good Hope in February of last year, though I am sure you have news of this already. It pains me considerably to think of you fretting after me. I need not go into all the storm's details since you are well acquainted with their ferocity. Consequently, we were laid broadside on a beach off the rugged coast of the Cape Colony. I am only thankful our resting place was sand and not rock, or we would all have perished. With the loss of Carpenter Hanson and lack of supplies, it took the men an inordinate amount of time to affect repairs in the desolate conditions.*

Thankfully the hull's integrity held, and the hold escaped with minor water damage, though we had to offload the cargo in order to refloat the Elias *with help from a Dutch East India Company ship. Reloading in those conditions was unpleasant, to say the least. We limped into Cape Town, from where I currently write. The* Elias *is undergoing extensive repairs. It is by God's grace alone that we made it here at all. It saddens my* heart to see our beloved ship looking so battle-weary. She was magnificent the first day we sailed, was she not? At least I still have that memory to cherish.

Besides Carpenter Hanson, we also lost Sailmaker Mayer to a falling yardarm during the repairs. Ben Blight lost another finger—jammed it in a metal clew—but he is in good spirits about it. I owe the man my life. I do not wish to alarm you with the details, but I made peace with my Maker in that cold water. Indebted to Toby Hicks for your life, I ordered Blight to save young Hicks first. I had not the strength nor the courage to hold on, but you were there, my heart, infusing me with your warmth. Blight returned after seeing Hicks safely to shore, though I profess I have no memory of his heroic deed. All I know is I am profoundly thankful he dragged my soggy hide ashore.

The rest of the crew are well, and they are keen to be underway again. If the repairs go well, and should Neptune grant it, we will arrive in Sydney Town before the end of September. I cannot believe that by then, it will have been nearly two years since I saw you last! A minute apart from you is too long—two years, unbearable. And how the children must have grown! Please tell Emily her letter delivered me much joy.

If all went to plan, the Saviour of the Seas should have arrived in Sydney Town by now. You will no doubt be relieved to have your beloved Dr Sykes returned to you. We could have sorely done with his services after the wreck. Alas, lamenting his absence does not change matters.

I have missed you more than is imaginable. Without you by my side, I am only half a man, capable of only half a thought, with my reserves of bravery depleted. It is one thing for me to be in love with you, but to have you love me back as you do, I feel such duty to your love. You are my north star, the pinnacle that guides me back, no matter where I may be. I will never be *lost with you to come home to, no matter how far off course I am blown.*

I ask for your enduring gift of patience, my heart. I am coming. I am coming.

With eternal love, your husband,
Seamus Alexander Fitzwilliam

Toby's wide, grey eyes and furrowed brow blurred before her as hot tears spilled through her eyelashes. "He's—" She hiccoughed. "He's well."

"He's alive?" he gasped, his astonishment filling the air like an exploded dandelion seed, each feathery tendril laden with hope and the promise of new life.

She nodded, a shaky laugh escaping her lips. "Shelby too."

Toby scooped her up and whirled her around and around with a whoop of delight. She gripped his lean neck tightly and buried her forehead against his furry, sweat-slicked skin. Who cared if he stank like a polecat? Who cared if their display drew censorious scowls? Seamus was *alive*!

Relief burst from her in hot, convulsive sobs. Her lungs, aching with agony, refused to draw breath until every ounce of sludge-coated doubt that had made it so hard to breathe these past months was expelled. Gasping, she inhaled a new lungful of air and cast her eyes heavenward. Not caring whether she became so dizzy that she collapsed in a heap, she extended her arms. The laughter tingling through her nerve endings was unfamiliar, but oh so welcome! *Her husband was alive.*

Chapter Thirty-One

SYDNEY TOWN, 27 SEPTEMBER 1843

The *Elias* slid effortlessly into the calm waters of Sydney Cove. Despite this voyage's tribulations, Seamus never grew tired of watching his well-practised crew eke every knot of speed from her. Up on the yardarms, the topmen thumped one another's backs, and the sailors on deck shook hands, congratulating one another on the achievement.

Above, Blight called out, "Huzzah! The Sydney girls have hold of the tow-rope!"

O'Malley, wholly unbefitting of an officer, capped his ginger brows and yelled upwards, "The *Elias* has the scent of land, lads. She knows where she's headin'!"

Surrounded by the beauty of the sun sparkling off the bay's blue water and the pale-grey cliffs of home, Seamus was not about to ruin the moment with a reprimand. Heavens knew how much he had looked forward to this moment. Why begrudge his men the same excitement?

Blight led young Hicks and Smythe across the deck, instructing them on their duties. "There'll be no going ashore after we've offloaded," he explained, scratching his fiery mane. "She's due for a tarring down before we step ashore. If the whole crew sets to it, we can have her finished off in a day."

With his fingers curled around the wheel's wooden spokes, and the green smell of land blowing in his face, Seamus's mind wandered to his days as a new joiner aboard the *Windfall*. With startling clarity, he remembered the pungent smells, sticky black mess, and arm-aching labour of his first time tarring a ship. He had followed the sailmaker across the deck, walking with his arms and legs outstretched to stop the tar-stiffened fabric from chaffing his armpits and thighs.

How young Hicks and Smythe endured those rags with such high spirits was beyond him. Perhaps the misery of it was lightened by their bond of friendship. Young Hicks grabbed a bucket of tar in one broad hand and a fistful of oakum in the other. He waggled his blond eyebrows at Smythe, who frowned.

"Mr Blight, how's a man supposed to hold on *and* tar?" asked Smythe.

Blight chuckled. "Why, 'tis easy, lad. You hold on with your eyelids." He flicked his head in encouragement at the blond- and dark-haired duo. "Come on you two. Wait until you're riding down the stays, then you'll be entitled to bemoan the difficulty. 'Tis a grand thing to be swinging aloft 'twixt Heaven and earth. Leave no holidays, mind. Miss any places with your tar, and I'll have you go over the whole lot again."

At the dock, Seamus stepped off the gangplank, surveying the bustling hive of Semi-Circular Quay. Every berth was filled with boats and ships of every size, a maze of ropes connecting the vessels to the pier's iron cleats like corded sinews securing infant to mother. It was low tide, and barnacles clung to the stone wall at the waterline, the choppy surface of the water churned by bobbing hulls. Occasional fish jumped into the air, disappearing in a circle of ripples.

Seamus quickened his steps towards Barclay & Co. Wool-store. Straight-backed, he cut his way impatiently through the assorted crowd of sailors, whores, beggars, and water workers along the wide stone walkway. A sailor on the vessel nearest to him tipped a bucket of water overboard, and the filthy water splashed into the sea, blooming into a brown cloud in the blue. The Union Jack snapped sharply in the breeze, and the gaudy sounds of a concertina carried across from the gin house opposite. Seamus was unsure if it was a manifestation of his own excitement, but the buzz of chatter and laughter seemed particularly festive. He was home!

He glanced at the towering Woolstore, searching the upper shipping-office windows, the grimy glass revealing nothing but a shadowed figure. Scowling, he adjusted his cocked hat and, gripping the stair's iron railing, hauled himself up two at a time.

CRAVING DISTRACTION, Grace sat beside Toby in the shipping office, poring over the customs and excise duties payable on the most recent load of goods and spirits delivered by the *Quintus Roscius*.

Below, in the Woolstore, men's muted voices filtered through the floorboards' cracks. Grace closed the ledger with a satisfying whump. "Ha! I challenge that self-important blackguard of a harbour master to find fault with *this* inventory." Not wanting her delicious anticipation of Seamus's arrival interrupted by Appleby's blustering ministrations, ensuring accuracy in the figures was necessary. She slipped the audited ledger to her right, and from the basket to her left she reached for the *Quintus Roscius*'s wool manifest for the return trip to London.

At a rustling above, Grace glanced at the exposed wooden

beams, searching for signs of the resident possum. Being noctur-
nal, the creature was likely tucked in a dark corner somewhere
awaiting its chance to come out and wreak chaos in the empty
shipping office later. Having learned the hard way not to leave
food lying around, she bit into her tongue-and-mustard sandwich
with gusto.

Toby scoffed smugly. "I've laid a trap for the little blighter.
It's only a matter of time before I catch him." He rose, empty
coffee pot in hand. "More coffee?"

She sculled the remnants of her mug, grimacing at the cold,
bitter dregs sliding down her throat in lumps. Stinking seaweed!
Why did she *always* do that? Scraping the gritty bits off her
tongue with her teeth, she nodded and held up the pewter vessel.

Stepping around the desk, Toby glanced out of the window,
his feet shuffling to a halt. He turned slowly, his eyelids wide.
"Mrs F., he's here."

Grace's breath exploded as though she had been headbutted
in the gut by a goat. Her instinct for creating order in Seamus's
presence kicked in, and she straightened the writing set and
recorked the inkpot. Snatching the loose sheaths of the wool
manifest, she tapped them on the desk, shuffling them into a neat
stack in the basket. She scanned the office, checking all was in
place. The wooden floorboards were rough but clean. The fine
layer of dust and the upside-down carcasses of two flies on the
windowsill could not be helped—the dry condition of this land,
and the unrelenting invasion of annoying insects, meant a daily
affliction of both. A third fly buzzed and bumped against the
begrimed glass of the window. Should she open the window to
let it out, three more would wretched-well swoop in and take its
place.

Toby stowed the empty mugs on the sideboard and shrugged
into his jacket.

Thudding footsteps, reverberating on the outer wooden steps,
grew louder. The chair creaked as Grace rose and stared at the

closed door. She shifted from one foot to the other, and the plank beneath her right foot squeaked. At the metallic screech of the turning knob, the door swung open, blowing in a scent of hot, grassy lanoline, bergamot, and—*him*. His signature citrusy fragrance dominated the underlying tones of musty, damp ship's bedding and smoky salted beef.

Not daring to blink in case he was only an illusion, she fiddled with the golden intertwined hearts of the brooch on her chest. The passage of time had not diminished his looks. His eyebrows seemed darker somehow, more like lightly browned toast than the golden colour of corn. His eyes were set deeper in his face than she remembered, but they still held the spark of intellect. Altogether more appealing for having the scars and lines on his face that told of a life well-lived, his bronzed skin highlighted the careful calculation behind his blue gaze. His straight, blond locks still shone like newly minted bronze— though was that a lightening at his temples? She liked what she saw now more than their first meeting at Mother's dinner table. Behind that unwrinkled shirtfront was her heart.

SEAMUS'S CHEST expanded and contracted deeply as he breathed through his nose. He clicked his wrist. Heavens above, she looked glorious!

"Captain Fitzwilliam!" Hicks filled the silence, his smile welcoming. He extended his hand. "Jolly good to see you, sir!" As though suddenly aware of how much too small the shipping office was for the three of them, he added, "If you'll excuse me, I'll pop down and say hello to the lads."

Seamus clapped Hicks's back amiably. "Good man, Hicks. Your brother will be pleased to see you too."

Hicks snatched his cap off the coat stand, crushing it onto his head as he drew the door to. Reaching behind, Seamus locked the door with a loud click.

"Seamus!" Grace lifted her skirts and bolted towards him. With a few strides, he met her in the middle. Tossing his hat aside, he lifted her up, kissing her hard. Her mouth was hot and urgent on his, her tongue probing deep. He kissed her back, tasting the peppery bite of mustard from whatever she had just eaten, and consuming her with all the missed passion from his dark, lonely nights. She gasped as he pulled back, staring wordlessly. Her deep, green pools said what her mouth did not, and at that moment, he knew *precisely* what she wanted. Good Heavens, when last had she looked at him with such vulnerability? His pulse sped through his veins.

"Dulcinea." Her name had never sounded so desirous. "Did you receive my letters?"

"Only the third one. The waiting nearly undid me."

"A stack of yours awaited me in Cape Town. They delivered such joy and hope. I wasn't sure you wished me to return."

"I never wanted you to leave." With a light touch, she traced his freshly-shaven jaw. She ran her soft thumb over his chapped lips and wiped the perspiration from his top lip. Her fingers smelled of lavender talc, freshly laundered cotton, and sweetened coffee.

When he did not kiss her again, or reach beneath her skirts, she laughed lightly, lowering her lashes. "Will you not do more than undress me with your eyes?" It was impossible to keep his eyes off her pink, moist lips as she spoke. "Come." She grasped his wrist, pulling him towards the desk.

He followed without objection and, locking her hips in a firm grip, lifted and slid her back on the leather inlay. He edged his way between her knees. Heavens above, he could devour her on the spot! She drew her skirts up and, leaning back, braced her hands on the desk behind her as though to welcome the full urge of his appetite. His unrequited desire flared as he gripped her hips again. By Neptune's forked trident, he had waited too long for this!

Her neck and cheeks pinkened as his gaze trailed from her head, lingering over the swell of her breasts, down to the curve of her bare knees. His gaze burned a return path up to her eyes, and his insides melted in anticipation. The tension in her thigh muscles vibrated like the hum of a wire strand pulled too tight. He was completely at her mercy, and the mischievous glint in her eye told him she knew it.

Seamus hummed desirously, peppering her warm neck with kisses. "By Christ, Grace, I've missed the feel of you!" He inhaled the smooth spot behind her ear. "And the smell of you."

Her skin warmed even further, and she angled her head to ease his access. "And here I believed you only married me for my wit and conversation."

He drew back and took her hands in his. Her fingertips were cool, but the centres of her palms were like warm sand on a beach. "Your wit and conversation were an integral part of the deal." She toyed with the white scar on his wrist, smiling when he shivered. His voice thickened. "Your wifely duties a welcome addendum."

She reached for his belt, her fingers fumbling. "Well, those duties might be a footnote to you, but they're the main title of *my* book."

She slipped the leather belt free of its loops, and the metal buckle clattered to the floor. It had been far too long since he had heard *that* sound!

With a glorious display of impatience, she guided his hands to her dress ties behind. "Take it off," she ordered hoarsely.

For pity's sake, his appetite for rekindling this intimacy with her surpassed any previous craving, for food or glory, but he needed to slow matters down. There were pressing issues to be considered first. He squeezed his eyes and dropped his forehead to hers. "Grace—"

She silenced him with a finger on his lips. "Shh, there'll be time for talk later." Cupping the back of his head, she drew him down. "Will you allow me to love you?" she whispered against his lips.

Oh, sweet mercy! They were the intimate words he had whispered to her on their wedding night. Clearly he was not the only one desiring a reinstatement of affection. He had not believed he could want her any more than he had that night, but now his longing combusted within him like a well-coaled firebox.

"Grace." He tried again, but she kissed him into silence. Her mouth, soft and unresisting—but resist he must. He broke away from her lips, keeping his forehead connected to hers as he spoke softly. "Wait, my heart."

Defiance dimpled the skin of her chin like lemon peel, and she met his gaze directly. "I'm done waiting. I've waited two years for this moment—"

"On the contrary, you owe *me* two years of my life without you. Separation now resides on the short list of things I forbid."

"Do you forbid *this*?" She squirmed before him and hooked her legs around his buttocks. He ran his hand up her nape, gently exploring and kneading her scalp. She groaned.

This was one battleground with which he *was* familiar, and one he typically won—though not today. With slow deliberation, he released his fingers from the spring of curls and trailed them down her spine. She writhed into him as his fingers ran over that tender spot where her lower back ended and her bottom began. His secret weapon.

He had her exactly where he wanted her—at his complete mercy! Hopefully, he had softened her sufficiently for what he was about to say. Making demands of any sort inevitably set off his feisty wife. He had to tread lightly.

"Make me a promise first." His voice was husky with emotion.

Grace's eyes narrowed. "What promise?"

With agonising deliberateness, he drew his hips to hers. Her nostrils flared, and she bit her bottom lip. Ha! Her little game to lure him into a state of malleability was just as easy for him to play. Growling, he raised one brow, not prepared to relieve her from this torment just yet. He breathed into her ear, "Promise first."

Goose flesh raced down her neck, and she wriggled, squeezing her eyes tight. "Promise what?"

When she opened them again, he shot one step nearer to submitting to her, desperately, completely. *Steady does it.* "Promise you'll remain by my side—*always*." He added an edge of gravity to his voice.

"But—"

"Promise you'll never remain behind again. No matter the circumstances." He remained stubbornly motionless. She tightened her legs around his, but she might as well be pulling against a mizzen mast for all his immobility. He would not sway until he had her assurance. "Promise me," he repeated with deadly calm. He breathed in her salted feminine scent. *By Neptune's forked trident, give me strength!*

Clearly frustrated by his height and inaction, she shuffled to her knees on the desk, bringing her eye to eye with him. "Seamus! You're killing me!"

She kissed him hard, her lips hot and demanding, and his senses swirled like the whirl of a dust storm. He had thought he could win this battle, but the little vixen had just thoroughly disarmed him. *And she knows it.*

He drew back just enough to make eye contact. His voice rasped and caught. "No, *you* nearly killed *me*. I thought I'd die with the need of you."

"I need you *now*. Cease torturing me." She bit him lightly on the chest.

He convulsed and protested with a laugh. Wrestling her aside and laying her lengthways across the desk, he pressed her onto her back and pinned her hands beside her head. Her gaze roved to his mouth. Her eyes, dark green in the poorly lit office, narrowed in humorous speculation. Oh, how he had missed this playful side of her. The sight of that little chin of hers clenched in rebellion tightened his throat. "Oh-ho, bite me, will you?"

He raked his chin against her soft neck, taking a nip of his own.

She gasped and bucked. "Don't you dare mark me!" Her firm tone dissolved into a giggle.

He muttered against her hot, damp skin. "You're my wife— I'll put my seal of approval on you any way I please."

"Don't!" She squealed, giggling and wriggling, but he held her fast. "Want me to look like a ship's biscuit gnawed by a giant rat?"

Seamus snorted and collapsed against her, laughing. Leaning up on his elbows, he gently brushed her soft, tight curls from her forehead. "You've *no* notion of torture until you've stood in my shoes." He forced a sombreness into his voice.

She frowned and shuffled upright, swinging her legs over the edge of the desk again. "What do you mean?"

He ground his molars, and the muscle in his jaw twitched again. "You once told me to never feel ashamed of showing you the depth of my love."

Her shoulders softened at the memory. "I remember. In Montevideo. Just after our Em was born." Worry fluttered across her face as he clicked his wrist.

"You're my Achilles heel, Dulcinea." He took a step back. It would be easier to speak his mind without touching her. His heart jammed in his throat, and fear grabbed his tongue, wringing it dry.

"What are you saying?"

"We're locked in a stalemate. Your desire to be with the children takes you away from me. My desire to be with you takes you away from the children." His chest expanded slowly, his breath releasing in a rush.

Grace nibbled her top lip, red and moist from his earlier efforts. "What are you proposing?"

"I fear I'm softening in my old age. My heart won't stand continual partings from you." He turned his gaze to the painting of the *Elias*. "Every day away from you was tantamount to ripping the scab off a festering wound over and over, but left unpicked it'll heal."

He stared at the two figures in the painting. Sykes had captured their likeness well. They had an ease about one another, both content and at home on their ship, despite the boiling sea about them. Heavens knew he sometimes questioned where he fitted in life's grand scheme, but no matter what course was charted for him, he had never doubted having his wife beside him to weather the storms. He swung his gaze back to Grace.

Shit!

Chapter Thirty-Two

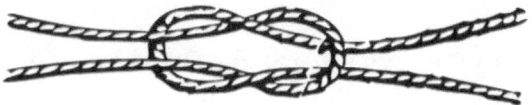

L eft unpicked? What did that mean? He was leaving her
so he could run off and lick his wounds, and hope they
would heal? An icy shiver fluttered over Grace's skin.
Fighting the urge to vomit, she thrust her palms against his
shoulders and slid off the desk. How *dare* the bastard still expect
her to choose, even after all that had transpired!

A knot of anger built in the pit of her stomach until it was the
size and weight of an iron ball of shot. How did he not understand? She had protected their children in a way Mother had
never done for her, and she would bleeding-well do it again!
Mother had never defended her against Father either. Well,
Seamus bloody Fitzwilliam had just declared war. It was time to
broadside her marriage and blast it to smithereens!

"Good!" Her voice hitched as though a bear trap's steel jaws
snapped over her vocal cords. "Then you've an idea of the pain
I'd feel leaving our children—especially after Elias!" She
coughed to clear the spasm of fear gripping her oesophagus.
"You might be able to return to sea permanently and reconcile

yourself to your new station without us, but if I go with you without the children, I'll end up hating you. I *know* I will." A sob burst from her soul.

She wanted to tell him to leave quickly and be done with it, but she could not force out the words. The stifling air in the shipping office made it difficult to breathe. She tried to still the quiver in her chin, but hot tears dribbled unchecked down her neck.

Seamus's eyes widened, and he yanked her into an embrace. "No, Dulcinea."

She came, unresisting, but she was *damned* if she would fold her arms about him. With her back and shoulders rigid, she tried to ignore the warm solidness of his chest against her cheek. Nothing made sense. *This* was where she belonged. Beside him. In his arms. But how? How could they make it work?

"Oh, my brave and honest Dulcinea." His voice thickened, and he pressed a kiss to the top of her head. She tried to withdraw, but he gripped her tighter.

"Don't, Seamus." Her voice quailed. "Don't make it harder than it already is."

"I'm not done." His words were muffled in her hair. He tilted her chin up with his elegant forefinger.

She glanced away from his look that burned her like the flames of a torch. "It's quite clear that you're *done*—with us— with me." Swiping angrily at her tears, she sniffed loudly. "You can't make me choose—not after everything I've been through."

Seamus reared back, the cobalt of his eyes magnified by emotion. "What *you've* been through? What about what *I've* been through? I lost Elias too." His voice hardened. "My oath, it's as though you forget that sometimes." The muscles in his neck tightened.

Sorrow and hopelessness welled up inside her, and she thrust her face into her hands, sobbing. Curse every hair on his wretched head for making her weep so pitifully! This was not how their reunion had evolved in her daydreams.

"I'm sorry, my heart. I never meant to upset you so," he whispered, his voice thick.

So, he thought her brave and honest, did he? She would show him honest! The heat of her resentment sizzled away her tears, and she jabbed a finger into his shoulder. His face was a teary haze, but she blinked it clear, ignoring her hot, puffy eyelids. "How did you imagine I'd react to news of your leaving me? Dance a happy jig?"

His chest bellowed, and his eyebrows rucked. "Heavens above! I may be a bastard at times, but I'd like to believe I'm not cold-hearted enough to keep you in a constant state of misery. You've misunderstood. I'm *not* leaving you."

Sniffing, she swallowed the thick slime of tears and folded her arms. "Then what are you proposing?"

"I left you behind once, but I'll not do that again. *Ever.*" Seamus laid his large hands on her shoulders. "I must have all of you, always. Having you half a world away... well, my life wasn't worth living. I was unbearable to live with aboard the ship. This I know because I was unbearable to myself. My desire to be with you left me railing and raging against my officers and men. So, I've made a decision. I'll remain here, in Sydney, with you and the children. Raising my family ashore will be my new adventure. The uncharted territory of this land promises boundless possibility."

The air between them sucked into a timeless void, and her voice quivered with those annoying hiccoughs that always followed a long, hard cry. She chewed her bottom lip to stop it trembling and drew her brows together in confusion. "What of your captaincy? Who'll sail the *Elias*?"

"With Captain Robertson already in command of the *Quintus Roscius*, I'll find another master to skipper the *Elias*. You'll have no doubt met Captain McKay of the *Saviour*?" At the mention of the immigrant ship, Seamus's eyes lit up. He drew his shoulders up to his ears, his head tilted. "Perhaps it's time for me to try life on land and leave my expanding fleet in the capable hands of others?"

"You can't do that, Seamus. Your life is at sea. I can't ask you to give that up, you'll miss it too much. What if you end up resenting this life... and blaming me for it?" The voice of reason in her head shrieked. *Hush, woman! Are you trying to scare him off?*

"Haven't you realised yet that *you're* where I belong?"

These were the promises her crumpled soul craved, his assurance the bedrock upon which she needed to rest. A place where she could lower her weapons, lower her defences without risk of further wounding. She permitted herself to believe him. Trust him.

His hands trailed over her hips and around the curves of her backside, where he cupped her cheeks familiarly. He pulled her a step closer, and instinctively, she wound her arms around his waist, playing with the stitching down the middle of his jacket. Stinking seaweed—so much for her attempted siege on his affection.

"I'm confident that between you, Hicks, and me, we'll manage the Elias Shipping Company quite well from Sydney Town. Besides, I've secured another agent in London—Max Delisle."

Grace arched her eyebrows and nodded. "Do I know him?"

"No. He's a clerk in the Colonial Secretary's office." He grinned like a cheeky schoolboy, the warm pad of his thumb gently wiping the cooling tears from her lower lashes. "The man has experience with shipping companies in France and in England. Soon, he'll know the lay of the land in New Holland too. Admiral Baxter—" He paused, his blond brows sliding together. "Oh..."

"Billy told me," she said gently. "Go on."

"The admiral greatly admired Delisle. That in itself speaks volumes for the man's character and dependability."

She pressed a smile to her lips. "If Delisle was good enough for Uncle Farfar, he's certainly good enough for the Elias Shipping Company."

"Indeed," said Seamus. "I've also offered for Delisle to stay in Abertarff House in London—wouldn't want Bartel getting lazy in his old age." He winked.

A surge of hope flickered in her core, but she tried to smother it with a deep breath. She wanted nothing more than to return his eager smile of confidence, but wasps of doubt fluttered about her belly, their stings sharp and ready to attack. Her mouth dried with unease. "Seamus, I don't want you to feel I'm forcing you to start a new life ashore."

"You aren't forcing my hand."

"With our Em and Eddy away at school, and Sally's excellent housekeeping at Cliffview Cottage, the memory of our life at sea together haunted me while my whole bloody world fell to bits. With Toby managing the Elias Shipping Company, I was left with duties an apprenticed clerk could tackle. And now you're back, I'll have even less to do. Am I destined to become little more than somewhere warm for you to furrow your plough?"

Seamus frowned. "How long have you found being my wife so disagreeable?"

Grace inhaled sharply and dug her nails into her palm, willing a civil tone. "Aboard the *Elias*, I'm your equal, your partner in the true sense of the word—but here on land, I lose this privilege."

"Christ Almighty, Dulcinea! Life isn't duty-bound to give us what we want. We take what's given, and are thankful it's no worse than it is."

Grace's neck and cheeks burned, which might not be so bad were it not for the hot tears again. Swiping her cheek with the back of her hand, she firmed her chin. "I'll not be cast aside and turned into a useless creature like my mother."

Seamus gave a throaty chuckle and tightened his hands around her back, his earnest gaze burning through her concern, straight into her heart. "Didn't I prove your worth to me when I entrusted the *Elias* to you—to bring her home safely when I couldn't? Haven't I praised you for your business acumen from the outset? Extolled your mothering skills on numerous, uncountable occasions? They weren't empty platitudes then, Dulcinea, and they're not about to become that now. Our fleet is growing. I need you more than ever."

She dipped her chin to her chest. The barrel of hope she had been clinging to all this time had become barely more than a few splintered planks, swollen and split apart by doubt. His words of comfort were like newly smithed hoops of iron, binding her courage into a water-tight and unsinkable cask once again.

He lifted her chin with his finger. "Understand this—you're nothing like that poisonous asp, and I could *never* cast you aside. You are the light in my soul, my every breath, my heart."

"We've barely begun life together," she whispered. "But it's as though we've lived a dozen lifetimes with everything we've been through."

He pulled her closer, and she tucked her shoulder under his armpit, her cheek resting against his chest. She had always marvelled at how perfectly snugly she fit under here. Her husband was still erect and square-shouldered—not too shabby for a forty-year-old man. His once lean-cut face had filled out, softening the sharp lines, turning him even more handsome. Grace's heart gave the same ludicrous lurch as it had when she noticed him in the gardens at Wallace House at nineteen.

He arched one blond brow, the crease line on his cheek denting as he beamed. "And I'd happily live a dozen more as long as it means having you by my side."

His love was as vital to her as air, both life-affirming.

"Without you, my life ceased moving forward. Of course, I was happy to have the children about, but... I wanted more... I wanted *you*," she whispered. "I thought that without the children, I'd lose my soul to the tempest inside me. But this storm within isn't because of you or them. It's born of dashed childhood ideals, of living without Mother and Father's love. The ache of it is still as raw as it was back then."

"Our children *know* they are loved, whether we are near them or not."

"I realise that now. They're as happy at Dubois House as they are to return home to me in the holidays. Mother's indifference left a seed of pain in my heart. I've reconciled that it will always be a part of me, but I can bear it better now, knowing I've not planted that same seed of doubt in my own children." She squeezed him tighter. "Oh Seamus, I vow to remember that you love me as much as I you. I need you to ground me in those moments of storm. Don't let me stay lost—come and find me."

"You're no longer lost, Dulcinea. I have you, and I'll never let go." Drawing her around, he kissed her as tenderly as the first time his lips had touched hers outside the roofless church in Tierra del Fuego. He grinned and gripped her hand. "Come on then, we've two little rascals to surprise."

THANKS FOR READING *GRACE ARISING*. I hope you had as much fun reading it as I did writing it. I have a surprise for you! Call it an encore encouraged by reader demand. *Christmas at Gilly Downs* (The White Sails Series, Book 4—A Christmas Novella) jumps forward ten years to see what the beloved characters from The White Sails Series are up to as they prepare to reunite for Christmas at Gilly Downs.

Buy this next-in-series novella here: https://books2read.com/ Emma-Lombard

KEEP GOING TO SEE OTHER BOOKS FROM EMMA LOMBARD

Discerning Grace
The White Sails Series, Book One

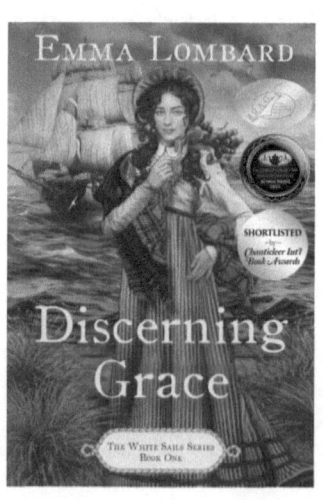

A ROLLICKING romantic adventure featuring an independent young woman, Grace Baxter, whose feminine lens blows the ordered patriarchal decks of a 19th century naval tall ship to smithereens.

Grace on the Horizon
The White Sails Series, Book Two

Continue Seamus and Grace's romantic sea adventures. Secrets and rumours abound as these two headstrong opposites try to expose the saboteur aboard their exploration vessel.

Grace Arising
The White Sails Series, Book Three

A new ship means a new adventure. With Seamus gravely injured, it's up to Grace to see the crew and her family to safety. Can she reach the New Holland wool market ahead of their competitors, and in time to save Seamus's life?

Christmas at Gilly Downs
The White Sails Series, Book Four: Christmas Novella

Jump forward ten years to see what the beloved characters from The White Sails Series are up to as they prepare to reunite for Christmas at Gilly Downs.

Buy this next-in-series novella here: https://books2read.com/Emma-Lombard

The Gold Hills Series
Coming soon

Continue on with the Fitzwilliam family saga from The White Sails Series. Follow in Emily Fitzwilliam's footsteps as she makes her mark on the world. Head over to the author's website for more information and developments of this series:

www.emmalombardauthor.com/the-gold-hills-series

ALSO BY EMMA LOMBARD

www.ingramcontent.com/pod-product-compliance
Lightning Source LLC
Chambersburg PA
CBHW030516120726
47904CB00005B/1491